THE INFERNAL AGE

I0599822

DEMON GATE

ANSON JOAQUIN

DUBIOUS DISTINCTION PRESS, LLC

ISBN: 979-8-9926139-0-2 (Electronic book)
ISBN: 979-8-9926139-1-9 (Paperback)
ISBN: 979-8-9926139-3-3 (Hardback)
ISBN: 979-8-9926139-2-6 (Audiobook)

Library of Congress Control Number: 2025902764

The story, all names, characters, and incidents portrayed in this production are fictitious. No identification with actual persons (living or deceased), places, buildings, or products is intended or should be inferred.

Cover Art by Jeff Brown

First edition 2025

Dubious Distinction Press LLC
1881 Grove Avenue
Radford, Virginia 24141

Trigger Warning: This book contains scenes of violence and gore, as well as (solely in Chapter 9) sexual assault and mild self-harm

ACKNOWLEDGEMENTS

I would like to extend my sincere and heartfelt thanks to all the people who helped and encouraged me on this journey. I never would have been able to finish this book without the help, forbearance, and support of my wife and our children; my father and Babcia; my meticulous editors/copy editors Claudia Jones and Siobhan Hayes; my writing coach Kathrin Lake; my Beta readers – including my wife, my father, TR (LLAP), Axsister, Jake, Anthony Smith, Jeff Perez, Martyn Lovell, Shando, Uncle Monkey, Eric Weigel, Robert Eugenell Johnson, and Stephan K; my Beta editors – Blue Fire Media, The Book Foundry, Audrey Logsdon, and Ink Slinger Editorial Services; course instructors Luis Alberto Urrea and Pam Houston; all my general encouragers; and to Aaron Butler, still much admired, who was the inspiration for most of the interesting parts of Tam Sinclair – I'm sorry I couldn't do better justice to such a singular individual. Additional thanks go to Jeff Brown for the incredible cover art, Travis Baldree for his gracious advice, John Pirhalla for an incredible audiobook performance, Lorna Reid for formatting, and the marketing team who all went above and beyond to help me get a professional and well-executed book out into the world.

For my wife, my partner, my heart

And when the Lord God saw the state of man,
whom He had kept whole, hale, and firm in His mind,
and observed that they had purchased through science and pride
a piece of His power over creation and destruction,
but were without conscience, purpose, or purity,
He withdrew His hand and allowed alien powers
and sour perversions purchase upon blessed Eden
so that man would be scourged and tested and winnowed
and those who might survive would learn purity
and brotherhood and faith, while those who did not
would be overrun and slain by demons.

- First Book of The Judgment, Chapter 22
Holy Scripture of the Citadel of the West
(Third Edition)

ONE

NEW MEXICO

Dr. Tamarind Sinclair stood in the control room, arms folded over his wrinkled lab coat, watching the Experiment Group scurry about as if he weren't even there. The scientists detoured around him as they bustled to and fro making the final preparations and pointedly avoiding his glare.

"We shouldn't be doing this," Tam muttered to no one in particular. It wouldn't have mattered if he'd shouted it, though; the team was moving forward now no matter what he said. A new configuration order had come in from the Theory Group that morning, with much higher energy, and his objections had been disregarded—again. This time, they hadn't even bothered to file a response.

He rubbed his stubbled chin and wondered if he should resign. Spectacularly, somehow. With an open letter? Or could he find some chains and lock himself in the experiment chamber? Looking into the room through the safety glass, though, he couldn't see anything to hook the chains to, and besides, he knew that if he tried, they would just send the guards in to physically remove him. That was if he even had chains, which he did not. And resigning wouldn't stop these experiments either. If he blew the whistle, he could only imagine what Command would do to him. Prison wouldn't be so bad, he tried to tell himself, but he wouldn't be able to help his mother and brother. He'd be abandoning them—just like his father had.

Tam glared at Lebedev, a handsome older man who was nominally in charge of the Experiment Group, as he sat at the control panel.

"You know we're not ready for this, right? We don't know a thing about using this much power."

Lebedev sighed and finally turned his head to regard Tam with his icy gray eyes. "This is point of science, yes?" he said dryly, his Russian accent somehow emphasizing his dislike of Tam.

The all-clear came as the rest of the team finished their final prep, and Lebedev turned back to the screen before him. Without another word, he pushed the button to initiate the sequence, and the equipment in the test room on the other side of the glass began to power up.

Five...four...three...two...one.

The hum of the emitters in the next room became audible even in here, the six beams they created intersecting at a single, tiny point, forcing rays of intense energy into the particles held there. Theory had decided that they were close to achieving large-scale remote particle pairing—a feat that, it was hoped, would facilitate instantaneous communication across any distance. But Tam suspected that the Director of the Theory Group, Ainsley Shannon, didn't care as much about the operational goals as she did about getting her New Unified Theory published.

She wouldn't care if she created a stable strangelet, or something even worse, he thought. The more unexpected the better, because that's how the greatest discoveries were made. In these experiments, they were playing with energies several orders of magnitude greater than those at play in the Large Hadron Collider. Ainsley and the rest of the Organization were of the self-serving belief that the risks were small enough and that if something did go wrong, the new zero-field generators would lock down all the energy and matter around the experiment and hold it in stasis until they could evacuate or figure out how to undo whatever it was they'd done.

In Tam's estimation, the chances of an *undesirable* outcome were far too high. It was as if Ainsley were spinning a giant roulette wheel, where black meant scientific discovery, red meant they lost their money, and if the ball landed on zero, they would execute everyone in the casino.

As he stood there, lost in thought, the emitters quickly passed the 100 TeV mark. They had never attempted to work with energy levels that high before outside of single-fire testing, and the particles in the manipulation field were already approaching states that were rarely, if ever, achieved outside of a singularity. The hum of the emitters was getting louder—too loud. It reverberated through the control room and rang painfully in Tam's ears.

He started to yell out, to beg Lebedev to abort the experiment, but even as he opened his mouth, one of the emitters overloaded and exploded with a staggeringly loud crack, the lightning temporarily blinding and stunning him.

The humming stopped; the rest of the emitters shut down. Tam blinked, trying blearily to clear the ghostly afterimages from his eyes. The sounds of a dozen alarms and warning beeps filled the air. His heart pounded painfully in his chest. He peered into the experiment chamber, his vision clearing, and saw it.

A huge, dark ball.

Hanging in the center of the room was a sphere of absolute blackness, at least fifteen feet in diameter. It was perfectly still and impossibly solid. There was a slight rainbow sheen around the circumference, as if the ambient light of the room could find no purchase on it, but when he tried to look beyond the surface, it was as if he were staring into an infinite well of elemental darkness. It made Tam's skin crawl, but he couldn't tear his eyes away. *This must be the effect of the zero field*, he thought, *but what went wrong with the experiment? What is the zero field holding in stasis?*

After a minute or so, Lebedev cleared his throat, startling several people who had also been staring at the thing through the glass.

"Uncontrolled experiment propagation detected," he announced. "But zero field deployed correctly and is stable. All systems online and nominal. We are safe."

"No," Tam replied, his voice leaden and bitter. "We're fucked."

TWO

WASHINGTON, D.C.

"Rodriguez! Why. The. Hell. Are. You. In. My. Office?"
Colonel Broadnax pronounced each word as if it were
a separate, increasingly loud sentence. Her Atlanta
accent got stronger when she was angry, and right now, it was
about the thickest he'd ever heard it. She stood toe to toe with
Gabriel, too close for comfort, and stared directly into his tanned
face, as if daring him to show an ounce of weakness. Her sour
thundercloud of an expression was so full of contempt that it
seemed it would strip the flesh from his bones.

Her question hung in the air long enough for Gabriel to
realize he was supposed to answer it. He considered saying it was
because she had summoned him, but thought better of it. He
had never seen her this angry before.

"Fighting, ma'am?"

"You're goddamn right it's fighting, you flippant son of a
bitch!"

Gabriel remained silent. He'd been through this enough
times to know that it would go better if he gave his commanding
officer all the time she needed to yell.

The colonel continued to stare him aggressively in the face.

Her smooth, dark brown forehead glistened with sweat, even though she kept the room cold enough to raise traitorous goosebumps on Gabriel's muscular arms. He wondered idly if she yelled at taller people with the same intensity, or if she took particular pleasure in yelling at Gabriel because he was the same height as her. *Okay, maybe she's an inch taller than me*, he thought. He could admit that much.

Broadnax briefly broke her glare and gestured to his file, which was open on her desk. "If I pulled half the shit they let you get away with, they would have drummed me out of this outfit, I guarantee *that*." She put her hands on her hips and shook her head as if amazed at his stupidity. "I swear to God, you could start an argument in a phone booth. This bullshit ends *now*, do you hear me? You're not the only decent agent we have here, *Captain Rodriguez*, and I will not have you drawing attention to our organization again."

Gabriel continued to stand at ease, staring straight ahead and keeping his face expressionless. Like a good soldier should, even though he wasn't technically a soldier anymore.

Finally, she relented a little, taking a half step back and crossing her arms, though her expression was still severe. She looked him up and down critically. "You put two people in the hospital tonight, captain."

"I regret the incident, ma'am," Gabriel said neutrally. And he did, to an extent. He'd meant to hurt the one—*Chad*, he thought it was—who had been an absolute monster to the lady Gabriel had been talking to and then called him a *spic*, which had earned him a shove. The moron had certainly tried to hurt Gabriel after that. But in retrospect, the other guy might have been picking up his bottle to take a drink, not to use it as a weapon. In his anger, however, Gabriel hadn't seen it that way at the time.

"Why is it that we have problems with you almost every time

you're not on assignment?" asked Broadnax, her voice still hard.

Gabriel frowned. "I don't think—"

"God knows I try to keep you busy, Gabriel," she interrupted. "I don't understand how you can handle being the adult in the room when you're surrounded by egomaniacal scientists and all this fuckin' red tape, day in and day out, for months at a time, but then turn around and blow up like this when you're off duty for two weeks."

Gabriel remained silent. *A fair question*, he thought. He wasn't quite sure why. He had a feeling it might have something to do with how irritating Georgetown students were when they were drunk, though he knew better than to say that out loud. Or maybe it was related to just being home, being around his perfect sister and his perpetually disappointed parents.

Broadnax sighed, eying him critically. "This fighting—you know it's childish as hell, right? You're twenty-eight, for Chrissakes!" She wasn't quite shouting anymore, but in some ways, this was worse. "I rely on you when I send you on a mission, but it seems like it's only a matter of time before your temper gets you into trouble then, too."

Gabriel didn't respond, though he did try to will his face to convey remorse. He wasn't sure how that expression felt, though, and he doubted he was doing a very good job of it.

"If we were still in the army, I'd have you confined to quarters for a few weeks," the colonel said, looking at him to gauge his response. He didn't give her the satisfaction.

"But that would have to wait anyway," she said after a pause. "Instead, I am going to dock you a month's pay for each person you put in the hospital," she continued, watching his face closely. Gabriel sensed something else coming.

"And then I'm going to send you out on an assignment," she said, too casually. "Tonight."

Gabriel's expression must have betrayed him this time,

because Broadnax's face showed the ghost of a satisfied grin, though her tone was still deadly serious. "This is the most important job you've ever been assigned—maybe the most critical situation we've ever had to clean up—and you'd better hope to God it lasts a very, *very* long time," she said, her voice rising again. "You fuck this up and I'll see to it that you spend the rest of your career on an offshore oil rig so small you'll have to hang your ass over the side to take a shit!"

Gabriel was well and truly shocked now, and not by the colonel's rather colorful threat. *A new assignment already?* He had a month's leave scheduled, which he'd been planning to spend with his family—his sister was due with her first baby next week and he wanted to meet his new niece. Was this part of his punishment? Or was it really that important?

"Where?" he croaked, hoping for Los Angeles—or maybe France.

The colonel's grin deepened into an expression of pure, sadistic delight. "Oh, you'll hate it," she said. "It's a little base just outside a dusty, boring hellhole called Betelgeuse, New Mexico."

THREE

An hour later, without even having had a chance to say goodbye to his parents and sister in person, Gabriel sat alone in the cargo hold of a large military transport plane, wearing a huge pair of ear defenders. He read through the briefing packet carefully, familiarizing himself with the experiments going on at the facility—seemingly the jewel in the Organization's crown—as well as the key personnel and the cover story and logistics plan for the nearby town of Betelgeuse.

He snorted, still amused by the strange name of the town.

He paid particular attention to the personnel file of the man who would be his second-in-command, Ombudsman Dr. Tamarind Sinclair. Sinclair had started as an undergrad at Berkeley at seventeen, earned two doctorates before the age of twenty-six, and then gone straight to work for the Organization. When he was being brought on board, the reference checks indicated that his professors either loved him or hated him. A man who excelled at thinking outside the box—and probably wasn't great at following directions as a result. He sounded like a pain in the ass—brilliant, smug, and a genius at worrying and nitpicking. Perfect for his role as ombudsman within the Organization, of course. His immense academic accomplishments, particularly at such a young age, might have been intimidating to some, but Gabriel had been working closely with PhD scientists long enough now for the shine to wear off. The ones he had worked with knew so much about their fields that they tended to be arrogant know-it-alls, yet managed to be less informed and worldly than the average Joe about almost everything else.

Next in the file, Gabriel found a couple of the Level 3 ombudsman reports that Sinclair had sent directly to senior management at headquarters. One passage was highlighted, though it would have caught Gabriel's eye even if it hadn't been.

...cannot mathematically rule out a number of outcomes that would be undesirable from a human perspective. In addition to the relatively small chance that each of these experiments will be executed successfully as predicted by their respective project leaders, there is a non-zero chance of any of the following foreseeable outcomes: (A) localized atomic disorder of unknown consequences (although carcinogenesis in facility personnel and among the population of the local town is possible), (B) atomic chain reaction explosion of unknown megatonnage (the most likely outcome in my current opinion), (C) a universe-altering Ice-nine-type scenario, or (D) a man-made Big Bang.

Heady stuff, complete with a sobering dose of science fiction. "Ice-nine" was from a Vonnegut novel in which the water on Earth begins to crystallize at normal temperature and pressure. Among the doomsday set, the term was used more broadly to represent the universe "discovering" a lower energy state that would then propagate, releasing incredible amounts of energy and reordering (or disordering) all matter in the universe.

A subsequent report also had a highlighted section about the fail-safe technology the facility had in place.

The zero field device is fascinating in its own right, and I understand how it purports to work. I have reviewed the data you sent me on its development, but I believe the endorsement studies for this technology have overestimated the level and certainty of the safety it provides. I estimate that there is only a 75% chance that the technology will initiate properly in the event of a catastrophic propagation, but in some of the possible scenarios there can be no way of knowing whether it will work at all. Furthermore, even if it does work, logic dictates that the field will be impossible to maintain as T approaches infinity. That is, it is only probable, and not certain, that we can contain a mishap during these highly unstable experiments, but it is IMPOSSIBLE to contain any mishap forever. Of the range of outcomes following a successful implementation of the containment field, I believe a stay of execution, so to speak, of somewhere between 2 weeks and 5 years to be the most likely. There are just so many points of failure in this system (125 by my last count—list attached), and not all of these have redundant systems behind them."

The end of the report concluded:
"These experiments should be halted immediately before something truly terrible happens. This is the third time I have made this recommendation."

Gabriel had to admit that he was already beginning to like this Tamarind Sinclair a little. Clearly, he was a good ombudsman. Still, having an ombudsman as his second-in-command was very strange—they usually remained outside the hierarchy for several very good reasons.

It seemed that Gabriel's main job would be to secure the facility, implement solutions to the deficiencies that Sinclair and others had identified, and above all, maintain the zero field to keep whatever was going on inside of it from getting out.

Though he felt up to the task, after reading the rest of Sinclair's reports, he had to admit that it would all depend on the technology. Gabriel realized that he was really looking forward to getting started on this mission, meeting "Tam" Sinclair, and figuring out what they needed to do first to keep things stable.

He was so wrapped up in the briefing folder that his first flight was over before he even realized they were getting close. As they prepared to land at Holloman Air Force Base in New Mexico, he gathered his papers back into the folder and triggered the destruction sequence. The binder resealed, then released a foul-smelling chemical into the inside compartment, turning its contents into a clump of disintegrating rags. As the plane taxied to a stop and the cargo door opened, he gathered his pack and walked down the ramp and out onto the tarmac. A soldier stood at attention beside a golf cart a short distance away, ready to drive him to the helicopter that would take him to the facility.

The chopper ride to the facility was bumpy, but the scenery was incredible—stark and beautiful in the bright morning light. The miles of mountainous desert glided by effortlessly. The ground varied mostly between tan and red, but here and there were stands of dark trees and even some small forests. The roads winding through the hills were empty, ribbons of asphalt that seemed to come from nowhere and lead back to nowhere. It was eerie, Gabriel thought, as if there were so much unused space and so few people here that the roads were both useless and unused. Why drive anywhere else when the roads just led you to exactly the same kind of place? Gabriel shook his head slightly, thinking that the countless miles of pavement seemed like a testament to human stubbornness and pride. How much money and effort went into building and maintaining these roads that were used so infrequently by the few hundred people who lived in these parts that they looked like relics of an extinct culture?

By the time they touched down at the lab, Gabriel's sense

of wonder at the desert and excitement at starting this new assignment had faded, replaced in part by hunger, thirst, and an urgent need to use the bathroom.

He grabbed his backpack and ducked his head as he stepped down out of the helicopter. He jogged out from under the whirling blades in the same funny little way that everyone exiting a chopper did, shoulders hunched as if to make him even shorter and keep his head from being lopped off. He addressed the first soldier he saw.

"You there!"

"Jenkins, sir," the guard said, saluting.

"Jenkins, I need food, drink, a piss, and Dr. Tamarind Sinclair—and not necessarily in that order."

"Yes, sir. That way, sir," said the guard pointing to the small building at the center of the compound. "Jonas will buzz you in, sir."

Once inside the facility, Gabriel asked Jonas, the administrator, to direct him to the head, which the man did with a courteous smile and a wave. He was a thin, well-groomed guy in his early fifties, wearing a smart floral button-down shirt and tight matching blue slacks.

After Gabriel came back out, he approached Jonas' desk again.

"Jonas, could you get me some food and water and ask Dr. Tamarind Sinclair to come find me, please?"

"Certainly," the man said sunnily. He bent over an old microphone, the kind they used to use for announcements in high school, and said, "Dr. Sinclair, to the cafeteria, please. Dr. Sinclair, please report to the cafeteria. We have a guest."

Then he stood up and motioned for Gabriel to follow.

"Right this way," he smiled, leading him past some double doors that opened at a swipe of the badge on his lanyard.

After passing an elevator and a few office doors, they reached the open double doors of the cafeteria.

"You can grab whatever you need," Jonas said, pointing to the commissary at the back of the room. He smiled pleasantly at Gabriel and turned to walk back to his desk.

"Thank you, Jonas," Gabriel said.

"My pleasure," he replied cheerfully, without turning around.

Gabriel went in and walked across the room to the refrigerated shelves to see what was for dinner. Or was it breakfast? There were three pre-packaged deli sandwiches, a stack of half-frozen personal pizzas, a browning salad in a plastic box, two individually wrapped hard-boiled eggs in a large container, and one jug of green tea. An unrefrigerated shelf to the right held a wide selection of potato chips and other snacks. Gabriel grimaced and took a sandwich and a bag of chips. He was looking around for a cup to pour himself some green tea when he heard a voice behind him.

"Our savior!"

Gabriel turned and saw Sinclair standing in the doorway. He looked just like the picture in his file, but now he was wearing a badly wrinkled lab coat over a red-and-mustard striped sweater. He was gaunt and pale with wild, coarse brown hair, prominent cheekbones, and intense dark eyes.

The moment, no doubt meant to be dramatic, was somewhat ruined for the man when two other staff members pushed past him not-so-politely and headed for the commissary, one of them muttering to him not to block the door as they passed.

"Sinclair," Gabriel said, his manner serious. Well, as serious as he could be when he was holding a sandwich and a bag of potato chips.

The man smiled. "Welcome to hell," he said cheerily.

The contrast between Sinclair's voice and his choice of words disconcerted Gabriel, who glanced over at the two people who had come in after Sinclair—a pair of grease-stained engineers, by all appearances. One of them, a tall, middle-aged woman with a ponytail of salt-and-pepper hair, looked back at him boldly.

"Don't mind Tam—he's completely harmless. You can just ignore him if he bothers you too much." Sinclair glared at her behind her back.

Gabriel arched an eyebrow. "Thanks..."

"Carla. Head of Engineering."

"Nice to meet you. I'm Captain Rodriguez. Gabriel."

Carla paled a little and stood up even straighter. "I'm sorry, sir, but I don't remember how to salute properly... sir." As if to demonstrate, she made an odd, stiff motion with her right arm that looked like a cross between a wave and an attempt at showing off her bicep.

"We're not technically in the military," Sinclair interrupted, "but this fellow's in charge now." In a half-mutter, he added, "Hopefully he listens better than Lebedev." Carla rolled her eyes.

"That's quite all right, Carla," said Gabriel. He ripped open his pre-packaged sandwich and took a large bite. He looked at Sinclair and, around the mouthful of food, said, "Let's talk about what we need to do here and then let's get to doing it."

The man's face lost something of its manic expression and fell into what could only be described as resignation.

"Yeah," he said. "Okay." Then after another half beat, he muttered, "We're probably already too late." Then he looked up at Gabriel again and grinned unexpectedly. "You can call me Tam."

FOUR

Over the next three hours, Gabriel and Tam went over status reports on virtually every piece of equipment and system in the facility. They started with the zero field generator itself, as well as its backups. From there, they moved outward to the power service, the conditioners, the backup batteries, the generators, and the wiring that connected all of them.

They stopped to get some coffee and water. Just down the hall from Tam's office was a coffee station with a mini-fridge stocked with bottles of two different varieties of water. Gabriel grabbed one of them and Tam said, "You know they put mineral salts in that one to make you thirsty, right?"

Gabriel cocked an eyebrow. "Actually, I did know that, but as far as I'm aware, there's no hard evidence that suggests it's bad for you," he said. "Besides, it tastes better," he added.

Tam grinned. "I know of several such studies, but there are just as many with contradictory results," he said with a shrug. "I prefer the other one though. That one tastes like salt water to me."

Gabriel cracked open his water and pointedly took a drink. It was deeply refreshing—he must have been parched from all the talking—but *did* it taste salty now that he thought about it?

He finished his drink and replaced the cap. "I will not let your power of suggestion affect my reality," he stated primly.

Tam smiled approvingly and nodded back toward his office. Gabriel moved cautiously in that direction, having filled his coffee mug almost to the brim.

Once they were seated again, Gabriel checked his watch. "I can't believe it's only noon!" he exclaimed. Tam shrugged, unappreciative of the fact that Gabriel had been keyed up and alert for approximately thirty hours straight.

Gabriel sighed. He didn't feel worn out, though. He realized he was enjoying himself—he felt as if he could really make a difference here. "What's next?" he asked.

Without hesitation, as if the answer to that question had always been on the tip of Tam's tongue, he began ticking off items, using his fingers to punctuate each one. "Monitoring and control systems for the facility, hardening and maintaining the facility's survivability, and most importantly, planning for the evacuation of the facility and the surrounding area, including Betelgeuse." He held up his three fingers, and when he met Gabriel's gaze, his eyes contained a hard glint of stubbornness.

Gabriel didn't take the bait, instead remaining silent and waiting for Tam to continue. After a moment, the defiance in Tam's eyes dimmed a bit and he went on.

"There's more, of course, and each of those categories has between ten and fifty sub-items that need to be addressed individually. And that's without even touching on the failure of the experiment itself and what actually happened in there." This last part he added almost as an afterthought, but his furtive glance toward Gabriel as he said it gave away the importance he placed on it.

Gabriel straightened his shoulders slightly. "Someone else in the Organization is working on what happened with the experiment, so we won't be spending any time on that. It's beyond our remit," he said. He waited until he caught and held Tam's eyes with his own.

"Our job is to keep the zero field and this facility stable and functional," he said carefully. "Until we've done everything we can do on that front, we're not going to spend any time planning for failure. And there will be no talk of evacuation unless things take a turn for the worse."

Tam gave a feverish half-smile and spoke slowly, emphasizing each word with an exaggerated pause before and after, as if he were lecturing a classroom of particularly moronic undergrads. "We. Have. *Already*. Failed."

Gabriel was taken aback, his thoughts scattering as he tried to think of the perfect way to respond, but Tam continued before he had a chance.

"Did you read my situation reports from before you arrived?" Tam asked, his face intense.

"Yes, I—"

"Then you should know all of this already!" Tam exclaimed, his voice rising. "The Organization never had a full understanding of what these experiments were going to do. The only answer I ever got from them, other than brief acknowledgments, was a single response report from Theory in Los Angeles." Tam paused, wiping his forehead absently with his hand. "Ainsley Shannon and her group—that's who was working on the experiment—as if she and her Stanford cronies know any better than me…"

Gabriel said nothing, his curiosity now piqued. He hadn't seen any responses from the Organization in his briefing packet, and he had to admit that he was curious to know what they really thought of Tam's theories.

Tam continued, looking down at his shoes now. "Her response was… optimistic. She acknowledged the risks I outlined but gave a rosier estimate of how likely each was. She used complex-looking math that no one in management would ever bother to even try to understand, but basically she was using an outdated model to calculate the overall chance of any disaster at less than one percent." He gave a bitter little laugh, then looked up as he went on. "But she is biased as fuck—the experiment was designed to test effects that her own work predicted. She's the leading voice for her own brand of n-dimensional theory, and she has a lot riding on these experiments. And for the Organization, the upside of success made the risk worth it—instantaneous, non-interceptable communication across any distance. But we didn't get that—we got an unknown propagation that shut down everything in the containment field."

Gabriel tried to get the conversation back on track. "Our mission *is* the zero field—"

Tam cut him off again, this time talking directly over him in a reasonable, measured tone. "Do you know how they tested those stasis devices?"

Gabriel hesitated, then nodded. "Sort of. They said they had been tested in a wide variety of reactions, including several explosions—even a small nuke." He looked at Tam for confirmation.

Tam grimaced mirthlessly. "Very small," he agreed. "Equivalent to about ten tons of TNT—so small they used to put them in artillery shells in the sixties, and we and the Russians both carried them around in backpacks." He looked up at Gabriel again, this time his eyes pleading and his voice earnest.

"They performed that test *once*, and they only tried to keep the blast in suspension for four hours. That was their one success criterion." He threw up his hands in exasperation. "And then they let it explode and literally threw a party. *They served cake!*"

This revelation rocked Gabriel. He was silent as he grappled with the implications.

But Tam didn't relent. "It's already been more than five times that long! Gabriel, they are asking us to save them from a lit bomb of unknown size by wrapping it in bubble wrap and sticking it in a very cold freezer."

Gabriel felt dizzy for a moment, holding his tongue until he could gather his wits. Eventually, a cogent objection came to him.

"Wait a minute, though. We don't know it's a fission reaction..." he began, but then trailed off as a brutally thin smile spread across Tam's face.

"Yes, let's discuss that," Tam said, with brittle, overemphasized patience, as if he were talking to an unruly child. "The typical energy released in a single sustained fission reaction is only about two hundred million electron volts," Tam said. "The experiment downstairs used our new Molina-Berman method to manipulate particles with up to a million times more energy—far more power than any particle accelerator on the planet. But you're right, we don't know for sure because we can't see inside the field without compromising it. Have we set the air on fire, as some feared in the first fission tests? Or created a strange star that will turn the Earth into dark matter? Is it enough to tear the fabric of the universe and suck everything through?" His voice rose with each question. "I don't know!" he shouted as a fleck of spittle flew from his lips.

He regained his composure with visible effort as Gabriel watched him mutely. "I don't know," he repeated, almost calmly by comparison, his tone now painfully incongruous with his words. "And neither does Ainsley or anyone else in the Organization. We should be working on figuring that out. And we should be arguing every day for the evacuation of Betelgeuse."

Gabriel tried to take Tam's words to heart. "How likely do you think it is that Betelgeuse would be severely impacted if the containment field fails?"

Tam considered this for a moment, then answered, "WHEN the containment field fails, you mean. My best model suggests an eighteen percent chance of this being a runaway fission reaction large enough to be of concern. An explosion larger than about a five-kiloton equivalent would wipe out Betelgeuse, but we're isolated here. The next nearest real town would be relatively unharmed, other than some broken windows, up to about five megatons—a thousand times more powerful. Not counting fallout, of course. That's a natural boundary for how far out we should evacuate," he said, holding up his hand to forestall Gabriel's response.

"But the thing that keeps me up at night isn't that—it's what else it could be." He looked at Gabriel. "A better-informed model might come up with other possibilities that are dangerous to Betelgeuse or beyond."

Gabriel frowned. "You didn't exactly answer the question," he said. "What do you think are the chances Betelgeuse will be destroyed if or when the containment field fails?"

Tam shrugged. "I don't know."

Now it was Gabriel's turn to throw his hands in the air. "Well, what do you *think*?" he exclaimed.

Tam shook his head. "There's no model in existence that I can apply to support any specific figure, but if you want me to pick one by gut feeling, how about twelve? There's a twelve percent chance that Betelgeuse will be destroyed, and a one hundred percent chance of containment field failure, over a long enough period…"

Tam rambled on, continuing to explain the various numerical assumptions underlying his guesstimate, but Gabriel ignored the rest. He had already heard the important number. Twelve percent.

Gabriel was silent for a while, pondering this information as Tam's physics lecture passed around him. Who knew this stuff better than this guy? Surely the Organization wouldn't have left Tam as his second-in-command if they knew he was wrong. And if he was right… Gabriel couldn't ignore the truth just because it was messy or difficult. There were nearly four thousand people in Betelgeuse, and he couldn't just shrug off their safety and still believe in what he was doing.

Gabriel thought of a question and interrupted Tam mid-drone.

"If you think there's such a chance of a major explosion, why haven't you left?"

Tam fell silent and looked at Gabriel blankly. "It's my responsibility," he said, shrugging. "My front line. And if I fail and this thing blows, being here is my just deserts."

Gabriel held the man's gaze for a long moment before nodding in approval. He settled on a decision.

"I don't think there are any unbridgeable gaps between what you want and what the Organization wants," he announced. "I'll request that you be given access to Theory's latest work on the experiment, and I will recommend the evacuation of Betelgeuse. In the meantime, you and I are going to do everything we can to put more bubble wrap around this bomb and then reinforce the freezer."

He glanced up at Tam to see if his attempt at levity was appreciated or not. Judging by the scientist's surprised expression, it was more than the man had expected. As Tam's expression changed to something more like haughty triumph, he dipped his head briefly in acknowledgment.

"Aye aye, Cap'n," he said, sarcasm cooling his words. "It's a start."

They worked non-stop for the rest of the day, compiling a list of the equipment they needed to order, tasks to assign to their engineering team, and things they needed help on from outsiders, and assigning a priority to each. For the most critical items and external services, Gabriel logged on to his company terminal and placed the requisition orders, flagging each as mission-critical priority.

Then they called in Carla Martin. She was tall and solid, with deeply-tanned, leathery skin and an air of honesty that frequently bled into brashness. Although Gabriel had only met her briefly in the cafeteria, he had already formed an appreciation for her. Gabriel discussed with her the current priorities for Engineering and how best to incorporate and prioritize the additions he and Tam had come up with. This started off well, as Carla had already figured out some of the necessary tasks and was supportive of the rest—at least at first, writing each one down in her battered notebook along with copious, indecipherable notes. As they continued adding more and more tasks, however, Carla's demeanor and expression became increasingly flat. Nevertheless, she continued to accept them, which was the important part as far as Gabriel was concerned. Carla and her team had always scored highly during evaluations and were reportedly some of the best engineers in the Organization.

Gabriel reviewed with her the equipment they had ordered that day and why it was critical, and Carla, after some mild grumbling, figured out where each piece could be installed and gave offhand estimates as to how long it would take for each to be operational. Something told him that her wild guesses were usually right on the money.

"When can you get us copies of your notes from this meeting?" Tam asked her after about two hours.

Carla stopped writing and looked around the room quizzically, as if trying to find something. Not finding it, she looked back at Tam.

"Are you talking to me?"

Tam nodded gravely.

"Because it sounded like you were talking to your secretary, and I don't know who that is," Carla went on, non-plussed.

"This guy," she pointed to Gabriel with the end of her pen, "is our boss, and I'm the Head of Engineering, an operational group that is critical to the functioning of this installation and everything we've been talking about for the past two hours." Her gaze fell on Tam.

"You, on the other hand, are some kind of professional critic whose job seems to involve complaining about the things others do. You have no direct reports and can order exactly zero people to do anything, except maybe Jonas. You could ask him to bring you a sandwich or maybe order some office supplies, but I don't think he'd listen to you either, unless you said please– which you didn't by the way."

Gabriel tried unsuccessfully not to grin.

"Could you *please* send us the notes from this meeting when we're done?" Tam asked, his face betraying not even a hint of embarrassment.

"No." Carla didn't even look at Tam, having already started to write something else in her notebook.

Tam grimaced and looked to Gabriel for help.

"Carla," he began, but she cut him off.

"Once you're done adding things to my list, Gabriel, my team and I will come up with the detailed implementation plan, timeline, and requisition list for your sign-off, which is required for me to order the equipment I'll need. This will all be in the system, of course, because we're not barbarians, and it will be accessible to you and various other people in the wider organization." Here her gaze flicked to Tam.

"Yeah, it will," Tam murmured, as if she had played right into his hands, and Gabriel laughed out loud.

Eventually, they reached a point where there were no further urgent issues they could address until the requisite equipment arrived. Gabriel looked at his watch.

"Jesus," he remarked. "It's seven PM!"

Tam just shrugged, but Carla looked shocked.

"Shit!" she exclaimed. "I need to call my fella—I told him he'd have to pick up my kid, but I didn't tell him to make dinner, and if I don't tell the two of them exactly when and what to eat, they'll starve."

Gabriel smiled. "Let's call it a night." He stood up and took a long, slow stretch. "Where am I bunked?" he asked, finally getting a moment to think about it for the first time.

Tam grinned. "We've got a corporate loft apartment in beautiful downtown Betelgeuse, perfect for the young urban professional." He stood up as well. "Let me get my keys and I'll drive you."

Carla nodded goodbye to Gabriel, the phone already at her ear.

Tam called out to her back, "You know you're not supposed to use phones in here!" but Carla didn't bother to respond. Tam looked back at Gabriel and complained, "Well, she's not."

Gabriel nodded. "We'll start enforcing protocol tomorrow. Sleep now."

FIVE

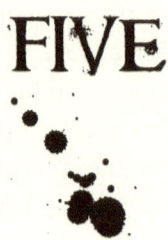

EARLIER

Hakk'rix, as it had come to think of itself, looked out over the barren landscape of vermilion rocks, shattered rubble strewn as far as it could see in every direction. It could hear the sky above roaring distantly, burning more intensely than it normally did, the light rippling and fluttering spasmodically. Two spots on the fiery horizon glowed even more brightly, where this world's two small, burning suns ignited the atmosphere. Ash and the occasional fleck of liquid fire fell in a scattering emberfall across the landscape.

The creature crouched behind a large wind-carved boulder, tasting the acrid air with its long, slithering tongue. It could detect no sign of a rival in the air this way, nor by any other senses it could bring to bear. The only living entities it could perceive nearby were the prey animals in the valley ahead, scrabbling hungrily at the moss that grew in the shelter of a steep ravine and singing softly to each other in polytones as they ate.

Its body was now perfectly adapted to life in this territory, and Hakk'rix was becoming more and more accustomed to it.

Its carapace was a ruddy red, very hard, and dusty like the rock it hid behind and the millions of other rocks just like it. The body's seven appendages were some of the most useful Hakk'rix had worn in its long life, keeping it low and close to the ground, always ready to attack or defend from multiple angles. Sometimes the claws clacked against the stones, but it was difficult to hear such minute sounds in this forsaken, wind-torn place.

The wind and the innumerable rocks and crevasses of these vast plains were welcome, as Hakk'rix's new size made it harder to hide. With its larger body had come a more fulsome, vital soulspark, along with a greater sensitivity to the soulspark in others. It was smarter, too, though Hakk'rix had always been cleverer than most of the rivals.

The most welcome change that had come with Hakk'rix's last ascension, however, was the energy it could feel crackling deep within its core, coursing to the ends of its claws along newly-formed veins with every beat of an entirely new organ. So far, Hakk'rix had only used this new potential on prey—a waste—but the effect was so powerful that it was almost eager for its next encounter with a rival. Hakk'rix could use it to paralyze, confuse, stop organs from functioning, or inflict devastating burns. There were probably even more possibilities, but these were all the creature had envisioned or required so far.

Hakk'rix finally advanced, skittering around the rock and following a depression in the terrain to stay out of sight of the prey animals. They likely couldn't see that far through the yellowish air and falling embers anyway, though, even with their huge, protruding eyes. It was always prudent to keep a low profile, and Hakk'rix had always been prudent, unlike so many of its rivals which seemingly coalesced from ambient soulspark only to attack and attack again until they were killed or ascended, growing ever larger until they met their end. Perhaps

Hakk'rix had not ascended as quickly or as often as other surviving rivals, but it had lived far longer than most. Hakk'rix suspected it was older even than some of the apex caste.

It squeezed its gnarled tongue out to taste the air again, then withdrew it into its fibrous, wet tongue-sheath to clean off the bitter dust.

The prey were still clustered in the crevasse ahead, but Hakk'rix could now make out one closer than the rest that was not feeding. Perceiving that it was instead facing in Hakk'rix's direction, seemingly guarding against approach from this side of the chasm, Hakk'rix began to climb the wall, moving closer still. Not all the way to the top where it would be exposed to the sky, but high enough on the wall to be out of sight of the animal.

As Hakk'rix approached the prey, it listened to the group's vocalizations. With a jolt that lanced from its core to the tip of each appendage and froze it where it clung, Hakk'rix realized it could understand the animals—at least some of them. Their whistles and clicks, which sounded no different than they always had, now carried meaning and information with far more complexity than Hakk'rix had ever suspected. It wondered if communication was common among this species, and it had only recently acquired the ability to understand them, or if these animals were exceptional.

Two of the long, spindly creatures clucked at the handful of young, warning them not to climb too high up the wall, while two others were deciding which way to go after they finished eating.

One of the animals in the main group whistled more loudly, but Hakk'rix couldn't parse the meaning of the sounds it made. Then a tense silence fell over the main group, and with a sudden inspiration, Hakk'rix realized that the loud whistle was a means of calling to the animal standing guard below. The sentry stirred uneasily, then called back uncertainly. Hakk'rix made its own presence as small as possible, hiding both mentally and physically, pressed flat against the rocks, thirty body lengths above the animal.

The loud one whistled and clicked again, and this time the lookout answered more affirmatively. Then those in the main group went back to eating and talking, apparently satisfied.

Hakk'rix thrummed excitedly, but quietly to itself. Not only could the animals use audible communication, but the one below was acting as if it was at least partially aware of Hakk'rix's presence. These were very fine animals indeed.

Now in place above its quarry, Hakk'rix began to broadcast its will—softly at first, buzzing in a way that usually calmed the prey animals and shrouded the predator's presence in a fog that was more mental than physical. This seemed to work, as the animal stood calm and still, its long, spindly arms hanging at its sides. Huge, luminous eyes took up almost the entirety of the animal's smooth, ovoid head, and it stared dully out into the emberfall. Hakk'rix could now see that this animal was holding the handle of a large stone club loosely in one hand, the head of the weapon resting on the ground. This animal used tools!

Hakk'rix crooned softly. With such advanced psyches, the animal and its offspring would be sure to make delicious meals. Hakk'rix's central maw, crowded with rock-hard, dagger-sharp teeth, spasmed open and shut in eagerness, its caustic saliva dripping onto the rocks below in what would have been a dead giveaway had Hakk'rix not already befuddled the beast it was stalking.

But even now, some part of Hakk'rix remained cautious, calculating. Was this pack of intelligent prey truly unclaimed? Out here, lost in the plains and far from any rival Hakk'rix had sensed, it seemed possible, but the predator's caution still sowed seeds of doubt. Could these animals truly be free and unbound, unnoticed by any other and ripe for the picking? Such a resource was unfathomably desirable and valuable. Was Hakk'rix even now in the territory of an apex rival? The loss of an entire clan of these prey animals would not go unnoticed by a member of the apex caste. It could even be a trap for unwary rivals—an exponentially more nourishing meal for one that could manage to secure it.

Hakk'rix was troubled. Conflicted. Even a few cycles ago, it would have been incapable of maintaining two strong feelings at once.

This one prey animal and no other—yet, it decided. It would not pass up this opportunity, but it would hold off on consuming any more of the group, instead observing them from afar, keeping watch for any rivals that might claim them. Perhaps if the rival was not too powerful, Hakk'rix might set a trap of its own. And if no rival came, Hakk'rix would claim all the animals, keeping the mature females and one or two of the males alive to make more. The very thought sent a thrill of pleasure through the predator's being.

The sentry was directly below, still becalmed and oblivious. Hakk'rix pushed off the wall slightly and allowed gravity to carry it hungrily downward, crashing into the beast below. The impact snapped two of the creature's limbs and knocked it off its two ridiculous feet and onto its side. Bipeds tended to be faster over long, flat distances, but Hakk'rix found their two legs incredibly impractical in every other situation. The animal couldn't even get off the ground now that it was injured. Hakk'rix used its new faculties to release a charge into the beast, stilling and silencing it before it could call out to the rest of its clan. Still, there was a chance that they might have heard the attack. Hakk'rix quickly began dragging the animal away, out of the ravine and toward the shelter of a huge pile of boulders that it had already picked out as a good hiding spot.

Once it had reached the relative safety of the rocks and

dragged the hapless animal through them and into the shielded center, Hakk'rix drew the paralyzed animal close. As tears leaked from its bulbous eyes, the thing's terror was palpable, intoxicating Hakk'rix and coating every pore on the sensitive underside of its limbs and body. All six of its eyes closed in involuntary pleasure at the powerful wave of fear and hopelessness emanating from its prey as Hakk'rix savored the complete surrender and relegation of whatever will and presence the creature possessed. Hakk'rix consumed all of it, absorbing the thing's psyche and will even as its maw settled on the animal's torso, latching onto the stiff, gray skin and slicing into the softer inner flesh. Even in its agony, the animal could not overcome Hakk'rix's dominating will and it lay there, submissive and unmoving.

Hakk'rix feasted gleefully and indulgently, only two of its eyes searching for threats.

Some time later, still sated and torpid from the meal and the resulting growth, Hakk'rix lay amid the pile of boulders. It could tell by the wind that the clan of prey animals had noticed that their sentry had been taken. They had mourned and raged, powerfully enough that Hakk'rix could still sense it from afar, but they had done so only briefly before fleeing in the opposite direction.

Hakk'rix vibrated softly in anticipation of the hunt.

It thought about the clan's ever-expanding trail across the plains, potentially perceptible to other hunting rivals, and how that trail now led back directly to Hakk'rix's current hiding place like a giant marker. The thought discomfited Hakk'rix, and it began to stir. It lifted itself off the ground and set out to examine the paths to the left and right of the chasm ahead, trying to decide which route would offer better cover as Hakk'rix tracked the animals.

It decided that the left was the more promising path, but as it took its first tentative steps from the pile of rocks, a tremendous CRACK reverberated through the air and rocks. It was more than just a sound; a terrible tearing sensation washed over Hakk'rix, disrupting its coordination and knocking its body flat to the dust as its legs twitched independently.

The sound faded, its echo fleeing across the plains, but the feeling lingered and changed. As Hakk'rix came to itself, searching in vain in all directions at once to determine the cause of its pain, it felt a wild, rich miasma of psychic vibrancy. It was an astonishing, heady sensation of incredible complexity and abundance. It was life—and on a scale that shattered the imagination. *So much* life and emotion! Hakk'rix stood stock still, tongue out, eyes wide, its whole body thrumming in astonishment.

Wondering if this was a trap, it began to gather its wits. What else could it be? But somehow it didn't feel like a trap. It felt... soft. *Naive.*

Hakk'rix was finally able to orient itself to the sensation and realized that the source was a long way away, back towards the southern lowlands. Far enough that it might lose the trail of this clan of prey altogether even if it wasn't a trap.

But this time, caution was ignored. Hakk'rix lurched unsteadily toward the new perception, even though it knew other rivals would surely come, too. Many others.

SIX

GABRIEL

G abriel awoke before six the next morning and was ready in plenty of time to grab a cup of coffee at the shop downstairs before Tam picked him up.

The place had large plate glass windows that looked out onto the street. The interior was vibrant with cherry-red countertops and round swivel stools. The glazed front door was fitted with a bell at the top that chimed pleasantly whenever it opened or closed. There was only one customer inside—an old, white-haired man sitting at a table by the side windows, reading an actual newspaper.

A well-proportioned young woman behind the counter took Gabriel's order—black coffee and a piece of fresh cinnamon bread.

"You're new here," the woman said frankly. Seemingly delighted at his novelty, she smiled broadly, showing a row of perfect, white teeth.

"I am!" Gabriel smiled back at her.

"Welcome," she replied brightly. "To the town and to The Morning Perk."

Gabriel thanked her warmly and walked over to a stool that

looked onto Main Street. He checked his watch as he sat down. He only had a couple of minutes until Tam was supposed to pick him up.

He opened the lid on his coffee so it would cool faster and held the cup to his nose. He felt the wet warmth of it wash over his chin and mouth and inhaled deeply, savoring the aroma of good, fresh coffee. *A harbinger of a new day and its possibilities*, he thought.

As he took a bite of his cinnamon bread, his taste buds spasmed, overwhelmed by the sugar, but the second bite went perfectly with his coffee, and he ate the rest with true pleasure.

When he was finished, he pulled out his phone and unlocked it to check his email. He had sent a brief status report to HQ last night, and he saw that he had already received a confirmatory reply, approving his approach and actions so far. In short, they wanted him to do more, faster.

He glanced at the time and noted that Tam was late. But that was just as well, Gabriel mused, since it gave him the opportunity to sit and enjoy the rest of his coffee at his leisure. However, it also reminded him that he needed to requisition a vehicle.

He held his coffee in both hands, relishing the warmth of the cup as he surveyed the scene outside the windows. There was a police station across the street and a fire station a block away. Next to the police station was a community bank and then an insurance office. Gabriel watched as a man carrying a thermos and a shoulder bag ducked into the latter and put on the lights, flipping the sign on the door to "Open" as he walked in.

The whole town was stirring, its people starting to go about their business for the day. It was quiet, sure, but not the boring hellhole Colonel Broadnax had threatened. It was nice, actually.

Gabriel heard Tam's ridiculous old Jeep pull up outside and looked at his watch again. *Eighteen minutes late*, he thought. He stood up, nodded and smiled at the young barista, and carried his coffee cup outside. Tam, who had been in the process of opening his door to get out, closed it again and then leaned over the passenger seat to unlock the door from the inside.

"Morning," Tam said pleasantly as Gabriel climbed in.

"Good morning, Tam. You know you're almost twenty minutes late," he stated rather than asked.

Tam frowned and ducked his head out his window to look up for some reason. *Is he looking at the sky to try to tell the time?*

"Oh. Sorry," he replied, with a hint of diffidence or perhaps confusion in his voice, as if he wasn't in the habit of considering what time even was.

Gabriel didn't know what to say. He couldn't help but grin slightly. Tam wasn't wearing a watch, but he had to have a phone that told the time, right? Surely he did. The company must have issued him one, even though he had yet to see Tam use or even carry it.

Instead of saying anything, Gabriel just shook his head. "Let's just get to the facility," he said.

"Aye aye, Cap'n!" Tam exclaimed bombastically. He pumped the accelerator twice and turned the key delicately, and the engine sputtered loudly to life. With an inadequate glance over his right shoulder, he threw the rig into reverse, giving it too much gas and jerking it into motion. Gabriel concentrated on not spilling his coffee.

As Tam rolled to a stop in the street, he shifted the transmission back into drive and stomped vigorously on the gas again, lurching them into forward motion and moving into the proper lane almost as an afterthought. Once again, Gabriel managed not to spill any of his coffee, but he didn't dare try and drink it until they were on a straightaway outside of town.

Gabriel was about to speak again when they hit a large, unmarked bump in the road so hard that they were both sent into freefall for half a second—long enough for his coffee to slop up and a portion of it to achieve escape velocity and slowly but inevitably sail onto the front of Gabriel's shirt.

He looked over at Tam, who was grinning like an idiot and not remotely surprised.

"Did you hit that bump on purpose?" he asked.

"Yeah!" Tam exclaimed. "Well, these days I do, anyway," he amended. "The first time it was an accident, but now it's like a free roller coaster." He was still grinning with childish glee. Gabriel sighed. He rolled down his window and dumped the rest of his coffee out onto the dusty desert road. He spilled most of it onto the side of Tam's Jeep, but he strongly suspected that Tam wouldn't care in the least.

The next few weeks were a blur. Gabriel worked sixteen-hour days at first—most of them right beside or across the desk from Tam, who continued to prove interestingly odd and extremely helpful. They mapped out every element of their power systems plan and saw to it that each was implemented. By the end of the third week, every part of the power system except the public utility itself had been equipped with multiple backups and automated failovers. The final link of power to the zero field generator now came from an array of eight power-regulating solid-state batteries, seven of which could fail without causing a single hiccup in power delivery. On that same loop was a failover switch that would detect a loss of power and throw the switch to the main loop in under five milliseconds, which was one-fifth of the field generator's minimum tolerance. The main loop itself had its own redundant power-conditioning and multi-path connections to seven power sources, including two sets of solar panels, four generators that cycled independently so that one was always on, and the public utility itself.

In addition to this system, of which Gabriel was

inordinately proud, they also installed some passive environmental monitors near the chamber that would provide a wealth of data to their monitoring systems on the other side of twenty-five feet of solid rock via a hardwire connection to avoid unnecessary EM radiation in the air. They then commissioned the project to install the blast damping material over every square inch of surface between the chamber and the stairwell and elevator shafts that were the only conduits to the upper floors.

Once that was done, Gabriel felt their tasks went from "most critical" to "potentially very important," with the primary goal of reviewing each component of the facility and evaluating whether there was a replacement that would be more durable and tolerant of various challenges, including power surges, EMP blasts, radiation, seismic activity, heat, sabotage, and wear and tear. When such an alternative was identified, the replacement was ordered and Engineering made each delicate substitution.

The Engineering unit was even busier than Gabriel and Tam because they had to actually implement the changes and draw up preventative maintenance schedules for all the new equipment. Gabriel got to know each member well and thoroughly vetted the four additional engineers the company brought in to help speed up the work. Carla, the Head of Engineering, was exceptional. She planned out everything she did ahead of time, gave accurate estimates of how long each task would take, and never needed to be reminded of anything. She wrote everything down in a notebook that she carried around with her at all times, even to the lunchroom, but never seemed to need to consult, even to answer the most complex questions.

Her attitude toward Tam, however, was both amusing and exasperating in Gabriel's eyes. She frequently acted as if she couldn't hear a thing Tam was saying, and sometimes when passing each other in the hall, she would walk right at Tam as if he weren't there, forcing him to dodge out of the way. Tam, for his part, either ignored this behavior or grinned at it as if it were a game they were playing.

She was perfectly dependable in personality and performance, however, and the only time she ever surprised Gabriel was when her boyfriend showed up at the gates of the facility one day on his Harley, yelling for her. Jonas summoned Carla over the PA system, which was so unusual that everyone in the facility wondered what was going on. Gabriel pulled up the video feed of the gate, worried that there might be trouble. Carla walked out the gate, facing away from the camera. She spoke so softly that Gabriel couldn't hear what she was saying over the microphone, but somehow she took the situation from him roaring at her to him begging for forgiveness over the course of ten minutes. The encounter ended in a hug, with Carla brazenly grabbing the guy's ass, and about five minutes later she was back at the worktable and ready for the next task. She flatly refused to talk about the incident, except to say that it wouldn't happen again. When asked about it, she simply smiled and shook her head. Gabriel decided that she was the best employee the Organization had.

No matter what they did, however, Gabriel could tell that Tam didn't think it was enough. There was a strained tension about the man that was infectious. Gabriel slept poorly most nights, which was unusual for him, and although he insisted on mandatory R&R for himself, Carla, and Tam in the hopes of keeping them sharp, he usually just felt guilty whenever he wasn't working.

SEVEN

TAM

Tam sat at the counter of Ruby's Cafe, sipping a hot cup of joe and watching the people in the restaurant as if they were a television show. For each group he looked at, he made up little stories to describe what was going on in their lives.

One couple was eating in silence—maybe they were nursing a grudge against each other. Tam decided the husband looked guilty about something and had blown their nest egg on a "Russian mistress" who turned out to be a fifteen-year-old hacker from Des Moines. Sitting at another table were three older men in short-sleeved button-downs, all with 1970s-style patterns. Tam thought they were talking about last night's bowling league, but would eventually get around to discussing the money the scruffy-looking one owed the others.

The door opened, and Tam saw that it was Gabriel, wearing rumpled outdoorsy clothes. He'd only been here a few weeks and already knew the surrounding area better than Tam did. He grinned at the man and motioned him over toward the stool beside him.

"Good morning, Tam," Gabriel said as he sat down.

"Morning," he replied. "Have you had the biscuits and gravy here?"

Gabriel smiled smugly, as if he had been expecting the question. Maybe Tam had asked him that before; he couldn't remember.

"I haven't," Gabriel admitted.

Tam nodded. "I insist you try them."

Just then, a waitress behind the counter brought Gabriel a napkin and some silverware. "What'll you have, sweetie?" she asked, her manner curt and efficient. She was a large woman, about fifty years old, and good at her job. She wore an apron over a thin, floral dress of modest cut, and her pinned-up hair was corralled by a visored hat that read *Ruby's*.

"Biscuits and gravy," Gabriel answered without hesitation. "Coffee." He paused for a second, then continued ordering. "Bacon… and two eggs over medium."

"And grits," Tam added.

"Yes, and an orange juice," Gabriel confirmed.

The waitress nodded, scribbling his order down on her pad, then ripped off the sheet with practiced ease and stuck the page into a holder by the nearest grill behind her. The cook glanced at it immediately, even though there were three similar sheets ahead of it.

"Where have you been?" Tam asked Gabriel, eying his uncharacteristically disheveled hair and wrinkled clothes.

"I went camping," Gabriel said.

Tam shook his head and tutted disapprovingly. "*I* socialized with human people for *my* required relaxation assignment and then watched old reruns of *Taxi* until I fell asleep in a bed indoors," he said.

Gabriel grinned. "To each his own," he said airily.

Tam chuckled. After a moment of silence, he said, "Carla,

Jenkins, and Weston from security and a couple of folks from town have a weekly poker game. You should join."

Gabriel probably already knew about the game, since he'd undoubtedly read a report on it from Security. It wasn't exactly forbidden, but regular interaction with the locals, especially when betting was involved, was something that needed to be reported in advance and required permission to go ahead.

He shook his head. "I like poker, but I'm not sure it would set a very good example for the troops."

Tam shrugged. "Suit yourself, but with all the things we're managing, it's hardly worth worrying about. Who knows—you might even learn something."

Gabriel raised an eyebrow. "Like what?" he asked.

"Like Jenkins is a terrible liar and Weston has a lot of women troubles. But with men." Tam took a sip of coffee, then spoke around a mouthful of it. "He's gay," he added, in case Gabriel didn't get it. He swallowed his coffee and continued, "And Carla hates the thought that her expression might give something away so much, she doesn't even look at her down cards until the second round of betting. Anyway, who knows what you might learn, and you *definitely* don't have anything better to do."

"Why do you say that?" Gabriel asked.

Tam grinned, then held up his hand and counted off the fingers. "First, I already suspected that you went camping last night because you have a piece of grass in your hair. Second, you came here alone—which is not surprising, as I have heard that women do not typically care for camping, and third, camping is dumb." He watched Gabriel's face fall at the comprehensiveness of Tam's argument.

Tam nodded to himself and lowered his hand. "Ergo, there are better things to do than sleep in a tent—and in any case, you need a better hobby than wandering off pointlessly into the wilderness. There are bears."

Just then the waitress came over, carrying a plate of eggs, bacon, and toast. "I'll bring the rest as soon as it's ready, shug," she said as she bustled off.

As Gabriel looked up from his plate, it seemed to dawn on him that Tam didn't have any food in front of him. Gabriel eyed him speculatively.

"Aren't you going to eat?" Gabriel asked.

Tam shook his head. "I ate before I came over."

Gabriel paused, a forkful of eggs halfway to his mouth. "Then why are you here?"

Tam shrugged. "It seemed like the thing to do. Interesting people watching, plus the coffee's pretty good." He took a slow sip to demonstrate.

Gabriel nodded. "That makes a lot of sense," he said, though the tone of his voice implied the opposite.

Tam eyed the man. "I can make eggs as well as they can, and I was hungry when I woke up," he said defensively.

"No, no," Gabriel said. "I get it. You ate at home because you were hungry, and then you came to a restaurant to sit and drink coffee."

Tam nodded slowly, still suspicious. "Yes. And to people-watch," he added.

"I got it."

"I like the atmosphere here," Tam muttered, half to himself. Gabriel could be a bit of a jerk sometimes.

"Definitely makes sense," Gabriel said again, still thinking it didn't at all, judging by his tone. He took a bite of the eggs and closed his eyes in an almost childlike pleasure that instantly endeared him to Tam once more.

After a few minutes of eating, Gabriel spoke again.

"Tam, why are you here?"

"I just told you."

"No, I mean why are you still at the facility, *really*. Given your projections, I would think you would want to get away. You could probably even do your work remotely." He looked over at Tam, his expression oozing earnestness.

Tam paused, ordering his thoughts.

"It's my responsibility. I have to help fix this. I told you that."

"But you don't even think it *can* be fixed," Gabriel said, arching an eyebrow.

Tam shrugged. "That's irrelevant. I have to try, and it's only right that I should suffer the same consequences as everyone else here."

Gabriel shook his head, his eyebrows furrowed.

"And before?" he asked. "Why didn't you leave when they wouldn't listen to your warnings about the experiment?"

"It was already my responsibility," he said, simply. "To try and help the Organization make better decisions by giving my opinion on the risks and ramifications of their plans. That's what I was hired to do and it's something I believe in. Science for science's sake is a worthwhile pursuit, but everything has consequences, and I needed to be involved and present to gather as much data as possible and influence things as best I could." Then, after a pause, he added, "Besides, with my level of clearance, I wasn't one hundred percent sure that they wouldn't disappear me if I tried to walk away." He winked at Gabriel, whose concerned expression gave him a rather constipated air.

The man held his gaze for a long moment, seemingly searching Tam's eyes for something, then nodded in what looked like respect. *Maybe he gets it*, Tam thought. Not everyone understood duty and obligation.

"Pass the hot sauce?" Gabriel asked.

Tam handed him the bottle and took a sip of coffee, which really was quite good. He sat back in companionable silence with his apparently very hungry friend, trying not to think about the zero field and whatever it was holding back.

EIGHT

GABRIEL

One Monday morning a few weeks later, after a surprise late-night video chat with his sister and his new niece, Gabriel made his way to the shop downstairs to get his coffee and cinnamon bread. He had snoozed his alarm and was running a little later than he would have liked. As he walked out the door of his building and toward the coffee shop, he looked up at the gray sky, thick with ominous clouds. The prospect of a storm made him nervous—their electrical system was designed with redundancy after redundancy for just such an event, but any test was stressful when it was life or death, no matter how well prepared you were.

After picking up his order, he walked out to his SUV, placing the bag containing the cinnamon bread on the passenger seat and popping the lid off his coffee so it would cool faster.

He started the vehicle to a low hum, eased it out onto the street, and picked up his coffee to cushion it against the jostling as he drove over the bumpy transition. He coasted toward the stop sign and was about to take his first eagerly anticipated sip, but just as the cup approached his face, a black cat shot out from underneath a parked car and ran across the street in front of him. He slammed on the brakes, perhaps a little too forcefully, and though he managed to keep his coffee from spilling all over the dashboard, the rebound sent a large slosh of the hot liquid surging onto his shirt and tie.

"Fuck!" he exclaimed. He looked over to where the cat had run, and immediately saw it, now sedately rubbing its face on a corner downspout. It seemed to be looking over its shoulder at him, its expression completely unrepentant. Gabriel looked down at his shirt and tie and sighed. "That *is* bad luck," he muttered. He hadn't spilled his coffee since his first full day here, when he had caught a ride to work with Tam.

He set the coffee cup, no longer full enough to be in any danger of spilling over, into the cup holder and leaned over to retrieve the bag of cinnamon bread from the passenger seat. He opened it and took out all the napkins the barista had helpfully included. He dabbed at his shirt and tie, trying to get as much of the coffee out as possible, but it didn't seem to be working. The tie and shirt might have gotten a little drier, but were no less stained. A car behind him honked, and he instinctively moved forward into the intersection, nearly hitting a pedestrian who was crossing. The man glared at him, but Gabriel, truly frazzled, was past him now and on his way again. He wanted to go back home and change, but as he looked at his watch, he realized that he would be late for a video meeting with the brass if he didn't go right now. He sighed and focused on the road.

By the time he arrived at the facility, he was hopeful that the stain had gotten far less noticeable. The guard at the gate didn't mention it, nor did Jonas when he walked in from the parking lot. Once he'd finished his morning meeting, he'd go into the bathroom and tend to it with some water.

"Wow, what a huge coffee stain! That's embarrassing!" Tam announced gleefully as he approached from down the hallway. One of the engineers walking down the hall turned to Gabriel and stared at his shirt.

Gabriel tried to scowl at Tam, but it ended up as something more like a lopsided grin—they had become friends over the past few weeks.

"Thank you," he managed, trying to be glib.

Tam nodded appreciatively. "You're welcome," he said earnestly. Sometimes it was hard to tell when Tam was joking.

"Did your communiqué have any new instructions today?" Gabriel asked, trying to change the subject.

Tam shook his head. "About your tie?" he asked. "No, of course not—they don't know about it yet. No, it's all the same stuff. I've been telling them that all the addressable issues now have redundant support, though I'd be happier if we could take the facility off the local power grid altogether." Gabriel nodded; he'd heard that request about twenty times in the past month, and the power system already had scrubbers, filters, generators, and enough instant backup batteries to power the facility for two months even without the gennies. He thought it was probably as robust as they could make it without having a nuclear power plant on site, and both Washington and Los Angeles seemed to agree.

Tam shrugged off Gabriel's lack of a response. "Anyway, what did you get up to this weekend? You missed the poker game on Saturday night."

"I take it from your grin that you took advantage of my absence by winning," Gabriel said. Tam's typically deadpan expression managed to exude an air of very false modesty.

"I've been on a good run lately," he allowed.

"I'll be there next week," Gabriel said. "Someone needs to help keep you from taking all of Security and Engineering's money. How can Carla be so good at mechanical things and yet so bad at cards?"

Tam took the question as non-rhetorical and began cataloging Carla's poker shortcomings. "She rarely bluffs, and it's obvious when she tries. She always folds when you signal that you have a better hand than her, but she'll always see you along the way as long as you don't bet too big. Very predictable." He paused, perhaps realizing he had gone off on a tangent, then said, "Anyway, where were you on Saturday?"

"I was camping in the National Forest, up on Sacaton Mountain," Gabriel said.

Tam shuddered. "Ugh. Camping again," he said predictably. "You do have a bed at your place, right? So you don't *have* to sleep on the ground where bears can get you? You know, there are only two reasons to go camping—one, if you don't have a home, and two, if you're sixteen and your parents won't give you the privacy you need to indulge your raging hormones." He paused. "Oh wait, did you go with someone? Was it that waitress at Ruby's? The ginger who seems to own nothing but halter tops and tight denim shorts? She's *lithe*, right?" He exaggerated the word lithe in a way that made it sound very, very dirty, which was even funnier to Gabriel because he had never seen Tam display an ounce of attraction to anyone on his own behalf—it was almost as if he were just trying to bond with Gabriel over Gabriel's attraction to women.

He just shook his head, his grin reappearing on his face almost against his will. As was typical, Tam had taken the conversation all the way through awkward and somehow back to amusing. He had gone camping alone, but his friend seemed to be enjoying himself so much that Gabriel didn't have the heart to correct him. Instead, he just smiled and said, "I'll see you at the ten o'clock session."

The storm he'd been anticipating didn't come at first, but the threat of it grew darker and darker as the afternoon wore on. A little after five, Gabriel received a message on his terminal from Tam that said, "Drinks?" After a long day of meetings and reviewing reports from a dozen systems and potential sources of disruption, Gabriel was more than ready for a cold one, and he could watch the weather reports on his phone from there. He responded, "Affirmative. OL in 5."

The Officers' Lounge, as they called it, was one of the few privileges of rank he'd instituted once things had slowed down a bit. It was a rec room for himself, Tam, and Carla with a brown corduroy couch, a TV, a ping-pong table, a couple of comfortable non-office chairs, a fridge, and a coffee table that was just the right height to put your feet up on. Against one wall was a dry-erase board that they frequently used in their brainstorming sessions. And since only the three of them were allowed in here, unlike the staff fridge in the commissary, their fridge usually contained a stock of alcohol along with their sack lunches, though only Gabriel and Carla partook. All in all, it was a cozy and relaxing place—one in which they often hung out. Gabriel had caught Tam napping here more than a few times, and even he himself had tried it once or twice. Pulling a twelve-hour day on site was enough to excuse taking a short nap in Gabriel's mind, and while Tam didn't seem to need an excuse, he tended to keep strange hours anyway. It was almost as if he generated his work schedule at random, which wouldn't surprise Gabriel in the least. He had never chided Tam about his schedule or his naps, though. The guy clearly loved his job and did everything that was expected of him and then some. Gabriel just hoped it would prove to be enough.

When he walked into the lounge, Tam was already on the couch, feet up on the table, a Coke in his hand. There was a baseball game on the TV. "Rockies are down two to one to the Cards in the second inning," Tam greeted him.

Gabriel made a beeline for the fridge, loosening his coffee-stained tie on the way. "Fine, yours?"

Tam grinned. "Good. Very productive, boss."

Gabriel grabbed a can of beer and flopped down on the

other end of the couch. They sat in happy silence for a while, watching the game.

In the third inning, the first batter for the Rockies hit a hard one-hopper down the third base line, but the third baseman made a terrific backhand stab and turned to launch a beautiful, barely arching throw across the diamond to beat the runner by a step.

"That was breathtaking," Gabriel said. "Baseball is such a beautiful game—a team versus team competition executed through a series of one-on-one battles."

Tam frowned. "It's okay. Some would say it's too slow. I saw an article in the *Wall Street Journal* a few years ago that analyzed some games and came to the conclusion that 90% of the man minutes spent during the game are spent literally standing there doing nothing."

Gabriel shook his head. "First of all, why were you reading the *Wall Street Journal*? Second, what does baseball have to do with Wall Street? Third, that's ridiculous! It's called building anticipation. Is waiting for a pitch to be thrown any less exciting than a backwards pass in soccer? Or the forty seconds between every play in football? There's planning and communication going on between the pitcher and the catcher, positioning of the infield and outfield based on the player's historical balls in play, and how the pitcher is going to try to pitch to him—inside, outside, off-speed, fastball—then the wind up and throw. It's the pitcher saying, 'Here's my best stuff, hit it if you can'. At the end of the at-bat, the batter either sits down dejectedly or gets on base. The pitcher wins or loses on each and every batter. The batters even get at least three chances during their at-bat, which is something that seems very American and very fair."

Tam shrugged, but now he was grinning. "Then why not watch chess? Or paint drying? A backwards pass in soccer means that the offense is resetting and trying to get the defense out of position—every player on the field is moving. It's basically the opposite of baseball. That's why baseball is a dying sport."

Gabriel adopted an air of affront. "Baseball is a bastion of perfection in an otherwise imperfect world."

Tam had his mouth open to offer what was obviously going to be a snarky rejoinder when he turned back to look at the television, which had lost its signal and gone snowy. "Did I mention they were calling for a storm today?" he said instead.

"Yeah," Gabriel said absently. "I get the reports twice a day. It started an hour ago, but it must be really bad out there to completely knock out the satellite signal. Hard to believe—it rains so little here." He shook his head. "Shouldn't matter anyway." Gabriel knew that despite everything they had done, Tam's analysis of the facility's power systems suggested that they were still a likely weak point, along with a half-dozen other categories. He wasn't sure if he was trying to reassure himself or Tam. "Still, it wouldn't hurt to go to the control room and look at the monitors directly."

Tam shrugged and put his hand on the arm of the couch as he braced himself to stand up. But before he could do so, the lights in the room flickered briefly. Gabriel and Tam locked eyes. Gabriel's phone emitted a loud, high-pitched beep. "That's the system switching over to the batteries," he said, already trotting toward the door.

"But the lights should never have flickered," Tam said, his eyes big as saucers. In one motion, he pulled himself up and sprinted toward the door after Gabriel. But before he was even halfway there, Gabriel had already reached the door and opened it.

A blindingly bright, weirdly sticky-looking light spilled through the doorway into the room, and then all he could see was the side of the room suddenly rushing toward him, smacking into him with thunderous force, before he crumpled to the floor.

His entire world was nothing but a deafening roar; then everything went quiet and dark as he slipped out of consciousness.

NINE

SARAH

The knife flashed, reflecting the light of the bedside lamp. Sarah stared at the blade with a blank, out-of-focus gaze, awash with feelings of numbness and an overwhelming rush of grief at the same time. And intense anxiety. *How could anyone feel so many different kinds of terrible at once?*

So she did what she always did when she felt this way. She pressed the sharp, cold blade against the pale flesh of her inner thigh and held it there. Her heart rate quickened, the fear and anticipation grounding her momentarily, redirecting her miasma of emotions toward something... actual. Then she sliced, the blade biting into her skin, marring it, separating it with ease so that the rich red blood welled out immediately. Just enough. The pain was sharp and warming. She hissed, feeling the endorphins flood her bloodstream as she held the folded-up toilet paper to the cut. She knew enough now not to leave any evidence, not to let her mother find out. *That's just what I need,* she thought, *Mom crying over me for two days instead of over Dad stumbling home on a Tuesday night and pissing on the couch.*

Once her leg stopped bleeding, she applied the antibiotic and the scar gel, then put on a Band-Aid from her secret stash. She'd gotten really good at this part, and the cuts always healed very well. They were barely visible after a couple of days.

She sighed, pulled up her sweatpants, and put her shoes back on—bright purple cross-trainers with a black flower print. *Twenty-three is too old to still be doing this*, she thought, but nothing else seemed to help when she was spiraling, and she was doing that a lot these days. Cutting didn't make her feel any less terrible or magic away all those negative emotions, but she felt more in control after, more able to put a brave face on and be there for her parents, to do whatever she could to try to help the people who couldn't help themselves.

As if on cue, her mom called out to her from the living room, probably looking for help getting off the couch and to the bathroom. Her Parkinson's was getting worse.

"Coming, Mom."

She crossed over to the door and had just put her hand on the doorknob when the lights went out. The TV promptly lost power as well, plunging the house into silence so that all she could hear was the sound of the rain and wind outside, and then a booming clap of thunder. An overwhelming wave of panic, disorientation, and nausea washed over her, and she fell to her knees. The intensity of her vertigo was astonishing—she felt like she was having a seizure, with all her muscles, including her heart, acting independently of one another. Nevertheless, she managed to avoid falling all the way to the floor as she knelt there, still gripping the doorknob with her forehead now resting against the wall.

When she came to, her first coherent thought was of her parents. Neither had said anything, or called for her again—were they hurt? How long had she been here? *I have to help them*, she thought. Using the doorknob to steady herself, she climbed shakily to her feet. She no longer felt the nausea or dizziness, but she was weak and wobbly like a newborn fawn.

"Get it together, Sarah," she hissed. She turned the doorknob and opened her door, still holding onto the knob for support. Then she let go of it and took her first tentative step. She almost fell, but caught herself by putting a hand on the wall. The next step was a little easier than the first.

"Mom?" she croaked. "Dad?"

Over the sounds of the storm outside, she could just barely make out the sound of a moan from the living room. The sound refocused her, and she was able to pick up the pace without falling.

Her mother was lying on the floor in front of the couch with her eyes closed. Her father was slumped back in his recliner, fresh vomit on his chest and shoulder. His eyes were open and staring, glassy. Sarah's heart thudded painfully in her chest, having finally found a steady rhythm.

Frantically, she felt for a pulse on her father's neck and couldn't detect anything at first. Then she felt a flutter and he blinked his eyes. Relief welled up in her and she turned to her mother, who was moving her head back and forth as if in denial.

She knelt beside her. "Mom?" she said, gently shaking her mother's shoulder. "Mom? Can you hear me?"

Her mother's eyes flickered open, and her gaze wandered around before finally settling on Sarah's face. Her slack features resolved into an expression of anguish that tore at Sarah's heart.

"Oh, sweetie, I don't feel good," she breathed, barely loud enough to be heard.

Her skin felt cold and clammy. Sarah helped her to straighten out her crumpled body on the floor in front of the couch, then hurried back to her room to get her phone. *I've got to call 911*, she thought.

Her phone was where she had left it, plugged in on her bedside table. She picked it up to make the call, but the screen stayed completely black, as if it were dead. It even *felt* dead—heavy and useless. *Maybe there was a power surge or something*, she thought. She put the phone down and ran back to the end table next to the couch, where her mother's phone rested. It too was completely dead, and, unlike Sarah's, it hadn't been plugged in. Sarah turned to her father, his chest still moving, albeit in shallow, irregular breaths, and dug around in his jeans pocket for his phone, making sure not to step in his vomit.

His phone wasn't working either. She was at a loss momentarily, then remembered their landline. She ran over to the house phone, which in her experience tended to receive mostly telemarketing calls, and picked it up. Nothing. She wasn't sure if that was normal in a power outage, but she thought she remembered that landlines had their own power source, since they weren't plugged into an outlet. In any case, it was now a dead chunk of plastic.

What am I going to do? she thought, panic rising within her. She ran to the front door of the house and jerked it open, pulling in a cold gust of rain.

"Help us!" she shouted at the top of her lungs. "Somebody help us, please!" Her voice seemed to be lost in the roar of the storm, and she feared that no one would hear her. So she screamed—a deafening, ragged, wordless wail loud enough to wake the dead. "Somebody please help us!" she shrieked, loud enough to hurt her own ears. She was pretty sure her scream had been audible in every house remotely nearby, but no doors opened, no flashlight beams appeared; there was no sign of life at all. Only the wind responded with its own tremulous howl.

She ran out into the driving rain, which immediately soaked her clothes and hair. She ran next door to the Johnsons' house. They were friends of her parents, sort of, and helped out sometimes. Plus they were always home. She dashed up onto the porch and banged hard on their door. It wasn't completely latched, and her banging jarred it open enough for it to bump into something on the floor. In the failing, storm-darkened twilight, Sarah could see that it was someone's leg. Mrs. Johnson was lying on the floor right behind the door. Sarah bent down and reached through the door, easing the woman away from it so that she could squeeze inside. Mrs. Johnson was completely limp and unresponsive. Sarah thought she might be dead. She felt for a pulse at the carotid, but couldn't find one.

Sarah stifled a cry of fear. She'd never seen anyone dead before, except during a trip to the morgue for a college anatomy class. "What the fuck is going on?" she breathed, fighting not to be overwhelmed. "Mr. Johnson!" she shouted. "Mr. Johnson, are you in here?"

"I'm here," she heard from the living room. Not shouted— barely loud enough to make out, in fact. The word was said in such a normal tone of voice, so shockingly out of place in the present circumstances, that Sarah wasn't sure she'd actually heard it. She rose and walked into the living room. Mr. Johnson was sitting on the couch facing the blank, lifeless television screen. He looked up at Sarah as she came in and said, "Oh hello Sarah—was that you shouting?"

At first, Sarah was at a loss for words and could only nod. Then, all in a rush, she blurted out, "Yes, my parents are sick and need help, but no one is answering no matter how loud I scream, and the phones are out. Your wife..." but she didn't know what to say after that, so she just lapsed into silence.

Mr. Johnson nodded. "She fell at the door and won't answer me. I don't think we're well." He gasped as if he was having trouble breathing.

"What's wrong with everyone?" Sarah asked, hating the weak and hopeless sound of her own voice.

Mr. Johnson didn't answer for a moment, but then looked up at her and said, "Judgment, I suspect." He closed his eyes and leaned his head back against the couch cushions. "God knows I deserve it," he murmured, seemingly to himself. "I'm surprised it took your mom, though—that woman's a saint for putting up with your old man."

The comment stung; her father's alcohol issues were common knowledge, it seemed, but her mother was no saint either.

"I'm going to the clinic to get help," she decided aloud. Once she had said it, it seemed obvious that she had to try. "Do you need anything before I go?"

The man just shook his head against the couch, eyes still closed.

Sarah turned and ran out the door, leaving it ajar in the rain. She leaped over a puddle in a vain attempt to keep her purple shoes dry and darted inside her house to get a rain jacket.

After throwing it on, she checked on her mom and dad. Her mom's condition was unchanged, but Sarah couldn't find her dad's pulse at all, nor could she see him breathing. She performed CPR on him through her sobs, but it was just like performing it on the mannequin she'd used for training—his still form remained lifeless and unchanging. Her sobs grew to a wail as she took his keys out of his pocket and pulled herself away, dashing out the door and back into the rain.

She ran to the car, jerked the door open, and slid into the seat, dripping water everywhere. She put the key in the ignition and turned it, but the engine didn't respond at all. There wasn't even the usual clicking-no lights, no sound. Completely dead, just like the phones. Somehow, she had expected this; she left the keys in the ignition as she lurched back out of the car and into the street, heading downtown toward the only clinic in the county.

She yelled for help periodically as she jogged down the street, but even though the wind and thunder seemed to be letting up some, no one answered her cries. *Is everyone sick?*

On Main Street, she had to pass a car stopped in the middle of an intersection. There was a woman in the driver's seat, unmoving, her head back against the headrest. She hurried on, afraid to look more closely.

The ten minutes it took her to get to the clinic were the longest of her life. Sarah ran to the automatic front doors, but they wouldn't open and she couldn't see anyone at the front desk or even in the waiting room. She stuck her fingers in the crack between the doors and pulled as hard as she could, sliding them fitfully apart a few inches at a time until she could slip inside.

"Hello?" she called, hopeful despite everything. But there was no answer. She ran past the front desk, where she saw the receptionist lying motionless on the floor. She went from door to door—there were only three exam rooms—and found the doctor in the last one, collapsed on the floor, practically on top of an elderly patient.

Sarah fell to her knees, sobs finally overcoming her. She had no idea how to help her parents or anyone else. Even as she'd passed more and more dead or dying people on her way here, she'd never applied that growing trend to the doctors. *So stupid!* She had always thought of this town as terminally ill but had never imagined anything as horribly literal as this. Had there been a chemical spill at the base or something-some poison that was affecting everyone but her?

She stood back up and wiped her cheeks with the back of her hand. Crying wasn't going to fix anything. *What should I try next?* She went back to the front door and looked out. The rain seemed to be stopping, although it was still dark and cloudy. She stepped out into the street and looked around, hoping for some inspiration on what to do now.

She saw movement and whirled toward it. There, walking down Main Street toward her, was a man she didn't recognize. He looked to be in his thirties or forties and seemed fit and healthy. He was bearded and a little scruffy, with a tattoo on his neck that was visible even from twenty yards away, but he moved toward her with an easy confidence. He passed the broken down car in the intersection without even glancing at the person inside.

"Hey there," he called out as he approached. He was *smiling*. "You need some help?"

Sarah nodded, eyes wide, trying to wrap her mind around how this man could be smiling. "Yes," she said. "My parents are ill and I can't find anyone to help them. Everyone seems to be sick." *Or dead*, she thought.

"Yeah, I've noticed," he said, seemingly amused by the understatement. "Everybody keeled over at the same time, just about, though some didn't die at first, and some, like me and now you, got over it real quick." He smiled reassuringly and then said, "Seems like some kind of kismet."

Sarah had heard the word before, but didn't quite know what he meant by it, so she said, "Can you help my parents? Do you have any medical training?" It sounded so naively hopeful when she said it that she almost winced, but incredibly the man nodded.

"I was an assistant medic in the military," he said. "I can help you. My name's Carl. But first, let's get some things from in there," nodding behind her at the clinic. Sarah moved out of his way, and as he brushed past her, she thought she saw him ogle her body even through her bulky rain jacket, which had made her feel like she was wearing ogle-proof armor. It creeped her out.

She followed him into the clinic. He didn't call out to or even look at any of those who had fallen. He walked back through the building, Sarah trailing behind, and tried each of the doors until he found a locked one to a room in the back. After trying the knob unsuccessfully, he reared back and kicked a booted foot into the door next to the handle. It flew open, part of the door frame splintering off as it banged against the wall.

Inside was a small storage room with a single window and a few wire shelves in the middle containing bottles and boxes of medicine. The man went straight to the shelves and began reading labels in the failing light. He took some needles and syringes and then grabbed every single bottle of hydrocodone and something called meperidine. No antibiotics, no bandages, no other equipment. *This man was after drugs, not medical supplies.*

Sarah had moved closer to read the labels over his shoulder, and when he turned back to her, she started, not liking being so close to him. He turned his unsettling smile on her in a way that seemed like it was supposed to be reassuring, then looked around the room until he saw a gray carrying case for some kind of cinderblock-sized portable medical device. The man upended the bag, dumping the expensive-looking machine along with its various fittings and tubes onto the floor with a loud crash, the device breaking open as it hit the hard tile. Then he stuffed his medicine bottles into the bag and pulled the strap over his head. Once he was done, he looked over at her and said, "Now, let's go see your parents."

Sarah hesitated, goosebumps of alarm spreading along her arms. She didn't want to be around this man anymore, but there was literally no one else. She remembered her poor mother and not being able to find her father's pulse, and tears blurred her vision. She nodded, not trusting her voice, and walked out of the room, feeling the man's filthy eyes consume her as she passed.

They walked down the middle of the deserted street in the waning twilight. The storm had abated, fading to a muffling, cloying wetness. The town was already darker than Sarah had ever seen it before because the streetlights weren't on. She shouted for help every block until her voice was raw, but no one ever answered. The man behind her never joined in, though he seemed content to let her yell.

Sarah's steps slowed as they finally approached her house. She was now certain that she didn't want this man's help after all, but she couldn't think of what to do. She was apparently utterly alone with this creep whose first action after everyone had fallen gravely ill was to steal drugs. *How could you be so stupid and naive*, she berated herself. She couldn't think of anything else to do now but run.

She was a good runner, or had been four years ago when she graduated from high school. She'd played soccer for a season and then run track, and had continued to jog on and off for a while after that, until her life had gone off the rails in the last couple of years.

So, when they reached the block before hers, she suddenly broke into a sprint. The man cursed behind her as she took off, and she heard him stumble as he tried to give chase. The roads were slick from the rain, and though she was not wearing athletic clothes, she was wearing her favorite purple sneakers and she flew across the pavement like an Olympic sprinter. The pent-up adrenaline from the last hour or two was churning her legs like pistons. She wanted to run straight home, but she didn't want to lead the man there, so she veered left and ran down a side street. She risked a glance over her shoulder and saw that the man was following her, no longer smiling. He was pretty fast, but not as fast as she was. She lengthened her stride and focused on putting more distance between them, her purple shoes splashing in puddles every few feet.

Two blocks farther on she finally saw another person who was still upright—an older woman, her hands on her knees in her yard, as if she, too, had been running. But when Sarah called out to her, relief welling up inside her, the woman abruptly rushed to the entrance of her house door and threw herself inside, slamming the door shut behind her. Sarah made it to the door immediately after and screamed, pounding on it with her fist.

"Help me, please! There's a man chasing me! Please help me!"

Sarah looked over her shoulder as she banged on the wood and saw the man still coming toward her. Winded and cautious now that she'd found someone, he had slowed to a walk but hadn't stopped.

Sarah hammered on the door even harder. "Please, ma'am, I need help!"

But the woman didn't answer. Sarah thought she heard her crying behind the door. "Go away," the woman said, her words barely audible over Sarah's pounding fists. "Go away and hide or they'll get you, too."

The man was getting too close now, and Sarah leaped off the porch on the opposite side, breaking back into a sprint and arcing around the back of the house toward Main Street in the hopes of then doubling back and heading home, where she could lock the door and hide inside, get a kitchen knife or her dad's baseball bat.

The man continued to follow her, like a wolf patiently tracking her scent, and Sarah began to experience a new emotion. Anger. *What the fuck is wrong with people?* She used the emotion to fuel her tired muscles and lengthened her stride again. She made a direct line back toward her house now, confident that she could beat the man there and lock the door behind her.

She reached her block. As she crossed the empty intersection, she saw movement out of the corner of her eye. Up the road, two dark blocks away, a young-looking man was running across the intersection. Sarah was about to call out to him for help, but her voice caught in her throat, and she missed a step as she saw some... *thing* step out into the street behind him.

It was at least twelve feet tall, and looked like a giant eyeball on four long, powerful legs. The whole thing was covered in hundreds or thousands of thick red strings that undulated and quested about, making the abomination look furry, or like it was infested with worms. As the thing strode across the intersection, Sarah was startled to see a woman stuck to the side of the creature's carapace, held in place by hundreds of the stringy appendages. The woman's eyes were open, and she was moaning loudly enough for Sarah to hear from down the street.

Sarah stared, her mind overwhelmed. *Is it eating her?* She forgot to keep moving her feet, and would have just stood there forever, trying to make sense of it all, but she heard her attacker panting behind her, prompting her to take off once more. She was almost home. She heard the man gasp in astonishment behind her—he must have seen the thing, too.

She made it to her front door and threw it open, but before she could dash inside, she felt him grab her rain jacket. He yanked hard, jerking her easily off balance and she fell backwards into him. Then he shoved her forward with shocking force, and she spilled painfully across the threshold and onto the living room floor of her house, crashing into the little wooden table where her mom kept her keys and the junk mail. The man stepped quickly inside and shut the door, locking it behind him. He peered out of the little window next to the door, puffing loudly, trying to look up the block to where the creature had been. Seeming reassured that neither it nor anything else was going to disturb them, he turned his attentions back to the little purple-shoed firecracker. Life was too short to pass up an opportunity like this.

Sarah scrambled to her feet and tried to run to the kitchen, but the man pounced on her like some kind of hateful wild animal before she made it five feet. His weight bore down on her, pinning her to the carpet, her shoes scrabbling uselessly against the floor. He began to tear at her clothes with his hands, making no sound at all.

Panic, revulsion and powerlessness flooded through her, as

if she'd fallen into a hole in the world, almost completely disconnected from her surroundings and her own brain, which was screaming incessantly for her to do something. But she couldn't. All she wanted was to get away, get to a knife, defend herself, but nothing worked. She couldn't even turn over to kick at him—he was so heavy—*how could anyone be so heavy?*

"Mom, Dad," she said, sobs and terror choking her voice. She looked over at her parents, still lying where she had left them. Their eyes stared unblinkingly at the ceiling, away from where Sarah lay pinned to the floor, the man writhing on top of her, wrenching off her clothes inch by inch.

Sarah closed her eyes so she couldn't see the world anymore either. She wished she could die. She thought of the monster she had just seen, and the thought struck her that she might be able to lure it here, that it didn't matter whether it killed her too.

So she screamed.

TEN

GABRIEL

As Gabriel began to wonder whether he was alive or not, the first thing he noticed was that it was dark. Disorientatingly, surprisingly dark. *Why was it dark?* He felt... odd. Almost like he was drunk and in the process of doing something stupid. He started to worry that he'd overslept, which reminded him that he actually *had* overslept today, and then all of it came flooding back to him. His stomach dropped, and he began to feel nauseated. And sore. He smelled smoke in the air.

"Tam?" he croaked, still not moving.

There was no answer. He levered himself onto his side and looked around the officers' lounge. As his eyes adjusted, he could dimly make out the outlines of the room and the wreckage inside. He pushed himself slowly up the wall into a standing position, then shuffled carefully over to where he suspected Tam lay, near a jumbled pile of furniture. Tam was lying on his back against the couch, one arm outstretched above his head. The framed poster of Albert Einstein sticking out his tongue that had been hanging on the wall by the door was now draped across his legs. The side of Tam's head had been bleeding, but it had stopped and the blood had dried. Gabriel wondered how long they'd been out. He knelt down and reached out to shake Tam's shoulder.

"Tam," he said. "Wake up." Tam's eyes didn't open right away, but his eyebrows furrowed like those of a kid fighting against waking up for school.

"Come on, buddy. Let me know you're okay," Gabriel said.

"What. The. Hell." Tam groaned. He cracked open one eye and looked up at Gabriel. Gabriel tried for a reassuring grin, but it was probably wasted in the near darkness and felt more like a skeletal rictus of death. "What happened?" Tam asked.

Gabriel answered quickly, as if he had been rehearsing it in his head, "Well, it's dark and there was a blast, so I'd say a containment failure is very likely. But we're still alive, presumably, so it probably didn't result in a nuclear explosion."

"But the power's still out," Tam managed weakly as he put a hand to his head where it had been bleeding. He winced. "Nothing that wouldn't kill us should be able to knock out all the backups. Not even an EMP should be able to do that—it's all shielded." He groaned again.

Gabriel was about to speculate when Tam's brow furrowed anew and he pulled himself into a sitting position against the wall. "Wait," he said, cutting Gabriel off. "How can we see?"

"What?"

"I mean, the power is out. We're underground. None of our lights are working, and I don't see any light source anywhere." His words began to pick up speed. "Yet I can make you out, and I can see the outlines of the room around us. Also, now that I mention it, I think we might be glowing."

Gabriel looked down at his arm, which, now that he was focusing on it, did seem to be glowing a little. At least he could see it relatively clearly. He brought his hand closer to his face for a better look, and as he moved, a small spark of light flitted from near his wrist toward his elbow like a miniature shooting star or will-o'-the-wisp, hugging the contours of his forearm. He stared down at his arm in confusion.

"Huh," he said in a dead voice. "That can't be good." He realized that he was probably in shock because this revelation simply didn't carry the emotional impact he felt sure it should.

Tam was now waving his own hands up and down like a panicked mime—he seemed to be feeling better physically anyway—as he watched his own skin-based shooting stars. He was wide-eyed and clearly freaking out. "I very seriously doubt this is healthy," he muttered, half to himself. "Maybe we've been irradiated or quark-ized or something. I certainly don't feel normal—I feel very, very weird."

"Maybe radiation could explain why none of the backup systems are working to power the lights?" Gabriel wondered. "Can you get up? I want to go check out the control room to see if everyone's okay and if there's any data."

Tam nodded as if to reassure himself and reached for Gabriel's hand. Gabriel dutifully hauled him to his feet and braced him there for a moment. After a slight wobble, Tam steadied himself and nodded more confidently.

"Let's do this," Gabriel said. The pair of them picked their way carefully over to the door of the officers' lounge.

"How long do you think we were out?" Tam asked. "My phone is dead."

Gabriel checked his own, then glanced at his watch. "Mine is too, but my watch is a wind-up mechanical and it says it's nine fifteen. We were out for over three hours."

Tam was silent for a moment, then said, "I'm surprised there aren't any rescue teams down here by now." He thought about it some more, then added, "Unless the surface is slagged, or more likely, the area is too hot."

Gabriel nodded; he'd been thinking the same thing. If the propagation event had released enough radiation, not only would they begin to burn and sicken, but it could delay any rescue attempt by hours or more. Despairingly, he tried again to think of any way the containment field might still be working, but to no avail.

They listened for any of their coworkers as they made it into the hallway, but the only sounds they heard were ominous structural groans and the distant crash of falling debris.

"Hello?" Gabriel called out. They waited in silence for a reply. "Is anyone there?" he shouted even louder. His voice seemed completely out of place in the silence.

After another moment of waiting for a response that never came, Gabriel said, "Come on, maybe we'll find the others on the way down to Observation," and they continued walking. As they reached the main passageway that ran along the center of the facility on each level and included access points to the elevator and stairwell that led from the surface down to the functional levels, the destruction became markedly worse. Rents in the floors and walls appeared to their right and left, even in the structural metal. The smell and smoke of burning things hung in the air, so foul that Gabriel assumed it probably carried some toxic fumes.

They reached the engineering office and saw that the door was ajar. Gabriel looked inside and saw an overturned bookshelf in front of the door, almost as if someone had tried to barricade the door from the wrong side—the doors opened outward. Gabriel stuck his head in, and Tam leaned forward to look as well. Just inside, next to the wall, there was something... *terrible* on the ground.

"Holy mother of God," Gabriel breathed hoarsely. "What the fuck is that?"

Tam leaned in closer, looking at the horrifying jumble on the floor. Arms and legs and viscera were strewn across the floor and part-way up the wall like wet leaves and sticks.

"Looks like two people," Tam whispered quietly. His voice

was strangely empty. "Parts of them, anyway." On the last word, his voice broke with a half-sob that he quickly cut off.

Gabriel swallowed ineffectually. He recognized something about the clothes. "Engineering staff, I think. Please tell me that's not Carla?"

Tam shook his head slowly and moved back out of the doorway, seemingly in shock.

"Tam, is it Carla?" Gabriel said, louder. Too loud.

Tam was still shaking his head mechanically, staring into nothingness, but he did not answer. He backed up against the wall of the hallway facing the office door.

"Where the fuck are their heads?" Gabriel yelled, his voice angry and echoing dully down the hallway. He continued to stare incredulously at the grisly scene before him. He saw the edge of a badge sticking out of the muck, but couldn't make out what it said in the darkness. Before he could think better of it, he leaned inside and reached out to grab it. The lanyard was caught on something, and he jerked it free with a wet sucking sound. Gabriel tilted the ID to catch more of the light emanating from his and Tam's bodies.

"Westin," he said. Jim Westin, Carla's right-hand man. Gabriel had spoken with him almost every day for months. "This doesn't make any sense," Gabriel breathed, savagely, taking in huge gulps of air through his mouth as he tried not to scream.

He scanned the other remnants until he saw the second uniform. It lay front down in the mess, so he would have to pull it up and turn it over to look for the badge. The idea was beyond revolting, but he had to know. Full of anger, at what exactly he didn't know, Gabriel grabbed the heavy, wet uniform with both hands and turned it over. There was enough light to see.

"Martin," Gabriel said aloud. It was Carla. He let go, and the remains slid wetly back onto the pile. "God DAMMIT!" Gabriel yelled, his voice hoarse. He looked back at Tam.

Tam's back was against the wall opposite the doorway. He was rubbing his forearm absently and staring dully down the hall. Gabriel thought he might be in shock, but before Gabriel could say anything to him, Tam whispered, "What kind of explosion could do that to them and not destroy the rest of the office?"

Gabriel didn't respond, turning back to stare at what had been two people he had known well, people he had depended on, who were now just piles of skin and guts on the floor. "I don't know," he said, his voice flat. His mind seemed sluggish, as if it didn't want to work on Tam's question, but now that it had been asked, the question grew into an unsolvable riddle. He stared for another half minute before turning away, then settled his attention back on Tam, who seemed lost in himself. Detached.

"Tam," Gabriel said, his voice calmer than he felt. Tam didn't respond.

"Tam," he said again, strained, almost yelling.

This time Tam's dead-eyed gaze slid back to Gabriel. "What?" he managed.

"What could have caused this?" Gabriel asked intensely, locking eyes with Tam, trying to *will* him to respond. His voice was a painful blend of fury and restraint. "You spent years studying what these experiments might do, planning for every possible outcome. This is your job. *What the fuck happened here?*" Gabriel realized he was panting with rage.

Tam's gaze moved to the doorway for just a moment before quickly snapping back to Gabriel. Now, though, his eyes were glassy with tears instead of detachment. He swallowed. "I don't... I don't *know*," he said despondently. "Nothing I predicted or imagined could do this." A tear slipped down his cheek and he brushed it away absently with the back of his hand. "I didn't predict this scenario," he said, helplessly, whispering. "I can't think of any explanation."

Gabriel's anger cooled. Tam's reaction made him realize that he wasn't angry at Tam. Of course he wasn't. He was angry at and scared of whatever it was that had happened—whatever thing had killed those people and snuffed the power out of what should have been a completely unbreakable system. He sighed, getting himself under control.

"If they had listened to you, none of this would have happened," he said to Tam. "We've got to keep moving. Let's get to Observation to see if we can get any data from there," he said, now trying to sound reasonable and encouraging.

Tam nodded but didn't move.

Gabriel stepped closer and took his arm, pulling him toward the door to the stairwell. Gabriel touched the doorknob briefly and glanced back at Tam. "You ready?" he asked. Tam shrugged and just stood there. Gabriel couldn't blame him. He yanked the door open and ducked inside, dragging Tam behind him.

As soon as Gabriel stepped into the stairwell, he felt the heat on his face and immediately noticed that the smell was worse in here. More like burning chemicals. Pieces of cement from the walls or ceiling, some the size of large watermelons, dotted the landing and stairs in front of them. Tam stirred from his stupor to reach for the wall, but stopped short of touching it. "Check out the walls," he breathed.

Gabriel took a step closer. The walls were warped and lumpy, as if a fire had been roaring up the stairwell. Or a herd of buffalo. Or a volcano. There was some heat radiating from the walls, but was there as much as there should have been just three hours later? Gabriel wondered. He didn't think so. He approached the edge of the landing. The railings he could see were completely destroyed. In several places they looked as if they had been crushed, smashed to the ground, or thrown into the abyss. In other places, they had melted into thin, slack ropes strung from one drunkenly leaning post to the next. He stepped closer still, his weight on his heels to avoid leaning forward over the edge. Below him, the stairwell zigzagged down to the lower levels, seemingly intact for the most part. There appeared to be more light here than in the hallway they had come from. As Gabriel looked even farther down, he saw that there was definitely light down there. It seemed to be coming from the doorway to the bottom level, and looked a bit like firelight, but not quite. It was blue instead of orange. Perhaps there were still some chemicals burning on the bottom floor, throwing light through the tiny reinforced glass window into the stairwell.

Gabriel glanced back at Tam, who was also looking at the railings. Their eyes met and Tam shook his head, as clueless as Gabriel felt. Gabriel turned back to the stairs and started down, hugging the wall. He could hear Tam shuffling behind him, following at a greater distance than before. At least he was moving on his own now.

They walked as fast as they dared, eager to get to the Observation Center, but hampered by the alien, threatening stairs. The flights of stairs were longer than in a typical building, as the lower floors were each separated by about fifteen feet of hardened concrete. When they finally gained the next landing, they could both see the thick, small window in the door that opened onto the lab level B3, two floors down. The safety glass window down there pulsed and flickered with a wicked blue light that made the entire ground at the foot of the stairwell dance with dark shadows.

The pair started down the stairs toward B2, which housed the Observation Center and most of Engineering, including the backup battery systems and internal generators. It was getting hotter. This set of stairs was even more battered, and as they approached the landing, the next flight leading down to B3 was even worse—more chewed up, with great gouges torn out, and the edges of the stairs closest to the center had melted away into rough slopes. Thankfully the hallway looked dark through the window in the door to B2, and the door itself was no hotter than the walls of the stairwell. Gabriel pulled the door open as smoothly and quietly as possible, then stepped through, pausing on the other side in a largely futile attempt to let his eyes adjust and also to listen for survivors.

"Hello? Is anyone there?" Gabriel called out a couple of times, but his voice was met only with silence. It was quieter here than out in the stairwell; it sounded and felt more like a tomb than a workplace. Through the gloom on their left was the engineering wing, including the multiple backup batteries and a pair of small generators that supplemented the larger ones on the surface. They should have been enough to prevent any power failures or fluctuations.

"What went wrong with our power systems?" he asked quietly.

Tam didn't answer, and Gabriel didn't press him. He didn't need Tam retreating back into his shell while they were still down here trying to figure out what had happened.

Gabriel turned them the other way and they began making their way toward the science wing. Ahead, they could just make out a set of doors standing across from each other in the hall. On the left was the door to Observation, a large room that served as the primary monitoring and reporting station for the main lab downstairs where the particle experiments had been conducted and also for the zero field generator that had been their focus these last few months.

To the right was another door, this one marked with the word "Lavatory." As they approached, Tam said, "Are we even going to be able to get into Observation? Doesn't it lock down in emergencies?"

Gabriel nodded. "Yes, but the power failure will have

disabled the automatic locking and opening system, leaving just the manual lock. If only we knew the master of this house, with his fancy master key…" He hoped his banter would keep Tam together. Gabriel fished in his pocket, suddenly worried that he'd lost his keys in the chaos after the explosion, but quickly produced them from his pocket and jangled them triumphantly. "Now I just need to find the right one."

The ghost of a grin flitted across Tam's face for the briefest of moments, and he said, "While you do that, I have some important business to attend to. Be right back." Gabriel was about to object on the grounds of every horror movie ever made, but managed to stop himself as Tam turned and walked over to the men's room. However, his faint amusement died instantly when he turned back to the door to Observation and saw from this closer vantage point a smear of what looked like blood running down the door at an angle and continuing on the floor, leading back down the hallway and into the darkness.

Gabriel closed his eyes briefly, his skin prickling up into goosebumps. He had never been so rattled before—not even when he had been deployed overseas, going from house to house, taking and returning fire. *What in the name of all that is holy is going on here?* He sure wished he knew.

"Let's just stay on mission," he muttered finally, trying to clear his head. He turned back to his keys and began going through them. It took several long moments to find the right one, and then another to locate the fail-safe lock. When he eventually found the opening with the tip of the key, he slid it in and turned it. Well-oiled and perfectly fitted, it felt very solid and made a satisfying *thunk* sound as he unlocked the bolt. He slid the key out and pushed open the door. Behind him he heard Tam emerge from the men's room.

"Took you long enough," Gabriel said, attempting a light tone.

"Yeah. There was another body in there, so it took me longer to go," Tam said dully.

Gabriel turned to face him fully, noticing that Tam looked pale even in the dark. "Who?"

"Rogers," he said. "Pretty sure it was Rogers. It was hard to tell. But I'm pretty sure." He paused. He seemed about to say more, but then lapsed back into the insulating quiet of shock.

Gabriel's stomach clenched, his anger at finding Carla's body coming back in spades. "Fuck," he said, stupidly. "What's happening?" These bodies made no sense, and it didn't seem right not to do something about them. *But what could they do now, from here?* He experienced a moment of dizzying confusion, which he fought back with pure anger. He turned to the yawning door that led into Observation.

"Let's see if we can get some data."

Gabriel entered the room first, pushing the door open. "Hello?" he called into the silence. The room was cool and dark, and from what little he could see, its contents seemed intact. Once inside, he grabbed the edge of a nearby desk and pulled it over to block open the door, thinking it might help them see better, but it didn't do much. It was much darker in here, though Gabriel could still make things out, if only dimly.

"Let's get whatever data we can and then try to get out of here. Hopefully some sort of rescue team will have arrived by the time we get up there," Gabriel said, moving toward his usual monitoring station. Tam started toward his, one row over, but they both stopped quickly as the same realization dawned on them at the same moment. The computers at their stations were useless without power. They looked at each other sheepishly in the darkness and silently decided not to discuss it further.

Tam thought for a moment, then—"The printouts!" he said.

They both turned on cue and hurried to the far right corner

of the room where a tall cubicle had been set up to hide the ugly and usually noisy monitoring printer and its stacks of paper streams. A day's worth of printouts lay collected in a large box off to one side. Since the event, Tam had insisted on regular printouts to monitor the status of the zero field generator and the experiment, and the printer had been spewing out details of power levels, propagation measurements, temperature, and vibration in the main lab below ever since. With the power inexplicably out, Tam's doomsday outlook had once again proven useful—the printouts might be the only source of data on what had gone wrong if the hard drives were as fried as the power systems.

The printer was undisturbed and had apparently been printing right up until the power outage, though it was hard to make out the information on the paper in the almost total darkness.

Gabriel spoke again. "We know there were no abnormal readings through yesterday. Grab today's ream and put it in a box or bag or something. We need to be able to carry it out of here so we can read it on the surface."

"What are you going to do?" Tam asked.

"I'm going to grab the removable hard drive from my station. It has the master facility logs, plus all this data. If it's not fried, both it and these printouts will be critical to help us figure out what happened here."

He walked back to the hard drive rack at his station while Tam began fussing with the printouts. Once there, he found the hard drive—it was designed to simply pull out so that it could be stored elsewhere or plugged into other systems, in Los Angeles or back in Washington, for example. He flipped the latch over, exposing the drive, then tugged gently on the handle, and after a moment of resistance, the drive slid out smoothly. It was surprisingly small and light.

Tam stumbled up behind him and said, "I've got the

readings," holding up a laptop bag he'd found and slung over his shoulder. Gabriel handed him the hard drive to stow with the printouts.

"Let's get the hell out of here," Gabriel said. He turned and hurried for the stairs as best he could in the dark.

The heat and soot hit them in the face as soon as they stepped through the door. Then, almost as shocking, came the noise. The sound of the fire downstairs was loud after the near silence of the Observation and Engineering floor. Gabriel tried not to breathe too deeply, for the smell was strong—strange and astringent. Whatever was burning downstairs was giving off some awful-smelling fumes, and who knew how dangerous they were to inhale. He started immediately up the stairs, once again sticking as close to the wall as possible, with Tam following behind.

They heard a loud screeching crash from somewhere below, then a dull boom. The heat seemed to grow even more intense on the stairs. As they hurried up the first flight and reached the landing, Gabriel risked a glance at the door at the bottom of the stairwell. He stopped. "Look at that," he said to Tam, half shouting over the din. Tam looked down and stopped as well. The glass panel in the door to B3, which was supposed to be blast-proof, had been blown out, and a violent inferno was raging behind it. More alarmingly, the dense metal door was glowing a vibrant blue. It looked warped and was radiating heat and light onto the stairs. Gabriel got the impression it was about to melt off its hinges and fill the stairwell with fire.

"Fuck me," he said, succinctly.

They started upward immediately. Speed was their main concern now, though the ascent was getting rougher as pieces of concrete, tiles, and slagged railing littered their path. They navigated the next landing without incident and passed the door back onto B1, severely winded and soaked with sweat. The wall and floor of the landing that marked the halfway point to ground level looked as if someone had let loose on them with a jackhammer. Or maybe they had witnessed a brief but intense battle between Wolverine and Freddy Krueger. As the pair picked their way carefully across the debris, Gabriel wondered if the structural integrity of the landing had been compromised to the point of collapse. Once they had crossed the jumbled walkway, they set their sights on the last flight of stairs but then stopped cold. The stairs were littered with body parts, innards, and work boots. There had to be three or maybe four more people here—most of the crew who had been working down here that day. Gabriel fought down nausea. Tam, however, was less successful and turned toward the wall to throw up. Gabriel felt a wave of anger wash over him—a dizzying, disorienting fury.

"*What the fuck!*" he raged. "What the hell caused this?! A goddamned anti-personnel mine?" His skin felt like it was on fire.

"Or a serial killer," Tam replied slowly. Gabriel wondered if Tam had gone into shock again. Then he realized he was panting and light-headed. He deliberately pushed his anger down to a low simmer, but still found himself longing to put his fist through a tangible, solvable problem.

There was no choice but to walk right through the disgusting scene. They had to get out of there. Gabriel took the first step, trying in vain to ignore the slick, squelching sound his boot made as he walked through the mess covering the stairs, refusing to see it or acknowledge what it was. After what seemed like an eternity, Tam followed.

As Gabriel emerged gingerly from the chaos, he risked another glance down to make sure of his footing. There, on the third step down from the landing, he saw the bloody footprint of someone who had come this way before them. *The problem*, Gabriel thought distractedly, is *that it looks more like a giant freaking claw print than a footprint.* It wasn't light enough in the stairwell to be completely sure, but the print seemed to consist of three thick, pointed toes, each the size of a large garden trowel with one shorter, thicker toe opposite them. Each of the large toes tapered to a point at the end, and though Gabriel was even less certain about that part, he thought the cement steps had been ridged and cut where the claws had dug in a bit. Without pausing, he shook his head and climbed the remaining steps to the landing. He thought about pointing the print out to Tam, but he was getting dizzy and thought he might pass out any moment if he didn't get some fresh air. In any case, he wasn't sure if Tam could take another shock right now. Besides, he might be hallucinating or something. When he reached the top, he pulled open the door to the ground level of the facility and held it for Tam, whose face was pale and sweaty. They both stepped through, and Gabriel shut the door firmly behind them.

They stood there, still sweating in the cooler air, listening and looking around in the dark. There were windows on this floor, but it was full night outside. The only sound they heard was a metallic groan from somewhere below them.

"No fire up here," Tam remarked. "There must have been a lot of radiation to keep the rescue and recovery teams out this long, but if so, why aren't we burned—or sick?"

Gabriel didn't answer, instead walking across the hall to the glass case next to the fire hose, opening it and grabbing the fire axe from inside. He turned back toward Tam with the axe gripped tightly in both hands, then pointed to the doors to the main hall. They approached the doors cautiously. Gabriel paused to listen, then stepped back and quickly yanked the door open. He stepped through, axe first, and Tam followed. They looked around them at the office area. Other than an office chair in the hall and a few loose papers on the floor near Jonas' door, Gabriel couldn't see anything out of place. He hoped that Jonas and all the other office staff and security guards had gotten out. He couldn't see any bodies from where he was presently standing, anyway. He turned to look forward, following Tam's gaze. The main doors were wide open—or rather, the doors were no longer there. The hallway ended in open sky and pavement, the doors lying haphazardly on the ground outside.

Gabriel walked toward the opening. His eyes were fixed forward, his hands gripping the axe like a lifeline. Tam followed a few feet behind, eyes glued to the doorway. They reached the opening and stood there, transfixed, as they stared across the parking lot.

ELEVEN

The sky was clear now, lit by bright stars and the nearly full moon, and they took deep lungfuls of the clean, dewy air. Gabriel continued to gaze around the still puddled parking lot in blank dismay.

A pickup truck parked near them was crushed, as if it had been trampled by an elephant or hit by a meteor. He pointed to it absently, but Tam was already staring at it. Once Gabriel was able to tear his eyes away from the sight, he noticed that the fence was down in several places. There were no lights on anywhere, and nothing was moving.

"Deserted," he croaked. No rescue teams, no fire trucks, no people. It was quieter here than it had been underground.

"This doesn't make any sense," Tam said loudly enough to startle them both. "Let's take a look at the printouts."

They walked over to Tam's old Jeep. Tam grabbed the strap of his satchel and ducked under it, swinging it up onto the hood of the vehicle. He took out a healthy stack of printouts and placed them on top of the satchel, bending his head down closely over the sheets and flipping them slowly over one by one.

Gabriel stood back, giving Tam space to find what they were looking for while he kept a lookout, axe at the ready—for what, he had no idea. It was hard not to try to look over Tam's shoulder; he really wanted to look at the data for himself. He wondered briefly what could crush a truck and take down the fence and then just disappear. Not an earthquake. A meteor, or maybe vehicle-sized hail, or, considering the storm, a series of lightning strikes was all he could come up with before pushing the thought aside to deal with later.

After flipping through about fifty pages in what seemed like ten minutes, Tam said, "Here," and moved over a little to make room for Gabriel to join him. Gabriel set the head of the axe on the ground with the handle resting on the side of the Jeep. He had to get really close to the sheets to make anything out, but not so close as to block out the light from the moon and stars.

When the numbers came into focus, they looked like random gibberish at first. This was not a prepared report with easy-to-read graphs. This kind of report sacrificed clarity in favor of having lots and lots of data. But that was good—that was what he wanted to see—raw data that would help explain what had happened. He read through the column and row headings and started to figure out what the various fields were. All the data on this page was from today. He saw all the normal readings, five minutes apart, throughout the day. The printer recorded five-minute intervals plus a continuous log of any deviations that lay outside the expected ranges. Then, at 5:47 p.m., the main power levels spiked and dropped again. Gabriel guessed this had been a lightning strike somehow getting through, but if so, the surge protector had mostly caught it. What should have happened next was that the subsequent set of batteries should have taken over, and if that didn't fix it, whichever set of generators that were running at the time should immediately have become the power source for the field, but that had never happened. It looked as though the containment field had failed in the split second after the power had gone out, but before the system could switch over.

Gabriel had known that that was the likely explanation, but it was still shockingly depressing to see hard evidence of it. For the past six months, his life had been consumed by doing everything he could to prevent this very thing from happening. He was reeling. He had failed at his one critical task, and everyone in their lab had died as a result. All their modeling and the Organization's testing of the zero field had supported the theory that the tolerance was well in excess of the time it would take for the system to detect a power fluctuation and switch to another power source. *Yet here we are*, he thought. He realized he was about to start hyperventilating and forced himself to calm down.

"I failed," was all he could manage to get out.

"Yes, but you shouldn't feel bad about that part—I've been telling you and Command that this was a doomed effort from the start," Tam said distractedly. "This is brand-new technology, and they were counting on it to stop a potential nuclear bomb from going off. Post-detonation!" he continued half wildly, eager to have something to talk about that he actually understood. "But the real problem is that they didn't know what they were doing. At no time and in no place in the known universe since the Big Bang, maybe outside of black holes, have particles behaved the way these guys were making them behave in this experiment. Instantaneous communication? That's great, but if you have to tear a hole through space-time to do it," here he made a face that suggested he found this behavior unbearably idiotic, "then of course you are accepting all the unknowable consequences of your actions." He paused, realizing he was on a rant.

"Anyway, they buried my white paper on it." He turned back to where his finger marked a place on the page and gave a bitter grin. "Here are the recorded artifacts of those consequences. Look at this. *This* is crazy."

Gabriel leaned back in and focused on the text Tam was

pointing out. He tried to make sense of the numbers. "Can that be right? Was there more than one explosion?" He could see all the different measures of the propagation suddenly pulse at 5:47, showing what looked like an explosive chain reaction escaping the field, then the room. But where was the pressure wave? The pressure sensors had barely registered anything about that pulse. Gabriel couldn't even begin to imagine what that meant. But within the next three milliseconds, five more pulses had been recorded with completely different values. There were pressure readings alongside increasingly high temperatures, but not really on the scale of the explosion they had all feared. Maybe they were thunderclaps or smoke bombs? Or just light bulbs exploding?

"The first propagation is what I find most unexpected," Tam said. "The later ones seem like asynchronous beats of a bass drum or something," he continued. "Which kind of makes sense to me—they were trying to prepare these particles for long-range pairing, and they had them so jacked up with energy and forced binding that they were expecting it to work like an antenna. Maybe these secondary pulses were what the antenna was receiving."

"So what was the first propagation—obviously not an explosion—at least not like we were expecting," Gabriel prompted.

"I don't know," Tam replied, his voice hoarse and shaky. "It looks like whatever happened when the propagation first started caused a chain reaction that finally escaped the field today," he continued. "But look," he pointed out, "the sensors picked up a huge number of tiny particles propagating outward. It's not just any old fission, though. The same particle, maybe from every single atom in the room. But the weight isn't right." He took a pen from his pocket and wrote down a series of numbers on a blank part of the page, doing some advanced-looking math. He looked up and met Gabriel's eyes. But instead of saying anything, he bent back to the numbers and started again, this time more slowly. Tam's eyes were bright and wide, his brow furrowed in concentration. Finally he looked up.

"Gabriel, there are no particles that size. I think we either discovered a new one, or my much crazier-sounding working theory is that we created one that never existed before."

Gabriel let that sink in for a moment, trying to think through the practical implications of it, and then gave up a few seconds later, because it was too big and too overwhelming to even consider right now. He leaned back over the readouts. "Tam, about the secondary pulses—do you think it was a physical effect of communication between this field and somewhere else?"

"Possibly, like a loud sound or something being rebroadcast," Tam responded. "In theory, the field particles could have been paired up with their counterparts literally anywhere else in the universe. Maybe inside a star, or possibly even in another universe in a different dimension." His eyes sparkled madly in the moonlight.

Gabriel paused. "A sound? One that comes out of nowhere and then just sits on the ground?" He pointed to the pressure sensor data from the floor as Tam pored over the sheet to follow what he was saying. The pressure sensors were all around the room, showing small pressure waves propagating throughout, but the sensors on the floor had captured much larger measurements that only kept increasing instead of resetting as the wave passed.

Tam swallowed loudly enough for Gabriel to hear. "Um," he said, "that's pretty weird, too." They were quiet for a moment, both at a loss for what to say.

"How many secondary pulses were there?" Gabriel asked.

Tam stared at the page. "Hard to say—the readings weren't fast enough to capture all the data before the sensors died. There are five quick cumulative pressure jumps here on the floor before all the equipment died. After that, who knows what went on."

"Other than a fire," Gabriel added. As if on cue, the structure behind them gave another shuddering groan, echoing a small, localized earthquake that rumbled softly and briefly beneath their feet. The smell of smoke and the sound of the underground conflagration became noticeable. Gabriel thought it likely that the explosion and subsequent fire in B3 would cause the structure and the ground around it to collapse.

"Maybe we should move farther away," he suggested.

Tam quickly shoved the printouts back into his bag and slung it over his shoulder. Gabriel picked up his fire axe and led the way to the guard shack near what used to be the main exit through the fence.

The gate had been a hard target entrance, with a double fence area for searching vehicles before they came all the way in. There were multiple positions offering cover for guards in case they needed to fire on people or vehicles outside the gates. Security cameras, ridiculously bright floodlights, and most importantly, considering the typical weather here, air conditioning in the guard station itself.

Now, however, it all lay in ruins. The inner gate had been thrown off its track and lay flat on the ground fifteen yards from the guard shack, while the outer gate was bent ninety degrees outward and barely standing. The structure itself was partially smashed on the side nearest the gate, the door hanging crazily from its bottom hinge and the roof line crumpled and broken down to about shoulder height. All the bulletproof plexiglass had popped out or been broken and lay strewn about the area. As Gabriel and Tam got closer, they could see what seemed to be yet another pool of blood near the entrance to the shack. Once they had gotten closer still, they could make out a leg sticking out of the smashed doorway. Tam was ready to head to the other side of the opening, but Gabriel angled toward the door, axe at the ready.

The leg was still attached to its owner. It was Jenkins. He seemed mostly intact, but he wasn't moving. Lying on top of his right arm was an assault rifle, looped over his head by its black strap. Gabriel eyed the crumbling structure, full of broken metal and sharp edges, and handed the axe back to Tam.

Hands now free, Gabriel bent down and grabbed the guard's legs to pull him free of the doorway. As he did so, Jenkins' eyes shot open and he began mumbling in a hoarse, high-pitched half-whisper—a stream of words like "weapons" and "shoot" and "lights," along with something about the gate.

"Jenkins!" Gabriel said loudly, trying to interrupt his barrage of unintelligible semi-conscious babble. Jenkins slowly wound down his hyperventilated monologue. His skin glistened with feverish sweat, and his uniform was soaked with blood from some unknown wound or wounds. Gabriel placed the inside of his wrist on Jenkins' forehead, which was dangerously hot. The guard's eyes slowly focused on Gabriel's face, and his breathing slowed as he seemed to come to.

Then the man spoke, more clearly this time. "You better run and hide, Gabriel."

"What happened, Alan?" Gabriel asked. But Jenkins was already losing consciousness again, slipping back into his waking nightmare. His eyes began to flit back and forth, seeming to see terrible things in every shadow.

"Get away!" Jenkins screamed suddenly, jerking erratically toward his rifle. Gabriel pinned the guard's arm to the ground and removed the strap from around his head. He slid the gun away from them and toward Tam. Jenkins struggled weakly for a moment, but quickly reverted to his feverish mumbling, eyes darting back and forth, breath ragged and uneven.

"Jenkins!" Gabriel said again, slapping him lightly on the cheek. The guard didn't respond, so Gabriel tried again, this time with a harder slap. Still no response. Gabriel went to try a third time, but Jenkins' arm came up to ward off the blow, catching Gabriel's hand and holding it against his cheek. His eyes swiveled around slowly to Gabriel's, as if he was grasping at the hand of consciousness before sinking back beneath the waves.

Jenkins, momentarily still, stared into Gabriel's eyes. He slowly began to speak, his face filled with earnest fear.

"Demons." Weak as he was, he managed to pour enough of his ebbing strength into the word to send a chill down Gabriel's spine.

Then, as if satisfied that he had sufficiently disturbed Gabriel and Tam, he passed out again.

Gabriel tried to bring him back but was unable to rouse him a third time. A pool of blood seeped out of Jenkins' body, surrounding the three of them and sticking to Gabriel's boots. Gabriel checked for a pulse and found one but it was very weak. Tam knelt on the other side of Jenkins and they each held one of his hands in silent helplessness. After two or three minutes, Jenkins' breathing simply stopped and his body went completely slack and still. Gabriel and Tam just sat there, tears welling up in their eyes—for Jenkins, for Carla, and for everyone else.

Gabriel shook his head and wiped his eyes and cheeks roughly with the back of his hand. He grabbed the assault rifle and stood up, absently rubbing his bloody palms on his shirt—first one, then the other. It was a futile exercise; both his hands were still bloody, as were the gun, his knees, and now his shirt.

He checked the chamber and the magazine, then reloaded, sighted a patch of ground a few yards away, and squeezed the trigger. *Click.*

He ejected the round and tried again. *Click.* He took out the magazine and dropped it to the pavement with a clatter that seemed to echo across the parking lot. He bent down to search the body for another clip and found one in a holster on Jenkins' belt. After examining the magazine carefully, testing the springs and inspecting the first round, he inserted the mag into the assault rifle, chambered the first round, and once again sighted and pulled the trigger. *Click.* Gabriel ejected the magazine and set the weapon down on the pavement.

Tam was still sitting on the ground next to the corpse that had been their friend. His face was vacant, void of any outward expression or spark.

"Tam," Gabriel called.

Tam didn't react.

"Tam!" Gabriel exclaimed, almost shouting.

Tam jumped a little, and then his eyes refocused, coming to rest on Gabriel's face, then slipping down to the assault rifle on the ground between them. He looked puzzled, then said, "Not working?" and nodded toward the weapon.

Gabriel shook his head. "Go see if you can start your Jeep or any other vehicle. I'm going to look for other weapons."

Tam nodded dully and struggled slowly to his feet. Jenkins' blood soaked his pants.

They didn't talk about watching Jenkins die right in front of them, or of his insane final word, but it was all Gabriel could think about.

Less than ten minutes later, Tam returned from the last vehicle he had been able to find keys for. Gabriel was already standing back at the gate, but a ways away from the no longer expanding pool of Alan's blood.

"None of them will even turn over," Tam said.

"Consistent with an EMP detonation," answered Gabriel. "We'll have to hope it was limited to this area only, and we can contact HQ from town."

"Yeah," Tam said. "Well, regarding the second part anyway—regarding the first part, I don't know if it's consistent with an EMP or not—vehicles are actually fairly well insulated against that kind of thing. Like rolling Faraday cages. For all the military vehicles to be out of commission like that—I don't know."

Gabriel didn't like the sound of that. "Maybe a really, really big EMP?"

"Could be," Tam allowed. "Maybe. But how big an EMP would it have to be to keep the Company from sending a crew here in the five hours or whatever it's been since it happened?"

Gabriel shook his head. Tam was right, and, second to all the horribly mutilated bodies they'd encountered, this seemed like it should be their biggest concern.

"Well, I don't know what we can do about it from here, and I'd like to leave. It seems like our best bet is to hoof it to town and see if they have power there. If so, we can try to contact HQ and report what happened and find out why the cleanup crew wasn't dispatched as soon as they lost contact with us."

"Aye aye, Cap'n!" Tam saluted. At the sight of Gabriel's cocked eyebrow, which seemed to demand a more earnest response, however, Tam added, "I mean yes, I agree that should be our next step. Sir. Captain, sir." Tam's forced levity was perfunctory and grating, but at least he was no longer catatonic.

"But you carry the axe," Tam continued after a moment. "It's too heavy for me to want to carry it thirteen miles."

"It's not thirteen miles," Gabriel began.

"It is too," Tam argued. "At least once you count the walk to the police station, or wherever it is we end up going."

Gabriel threw up his hands in surrender. "Anyway, I'm not going to carry it either. It's too heavy to use as a proper weapon. I found a couple of belt knives that will hopefully be enough to deal with any exceptionally bold coyotes. Anything larger than that, we'll have to resort to our wits." From his pocket he produced a thin, lightweight knife in its holster.

Again there was a silence as they both thought about what could have killed Carla and Jenkins and the others, unable to discuss it yet. *Would a knife suffice to fight that?* Gabriel wondered, but he wasn't quite ready to ask that question out loud.

Gabriel bowed his head slightly and motioned with his arm toward the opening where the gate used to be, as if directing Tam to his seat at a fancy dinner.

"Monsieur, your journey," he said hoarsely, unable to muster the cartoonishly thick French accent he imagined. The humor was on autopilot, but it somehow seemed to help him keep from breaking down into gibbering insanity right there on the pavement.

"Merci, garcon. Où est la salle de bain?" Tam replied dutifully and began walking toward the opening.

"I don't think that's how you say it," Gabriel remarked dully as they walked away from the awful, smoking remnants of their station. He couldn't help but think of it as the physical evidence of their failure.

TWELVE

TAM

They had been walking in complete silence for almost an hour, their path illuminated by the bright light of the moon and stars. Tam's mind buzzed erratically, lurching from one set of facts to the next. He still felt weird—as if his inhibitions had been artificially lowered, like the time he had gotten drunk as an experiment.

The silence had already become the new normal for him and Gabriel as each replayed the events of the past few hours in their minds. The only thing that kept Tam from discussing his theories aloud was the thought of how crazy anything he might say would sound. But the quiet was beginning to become its own kind of oppression. Tam began to struggle with the irrational fear that if he didn't say something—anything—, he might fade into non-existence. Gabriel and Jenkins were the only living people he'd seen since the explosion, and Jenkins was dead now, too. Tam felt almost defined by the anchor of Gabriel's physical presence—he wondered briefly if the strain of today's events would have overwhelmed him and caused him to completely lose his mind if Gabriel hadn't been there, seemingly sharing the same delusion.

"So, um, strange day today," Tam said, trying to master understatement in one ambitious stroke. He rubbed at his arm absently. It was a cold night in the desert, but after an hour of walking they were both warm enough to stop their teeth from chattering. Tam's feet ached already, and he thought he might be getting a blister. Gabriel kept having to slow down to match his pace.

"Yes, I found it a little weird too," Gabriel replied. He obviously didn't want to rush into this conversation, either.

Tam tried a different tack. "What part of the day did you find most strange? Other than the Rockies not being able to score on the Cardinals, of course."

Gabriel smiled at last, pondering the question. "Aside from the ball game, I'd have to say the fact that no one has shown up yet. Even if the place were hot with radiation, which seems unlikely given that we are not dead, I would expect a team to have been on the ground hours ago." He paused. "How about you?"

Tam didn't answer right away. He was suddenly afraid all over again, as if he'd woken up to find himself standing on the edge of a deep crevasse with the wind blowing fitfully at his back. He was tempted to talk about the mess on the floor that had been their friend Carla but bit his lip instead.

Finally he spoke, forcing his voice to be perfectly neutral. "It's the pressure readings... along with some other stuff."

Gabriel waited for him to go on, but the pause expanded until it became a pregnant silence. "What about the pressure readings—and what other stuff exactly?" Gabriel eventually asked.

"Oh, um. Well, I suppose I'm wondering what killed our people but didn't kill us and didn't destroy the walls. Seems like something an animal or a meat grinder would do, not an explosion. Then there are the readings that show a weight on the floor with each of those pressure waves, suggesting that something solid was created or came through..."

"Came through?" Gabriel interrupted incredulously. But he didn't say anything else. Tam assumed he must have come to the same, dizzying conclusion.

Tam started talking again. "I think the particles in the zero field achieved what they needed to achieve in order to pair up. When the propagation started, it ran wild, with more and more particles on this side pairing up and changing to match the particles they were pairing up with." He cleared his throat. "What I thought was a drumbeat, rebroadcasting a sound or something from wherever it was paired with, might have been actual matter, or maybe even living things, translating from wherever. To here."

Gabriel stumbled in stunned silence, and Tam kept quiet so that they could both process this idea.

Eventually, Gabriel spoke.

"Everything you're saying seems nearly impossible— unlikely to a degree that defies comprehension, but the problem is that I haven't been able to think of any other more likely explanation, either." Gabriel hesitated, then continued. "There was one other thing." He paused again, for one breath, then two. Then another. Tam waited him out.

"In the stairwell, near the bodies and the blood? I am now fairly certain that I saw a large, non-human claw print."

Tam just nodded. "I saw that too."

Gabriel was silent again for a moment. "And then there was the thing Jenkins said."

Tam nodded even though Gabriel wasn't looking at him. "Yes, there's that too. In terms of crazy, unsubstantiated, and completely unlikely theories, this is the one I'm going with for the moment. Also, I now regret leaving the axe behind."

"I regret not being able to find a working firearm," Gabriel responded. "I tried five different ones, so I'm forced to assume that whatever happened to the electronics also caused the gunpowder to go bad."

Tam wondered what kind of radiation could do such a thing. Other than a good soaking with water, maybe-and it had been raining, after all—he couldn't imagine anything rendering the weapons they had found so useless. Still, he doubted that a rainstorm could have disabled every round they had tried.

Gabriel continued, obviously thinking the same thing. "At least it makes more sense than all the rounds I tried randomly being duds, or all our guards intentionally carrying nonfiring ammunition as part of a very subtle peace protest, or anything else I can think of."

They walked on. The uneven landscape was dark around them, though the sky was bright with the crystal clear stars so typical in the desert. Each of them focused on the ground in front of them lost in their own swirling thoughts.

A few minutes later, as Tam pondered the unlikelihood of water or some water-like substance ruining only black powder and electronics, he glanced up at the horizon, where he could now see lights. Gabriel hadn't looked up yet to notice.

"I think the propagation may have been larger than we assumed," Tam said, a little too conversationally.

"Why is that?" Gabriel asked.

"Because the town seems to be on fire. And the fire is all blue."

As they drew closer over the next hour, Tam could see that one of the buildings on the small hill overlooking the town was entirely engulfed in flames, casting an angry and bizarrely blue-tinged light over the buildings below. There were also a few smaller blazes scattered throughout the town. These, too, were blue instead of red—an eerie and disturbing effect, as if the entire town were bathed in some chemical pollutant.

Betelgeuse, New Mexico was a small, jumbled crossroads town situated in the desert in the middle of nowhere. It had sprouted up like a big patch of weeds at the intersection of two roads, each leading to similarly dusty towns hours away, all of them nearly cut off from the grid by the construction of the interstate highway system in other parts of the state. But Betelgeuse wasn't dying—or at least it hadn't been until today. Home to the government facility, the county's only high school, and several small bars and restaurants, it had been thriving. It was a nice place to live. Tam rented a small white adobe-style house on the edge of town, with a yard and a roof terrace overlooking the desert.

Now the town looked like a corpse. All the streetlights were out leaving it in darkness except for the fires, which no one from the fire department was out fighting. No police had come to investigate a car abandoned in the middle of Main Street as it entered the town. A few shop windows on Main Street had been smashed, the shattered glass on the sidewalk below glinting blue in the firelight, but no one was investigating that either. In fact, no one was moving anywhere as far as he could see. From this distance, the town looked dark, ominous, and deserted. Tam's heart thundered; he was terribly afraid they'd find more bodies in town like they'd found in the facility. Gabriel seemed lost in thought, perhaps processing it all, but it was all Tam could do not to scream. He hadn't felt this out of kilter since high school, when his family had fallen apart and his brother had gone off the deep end.

When they had finally stumbled close enough to hear the crackling of the flames, they crouched behind a small stand of skinny trees. Well, in Tam's case, he just sat down on a patch of grass, his hands clasped around his shins. Gabriel regarded him with a flat, serious expression. "We need a plan," he said softly.

"I'm starving," Tam piped up. "And I've got a terrible blister that I need to see to while I eat."

Gabriel hesitated, then nodded. "Okay. You go straight

home then—it's not far from here. I want to run over and collect some things from my place. Let's split up."

"Ooh—dibs on being the sole surviving protagonist!" Tam exclaimed in mock excitement.

Gabriel ignored him. "We'll meet back at your house. If there's a problem when you get there, leave the door ajar and get out, and we'll meet back here with as many supplies as we can gather within the shortest possible time." He paused for a moment. "It might be an hour or two before I make it back. If I'm not back by noon, leave town and try to find the edge of the area that's been impacted and make a report. Maybe Ainsley Shannon in Theory can figure out how to suppress or remove this field and start the cleanup."

Tam raised his right hand to his forehead in a stiff salute. "Sir, yes, sir!"

Gabriel didn't react to the slight mockery. Or was it pseudo-mockery? Tam wasn't really sure. Gabriel just nodded as if the salute were his due, which was irritating.

"I'll try to be at your place in two hours," he said.

Tam had no idea how he was supposed to keep track of time at night without a working watch, but he didn't say anything— at least Gabriel had a plan. He nodded and swung his legs around under him to stand up gingerly on his throbbing feet, brushing the grass absently from his pants. They turned back to face the town, and after an awkward pause, Gabriel slipped away, leaving Tam alone in the sinister night, like a candle guttering in the dark.

Tam stood there, his heart lub-lubbing palpably, watching Gabriel's broad shoulders and squat frame flit furtively from one piece of cover to the next as he headed downtown. He moved like soldiers did in the movies, somehow keeping his head and arms still and level while his lower half bounced and danced over the terrain. It looked cool on screen, but here, it struck Tam as ridiculous.

"He knows he doesn't have a gun, right?" he whispered to himself.

Once Gabriel was out of sight, Tam was truly alone. He listened to the sounds around him, hearing only the faint crackling and roaring of the fires. He couldn't even hear any of the crickets or coyotes he always listened to from his roof at night. The absence of other sounds was disconcerting and unnatural. *At least no one is screaming*, he thought, and decided to follow their example.

He started walking, not sneaking, but limping along at a normal pace through the flickering shadows in the direction of his house. What good would it do to sneak?

Normally, he liked being alone. He could think better that way. It was much harder to live by logic and principle if you spent too much time around others. Most people were slaves to their emotions and baser instincts, and so frequently behaved in the most obvious, boring, and disappointing way possible. Tam generally thought that almost everyone walked around with their ids—their lizard brains—in charge almost all the time, rarely rising up to break away and do anything remotely surprising or interesting, something driven by philosophy, creativity, or ethical virtue.

But… there was alone, and there was being completely cut off and adrift. With monsters around, probably. This wasn't the good kind of alone. Where were all the people? Was everyone here dead, too?

As if the thought had manifested itself into being, it didn't take very long to find the first corpse—an older woman dressed in a waitress uniform, lying on the side of the street in a pool of her own blood. Parts of her flesh were missing—great, ragged holes were torn through her shirt and pants and skin. From her stomach down, she was a mess of blood and injury, and her glassy, dead eyes stared unblinkingly up into the sky. Tam sank down beside her and burst into silent tears. He couldn't bring himself to look at her anymore, but he could at least be with her for a little while, giving her the dignity and companionship she'd been denied in her last moments.

"Are we responsible for this?" he whispered aloud. The answer was obvious, *had been* obvious for hours. Collectively, they were almost certainly 100% responsible. Individually, too—he was responsible for not convincing the Organization to abandon these experiments, or even just wait until the risks could be assessed properly. He was also responsible for not foreseeing how the failure could happen, for failing to protect the zero field generators, and for not realizing the risk of... whatever had happened to make it seem like murderous monsters might have poured out of the experimental propagation.

Yes, he knew he had tried every day in one way or another to do all those things. But his efforts hadn't been enough to keep this poor woman from being murdered and mauled as she made her way peacefully home from work. What had he missed? He was sure there was some blind spot that had just never occurred to him. Some vulnerability in the system that he had stupidly overlooked because of his flawed, human brain. Something he could have said in his reports, some general or project leader or politician he could have reached out to within the Organization, *something* that would have made a difference.

Instead... *this*. Hundreds of dead, probably, or maybe many, many more. Had they destroyed the whole world or just this town?

Tam didn't know how long he'd been sitting there, tears and snot streaming down his dirty face, staring off into nothingness. The stench of the woman's insides began to press into his nose, turning his stomach. He thought for a moment about deliberately exposing himself to more of it as his just reward for his failures, but he immediately recognized that as pathetically illogical. He might actually be able to do something about this. Right now, no one in the world knew as much as he did about what had happened. If the effects of this accident could be understood, it could be possible, between himself and Ainsley Shannon's group at the Los Angeles facility, to devise a way to address it, or even fix it, if there was anything left to fix. He could wallow in impotent self-blame and madness like Cassandra of ancient Troy, or he could try to be a part of the solution—to add something beneficial to the world. If anyone *could* put the genie back in the bottle, it was the group that had let it out.

So he wiped his face on his sleeve and got up. He needed to get to his house, and he also had to watch out for whatever had killed this woman and the people back at the lab. Given that he'd just sat in the open on the side of the road for an extended period without being killed, he probably wasn't in any immediate danger, but that wasn't how he felt. Every few minutes, he thought he saw movement in his peripheral vision, and he heard the rustle of murderous animals in every hedgerow and tuft of grass. By the time he neared his house, his heart was hammering in a staccato rhythm, and he was limping as fast as he could without breaking into a jog. Then he really did hear something, and it was definitely coming toward him.

He jolted into an uneven run.

THIRTEEN

GABRIEL

"Almost there," he muttered under his breath. Just three more side streets to his apartment. As he neared the end of the block, he heard what sounded like two dogs fighting. He paused, pressing his back against the building, and peered around the corner down the street. Two dogs were fighting like wolves over a mutilated body in the middle of the road. One of them was a Doberman with a spiked collar, but the other one was just a regular medium-sized mutt.

Gabriel's stomach turned, and he would have stepped out to chase them off if he'd had a stick. Instead, he looked around, trying to figure out the best way to get past them safely.

Just then, the dogs stopped growling and barking and turned to look farther down the road. Gabriel couldn't see what they were looking at and was suddenly afraid to lean out any more to get a better view. The dogs began to growl again, this time in unison.

A terrible dread seized Gabriel's insides. He pressed himself back fully against the bricks, too afraid to move. He felt an overwhelming desire to melt back into the building instead of being exposed on the street. His heart thudded painfully in his chest. All he could think of were the dead bodies he had passed, a fate that now seemed more and more likely for him, too.

Suddenly, the Doberman took off, bolting toward whatever it had been growling at, the other dog following close behind. Both dogs barked and slavered madly as they sprinted down the street. Gabriel heard their continued barking punctuated by a vicious snarling as they attacked whatever it was they'd gone after. It couldn't have been more than a block or two away.

Almost immediately there was a sickening crunch and snap of bones, and one of the dogs let out a piteous, piercing yelp followed by a second. Then there was another crunch and the yelping ceased. A second later, the Doberman sprinted by in the opposite direction, its short tail tucked between its legs. It careened heedlessly down the street, and Gabriel stood perfectly still and silent, watching it.

A second or two later, something gave chase.

Gabriel's first impression of the thing was one of bulk, but it moved with a confident, predatory grace. And it was fast. It had five long, multi-jointed legs ending in hard claws that clacked rapidly against the pavement as it flowed down the street. Its puffy body was a dull, bulbous yellow, large and low, like a platform with no discernible head. Instead, two appendages sprouted from the top of its body like thick, articulated tentacles. As the thing scurried past, Gabriel caught a glimpse of the end of one of the tentacles and was horrified to see a glowing red eyeball set above a pair of nightmarish, jagged-toothed jaws. Both tentacles strained toward the fleeing dog, which had ducked under a parked car to hide near the end of the next block.

The monster approached the car and its tentacles snaked underneath. The dog yelped and sprinted out the opposite side, down the next street. Once again, the creature gave chase, gliding across the hood of the car as if it weren't there and stalking after the fleeing dog. As it rounded the corner, one of its tentacles trailed behind it, pointing rearward, and the last thing Gabriel saw as the abomination disappeared out of sight was the gibbering open mouth and the huge red eyeball looking right at him.

Gabriel's fear of moving instantly became a fear of standing still, and he took off running himself, throwing caution to the wind as he raced as fast as he could toward his apartment. He sprinted down the street, willing his pounding footfalls to be as silent and as swift as he could make them. His eyes darted around wildly as he ran.

On the next block, his heel skidded in the blood of another corpse lying in the shadow of an abandoned car, and he almost fell, his arms pinwheeling involuntarily in the air as he righted himself and regained his footing midstride.

He bounded onward, and the back of his apartment building finally came into view. The entire block on this side was in deep shadow, the building itself blocking most of the firelight, but he couldn't stop. The panicked pounding of his heart and the adrenaline coursing through his veins wouldn't even permit him to slow down. He couldn't hear anything behind him, but he couldn't risk looking back.

A pair of galvanized garbage cans lay overturned between him and the rear door of the building. He tried to leap over one of them without breaking his stride, but his foot caught the top of it at the apex of his jump, causing it to spin and clatter noisily, its open maw reverberating and projecting the sound like a sonic bomb.

Barely regaining his footing, he fled to the door, jerked it open, and ran inside. It was even darker in here, and his instincts told him to slow down and be careful, but his feet wouldn't listen. He sprinted to the stairwell, grabbed the banister to redirect his momentum, and took the stairs three at a time.

The shadows pressed in on him, but no claws were reaching

out of the darkness as of yet. He ran up the side of the stairs closer to the wall, but no tentacles snatched at his ankles through the railing. He shook nonetheless, his breathing ragged and painful in his throat.

He made it to his door and plunged his hand into his pants pocket, extracting his keys, only to drop them noisily from his shaking hands onto the wooden floor, the sound echoing through the hallway. He bent down and snatched them up, jerking them up to his face to find the right one, then jammed it into the lock and turned the handle.

In half a second he was inside, closing the door and locking it, the sound of the deadbolt sliding home music to his ears. He leaned against the door, trembling. He could barely hear over the pumping of his heart and the roar of blood in his ears, but still he strained to listen for sounds of pursuit.

Even as his breathing slowly returned to normal, he could hear nothing. No dogs, or fire or… whatever that thing was. Just silence. It took him almost five full minutes to muster the courage to take another step, afraid he'd make a noise and be heard. His mind whirled like a storm, scattering every thought like dry leaves in the wind until all he could think about was the sight of that monster.

Eventually, though, he recalled why he had come here in the first place. To gather useful supplies. That reassured him somewhat—a mission he could accomplish. To get food and a weapon. He wasn't going to fight that thing out there with a tomahawk, but something was better than nothing, so he set about his business. He was afraid that if he didn't start getting ready right now, he would never summon the will to leave his apartment again.

His loft seemed bright compared to the side streets because his blinds were all open, letting in the firelight. Maybe the sky was brightening too—he couldn't tell for sure.

He went to the closet where he stored his camping gear. His backpack already had the essentials. He and Tam might need to sleep outdoors as they traveled. *Dios mío*, he thought—he had to warn Tam about the abomination that was prowling the town.

He moved as quietly as he could, pausing often to listen. He changed into his hiking boots and threw a pair of jogging shoes into his backpack as well. He checked his headlamp and a flashlight just to be sure, but neither worked. Then he grabbed all the nonperishable food he could find in the house and some candles and put it all in the pack.

As for weapons, he had a large survival knife in his pack and a tactical tomahawk and holster, which he attached to his belt. Out of the back of his camping closet, he pulled his old walking stick—a strong, solid family heirloom passed down to him by his grandfather. It was smooth and unadorned, other than some carvings at the top, and had brass caps on both ends. It had always felt good in his hand and seemed to feel especially so now.

He crept over to the front windows that overlooked Main Street. The only movement he could see was from the dancing shadows cast by the scattered fires.

As he watched the blue firelight flicker across the desolate town, he felt a sharp pang of worry for his family—almost physically painful. Was Betelgeuse the only town affected? Surely his family was safe back in Baltimore? But there was no way to know for sure right now.

He shouldered his backpack and picked up his walking stick, then crossed the room to the door. Decisively putting all doubts out of his mind, he set his jaw, opened the door and slipped out into the hallway.

On his way down, Gabriel knocked softly on every door he passed, but no one answered. The entire building was deserted. Or so Gabriel decided to believe.

Now that he was somewhat armed, he felt a little more confident about checking out the scene on Main Street. He pushed open the door to the street as quietly as he could and peered around it. There was a small pool of blood on the sidewalk, with a couple of sets of bloody footprints coming from it, both heading down the street. *Whoever made those prints was distracted and in a hurry*, Gabriel thought. As he followed the prints with his eyes, he spotted a police cruiser parked near the town's drugstore, its driver's door and trunk wide open. A crumpled form, undoubtedly a body, lay on the ground in front of the car. There was no movement that he could see, so he began to walk slowly down the sidewalk, sidestepping the pool of blood.

He went to the coffee shop first, almost by force of habit; he'd visited the place every morning since he'd arrived and had come to be on nodding terms with the barista and most of the clientele. The windows on the side nearest to him were still intact, but those closer to the corner were smashed inward, open to the predawn light. He tested the door, pushing it slowly open. The stupid bell at the top jingled loudly, and Gabriel froze, cursing silently and listening for anything that might be attracted by the sound. Five seconds of silence. Ten.

When he reached thirty seconds and nothing had sprung out at him, he let out the breath he only now realized he had been holding. Reaching up, he wrapped his hand around the bell to muffle it and yanked it off the door frame. He set it carefully on the counter next to the door and turned his attention back to the interior of the shop.

Inside, the place was a wreck. Chairs lay everywhere, broken and toppled. Tables were overturned. Even the equipment behind the counter seemed to be smashed. *Why?* Gabriel wondered. He picked his way carefully across the floor. When he was standing in the center of the place, he saw a body, immediately recognizing it as that of the old man who sat in here every morning reading the paper. He seemed to be intact—not ripped apart or even bloody. He was slumped almost peacefully over his regular table. His newspaper had fallen from his fingers and now lay scattered on the floor. Gabriel put a hand on his shoulder to shake him, but his body was cold and stiff. Gabriel dropped his hand and turned to explore the rest of the cafe.

Behind the counter he found the savaged body of the barista, her apron sliced to ribbons over her mutilated flesh. She lay in a pool of blood, one hand raised and clenched around the stainless steel handle of a cabinet and her sightless eyes wide and still. Gabriel's stomach lurched and he turned away quickly, a tear welling in his eye. He left the shop as quickly as he dared, stepping back out onto the street, and heading toward the police car.

As he neared the cruiser, he saw that the body in front of it was a middle-aged woman wearing high-waisted mom jeans and a loose floral shirt. Gabriel didn't recognize her as anyone he'd seen before. She lay on the pavement, folded up backwards as if she had been snapped like a dry twig. As Gabriel got closer, he could see what looked like a large bite wound in the front of her neck.

Behind the car, the uniformed policeman lay among a scattering of unused shotgun shells and blood. His face had been slashed and his partially eviscerated remains already stank terribly. His nightstick was still in his hand, charred and crusty from use, but it obviously hadn't been enough to save his life. Gabriel knelt down beside him and pried his fingers off the wooden baton to add it to his pack in case Tam wanted it. It was kind of comforting—a talisman representing law and order, although the fact that it had failed the policeman had its own symbolism, Gabriel thought.

As he finished shoving the police baton into his backpack, he heard a noise coming from the pharmacy ahead. Gabriel now noticed that the tempered glass door had been smashed in and that someone or something was moving around inside. As he tried to decide which way to run, two men stepped gingerly out of the opening. Relief flooded Gabriel, and he started walking toward them. He wanted to talk to them, but not out on the street—he needed to warn them about the monster, if they didn't already know.

Each man had a number of small plastic bags in one hand, and both were armed—at least in some fashion. One of them was carrying a shotgun—maybe the cop's shotgun. *No immediate threat*, Gabriel thought, trying to bolster his courage though with little success. The other man was holding a metal crowbar. They both wore jeans and motorcycle jackets. Once they were on the street, they looked over at the police cruiser and saw Gabriel. They seemed surprised rather than pleased to see him.

Gabriel's steps faltered a bit when he saw their reaction, but as he was already halfway over to them, he kept going. Their posture became even more tense as he approached. Once he was close enough to talk to them without raising his voice above a loud murmur, he spoke.

"Did you guys see what happened here?"

He used the hand holding his walking stick to indicate the town around them, attempting a reassuring smile.

The guy with the crowbar shifted a step to his right, toward the street, and shook his head.

"Not really, man." He spoke too loudly, and Gabriel winced. Was the man going to bring the creature down on them all? "We were just gettin' dinner when the shit hit the fan," the man continued, only a little more quietly. "The lights went out and I got real dizzy and had to sit there till I came around. By then some people were screaming and running all over, others were lyin' on the floor, sick as dogs. We hid in the storeroom for a while till it quieted down." He took another sidestep into the street, putting more space between himself and Gabriel. "Saw some shit after that, though. End of days shit." Then he smiled, a toothy, mirthless grin that sent a jolt of alarm down Gabriel's back.

He means me harm, Gabriel realized. He wasn't sure how he knew, but he was absolutely certain of it.

The man with the shotgun had been standing still in front of the pharmacy, but now he slowly walked around Gabriel in the opposite direction, saying nothing. Gabriel noticed a large kitchen knife stuck through his belt. He thought he saw some blood still on the blade. It was getting hard to see both of them without turning his head. Gabriel's sense of alarm swelled—these guys were circling him like hyenas.

"Why?" Gabriel asked simply, sounding far calmer than he felt.

"Why what?" the crowbar guy asked.

"Why are you going to attack me?" Gabriel replied. He felt completely dumbfounded that the first living townspeople he had encountered were threatening him. *Maybe that's why my training hasn't kicked in yet*, he thought.

"Who said anything about attacking you?" said Crowbar. "This shit has made me realize that I can do abso-fucking-lutely anything I want, and I think I could use me a big ole backpack." He stared hard at Gabriel. "I bet you got some useful stuff in there," he continued. "If you set it down, and your tomahawk, ain't nobody attacking nobody," he said. His voice dripped with false reason, and there was a strange, discordant overtone, as if Gabriel could *hear* him lying.

Gabriel's mounting panic suddenly erupted into a cloud of incandescent rage. As the world fell apart, these dipshits were feeding on the corpse of society before it was even cold. Gabriel felt lightheaded with fury. He stood up taller. "All I'm giving you is a chance to leave now," he said, his deep voice strained with emotion.

The man with the crowbar chuckled. Gabriel heard a click from behind him as the guy with the shotgun pulled the trigger, presumably at him, though the two men were now on nearly opposite sides and impossible to see at the same time. Gabriel watched the man in front of him. Behind him, he heard the sound of the other man setting his shotgun on the ground. Gabriel glanced back at him to see that he was now drawing his knife.

In what seemed like a mutual decision, both stepped toward him—and past the point of no return in his eyes. Gabriel had trained to fight in the military and continued to take martial arts classes after leaving. He thought he should probably know what to do in this situation, but his mind was awash with pure rage, rendering him unable to think with any degree of clarity. He wanted to hurt these men, to put them down like rabid dogs. His anger felt physically palpable, making the skin on his back and shoulders feel tight and tingly.

Gabriel feinted as if to run directly away from the drug store. The man with the crowbar leaned forward and took a step to give chase, but Gabriel reversed direction and lunged right at him and away from the guy with the knife. He whipped his walking staff in a vicious circle at Crowbar's head, and the banded end smacked into the man's left cheekbone, snapping his head back with a shocking crack. He began to topple over backwards, seemingly already unconscious.

Gabriel whirled to face the guy with the knife, his staff arm already in motion again, and as he turned, the knife-wielder was almost on top of him, knife held high and arm extended. Gabriel twisted and ducked to the side, slamming his stick down on the guy's knife arm. Bones shattered and the knife clattered to the ground. The man dropped to his knees beside his knife, making no immediate move to retrieve it.

Gabriel paused, amazed at how quickly he had moved and how strong he felt. He glanced down at his arms, which seemed more muscular than usual. He felt suffused with energy. He saw, or thought he saw, a tiny flame dancing up his arm and flickering through his shirt, across his bicep, around to the back of his arm and up to his shoulder. It stung. He stared right at it for a moment, practically cross-eyed, still almost sure he was hallucinating it, when another tiny lick of flame sprang up over his forearm momentarily before winking back out. The material of his shirt had been blackened, leaving a record of the flame. Somehow this additional evidence was far more convincing, and he experienced a moment of hysteria and began grinning wildly. This had to be the strangest and most interesting case of radiation poisoning he had ever heard of. He looked back down at his would-be assailants. They had picked the wrong guy to attack.

Moaning incoherently on the ground, the knife-wielder finally reached out with his left hand to reclaim his weapon. Gabriel stepped on his fingers, then stomped down on the guy's wrist with his other boot. He could hear and feel the bones snap. *Let's see this guy attack someone with two broken arms*, he thought. Gabriel's head swam with the unreality of it all.

He kicked the bloody butcher's knife under the police cruiser and walked over to the white plastic grocery bags Knife Guy had dropped next to the shotgun. He emptied a few, reading the labels of the packs that fell out. Prescription painkillers, mostly. And anti-anxiety meds. They seemed like things junkies or drug dealers would be after. He grabbed a bottle of pain medicine and walked back over to the men.

The man who had held the knife struggled weakly into a sitting position, holding both arms awkwardly close to his torso.

His right forearm was bent at a sickening angle. Gabriel walked over to him and held out the bottle of pain pills. The guy didn't move or react in any way. *He might be in shock already*, Gabriel thought. He slipped the pill bottle into the guy's breast pocket and hauled him to his feet by the front of his jacket.

"You could have just let me go," Gabriel murmured in the guy's face. The man didn't respond, but at least he had the decency to look terrified now. *The flames might be helping*, Gabriel thought. There were more of them now, several perched on his shoulders and visible in his peripheral vision. He growled at the back of his throat. "Now get out of here before I break your legs." He gave the guy a small shove and watched him stumble into a shambling run, back toward the edge of town.

Gabriel turned back to pick up his staff again, looked up and down the street, and then walked over to the first guy, who was still stretched out on his back, one leg straight and the other bent up at the knee, as if he were taking a siesta on the pavement. The side of his face looked wrong. His cheekbone was probably shattered. He wasn't stirring at all, so Gabriel stooped to feel for a pulse at his neck. He couldn't find one, so he switched to the man's wrist, watching his chest closely for signs of breathing. Nothing there either.

Gabriel's anger ebbed away quickly now. He wasn't panicking again, though—he just felt drained. *What have I done?* he thought incredulously. The guy had attacked him with a crowbar, it was true, and had probably intended to kill him. It was pure self-defense, and he didn't expect there would be any legal consequences even if things went back to normal in a few days or weeks—there was so much death around! But killing someone felt sickening—especially here, in the heart of small-town America. *I killed that man! Am I any better than the looters?* His body shook. And the spontaneous combustion? *Am I going to die of radiation poisoning?*

He took a deep breath and got to his feet. He stood there for a moment, staring at Mr. Crowbar, trying to think of something to do other than just walk away. He knew the two men weren't responsible for all those dead bodies—at least not alone. That creature could come back. He had been out in the open too long already.

He walked back to his pack and slung it over his shoulders. The parts of his skin that the flames had touched felt tender and brittle, and his bones ached. He felt as if he had fallen naked down a long flight of exceptionally abrasive stairs.

He left the shotgun where it lay, but rifled through the looted pill bottles again. This time he found some antibiotics and ibuprofen, and tucked them into his pockets along with two bottles of hydrocodone. He didn't linger any more, hurrying furtively over to the more shadowed side of the street. He crept from one hiding spot to another as he worked his way down the street, listening for the sounds of the creature at every pause.

As he approached the police station and the fire department, he surveyed the scene before him. The fire department had apparently pushed the fire truck into the street, or maybe it had just died there. One of the town's burger joints a block off Main at the next intersection was now a burned-out, still-smoking shell, and there were several other fires burning unchecked elsewhere around town.

Numerous bodies lay around the fire truck. As he approached, he counted six, all lying on the street, broken and torn apart. The pavement nearby was burned black—could the street itself have been on fire? Some of the body parts were also burned. One of the bodies lying in the blackened area of the road was charred to a crisp. It was still wearing a sooty, sticky-looking fireman's hat. Gabriel quickly turned away from the nauseating sight.

Across the street, in the open garage bay of the fire station, he saw a body hanging from the ceiling with a rope around its neck.

"What the hell?" he mouthed to himself. He stopped for a moment and stared. *Had the man killed himself?* He was wearing firefighter's pants and boots with a white t-shirt, as if he had been getting dressed to go help, but then decided that hanging himself was a better option.

Gabriel shook his head and made his way over to the window of the police station next door. Through it, he could see a clean waiting room and reception area with a hallway leading farther into the building. There were no officers in sight. He slid over to the door and tried to push it open, but it was locked. Gabriel was seized with the idea that if it was locked, someone might be inside. He used the meaty part of his hand to pound quietly on the door, looking around at the street as he did so. He waited a second and was about to pound louder when an officer poked her head out of the doorway to the right of the reception desk. She stared at him blankly. Gabriel froze, joy surging in his gut. Then he waved and tried to mime unlocking and opening the door in front of him.

The officer looked at him a moment longer, then reluctantly came all the way out of the hall, hugging the wall to the right as she approached the door. She was in uniform but looked rough—bedraggled and sick. Her face was sweaty, her pixie-cut matted to her head. She was holding on to the wall with one hand and in the other, she gripped a nightstick. She stopped about six feet from the door.

"What do you want?" she asked. *Protect and serve indeed*, Gabriel thought.

"Let me in," Gabriel said as quietly as he could while still being heard.

She shook her head. "We're on lockdown," she said. "The sheriff and all the other deputies are out there." She paused and glanced down the street toward the fire truck. She licked her dry, chapped lips and then looked back at Gabriel. Her eyes were wild. "I'm just here to monitor dispatch in case the systems come back online."

Gabriel tried his most reassuring *we're at a funeral, sharing a moment* smile and said, "Can you let me come in for a couple of minutes, please?"

The officer shook her head slowly, eyes glassy. "I'm sorry, sir. That's not going to happen—you... you're going to have to move on down the street. Find cover and wait for rescue."

Gabriel said, "Please!" again, but the officer just shook her head sadly.

He tried a different tack. "What happened out here?" Gabriel asked, nodding back toward the fire truck.

She didn't answer at first, but she clearly wanted to say something. Finally, she began to speak. "I don't know—the power went out, but our backup generator didn't kick in. Jones and I worked on it for a while. The sheriff came back in and grabbed Jonesie and Smitty to help him patrol the town. None of us felt good, but the sheriff has a way of motivating you. A while later he came back in to get his assault rifle, but it didn't work, so he told me to lock up." She paused, looking even sicker. She met Gabriel's eyes again, but didn't continue. Her expression tore at Gabriel's heart.

"What did you see out here?" he asked. "What did all this?"

She shook her head again, a pained expression on her face. *She's seen something,* Gabriel thought. "It was dark," she said. "Billy had the volunteers—everyone who was still on their feet— help him roll the fire truck out into the street. Said they had some manual pumps. Jonesie was with them. I don't know where the sheriff or Smitty went. They..." she paused, staring at the ground. "People started screaming and pointing at something... I couldn't see what it was at first." Her gaze was vacant now. Her mouth worked, but if she was saying anything, Gabriel couldn't hear it.

"What was it?" he asked more forcefully, glancing over his shoulder to make sure the road was still clear.

The officer looked up at him. "A thing... or a man or something. I don't know. It was huge. As tall as the fire truck. It walked up to everybody... God, it was on fire! Like head-to-toe flames and blue, burning skin. But it just kept coming at them, and people were all huddled up against the truck. Billy tried to get in the way of the thing—he's the fire chief. But it just... just reached out and kind of set him on fire. He went down, and Deputy Jones came over and tried to shoot it, but his sidearm didn't work. Nothing has worked since the blackout. Then that thing killed Jonesie and everyone started running and it started grabbing people and biting them. I opened the door and tried to shoot it from over here, but my gun didn't work either."

"How long ago did this happen?" Gabriel said.

She shrugged. "A while ago. None of the clocks are working," she replied. "And it's been a really long night." She slumped over, leaning against the wall now and sweating profusely. She did not look well at all.

"Can you let me in?" Gabriel asked again. But she didn't seem to be paying any attention to him anymore. She turned away, muttered something about "lockdown," and walked back through the door she had come out of, steadying herself against the wall with her hand as she went. Gabriel lowered his shoulder and tried to use his whole body to open the door, but it was rock solid and didn't budge in the slightest. He considered looking in his pack for something to help him get in, but then thought better of it.

He turned to survey the street again, trying to make sense of the story the cop had told. It could have been a hallucination, given her obviously febrile state, he thought, but it matched what he saw at the scene. And it gave a troubling new angle to the flames on his own body. Gabriel decided he couldn't think about that in detail right now, out in the open as he was. He'd worry about it later.

He listened to the night as he looked up and down the street. The scene in front of him seemed even more frightening than before, but there was no movement and nothing to do but keep moving forward, so Gabriel began to creep back down the road, stopping to peer around the corner of the side street that would take him back toward Tam's.

Once he was off Main Street, things were less horrific, at least on the surface. As he walked, gliding from one shadow to the next as quietly as he could, he watched his surroundings carefully. Nothing moved, and the only sound to be heard was the static of a few scattered, smoldering fires.

As the street transitioned from downtown to residential, he saw another body—intact and lying relatively peacefully on a patch of grass next to the sidewalk. Then another two blocks away, positioned similarly, though this one looked as though he had been in distress when he had died, crawling toward the street from the open door of the house. Two houses down from there was the body of someone's dog, which was somehow worse, though Gabriel couldn't say why. Novelty, perhaps.

He made his way furtively down the street, toward Tam's. The rest of the way, he didn't see anything else out of place except for another dead dog. Maybe there were people in some of the apartments and houses, but Gabriel didn't see or hear any sign of them as he passed by, drifting like a ghost through the gray light of dawn. He turned off Progress Street and after a couple more blocks, he caught sight of Tam's place, which was the last, dumpy house on Fifth Street. The bright blue conflagration consuming one of the school buildings that overlooked this part of town bathed everything in a sickly blue hue. The sound of the fire was louder here.

Tam's yard was overgrown with weeds in some places and sported bare dirt in others. A cheap old lawn mower, which had been dead for months, sat abandoned next to the driveway. Tam's Jeep wasn't there, of course, since they had left it at the facility, but hopefully—*please God*—Tam had made it.

Gabriel approached the front of the plain white house. As he got closer to Tam's door, he saw that it was padlocked from the outside—Tam used a padlock because his landlord had reportedly lost the key to the door itself—and fear filled Gabriel. *Had Tam not made it here?* He looked behind him and around the other houses before knocking on the door. There was no immediate answer and his heart began to pound in his chest. He waited another few seconds and knocked again, louder this time.

"Tam!" he said in a loud half-whisper, half-shout. He glanced up just as a head poked over the edge of the roof, looking down at him.

"There you are," Tam said in his typical conversational tone, which seemed shockingly loud to Gabriel. "No need to shout," he said, almost twice as loud as Gabriel had "shouted." Tam ducked out of sight for a moment, and when he returned, he threw down a rope ladder, which nearly hit Gabriel in the head and clattered against the door as it fell.

"Rapunzel, Rapunzel, let down your hair," Gabriel muttered.

FOURTEEN

When Gabriel got to the top, they embraced, each giving the other a vigorous slap on the back before letting go. Then Tam slowly pulled the rope ladder back up while Gabriel unslung his pack and surveyed the roof. Two classic woven-strap lawn chairs sat facing out into the scrubby, desert-like fields with a white plastic table between them. On the table were a butcher's knife, an entire wheel of cheese with one slice already cut out, and a pack of kids' juice boxes. Sitting in front of it were a canvas rucksack, an old machete, a first aid kit, and a sleeping bag.

"Nice setup," Gabriel murmured. "How'd you get up here, anyway?" He looked around Tam's neighborhood from this higher vantage point but didn't see anything moving. He walked over to one of the canvas chairs and lowered himself into it. He sighed, relaxing for the first time in hours.

Tam didn't answer right away, and Gabriel thought maybe he hadn't heard, but just as Gabriel was about to repeat the question, Tam seemed to come back to himself.

"I've got stairs leading up here from my kitchen," Tam said, indicating the lone door behind them. His voice sounded distracted—out of it.

"No, I mean, your front door is still padlocked from the outside—did you climb down and relock it?"

Tam's eyebrows furrowed. "No?" he said, sounding puzzled. "I don't think so. It's kind of a blur. On my way here, I saw another body, like the ones back at the lab, and then I heard something in the shadows behind that green house on the next block. I overreacted and kind of panicked and ran over here... the next thing I remember clearly is looking out the living room window, but I didn't see what made the noise." He shrugged.

"Yeah, about that," Gabriel began, somber and quiet. "I saw a... creature over near my place that could have been the thing that left the footprint at the lab—the thing that killed our friends. Or one of them, anyway."

Tam didn't say anything at first, but then his curiosity seemed to get the better of him. "What did it look like?" he asked, much more quietly than before.

Gabriel paused, trying to put the horrific vision into words. "Um. Like a giant, yellow, mold-encrusted, five-legged leech with two fat tentacles coming out of its back, each with a giant eyeball and teeth at the end. Maybe six feet long in the body, and about five feet tall at the back. A demon, basically."

Tam was silent for a moment, taking in Gabriel's description. "Was it tall enough to see us up here?" he asked. "Can it climb?"

Gabriel shrugged. "It could probably see us, but I don't know about climbing. At least we could see it coming from up here."

Tam was quiet a moment longer as he looked around the silent streets. Eventually, he spoke again. "I don't think we should call them demons," he said. "They're aliens."

Gabriel frowned. "In that they have no legal documents allowing them to be here, yes," he conceded. "But aliens arrive in spaceships, not through accidental portals to hell."

"Hell is a fairy tale told to encourage people to behave in a socially acceptable way, not a real place," Tam said. "We don't know where they came from, and demons are just bogeymen for adults anyway."

"It doesn't matter how we came up with the concepts of hell and demons—whether they're Jungian archetypes from humanity's collective unconscious or just ancient fictional memes. The concepts exist, and the facts fit the situation depressingly well. 'Aliens' implies a rational species from outer space exploring Earth, while 'demons' implies murderous embodiments of evil from another dimension set free to wreak havoc."

Here, he gestured at the world around them to illustrate his point, then continued. "With an infinite number of worlds that they could have come from, it is certainly possible that theirs resembles hell in every conceivable way."

Tam opened his mouth to argue further, but Gabriel cut him off.

"In any case, the way we do things on this planet is generally that the first man of European descent to see an animal gets to name it for everyone, regardless of whether it already had a name. Jenkins called them demons, so demons they are."

Tam frowned stubbornly, but didn't continue the argument. Instead, he walked back over to his chair and sat down to slice some cheese.

"I guess that's why you were gone for so long. I was getting worried," he said around a mouthful.

"Yeah, I can tell," Gabriel responded dryly. He looked out over the desert. It was going to be a clear, hot day, but it was still cool now, which Gabriel was just noticing.

"Juice? Or cheese?" Tam asked, one eyebrow arched inquiringly.

Gabriel grabbed a juice box—of course Tam would have

actual children's juice boxes. "Yes, thanks," he said. He pulled the straw from the box and peeled off its plastic.

"To Carla," Gabriel said, his heart thudding in his chest. "And Jenkins."

"To Carla," Tam replied solemnly. "And Jenkins."

The drink walloped Gabriel's taste buds with an overwhelming tide of sugar, but it was also strangely satisfying. He set it down after draining half the contents, then sliced off a piece of cheese with Tam's proffered knife.

They passed the next few minutes in silence, keeping watch over the neighborhood and finishing off all of Tam's rather unorthodox breakfast except for a couple of the juice boxes, which Tam tossed into his pack. Then Gabriel related what he had seen since they had split up.

"I'm guessing people had a reaction to whatever is blocking the power and turning the fire blue," he concluded.

"I didn't feel well when we were walking to town," Tam said. "Drunk, overwhelmed, and self-indulgent; but my immune system is very strong. I almost never get sick. In fact, I had already started feeling better by the time you left for downtown."

"One other thing happened," Gabriel said. "I surprised two guys coming out of the drugstore. Looters." Tam raised an eyebrow. "Remember how our skin seemed to be glowing when we first came round?" Gabriel asked.

"I think I can recall it," Tam said, completely deadpan.

"My skin did that again, only more so," Gabriel continued. "Like little tongues of flame running up from my wrists to my shoulders, and my arms got more muscular somehow, although they've gone back to normal now." He didn't mention how his skin and body had ached afterward—his father had taught him that suffering in silence showed strength of character.

Tam made no comment on this revelation, his eyebrow still raised. Gabriel waited another moment, thinking about how crazy it all sounded, then went on. "They attacked me from opposite sides and I put both of them on the ground." Gabriel swallowed. "One of them—I broke both of his arms... and the other I accidentally killed. I didn't know he was dead until after the other guy ran off." He stopped there, waiting for Tam's reaction.

His friend was quiet for a moment, then said, "I'm sorry they put you in that position. There's enough death and horror already." He didn't look at Gabriel as he spoke, and there was a great deal of sadness in his voice. "I don't mind the looting—these circumstances qualify as exigent even by the most extreme definition. But people should be working together, not attacking each other."

Gabriel considered the situation. Despite Tam's words, the sadness in his friend's voice made Gabriel feel judged, somehow; his stomach clenched with guilt for killing the man with the crowbar, and maybe the other would die, too, without the use of his arms. But then he remembered his rage. They had come at him. *Why couldn't they have left me alone?* But Gabriel wasn't going to argue with Tam about it. He hadn't been there. Gabriel decided he wasn't going to apologize or feel guilty for defending himself or others from predators—it was as if someone else's doubt was feeding his own certainty.

He changed the subject. "Anyway, I'm now embracing an Incredible Hulk, Doctor Manhattan-style theory about what happened to us," he said.

"The Hulk was based on Heracles," Tam replied absently. "The Greek demigod who was so strong that he accidentally killed his family in a fit of rage and had to perform all those incredible feats of strength to seek redemption. I'll take Doctor Manhattan. I'd love to go build science projects on Mars whenever I want."

Gabriel nodded. "Remember the scene where he and his

girlfriend are being intimate and he grows extra arms so he can pleasure her better?" He smiled as he remembered it himself, but Tam just looked at him blankly, vague disapproval etching his features.

Gabriel shrugged, still smiling. "It's a very practical superpower," he said.

Tam shook his head, but he started to smile a little, and Gabriel thought how nice it was to talk about something less real and scary than their present circumstances for a moment.

They lapsed into silence, though it was not as tense now. Gabriel looked out over the desert and Tam followed his gaze. Dawn was well and truly breaking, and it was magnificent. The rim of the sun looked like the edge of a beam from a giant, world-cooking laser. He felt the heat on his face immediately. He closed his eyes against the glare and basked in the warmth. It was very relaxing and he was very tired. They just sat there for a while, listening to the too-quiet town around them, and were both surprised and absurdly pleased when a bird began to sing.

They sat like that for some time, enjoying the tactile pleasure of the new sunlight on their skin. Gabriel wasn't one hundred percent sure that he hadn't briefly fallen asleep. After what seemed like thirty minutes, Tam broke the silence.

"Now what the fuck are we supposed to do? We're in some real pretty shit now, man." Tam said in a whiney voice, quoting the classic sci-fi movie *Aliens*. "I take it we don't think anything works in town either," he continued more normally.

Gabriel cracked open an eye and looked over at his friend. "No, I don't think so. Hard to tell how big the field of effect might be," he replied. "If it's a large, persistent field, that could explain why no outside help has arrived yet." Gabriel thought about it. "Actually, if the field is several hundred miles wide, people might not even know where it's centered or what caused it at all."

"Anything is possible at this point," Tam agreed.

Gabriel sighed. "We have to get outside the area of effect and contact LA with our news and the data we've managed to collect on the experiment." He glanced over at Tam, who nodded slowly. Gabriel continued, "So with that in mind, and assuming that the area of effect is not that wide, the best solution would be to pick a direction to travel in for a few days until we find a working communication device we can contact our bosses with."

"With which we can contact our bosses," Tam corrected, half under his breath. "Which direction?"

"I say west," Gabriel answered. "Phoenix is closer than any major city to the east, plus on the off chance that's not far enough, we could continue all the way to LA if we had to. We could join the team there and try to figure out how to fix this."

Tam frowned. "They *caused* this," he said, irritably.

"Regardless of who caused it, I feel responsible for not stopping it," Gabriel said. "And it seems that getting our information to Theory is the best chance we have of fixing it."

Tam didn't respond at first and Gabriel wondered if he was preparing an argument, but then Tam burst out excitedly, "We should get bikes! And tents and, and... water-carrying devices."

"Yep," Gabriel replied. "Hopefully the outdoor outfitter has water-carrying devices, or as we humans call them, 'water bottles' or 'canteens.'" He gave a wry grin. "But before we leave town, we should get some sleep here. You have a spare couch?"

"Affirmative," Tam responded, waving toward the door behind him that led to the stairs.

Gabriel struggled to his feet, grabbed his pack and staff, and moved toward the opening, his limbs leaden with exhaustion.

"Wake me up when I'm not sleepy anymore," he mumbled.

FIFTEEN

When Gabriel finally awoke, he lay on the couch trying to remember where he was and what had happened. As he recalled yesterday's events, a cold, calm detachment settled over him. Reluctant to get up just yet, he tried to fall back asleep, but his mind began to race with questions and theories. What had really happened with the experiment? What had happened to him? How many people had been killed? He sighed. At least the questions kept him from giving in entirely to depression, he thought. He also had a job to do. They had to report what had happened here to the Organization.

He sat up and checked his watch, which said it was already after three. It had been a long and much-needed nap, but if they wanted to leave today, or even get fully supplied, they had to get moving. "Tam," he croaked. He cleared his throat and tried again. "Tam!" *Better.*

"What?" Tam said from the bedroom, speaking directly into his pillow.

"Let's go shopping—it's getting late."

"I'm up," Tam said, still muffled by the pillow.

"I mean it," Gabriel said.

"I mean it more," was the muted reply. Gabriel leaned over to his backpack and rummaged through it for a moment, pulling out his kit and opening it to get his toothbrush. He stood up slowly and found his way to Tam's messy bathroom. The whole house was messy, actually. Tam's bedroom floor was almost completely covered with junk. You could only see the floor in two places—right by the door and right next to his bed. The rest was buried under books, storage bins, clothes, folded-up blankets, vintage stereo equipment, board games, and even a couple of large stuffed animals. He had seen Tam's idea of home decoration before, but it never ceased to amaze him. Once again, Gabriel thought how insane it would make him to have to live in such an environment. He ducked into the bathroom to freshen up.

"When we go looting, I'm going to get a better pack—mine only has one strap," Tam said, finally sitting up on the edge of his bed. "And some beef jerky!" He seemed excited at the prospect of a shopping trip.

"I just hope we don't run into that creature," Gabriel said. The image of it flashed through his mind, stirring up feelings that made him flinch as he spat out his toothpaste.

As he went back to his pack to put his toiletries away, he said "I'm hungry. Do you have any other food in here we can grab before we take off?" Then he thought of another essential. "Also, do you have a non-electric coffee maker?"

"Probably yes on the food," Tam said from the bathroom. "Probably no on the coffee maker—mine's electric." He paused for a beat, then added, "Boogie woogie woogie," a little more quietly.

Gabriel grinned. "That song's over fifty years old! I think you might want to retire the reference."

"NEVER!" came a defiant cry from the bathroom.

Gabriel walked into the kitchen to start rummaging around

for anything edible that wasn't Tam's wheel of cheese. He quickly found some frosted Pop-Tarts and a loaf of bread, and in the fridge, which was no longer cold, he discovered some packaged turkey slices. He portioned out a little of everything for them both and had already begun eating when Tam came into the kitchen.

"Breakfast of champions," he mumbled, his mouth full of turkey.

"Too bad the generators probably won't work," Tam began. "If they did, we could go get one, and get some gas, and an electric dehydrator, and we could make tons of jerky for our expedition!" He looked proud of his idea.

"If 'ifs' and 'buts' were candy and nuts, then we'd all have a merry Christmas," Gabriel said, his mouth turned up at the corners and his eyes sparkling.

Tam sighed, unamused. "As a matter of fact, candy and nuts haven't constituted a merry Christmas for American children in over a hundred years," he said, looking at Gabriel pointedly. "Now who's using the most outdated reference?"

After breakfast, Tam finished packing his bag, then climbed back up to the roof and down the rope ladder to the front door, which he unlocked from the outside before coming back in the simpler way. He and Gabriel put their traveling clothes back on except for their jackets, which they each tied to their packs. They slung their bags onto their shoulders, picked up what weapons they had, and had a look around for any last minute items they might want to take with them. Tam grabbed a deck of cards and put it in his pants pocket. They both stood in the living room, looking at each other for a few more seconds before Gabriel opened the door with a shrug and walked out into the late afternoon sun. Tam padlocked the door behind them.

Their shopping trip was eerie and nauseating, but uneventful. Walking around in broad daylight with a companion and a thick stick in his hand was far less scary than his outing the night before had been, though he still kept a careful watch out for any sound or sign of the creature he had seen.

They stopped by the drugstore, where the man Gabriel had killed still lay on the sidewalk. After clearing out the store's entire supply of beef jerky and granola bars and grabbing a few other items, they picked up more food at the grocery store, passing by the partially eaten remains of several people as they went inside. Finally, they walked the final three blocks to the outdoor supplier. This was a stout, windowless brick building with a strong metal pull-down shutter covering the entrance, secured to the ground with a thick padlock.

"Well, that's discouraging," Gabriel said.

Tam nodded. "Positively unwelcoming."

Gabriel walked over to a car that sat abandoned in the middle of the street. Both the hood and trunk were open, but there was no sign of the driver. In the trunk, Gabriel found what he was looking for—the tire iron. He grabbed it and walked back to try wedging the iron under the gate and prizing it open. When that didn't work, he tried to pry off the lock, but the end of the tire iron was too wide to fit inside the thick metal loop, and even when he found purchase on the edge of the lock or the latch of the gate, they proved to be tougher than the metal of the tire iron. He paused, frustrated, then stepped back. "Any other ideas?" he asked, dropping the iron on the grass by the door.

Tam shook his head slowly. Gabriel racked his brains for a solution. They simply had to get into the store somehow—it held essential supplies that could be the difference between survival and death.

At last, something came to him. Gabriel bent over to pick up his staff, then planted his feet in front of the lock. "Gabriel smash," he murmured. He took the staff in both hands, resting the hardened tip on the lock as he adjusted his stance, preparing to try and use the staff like a pile driver to break the lock. He thought that actually hitting it at all would be the trickiest part. Then he gathered himself for the effort. His muscles bunched and rippled, and he thought he saw a spark shoot across his triceps as he prepared to raise his arms. But before he could even lift the staff at all, the lock popped open spontaneously. At the same time, he saw another spark shoot from the back of his hand onto the staff itself, which was vibrating distinctly. His head swam, and the only reason he didn't throw the staff down in shock was because it was over so quickly. Instead, Gabriel stared at the staff, noting a small burn mark near the top that gave off a tiny wisp of smoke.

"What the hell was that?" Tam asked incredulously, staring at the lock and then the staff.

Gabriel had no idea. At first, his shock robbed him of words, but he eventually managed, "That? That was nothing."

"I think it may have been something," Tam replied cautiously.

"Well, okay, fine, it was *something*," Gabriel muttered. "I don't know. I was getting ready to try to break the lock, thinking about getting in, and it just opened by itself." He shook his head in wonder.

After a moment he remembered to look around again then said, "Let's go in and get the stuff we need."

Tam followed right behind Gabriel, still talking.

"Don't be flippant—you just did magic, basically, and I think we should talk about it."

Gabriel shrugged, looking around the dim interior of the store.

"I just told you how it happened—I'm not sure what else to say about it right now." As he spoke, he moved toward the sales counter, where a long glass case displayed the chief object of his desire.

"One comment does not science make," Tam complained. "We need notes, interviews, and experiments with multi..." He trailed off, watching as Gabriel opened the case and reverently removed the target of his attention.

"What is *that*?"

"This," Gabriel said, sounding almost lustful even to his own ears, "is a Vengeance Lord Apocalypse Axe, which, as you can see, is an honest-to-God battle axe that has the advantages of modern materials and design and the disadvantages of being very expensive and also completely worthless in just about any situation... except maybe the one we're in right now."

Gabriel leaned his walking stick against the counter and found a relatively wide space, taking a couple of practice swings with the axe. It was very sturdy, with a long, subtly curved handle made of some kind of lightweight black metal that was etched for a better grip and topped with a wicked-looking axe head. An angry, vivid green line ran along the edge of the whole thing as its only non-functional embellishment. A cross between a modern fire axe and a zombie hunter cosplayer's wet dream, the thing was a powerful and menacing work of art.

Tam shook his head. "I have to admit you look pretty badass," he said.

Gabriel turned around, grinning. "Good," he said. "The scarier it looks, the less likely it is that I'll actually have to use it." He went back to the counter and pulled out a ring and harness for securing it to his waist and thigh. "There are a few other weapons in here if you need one. Knives, higher-quality machetes, and tomahawks like the one I have," Gabriel said. "I'll go get a water filter."

Tam stepped over to the display case and looked inside. After a moment he drew out a machete. It was black and modern looking with a similar bright green trim to Gabriel's new toy, and the back of the blade was jaggedly serrated. He picked it up and gave it a few test swings. Seemingly satisfied, he slid it back into its sheath and then set about exchanging it for the old, thoroughly battered one on his belt. After that, he noticed a belt pouch containing three large throwing stars, which he added to his haul.

Gabriel returned with a water filtration pump and then found a small container of Swedish fire starters at the counter. He took one out and tested it on the countertop, sending disturbingly odd-looking sparks scattering across the glass. They looked blue, like the fire at the school, and they didn't fly around as sparks normally did. They looked like they were dripping, somehow. Fatter and far slower than they should be. Gabriel and Tam exchanged glances, but neither said anything. Gabriel put the container in one of his shirt pockets and grabbed a couple more, placing one in his bag and sliding the other over to Tam. Then he walked over to a rack of sunglasses near the counter, most of them more functional than fashionable. He spun the rack around slowly until he found a pair he liked. He peeled off the sticker before trying them on, looked at himself in the little mirror and nodded. Tam followed suit and selected a pair of large, amber-colored shooting glasses that would provide excellent protection from dust and wind, as well as relief from the merciless desert glare. He slid them up on top of his head.

"I think they have some iodine tablets for backup water purification," Gabriel said. "I can't think of anything else I need. If you need a lightweight tent or rain gear or a jacket or anything, this is the place. They also have water-carrying devices."

Tam grinned, unslinging his pack and dropping it to the floor. Then he walked around the place, gathering the things Gabriel had mentioned, plus whatever else he thought he might want later. He also picked out a larger backpack to replace his own. When he brought his loot back, he set it all on the ground and opened his old pack, taking out a bulky winter jacket he had stuffed inside and tossing it casually over a nearby clothing rack. He put his stuff into his new bag and tied the flap shut, then struggled to lift the thing back onto his shoulders. It seemed considerably heavier. "We're going to be in such good shape," he said, his voice completely sincere.

Gabriel reshouldered his pack as well, and dropped his battle axe through a thick black metal ring on the harness. Then Gabriel picked up his old walking staff and jumped around a little, looking down at his axe to see if it would fall off or cut his leg or trip him.

"This is no time for dancing," Tam said.

"It's always time for dancing!" Gabriel responded, half-heartedly. Satisfied that his axe was secure, he started toward the door. Tam followed Gabriel out into the sun, where they both put on their new shades. Gabriel felt more ready to face the world than he had at any point since yesterday. He turned and pulled the gate down behind them, relocking the padlock as if nothing strange had happened to it earlier.

Gabriel walked point, leading them back up toward Main Street. Tam didn't bother to ask if he had a reason for choosing this route, but after a moment Gabriel said, "I want to stop on the way and see if that officer is still at the station. Then we can go get bikes."

"Suits me—I'd actually like to report some crimes," Tam said. "And see if she'll put out an APB on something murderous with claws."

"Good idea," Gabriel said, nodding gravely. "Also, there's a guy on fire who's wanted for questioning in connection with the murder of a fireman."

"He's certainly guilty of irony," Tam said emphatically.

Gabriel sighed. "I regret encouraging you."

A few minutes later they arrived at the station. Gabriel rapped loudly on the door frame with the knob of his staff. Tam watched the street around them. After a moment Gabriel rapped again, this time more insistently. Still there was no answer. "Should we break in?" he asked.

"Let me see your staff," Tam said. Gabriel cocked an eyebrow at him, but proffered the staff anyway. Tam took it and stepped toward the door. He rotated the staff until he found the mark that had appeared when Gabriel had opened the lock at the outdoor shop. He examined the design carefully, tracing it with his finger, then took a deep breath and reached out with the bottom of the staff to touch the locking mechanism next to the handle. Gabriel felt... *something* in his head and heard the lock snap open.

"Cool!" Tam exclaimed, then glanced up and down the street once he realized how loud he had been. Gabriel's mouth hung open.

"What?" Tam asked. "You did it first."

"Yeah, but," Gabriel said. "I thought that might have been a freak coincidence. How did you know it would work?" he asked.

Tam shrugged. "I didn't. It was an experiment," he said. "When you did it earlier, I saw this mark appear on the staff. It didn't look random, and I wanted the chance to test it," he continued.

"It doesn't seem like you to jump into an experiment without a mind-bogglingly exhaustive understanding of what you're about to try," Gabriel remarked.

Tam shrugged. "This is something truly new. We need data if we're going to learn the new parameters. Besides, we've already triggered the consequences—we might as well learn as much as we can, including how your stick now uses Evocation to open locks."

"Evocation?"

"Calling into being," Tam shrugged. "I don't know what to call it. Magic."

Gabriel breathed softly as it began to sink in. "Fucking A! I'm Gandalf the Grey!"

"Who?" Tam asked.

"Gandalf." Gabriel said, awaiting recognition in Tam's eyes. But he was left waiting. "Gandalf. The wizard from *The Lord of the Rings*?"

Tam shrugged.

"You've got to be kidding me," Gabriel said, exasperated. "You don't know who Gandalf is?"

"A wizard?" Tam asked tentatively.

Gabriel's mouth dropped open again. "Perhaps this is a bit of an overstatement," he said, "but right now I think this is the most shocking revelation of the past two days. How could you not know The Lord of the Rings?"

"I don't read much fiction," Tam said haughtily.

"But you were quoting Aliens yesterday," Gabriel said.

"That's a movie."

"The Lord of the Rings has been made into THREE movies!" Gabriel exclaimed.

"I haven't seen them, I guess." Tam said. "Do they have elves and dwarves?"

Gabriel nodded, still dumbstruck.

"Stories with elves and dwarves are transparent affirmations of the idea that people who look different should live separately. Enemies at worst, benevolent visitors at best. Elves were often thinly-veiled symbols of white supremacy, and dwarves were usually just representations of antisemitic tropes. It's society porn for racists."

Gabriel stood and stared at Tam, who just stared back, obviously confused by the severity of the reaction.

"We'll circle back to this later," Gabriel finally said. "Much later. Let's go talk to that cop, if she's still alive."

He pushed open the now unlocked door and walked into the deserted police station. Tam had one hand on the handle of his machete, but kept it holstered as Gabriel called out, "Hellooo—anybody here?"

There was no answer.

"Maybe she went to get some coffee," Tam said. They had both joked in the past that the local police force seemed intent on living up to the stereotypes about cops, coffee, and donuts. Now, though, it just reminded him of the coffee shop and the bodies he'd found there.

Gabriel locked the door behind them, then walked past the vacant reception desk and into a large office with three or four workstations, rolling chairs, and a variety of mismatched filing cabinets. Tam stopped to check the dispatcher's communications equipment to see if it had been affected like everything else. He flipped every switch and pressed every button, but nothing worked. He shook his head dejectedly.

"Found her," Gabriel called from the door at the far end of the large office. Tam walked across the room to join Gabriel, who was standing in the doorway of what looked like the captain's office. His eyes were fixed at the officer lying on the floor, seemingly comatose.

"Officer!" Gabriel called loudly, but the woman didn't stir. The skin of her face and neck was sweaty and terribly blotchy. Her lips were badly chapped and covered in white scabs. Her nose had been bleeding, leaving a dried crust that trailed across her upper lip, back down her cheek and into the hair behind her ear. Her chest rose and fell shallowly.

"She's alive, but she looks like hell," Tam said. "She's very ill." He started toward the woman, but Gabriel put a hand on his chest to stop him.

"I'm going to float a position to you for feedback," Gabriel said. "Not necessarily my position, just talking out loud."

Tam eyed him suspiciously. "Go ahead."

"It's critical that we get our information to LA," Gabriel said. "And I think this lady may die regardless of what we do here, and she may have a disease that could be catching."

Tam said nothing.

"And our access to medical help is nil."

Tam remained stubbornly silent.

"So I might suggest that the smartest and safest thing for us to do is to roll this lady a couple of water bottles, shut this door and be on our way," Gabriel finished, looking at Tam cautiously.

"That's a sensible plan," Tam offered, and Gabriel started to relax.

"Except for one thing," Tam amended.

"Which is?"

"We're not fucking monsters." His tone was icy.

Gabriel was taken aback. As he attempted to formulate a defense, Tam brushed past him and went to where the officer lay. There he knelt, placing a hand on her forehead and then unbuttoning the top button of her shirt. She didn't react at all.

"She's obviously been locked in here alone," Tam said absently. "And it seems like the majority of people got sick at once—it's most likely not a communicable infection." He stripped off his backpack and began going through it, pulling out a couple of bottles of medicine—potassium iodide and an antibiotic. "It could be some kind of radiation poisoning," he speculated.

"I've got some medicine for you," he murmured gently to the woman, then pushed several pills into her mouth and held a bottle of water to her lips. She swallowed reflexively, coughing weakly, but then fell back into silence.

Tam sat back and watched her for a moment. Then he

stood up and looked at Gabriel. "I'm going to stay here for a little while, see if she comes around," he said.

Gabriel nodded somberly, somehow feeling both guilty and relieved. "I'll go check on their generator," he said, and turned to walk down the hall, past some empty holding cells to an area that looked like the maintenance room. The generator was indeed back here, and easy to spot, as it had been uncovered and there were a couple of wrenches and a can of lubricant or primer or something on the floor next to it.

For the next twenty minutes or so, Gabriel tried everything he could think of to get the generator running, but the thing seemed completely dead. The voltmeter wouldn't budge, even when he pulled the manual crank cord. Not only did the engine no longer work, but it seemed like the thing wouldn't produce any power even if they somehow managed to hook it up to a treadmill. He hadn't really expected it to work, but it was still frustrating.

"Let's go get some bikes," Tam said, suddenly appearing in the doorway. His expression was grim.

Gabriel eyed him and deduced that the officer had died despite Tam's efforts. "I'm sorry," he said.

Tam just shrugged, but Gabriel could tell he was upset. He looked like he was about to cry.

"Let's get the bikes and sleep back at your place tonight," Gabriel said, focusing on moving forward. "We can leave town in the morning. We only have a few hours until sunset, and I'd rather get an early start and travel all day tomorrow."

Tam pulled himself together with a single sniff, then nodded. "That sounds good," he said. "I assume I won't have to call shotgun for my own bed," he continued, a perfunctory, superficial half-grin appearing on his lips.

Gabriel snorted. "I probably couldn't even find your bed in that junkyard you call a bedroom." It felt strange to joke when the world had apparently ended, or at least the part of the world they were in, but Gabriel didn't know what else to do. He felt like habit and the mission were the only things keeping him functional.

"Let's get moving," he said.

Back out on the street, sunglasses on and hands on their weapons, they walked stealthily toward the bicycle shop. It was on the other side of town from Tam's house, but not far from the police station. Really, nothing in this town was all that far from anything else, Gabriel thought. As they turned onto the mostly residential, rather ironically named Madison Avenue, they saw several bodies in the street that looked like a group of people who had all been run down at the same time. Each had been eviscerated and partially consumed. As they approached, a small, wiry dog slunk away with its teeth bared. The stench was horrific. Tam pulled his T-shirt up over his nose as they walked past, each of them trying to see as little of the corpses as possible. There was no sign of whatever had done this, but Gabriel couldn't shake the image of the thing he had seen—the demon—from his mind.

As they approached the bike store, they could see that it was intact. The door was locked, but Gabriel was able to perform the door-opening trick again with his staff, which felt just as dizzyingly bizarre as it had the first two times. They still hadn't discussed it, and Gabriel didn't want to start now. Later. They could talk about all the weirdness later.

Inside, the shop revealed maybe thirty bikes on racks along one wall and a selection of accessories and sportswear toward the front. The entire back of the store was a workshop with bicycle parts and tools strewn about on two dirty benches, a cluttered wooden table, and even the floor. Tam walked straight to a red bike about halfway down the store, one he'd obviously had his eye on. It was a rugged looking hybrid, good for riding on or off road, with shifters and brakes on each handlebar. It seemed like a good choice. He got it down and tested rolling it, stopping it with the brakes. He stood next to the seat and eyeballed its height, then decided to lower the seat a little. He went behind the counter and found a small multi-tool designed for bicycle repair, as well as a water bottle and holder. He brought them all back to the bike and happily set about attaching and adjusting everything.

Meanwhile, Gabriel looked through the rest of the bikes, searching for one similar to Tam's. There was a white one that looked very like it, though of a different make. He got it down and looked it over more closely, deciding that it was acceptable. It felt light and sturdy, both top of his functional wish list. Following Tam's lead, he found a bottle holder, attached it to the frame and grabbed a plastic water bottle. He also looked around until he found a couple of bike repair kits and a small air pump. He looked longingly at an extra wheel, but decided it was too bulky and difficult to carry. He glanced back at Tam standing idly beside his new bike and said, "You ready?"

Tam placed a small stack of twenties on the counter and replied, "Sure." Gabriel rolled his eyes, but didn't begrudge Tam this act of civility.

They rolled their bicycles through the door, leaving the store unlocked behind them, then paused to mount up outside. It was surprisingly difficult and awkward to get on the bikes and stay upright while wearing large backpacks, but it got a little easier once they picked up speed. Gabriel had to lay his staff across his handlebars, but his various other weapons seemed to be out of the way. Even the axe hung far enough out to the side so as not to interfere with his pedaling.

After each of them had nearly fallen over once or twice while trying to get used to riding this way, they began pedaling toward Tam's place, gliding past the bodies on Madison and out onto

Main Street. They didn't see anything moving, except for a dog, maybe the same one they'd come across earlier, which took off running as soon as they saw it. The town whizzed by, and although Gabriel fretted about the noise the bikes made as they coasted, they made it back to Tam's house quickly and without incident.

When they reached Tam's front door, they dismounted, and Tam let them in. They walked their bikes into the living room and propped them up against the wall next to the door.

Both men shrugged off their packs and removed some of their weapons. Gabriel flexed his right shoulder and rolled his arm back and forth. "I think I'm sorer than after a weekend of backpacking."

Tam dropped onto the couch. "You probably don't spend as much time in fear of your life when you're camping," he said. "That's likely put some extra tension in your shoulders... if I had to guess."

Gabriel nodded and joined his friend on the couch. He dragged his bag over between his legs, opened it, and began taking things out and setting them on the coffee table.

"Are you moving in?" Tam asked.

"Just rearranging stuff," Gabriel replied. "More efficient use of space."

Tam sighed. "I should do that, too." He sat up and leaned over far enough to grab his own bag and pulled it toward him. Within ten minutes, the table, floor, and couch around them were covered with piles of food, equipment, clothing, and weapons. In the end, they moved the food and some of Gabriel's camping gear into Tam's bag, leaving out a few unnecessary items.

When they were done, they each leaned back on the couch to rest for a moment. Within minutes, they were both asleep.

When Gabriel awoke from his nap, Tam was rummaging

around noisily. Gabriel stretched mightily and yawned, then slowly made his way to the kitchen, where Tam had laid out some food on the counter. Well, maybe "food" was pushing it—all he saw were some peanut butter, crackers, a can of pork and beans, and a small jar of Kalamata olives. "This... actually looks delicious," Gabriel admitted.

"We must be adapting already," Tam said. He grabbed a couple of plates from the cabinet and divided everything between them. "You want to eat on the roof?" he asked.

"Sure," Gabriel said. Tam picked up his plate and walked over to the stairs and up, with Gabriel following.

On the roof, they found their lawn chairs right where they had left them, but the real attention-grabber was the fire that was still burning at the school on the hill. One of the buildings had already burned to the ground, but now the one closest to it was fully engulfed. The angry, flickering blue light of the flames reflected off the plumes of smoke billowing up from the conflagration illuminating them from below. Some of the flames were a dark, malevolent red around the base, but all the rest were an eerie, vibrant blue.

Tam sat down in his chair and turned it to face the school. After a moment, Gabriel did the same. They sat in silence for a while, eating their strange meal.

After a bite of peanut butter and olives on a cracker, Gabriel broke the silence. "I mean, that's not the color fire's supposed to be," he said with adopted indifference.

Tam continued to gaze at the spectacle before responding. "No, it really isn't," he agreed. "But that's not even the weirdest part—look how slowly it's flickering. I've never seen anything like it."

Now that Gabriel was focusing on it, it did seem very strange. The flames themselves were high and almost constant, wavering or winking out periodically, but without the merry flickering and dancing of any fire he'd ever seen.

"Could be some kind of chemical up there making the flames do that," Gabriel suggested, but even as he said it, he remembered that all the fires he'd seen since the incident had looked the same.

Tam didn't answer.

They finished their meal, gazing at the odd blaze in fascinated silence. Gabriel noticed that the two other buildings up there seemed to be intact. He wondered if they would catch fire as well. Both seemed to be far enough away from the one that was now burning to escape harm, barring a collapse or an explosion or something. The building on the left particularly caught his attention. He wasn't sure why, but now that he had noticed it, he couldn't stop looking at it. It was a pretty typical school building, really. Cheap, concrete block construction, with windows for every classroom, taunting all the students with an amazing vista of the town below. It looked like thousands of other schools built around the same time. Gabriel imagined the students who attended that school looking out those windows every day, waiting for the final bell to ring and give them their freedom. He thought he saw something move in one of the windows, snapping him out of his reverie. He looked again but couldn't see it anymore. He looked at other windows, but didn't see anything there, either.

"I thought I saw something in one of the windows," he said.

"In the building that's on fire?" Tam asked.

"No, the next one over," Gabriel replied, still trying to catch another glimpse of it. "I don't see anything now." Tam looked at the building Gabriel had pointed out, but shrugged after a moment and went back to eating.

Gabriel followed suit, chewing thoughtfully and looking at

the windows of the as-yet unburned building. He realized that he wanted to go investigate, but he couldn't articulate why he wanted to do it—not even to himself. Before he realized it, he was saying out loud, "I want to go up there and check it out."

Tam looked up at the building again and simply said, "Okay." Gabriel couldn't help but smile at that. He felt that going along with just about any suggestion was one of Tam's best traits as a friend. He wasn't like that at work, but off the clock, Tam was always up for anything. Except camping. They finished the remainder of their meal, continuing to observe the quietly raging blue inferno in silence.

After dinner, they went back downstairs and began to gear up. They each put on a long-sleeved shirt to ward off the cool night air and then began gathering their weapons. Tam went to the kitchen to get candles so they could see better. When he brought them back to the living room, he held them out to Gabriel as if for show and tell. The flames on these candles were blue too, just like the ones currently consuming the school.

Gabriel sighed. "Were they like that when you lit them?" he asked.

Tam shrugged, then set them down on the coffee table. "I dunno," he responded. "I wasn't really paying attention before, plus it isn't really dark yet."

Gabriel didn't know what to say. If the air was full of some strange chemical that was affecting fire he couldn't smell it and it didn't seem to be impacting his breathing, so he might as well ignore it for now. He went back to gathering his weapons. He decided to carry his new axe in his hands instead of the staff, setting the latter against his pack.

Tam noticed this and asked, "If you're not going to carry the staff, could I? We might need it to unlock a door or something."

Gabriel picked it up and extended it to Tam, who took it

almost reverently. He looked it over and tested its heft in his grip. When he was done he nodded to indicate his readiness, saying "Do you want to ride the bikes up there? It's really steep."

Gabriel considered it, but the thought of sneaking quietly on foot was slightly more appealing to him than laboring uphill on their bikes. "Let's walk."

Tam assented and led the way to the door. They slipped out into the rapidly cooling night and Tam locked the padlock on the door behind them.

After they had walked halfway up the hill, looking and listening intently for any threats nearby, they heard a distant scream. It seemed to be coming from the school.

"We need to hurry," Gabriel whispered.

SIXTEEN

T
he rest of the town seemed quiet as they walked toward the school, and they didn't hear any more screaming. They *could* hear the eldritch fire raging at the top of the hill. At least the sound—a dull roar punctuated by snaps and pops—seemed normal, if that could be said of a fire slowly burning a school to the ground without anyone raising a hand to stop it. They followed the road to the foot of the hill without incident. The town appeared completely deserted. Either everyone was dead or they were hiding, and whatever had killed so many people seemed to have moved on.

Once they started up the hill, Gabriel led them around so they could approach the building where he had seen the movement directly, rather than having to pass close to the fire. The school grounds were eerie. The buildings were plain and blocky, but still impressive in their commanding position, perched atop the hill. Now, however, deserted and still in the flickering blue light, the whole place seemed off. Terrible. A reminder that scores of children must also be dead or missing in all of this.

Gabriel tightened his grip on the axe and walked on. As they approached, he examined the building more closely. It was an old concrete block construction with a brick facade and a notable lack of design or aesthetic frills. It was three stories tall with cheap-looking windows about every ten feet. Gabriel imagined the place was probably hot in the summer and cold in the winter. He had spent his elementary school years in a very similar setting. The gymnasium had been larger, at least before it had burned down, but this one was huge too, relative to the size of the town. Gabriel suddenly realized that this school must be K-12. Three schools in one. He hadn't really thought about it before, but it made sense in such a small town.

They went to the main entrance and up three concrete steps to the double doors. Gabriel put a finger to his lips and tried the handle, finding it locked. He gestured for Tam to perform their newfound trick, and Tam gently brought the brass cap of the staff into contact with the lock casing, producing a barely audible buzz followed by a click as the door unlocked. They grinned wildly and looked at each other, realizing once again that they still had not even tried to figure out the mechanism by which they were now able to unlock doors. Gabriel imagined they were both thinking the same thing—it was hard to talk about something when you had no idea how it could be happening—it just *was*.

Gabriel waited until Tam nodded his readiness, then he pulled the door open and they slipped inside.

The interior of the school matched its exterior perfectly—a wide tiled hallway ran from the entrance all the way to the other end, with classroom doors standing open on either side, dark and ominous. With the door closed behind them, the roar of the fire outside was quieted. The inside of the building was lit only by the slowly flickering blue light entering through the windows. Gabriel and Tam both had to wait a moment while their vision adjusted as the afterimage of the ghostly fire outside faded slowly from their retinas. A staircase to their left led to the floors above.

Gabriel stopped in front of it, holding up a hand to still Tam as he listened.

There was a murmur of speech coming from somewhere upstairs. Gabriel was about to motion for them to go up when another scream echoed shrilly down the stairs. Without exchanging a word, both men started up the stairs, taking them two at a time while trying to be as quiet as possible. As they made the second floor landing, the scream came again, a ragged, brutal sound that hurt to hear, let alone make. It sounded like a woman.

Before they had taken three steps down the hall, a man's scream joined the first voice. Gabriel adjusted his grip on his axe and hurried forward grimly.

Then another sound cut through the screaming and shouting—a loud, pervasive buzzing that seemed to reverberate through the floor beneath them and the very air they breathed. Though not deafening, it could certainly be heard and felt over the cries coming from the room in front of them. Gabriel also noticed a stench, like a cross between wet, fermenting dead grass and rotten eggs.

He edged into the open doorway and peered inside, but he didn't understand what he was seeing at first. In the far left corner of the classroom, shrouded in flickering shadows, stood a large creature of some kind. Every bizarre angle and line of it was an impossible nightmare of wrongness. Its skin was black, or perhaps dark green. A predator. Gabriel couldn't even tell how many legs or arms it had, as it seemed to sprout limbs asymmetrically from random places on its body. The monster was large, but it looked *folded up* somehow, with too many joints in too many places. Sharp, thick spines protruded in serrated ridges from the sides of its vaguely lizard-like head, and more grew along the edges of its largest appendages and back. Its many small dark eyes glittered like malevolent will-o'-the-wisps in the shadows, reflecting the dancing blue firelight. The terrifying buzzing sound seemed to be coming from the creature, though it was not at all clear how it was making the noise.

After what seemed like two full minutes of staring at the thing, but could in reality have been no more than a few seconds, it came into better focus and Gabriel saw a human being cradled in one of the creature's appendages. The man's back had been broken in half like a green twig, his lower half hanging loose from the monster's grip at a stomach-turning angle. The creature took a bite out of the man's throat, its long, ghoulish fangs crushing and ripping his flesh. Lazily, it eyed Gabriel and Tam, probably the only people on Earth who had heard the screams. Then it turned its head sideways and latched onto the corpse's head, biting down with immense force and crushing the skull with a sickening crunch. Gabriel put his hand on the doorframe to steady himself as Tam threw up in the hallway behind him. Had his failure at the lab unleashed this creature? *Had this thing killed their coworkers?*

Something at the front of the room seemed to attract the monster's attention, and it casually dropped the partially eaten corpse to the floor with a blunt thud and turned, completely ignoring Gabriel and Tam.

At the front of the classroom, next to the blackboard, a young woman was huddled in a ball, her arms clasped around her drawn-in knees as she stared in abject horror, her mouth open in another ragged and wordless scream.

She looked to be in her early twenties. Her face was dirty and tear-stained, both her T-shirt and pants were ripped to shreds, exposing patches of pale, sweaty skin, and she wore a pair of incongruously bright purple sneakers.

The demon, *because that's definitely what this is*, Gabriel thought, cocked its head to one side, then seemed to unfold, making itself taller, and lumbered across the room toward the young woman. As it drew near to her, it crouched down and lowered its head to her face, as if to examine her more closely.

The girl's eyes stared straight ahead, as big as saucers; she had gone mute and still. She didn't even flinch when the creature reached out a dark, backwards-jointed appendage to touch her, lightly at first, on her side, beneath her ribcage. Then she stiffened and hissed in pain as the thing's claw sank through her shirt and into her flesh, blood spurting out as the creature stared into her face. The monster's buzzing now sounded like a croon of pleasure as it seemed to breathe in her terror and pain.

Screams filled the room again, but the woman's mouth and eyes were now closed. It took Gabriel a second or two to realize that the sound was coming from his own throat, and that he was sprinting through the desks, axe held high, straight at the back of this unholy monster.

He only had time for one last thought as he hurtled across the room. *I really hope I know what I'm doing.*

SEVENTEEN

TAM

Tam watched in thoroughly overwhelmed detachment as Gabriel took off, sprinting straight toward the nightmare creature. The whole thing was an incredible spectacle, from the bizarre wrongness of the monster to the fact that Gabriel seemed to be on fire. Little blue flames erupted all over his body, especially along his back and arms, poking through his clothes and flickering as he ran across the room. Even his axe, raised in the air and ready to strike, was now limned in flame.

The monster seemed to react too slowly; it was only beginning to turn to face Gabriel as the axe slammed into its lower thorax with the force of a thunderclap. The creature, already pivoting, was sent staggering backward, slamming into the teacher's desk and overturning it before regaining its balance. The buzzing grew louder, sharp, as if in outrage, and Gabriel backed away six or seven paces, trying to keep his distance now that he had the thing's attention. The head of Gabriel's axe smoked as the creature's blood burned in the slowly dancing flames.

One of the monster's larger limbs now hung uselessly,

dragging on the ground beneath it, but even as Tam noted this, two other appendages popped wetly from its body with dull, deep snaps like giant knuckles cracking. The nightmare took a step forward, and Gabriel took an answering step back, away from the girl.

With a start, Tam realized he should do something to help. He wasn't sure exactly what that might be, but as he considered his options, he remembered the throwing stars in his belt pouch. He grabbed one—it felt solid and deadly in his hand, though he wondered if he ought to have practiced with it.

Without further thought, he wound up and threw the thing with all his might at the creature's core. Amazingly, it flew true, right on target, and far harder than he had anticipated.

It struck the creature's carapace with a dull *dink* and bounced away harmlessly to clatter on the tiled floor. The creature didn't even take its eyes off Gabriel.

Well, it was worth a try, Tam thought.

He began to edge toward the girl, eyes glued to the alien creature and Gabriel's staff clutched across his chest in both hands. The thing seemed not to have noticed Tam at all; maybe he could make it to the front of the classroom and at least put himself between the thing and the girl, who looked to be in utter shock.

Three wide, careful side-steps. Four. Five—he was halfway there. Six. Past the first row of desks.

Then, when he was at his most exposed, too far from the door for that to be an option and without any cover whatsoever, the creature whirled and rushed at him in three herky-jerky steps, one limb lashing out at his face. He barely got the staff up in time, and the thing's claw hit it so hard that he almost lost his grip. But the monster didn't stop; instead, it took another step closer, towering over him, and reaching for him with several shorter claws at once.

There was nowhere to go. Tam sank back against the wall, all his senses overwhelmed by the proximity of the creature—its caustic, wet grass and ammonia stench nearly as powerful as the buzzing sound, which throbbed so strongly he could almost feel it vibrating in his skull.

He closed his eyes and willed himself to disappear, waiting for the creature's claws to sink into his flesh.

EIGHTEEN

GABRIEL

Gabriel watched the thing turn its back on him and rush at Tam, who was cowering against the wall of the classroom in a ball, almost as if he had resigned himself to being shredded and eaten. Gabriel took the opening and lunged forward to attack again, fearing he would be too late. Gabriel closed with the creature, preparing for another axe blow to its back, when Tam seemed to duck right through the monster's many legs, running past him and toward the girl. Gabriel didn't understand how Tam had managed it, but he didn't have time to think about that as the creature spun around to face him, arms spread wide again. Gabriel was already well within the thing's reach; he could only try to do as much damage as possible before it killed him. He brought the axe back, coiling up for another huge swing.

The creature staggered as it finished its turn, nearly falling before catching itself with two of its smaller limbs. Its hideous head was cocked sideways at Gabriel. Eight—*no, ten?*—flat, emotionless eyes stared at him from multiple surfaces and the thing's maw hung open, angry and hissing. Gabriel stepped into his swing, feeling fire and energy coursing through and around him, and aimed for what might have been a neck. The base of the head area, in any case. The blow had no proper form—it didn't even resemble a baseball swing—but it contained every ounce of force that Gabriel could muster and sent the blade of his axe sinking deep into the creature with a wet crunch, nearly cleaving its head from its body entirely. The small tongues of flame on the axe seemed to leap onto the demon with the blow, igniting it as well. The thing crashed sideways to the floor, head hanging by what looked like a handful of bloody black leather strips. Its limbs twitched uncontrollably as the flames danced over its wet, leathery skin, and the buzzing finally, mercifully, stopped.

Gabriel stepped away from the flailing creature, axe at the ready in case being nearly decapitated didn't kill it, but the beast made no effort to come after him. Its twitching gradually slowed and the flames spread voraciously to consume its whole body, filling the air with a new and different sickening stench that resembled smoldering rotten eggs and cabbage.

When the creature finally stilled, an amazing sense of peace and rightness came over Gabriel, suffusing him with a wild euphoria. He looked at Tam, who was staring blankly at the burning remains of the demon. The man's eyes were glazed over, as if he were lost in deep thought. The flames around the creature turned from blue to a natural orange, surprising in its normalcy. *A beautiful sight*, Gabriel thought.

The fire continued to dance across the creature's skin, converting its flesh to ash before their eyes one layer at a time. Gabriel turned to see about helping the girl with her wound and caught sight of the burning building across the way. The flames there were still blue.

Gabriel bent to examine the young woman, his brittle, raw skin and general body aches causing him to wince as he did so. The young woman shied away from him at first, and when he tried to take her arm and coax her out of her crouch so he could see her bloody, wounded side, she tore her arm from his hand, hissing in pain. The arm looked broken, the forearm sagging slightly out of line in the middle, but she didn't seem to want his help at that moment. She looked pitiful.

"Tam," Gabriel said, realizing that Tam was still just standing there, staring blankly at the burning creature. Tam didn't stir.

"*Tam*," Gabriel said, louder, and this time his friend gave a little jerk as he came back to himself.

"What?"

"Can you find something to splint her arm with, please?"

Tam nodded and started looking around the room dazedly, eventually returning with a random assortment of items including a light cotton sweater, a couple of oversized, paint-stained art smocks, and a plastic cup full of rulers.

Gabriel persuaded the girl to lie down on her side, though she looked almost catatonic, her face completely devoid of any emotion. Gabriel murmured to her encouragingly, a constant stream of optimism, "You're tough, you're strong, this will all heal," and the like, which seemed to be working, as the girl allowed him to lift the back of her shirt over the wound to examine it. It looked bad, covered in gore. *Without a hospital, she's a goner*, he thought. Yet when he took one of the smocks and gently wiped away the blood, almost all of it smeared away, including what he'd thought was the wound itself. The skin looked unbroken, if grimy and blood-soaked, with only a slightly puckered red line marking where the creature had gouged a furrow into her side.

Tam leaned in to take a closer look, finally starting to re-engage in the proceedings. He turned to meet Gabriel's eyes in confusion.

"What is going on here?" he asked.

Gabriel shook his head in silence and lowered the girl's shirt. She glanced at them sideways without turning her head.

"We can splint your arm with rulers and strips of cloth," Gabriel said aloud, and he reached carefully for the girl's arm again. She flinched, but then subsided. As gently as he could, he felt along the ulna and radius for the break. He couldn't find it. The arm was bruised, but the bones seemed straight and true now.

"Okay, this is just weird," Gabriel said, abruptly enough to startle the girl.

Tam cocked his eyebrow in query.

Gabriel frowned. "I'm sure it was broken before," he said. He felt along the young woman's forearm again, and though she shifted away after a couple of seconds, he was able to trace the entire, intact bone. There was no break now.

He sidled around to the front of the girl and held out his hand to help her up. She didn't seem to notice, however. "Listen, miss," Gabriel said. "We've got to get you out of here, okay?"

The woman just kept staring at the floor.

"Can you walk?" Gabriel continued, again with no appreciable response. He said, "Please, I need you to walk with us so we can get out of here and go someplace a little safer. Can you walk with us?"

The girl's eyes had shifted to the creature's burning corpse, but at his question, she flicked her eyes to him and gave a slight nod. She struggled clumsily to her feet despite her evident discomfort.

"Okay, let's go," Gabriel said, turning to Tam. "Back to your place for the rest of the night, and we'll figure out what to do with her tomorrow."

The girl had some trouble keeping up with them on the way back down the hill, stumbling several times despite not looking up from her shoes the whole time, but she was at least very quiet.

Tam, on the other hand, seemed to come back to himself as they walked. When they reached his house, he unlocked the door and motioned them inside, Gabriel going first.

The girl stopped cold in the doorway and refused to enter. Gabriel, who was already inside the house, turned and looked at her. Her brow was furrowed and she was breathing more heavily than she had been on the walk. Guessing what the problem might be, he took his large survival knife from his belt and handed it wordlessly to her, handle first. She looked up at him and frowned, but then reached out and took the knife. After another second, she entered the house and looked around, clutching the weapon in both hands in front of her.

She was tall, Gabriel thought. Easily as tall as he was—taller, if he was being honest. She had long blonde hair that looked duller than it should, probably from sweat and dirt. She was athletic and trim, with a finely sculpted, vaguely Scandinavian face. Gabriel thought she was probably in her early twenties. Under almost any other circumstances, she would be considered really pretty. Now, however, she looked like a disaster survivor— a heart-rending combination of shell-shocked and exhausted. Her expression was slack, but her darting eyes watched them warily, and she kept the knife upright in front of her even as she sank into a chair.

Gabriel went to his pack and rummaged through it until he found one of the first aid kits. He brought it over to the girl and knelt down next to her. "Miss, I'd like to use some disinfectant on your side, just to be sure, if that's okay with you." She didn't immediately offer any response, instead staring at him expressionlessly.

"Alternatively," he began, but then she slid slightly forward in her seat and leaned away, over the armrest. Keeping hold of his knife in one shaky hand, she used the other to hike her sweater up past the wound. Her head was cocked to the side, one eye fixed on him, her expression unreadable. He tried to keep his face blank as well, his hands firm and steady as he used the disinfectant wipe to clean away the rest of the dried blood. There had been a lot of it, crusting thickly over her skin and into her shirt, but as he cleaned the area thoroughly, he could see that the wound was completely healed, at least externally. Even the puckering and redness had subsided, leaving only a faint white line.

Tam returned from the kitchen carrying two lit candles, and Gabriel suddenly wondered if he had been seeing in the dark again and if the girl thought that was weird. Tam walked over and looked over Gabriel's shoulder at the wound. He came closer, studying it by the light of the candles in his hands. He gave a low whistle, which caused the girl to flinch. "Yes, that is unusual," Tam remarked.

Gabriel thought about it but couldn't come up with an explanation. "Miss, does the wound still hurt? How did it heal up so quickly?"

The girl shook her head slowly, then gave a small shrug— the most extensive interaction they had had with her since first seeing her. She pulled the hem of her sweater back down and scooted back away from them as far as the chair allowed.

"What's your name?" Gabriel asked. The girl just stared at him as if he were a bug. An evil bug.

"Unless you don't want to tell us your name, which is fine..." He paused, but she didn't react at all and didn't seem like she was going to.

"Well, we'll need to call you something, at least until we can take you home or wherever you want to go," Gabriel said.

"Since we were just talking about the movie *Aliens*," Tam said, "how about Newt?"

Gabriel shook his head as he watched the young woman, trying and failing to read her expression. "Newt was a little girl," he said. "How about Ripley, the bad-ass who saved them?" He pulled out a bottle of painkillers that they'd taken from the drugstore and offered her what he guessed might be the largest safe dose for her. The girl's face softened just a touch, though whether it was at the name or at being handed some pills for the pain, Gabriel couldn't tell.

"Okay, we'll call you Ripley for now, until you tell us your name," he said. "I'll get you some water and whatever food we have left, then you should get some sleep. We will take you wherever you want to go in the morning."

By the time he returned with the water and a heel of bread, the girl was already asleep in the chair. She didn't wake even when he picked her up and set her down on the couch so she would be more comfortable. Tam went to his bedroom with a yawn and a wave. Gabriel got out his sleeping bag and laid it on the floor, taking one of the couch cushions to use as a pillow. Despite his reservations about how quickly he would manage to fall asleep on the floor, he was out for the count less than two minutes later.

NINETEEN

L ate in the morning, the girl suddenly gasped, waking Gabriel instantly. She looked around from the couch, her eyes blinking and confused, but not as glassy as the night before. Gabriel stretched mightily on the floor and said, "Good morning."

The girl got up from the couch, once again holding his knife. She looked at him blankly, saying nothing, and walked quietly to the bathroom. He could hear her running and splashing the water liberally. It occurred to him that the water would be very cold, and probably wouldn't last much longer, now that the town's power was out.

Gabriel picked himself up off the floor and stumbled into the kitchen to gather whatever edible substances he could find, preparing a breakfast of a large jar of olives, a package of stale crackers, a variety of condiments for dipping, and the heel of bread that Ripley hadn't eaten the night before. For drinks, he poured three tall glasses of water and a beer that had been under a package of rotten spinach in the vegetable drawer, probably intended for guests.

He poked his head into Tam's room, announced loudly that breakfast was served, and took the food into the living room, arranging it on the coffee table in front of the couch. Sitting down at one end, he put some mustard on a cracker and topped it with an olive. He popped the creation into his mouth and began to chew. It was so tart that his eyes began to water.

"That good?" Tam asked, walking toward the couch. Without waiting for an answer, he sat down and reached for a cracker and a packet of mayonnaise. "I take it um… Ripley's in the bathroom?"

Gabriel nodded and prepared another cracker, this time with a combination of mustard and mayonnaise. "She took a surprisingly long shower, considering there's no hot water." He paused to eat his cracker. "We need to decide what we're going to do with her," he continued.

"Hopefully she has some family still alive in town," Tam said.

Gabriel nodded slowly. "If not, we'll need to outfit her and either drop her off somewhere or maybe find some people who might help her. I'm not sure she'll make it on her own."

"And if there's no safe place to drop her off or people she can trust?" Tam asked.

Gabriel thought it over and shook his head. "We can't take her with us—we'll be traveling light, as fast as we can, avoiding people. She will slow us down."

Tam's face hardened into a stubborn expression. "We can't just leave her here alone unless she absolutely insists." He paused for effect. "I don't think it's safe here."

Gabriel frowned. The understatement was ridiculous, but Gabriel knew that if they tried to take along every traumatized person they encountered, they would dramatically reduce their chances of making it to a place where they could contact their superiors. They ate in silence for a while.

Gabriel had eaten all the crackers, olives, and condiments he cared to before the girl emerged from the bathroom. Her skin was pink from toweling off, and she was wrapped in three towels, leaving only her shoulders, arms, and face exposed. She carried Gabriel's knife casually in one hand at her side, the other holding the dirty, bloody clothes she had worn last night. She tossed them unceremoniously into the trash can just inside the doorway to the kitchen before walking over to the coffee table. There, she sat down gracefully in front of the food, surveying it briefly without expression before reaching for the mayonnaise and the lone piece of bread.

Gabriel couldn't help but smile. "Tam, do you have any clothes that would remotely fit Ripley?"

Tam stuffed one last cracker and olive into his mouth and said something that was probably, "I'll go look."

Ripley chewed her sandwich thoughtfully, not making eye contact with Gabriel. She picked up an olive and sighed mournfully, causing Gabriel to laugh out loud.

"It's not that terrible! Just unusual, that's all. Anyway, you should eat as much as you can—it'll make you strong." Ripley glanced at him, but remained silent. She put the olive in her mouth, chewed, and swallowed. Her face was a combination of tragedy and horror, but she picked up three more and ate them all as rapidly as she could, then took a long drink of water.

Tam came out of his room carrying an armful of clothes. "I brought several options." He held them out to Ripley. "You can try them on and keep the ones that work. We can also stop someplace later and get you something that fits better."

Ripley stood up and took the clothes. She walked back to the bathroom with them and closed the door.

Tam sat back down on the couch and picked out another olive. He was quiet for a moment, then said, "Do you think that thing last night was—somehow—one of the things that came through the anomaly in the lab? Was it like the one you saw before?"

Gabriel thought about it, although it was so much easier not to think about such things, and then nodded slowly. Things were getting worse and worse. "Yes, I do. The one I saw looked different, but yes, they were probably both from the... black ball, or dimensional rift, I guess, in the lab. Those two, and the one the police officer described. It fits our theory, anyway."

Now Tam nodded. "I wonder how many came through," he whispered.

"And where are they all?" Gabriel asked. "And what are they?" He went on, "And while we're at it, why do we sometimes glow or see in the dark or catch on fire or open locks without a key?" He cut his wonderings short before he became hysterical, and they both sat in silence for a moment before Tam ventured a response.

"Those are all very good questions," he began cautiously. "I would guess that it has something to do with the new particles that propagated. As well as some interaction with whatever environment is on the other side of that conduit, if we were right about that."

Gabriel sighed. "I think so, too, but that doesn't get us very far in terms of understanding what's going on right now."

Ripley emerged quietly from the bathroom, wearing some of Tam's old clothes in place of the towels. Her hair, now partially dry, was already lightening, and her cheeks were still pink from scrubbing. She looked much more alive and aware than she had last night. Gabriel saw that she was indeed very beautiful. She dropped the extra clothes on the floor and spoke to them for the first time.

"Thanks," she said, looking at each of them in turn. Her voice sounded rusty and hesitant.

Gabriel, his heart warmed by the improvement in her mental state, replied, "You're welcome." He thought for a moment, then continued, "Will you tell us your real name?"

She looked at him briefly, then fell back into an impassive stare. Finally, as if having considered it fully, she gave a small shake of her head.

"Fair enough," Gabriel said. "We can take you home now..." Here he trailed off, because Ripley gave a shake of her head that told Gabriel all he needed to know about the situation at home.

"In that case," he said, starting again, "we'll take you downtown to get supplies and weapons, and then you can decide where you want to go—Tam and I have to leave after that; we're headed west." He looked for understanding in Ripley's blank face. "Okay?"

Ripley nodded slowly.

"Good enough," Gabriel said. "Let's go."

After gearing back up, Gabriel and Tam grabbed their bikes, wheeling them out onto the porch, and padlocked the door behind them. Ripley carried only Gabriel's knife, while Tam carried the walking staff. Gabriel wore his axe on his belt and guided his bike with one hand while holding Tam's last juice box in the other. He took a swig and passed it to Tam, who handed it to Ripley. She took a long drink.

The morning was cooler than Gabriel had expected, and clear. There was no sign of movement, human or otherwise, as they made their way cautiously downtown. Gabriel took them to the drugstore first. He and Tam led the way in, carrying their bikes through the broken window and checking to make sure no looters, or worse, were inside. The place was deserted. Gabriel listed off things that Ripley should get—pain relievers, snacks, first aid kits, plus whatever "women's stuff" she might need. For her part, she seemed to be ignoring him and eventually he trailed off into silence. Tam handed her some plastic bags and she searched through the aisles. Gabriel and Tam removed their packs and sat on the two cash register counters at the front of the store. Tam poked idly through his register drawer, which was ajar, but someone had already taken out all the cash.

At one point, Gabriel couldn't help but notice Ripley step behind a shelf in the back of the store and start taking off her clothes. She hung her shirt and then her pants over the top of the shelf before opening a package of underwear and a bra she had grabbed. After putting these on, she put the pants and shirt back on and continued down the next aisle.

When she was finished, she came back to the front of the store with several bags full of stuff. She nodded to them and stood waiting, facing the street. Gabriel led the way out and turned his bike to the right, toward the outdoor store.

As they approached the first group of bodies, carrion birds and a wild dog scattered ahead of them. Gabriel and Tam looked at Ripley to gauge her reaction as they got closer.

"Are you from Betelgeuse, Ripley?" Tam asked. Ripley gave a tense nod, her eyes still on the bodies, which to Gabriel's eyes already looked less like people and more like piles of rotting garbage on the street. Ripley looked paler than she had earlier, her eyes tracking each form as they walked by. She made it past them, though, even if she looked queasy. At least she hadn't screamed or cried or run away. Gabriel thought the girl was probably still in shock, but as long as she kept quiet and kept up, she could process things on her own schedule.

Soon they arrived at the outdoor outfitters. The door was locked, just as they had left it. Gabriel gestured to Tam to wait a moment, then propped his bike against the wall and bent down to the lock, shielding it from Ripley. He wanted to try the opening trick without the staff. From the start, he hadn't felt that it was the staff that was doing the unlocking. He laid his hand on the lock, but nothing happened. He thought briefly, remembering the symbol that had appeared on the staff that first time. He could recall it clearly, even without looking at the staff.

As he envisioned it, tracing the lines in his mind, the lock popped open, softly and satisfyingly. He pulled open the door and bowed, welcoming Ripley and Tam with a wave of his hand. Ripley, not having seen him open the lock without a key, looked at him as if he were a bug again, not responding to his playfulness at all. Tam, however, grinned and raised an eyebrow as he wheeled his bike past Gabriel, logging the new information about not needing the staff to open the lock. Gabriel imagined they would discuss this later.

"Ripley, come with me and I'll help you pick out your gear," Gabriel said. "You want *backpacking* gear, not camping gear, mostly. It's lighter." He led her to the packs first so she'd have something to put the rest in. He didn't have to tell her not to pick the bright orange one—not that they had any inkling as to whether the creatures saw colors the same way they did.

After that, he guided her all around the store, getting her just enough equipment to be self-sufficient. Then he showed her where the hiking boots were kept and suggested that she pick out a comfortable, lightweight pair. While they were in that section, he and Tam both grabbed a couple of extra pairs of anti-odor socks made from bacteria-resistant wool. Ripley spent the next few minutes trying on boots, then picked out a pair of hiking pants and some undershirts and tops, and finally a sturdy jacket. When she came back to where Gabriel and Tam were resting on the floor, Tam indicated the counter and the side wall where the weapons were and said, "Arm yourself, but don't bother with the guns—they don't work here anymore." She nodded and turned to look over the options.

They watched as she considered each weapon in turn, searching for just the right one. Or the right ones, as she kept looking after selecting a useful belt knife, which she immediately strapped on. After a few minutes, Gabriel was sorely tempted to step in and help her choose her second weapon, or at least to tell her to hurry up, but he held back, knowing how important it was that she pick something she was comfortable with.

Ripley moved from rack to rack but didn't pick anything out. She finally drifted to the next section on the far wall, where some used sports equipment was displayed. Gabriel's puzzled gaze followed her as she rifled purposefully through the items. She pulled out, evaluated, and replaced several items before settling on a group of strap-on pads from a variety of sports, which she attached to her thighs, knees, and elbows. Then she found a set of shoulder pads and a dark blue helmet featuring what Gabriel assumed was supposed to be a bronco. Gabriel glanced at Tam, who was grinning widely at the spectacle. Finally, Ripley pulled an aluminum baseball bat from a rack and tested its weight with a few swings. Seemingly satisfied, she finally walked back over to them and held out her hand to Gabriel, proffering the knife he had loaned her.

Gabriel took it, marveling at the transformation. He would have expected her outfit to look silly, but she actually looked like a perfect road warrior, and it was all oddly practical as well.

"You look badass!" Tam exclaimed, still grinning.

Ripley gave a tight smile but didn't say anything. Gabriel and Tam got up and gathered their gear. Ripley set down her baseball bat for a moment and picked up her own backpack. Clearly surprised by the weight of it, she had to set it down and try again. This time she swung it onto her shoulders and stood up, bouncing it up and down a couple of times to position it comfortably before connecting the straps across the front.

"Ugh," she said distinctly. Gabriel tried not to stare at how the cross straps went across the top of and just below her breasts, as if deliberately accentuating them. She finished adjusting her pack, grabbed her baseball bat, and looked at them, indicating that she was ready. Her expression made her seem more mature and confident than she had before, and Gabriel revised his estimate of her age to mid-twenties.

"Ripley, as I mentioned before, Tam and I are leaving town and heading west," he said. "Do you have someplace to go in town, like your house, that you want us to check out with you? We can help make sure it's safe, or, you know, clean it out or whatever..."

She shook her head. Just once, but firmly.

"Do you want to come with us, at least until we find a safe place?" Tam asked. Gabriel had not wanted to offer that, at least not right away, but it was done now.

She thought for a moment and then nodded her head.

"Well, okay then," Gabriel said, neutrally. "Let's go to the bike store."

The only bike they could find that Ripley could imagine feeling comfortable riding with her backpack on was an utterly ridiculous pink girls' model, with a banana seat covered in alternating pink and white plastic, a glittery finish on the pink paint, colorful plastic streamers coming out of the ends of the handlebars, and a basket in front.

Tam laughed for two solid minutes when they got it off the wall and into the main aisle of the store for Ripley to examine it. He seemed to like it even more than she did. They wheeled it out into the parking lot to try it out.

She took a breath and forced the thing into motion, weaving circles around them. She rode as if she were drunk, swerving every time she pedaled. She didn't fall over, though, which was the important part, and it was certainly faster than walking, so it would do. Ripley half-smiled at the bike after she got off, maybe because it was so ridiculous, and for Gabriel, that was reason enough to take it.

Back inside, near the kids' bikes, there were some two-wheeled pull-behind trailers, the kind parents could use to pull their children along behind them. Gabriel wondered if it would be worth the hassle of taking one to put his gear in. Since he was already feeling the strain on his shoulders and back, he thought it was worth a try, so he got one down and figured out how to put it together and attach it to his back wheel. After seeing the experiment, Tam grabbed the other one and set to work.

Gabriel's had a light blue plastic canvas stretched over a lightweight black metal frame. If he pulled down the clear plastic window and connected it to the front of the frame, it would keep his gear dry inside as well. *And make it marginally less conspicuous*, he thought.

He rode out of the parking lot and turned west, leading them past the fire truck and the police station, past all the bodies, now bloated in the sun. Past the empty stores and broken windows. Away from the terrible memories of the past few days and the eerie silence of the dead town.

TWENTY

Their journey began inauspiciously, as the first leg seemed to be one hundred percent uphill. Gabriel had taken them north heading out of town and up to Route 180. The road ran along an old mountain pass, leading between two bald peaks that stood out starkly against the surreally crisp light. They would follow it for a few hours before taking 78 west toward Arizona and heading for Safford, the nearest town in that direction, though it wasn't all that much bigger than Betelgeuse.

At their current pace, he estimated it would take them three to five days to get there, if not more. It wasn't a steep gradient, but it was constant, and Gabriel thought he remembered it staying that way until the turnoff to 78. If that was so, it would take them all afternoon to reach the turn.

If things in Safford were anything like they were in Betelgeuse, they wouldn't hang around, and Phoenix was about two or three times farther away again. The final stop on his tentative route was Los Angeles. When they had discussed the plan as they pedaled away from the town, Tam had talked at some length about what would happen to a major city without power. Water and food shortages would lead to looting and violence, not to mention the possibility of finding more of those creatures. "Big cities are perhaps *primarily* giant engines that bring in food and water from the surrounding regions," Tam had said, as if delivering the "exciting" intro to a dry anthropology lecture. Without power, people would have to scatter to survive, and that was before even considering all the violence likely to occur in a desperate, starving population.

Although they had to stop and rest several times, they made it to 78 in just under four hours. Toward the end, the road got so steep that they had to walk beside their bikes, sweating in the sun despite the unseasonably cool air. They had all shed their jackets, and Gabriel rolled up his sleeves. His skin was already on the darker side from his camping trips, so he didn't bother with sunscreen. He got pretty pasty in the winter, at least relatively speaking, but as soon as he spent any time in the sun, his skin tanned quickly, probably thanks to his father, who was as dark—and short—as one of their full-blooded Nahua ancestors.

As they approached the turnoff to 78, they saw a couple of apparently abandoned vehicles at the intersection looking as if they were waiting to turn. The one coming from 78 was a Ford Taurus, its white paint gleaming so brightly in the sun that it almost obscured how filthy it was. The other was an old, beat-up pickup that looked like it was from the seventies. Both appeared empty from a distance.

He and Tam approached the vehicles cautiously, Gabriel holding his axe in both hands and Tam with his machete at the ready. Gabriel walked to the driver side door of the old pickup and looked inside, then glanced back at Tam and shrugged. It was empty.

Then he started toward the Taurus. As he got closer, he could see the driver, an old man, slumped over in his seat, his body sprawled across the center console and into the passenger seat. His combed-over hair hung straight down from the side of his head like limp string, grazing the fabric of the seat. Given the man's near-baldness, the comb-over was impressively long and thick.

Gabriel tapped on the window of the car with the side of his axe. The man didn't stir. "Look at his pants," Tam said. Gabriel glanced back at the man's lap and noticed that it was stained with dried vomit. "Could be a failed pacemaker or a stroke or something, or maybe an illness similar to what the woman at the police station suffered from," Tam continued.

Gabriel turned back to the truck. "And whoever was in the truck probably took off on foot," he said. "Which means that the truck died, even though it looks like it was made before electronic parts became common in engines."

Tam shrugged uncomfortably. "I agree, but the engine could have been replaced since then." He walked over to the truck. "I'll give it a try just to be sure," he said. "You try the Ford—at least we know the keys are in that one."

Gabriel went about gently pulling the dead man, stiff and cold, out of the pungently disgusting car and laying him on the grass at the side of the road. He tried the key—a failure. Tam had searched unsuccessfully for the keys to the truck for a few minutes, and then tried the point of his knife on the ignition, but to no avail. Ripley tried to arrange the old man's hands together across his chest, but his arms were too stiff. She ended up gathering a few wildflowers and just putting the stems in his hand. She also fixed his comb-over. Gabriel got out some hand sanitizer from his pack for both of them.

Tam sighed from the driver's seat of the truck. "Shame they didn't leave their keys," he said. Gabriel laughed out loud. Tam looked at him, then continued, "This truck is the best chance we've had so far of getting a vehicle operational. Even if the ignition doesn't work, it wouldn't take much to turn it around and freewheel it down that hill. Then we could try to jump start it." Ripley looked puzzled but didn't say anything.

Tam noticed her expression and explained, "Back in the old days, if your battery was flat, you could roll down a hill with the ignition and the clutch in, and then quickly release the clutch to start the car." He pumped the clutch pedal down and then let it pop up to demonstrate. Ripley smiled like he was being funny. He frowned at her absently, which seemed to amuse her even more. The whole thing entertained Gabriel as well; it made Tam seem so much older than he was.

"Anyway," Tam continued, "I can't unlock the steering wheel without the key, and I don't really know enough about old cars to figure out how to bypass the mechanism manually."

"So... bikes?" Gabriel asked.

"Bikes," Tam agreed.

"Bikes," Ripley murmured, unusually chatty.

They made much better time over the next two hours. The road led downhill at first, then flattened out. It curved after half a mile, then seemed to run straight as an arrow west for as far as they could see. The road was a simple two-laner, its surface worn and pitted in places. It ran through a grassy plain, broken by the occasional tree or dry creek bed. They saw fences, but no livestock. Gabriel wondered if animals had been affected the same way as humans had.

They passed a few more cars, mostly abandoned, but a couple containing other bodies. They didn't see any vehicles as old as the truck from earlier, much less one that had conveniently been abandoned with its keys in it and parked near the top of a hill, so they didn't get to try the jump-start idea.

The third vehicle they came across that had a body was a maroon Nissan SUV. The man inside it had rolled down the windows and moved his seat way back. Perhaps he had lain down when he'd started feeling ill, waiting in vain for his cell phone to start working again so he could call 911 or AAA. Then he had drifted off to sleep, never to wake again.

"Cars are like fancy coffins now," Ripley said. Gabriel was so surprised to hear her utter an actual sentence that he couldn't think of anything to say in response. He just felt a pang of sadness that this was how she was beginning to reengage with the world.

Tam nodded, impressed with Ripley's observation. He said, "Automotive mausoleums, protected from scavengers." After a pause, he continued, "The only thing missing are the curtains—the bodies are already starting to decompose, and all these sarcophagi have windows so everyone can see the grossness up close."

Ripley fixed him with an irritated look and began pedaling again, riding away from Tam and the car. Tam shrugged at Gabriel and remounted his own bike.

By early evening, the companions felt they had covered a lot of ground, though they probably could have driven the same distance in an hour or two. Gabriel began to think about finding a spot out of view from the road to set up camp.

He coasted up a small hill and saw a tractor trailer in the distance ahead of them, half on and half off the road. All of the tires on the right side were in the dirt, but the thing was still taking up most of the lane. As he pedaled closer, he saw that the driver's door was ajar and that a man was lying on the ground in front of the truck, his hand raised slightly toward them, as if trying to wave.

Gabriel slowed down and looked around to check if there were any other people around, but saw none. He rode past the trailer to scout a little farther ahead, then turned around, changing gears and pedaling slightly uphill back toward the front of the truck. By the time he got there, Ripley and Tam had stopped beside the man, and Ripley was already off her bike.

The man was alive and conscious, though barely. His skin was deathly pale and covered with an even sheen of sweat. Blood seeped from a few scabby blisters on his cheek and lips. He was badly sunburned, but Gabriel thought it possible—likely, even—that he was suffering from the same sickness that had killed the police officer at the station.

"Ripley, this man is sick and it could be catching," Gabriel said gently. "We should stay away from him."

The man's head jerked slightly toward Gabriel as he spoke, and he croaked out one pitiful word, "Water."

Ripley immediately turned back to her bike, but Tam handed her a bottle of water before she reached it. She nodded and gave him a small smile, which he returned.

Gabriel, alarmed, said, "Guys, not only might YOU need all of your water to survive, but there's also a chance he could infect you." He tried to sound reasonable and convincing, but it was as if Ripley had gone deaf, while Tam just stared back at Gabriel, nonplussed.

Ripley knelt beside the man and slipped her hand behind his sweaty head to raise it up a little. When she had done so, she poured some of her water into his mouth in a tiny stream. The man's tongue and lips worked as he swallowed once, then again. After a third swallow, he coughed weakly and Ripley stopped pouring.

"Call… ambulance…" the man wheezed weakly.

Ripley shook her head sadly. She didn't answer aloud, though; the man's eyes were now closed.

Tam spoke up, saying, "Phones and cars aren't working anywhere around here, as far as we can tell." The man didn't respond, and Tam continued. "The nearest town is Betelgeuse, and if there are twenty people alive there, that's the height of it."

Gabriel glanced at Ripley and was startled to see that the man's hand had found hers, or vice versa, and she was holding it gently.

"So's not just me, then," the man muttered. His beer belly

peeked out from the bottom of his shirt, rising and falling shallowly. Yellowish sweat and streaks of blood soaked through every inch of his shirt.

"No, it's everything, at least around here," Tam said quietly. The man may have nodded, though it was hard to tell. Ripley sat there, eyes wide, holding his hand, and he seemed at peace. Gabriel felt dreadful, whether over his inability to help the man or Ripley's willingness to expose herself to whatever illness the man was suffering from. He didn't like feeling like this, but it was hard to blame Ripley for comforting the helpless, hopeless man.

Tam sat down on the pavement while Gabriel remained standing. They all stayed that way for another fifteen minutes—all the time it took for the man to pass away, still holding Ripley's hand. When it was over, Ripley rose unsteadily to her feet, walked a few feet away, and vomited into the brown grass.

She stood there for a moment, bent over with her hands on her knees, then spoke in a barely audible croak.

"Why is this happening?"

"We're not sure, exactly," Gabriel said. "People are getting sick and—"

"Why?" Ripley's voice rang with anguish.

Gabriel looked at Tam, who frowned as if in pain, shaking his head sadly. A large part of Gabriel wanted to tell Ripley what they knew, but mostly out of habit he stuck to what he thought his job required him to say.

"We don't know for sure," he managed. "It seems to be related to the failure of electricity and combustion—things don't work, or, at least, they don't work the same. Even people's bodies."

Ripley shook her head wordlessly, as if to indicate how pathetically inadequate she found Gabriel's explanation. *That's how it felt to say it, anyway,* he thought. She straightened up and, still avoiding his eyes, walked woodenly back to her bicycle.

Gabriel sighed. Unless he was going to tell her everything, there wasn't much more to say.

"Let's roll out then," he said. "We'll ride for about thirty minutes and then try to find a good place to get off the road and set up camp."

Soon the road bisected a dry creek bed lined sporadically with trees, and Gabriel stopped his bike there, waiting for the others to catch up. When they pulled up beside him, he said, "Let's walk our bikes up this way for a while until we find a good place to camp. I want to be far enough off the road to be out of sight and earshot."

He led them along the creek bed—upstream, he thought—until it was nearly dark. Once he estimated that they were at least half a mile off the road, he looked for a good spot to stop for the night. They soon found the perfect place—one where the creek bed had cut through a soft hill creating a miniature ravine, where the bed was ten feet below the level of the surrounding land. The ground itself was soft with dried silt, and trees sheltered the location from the surrounding countryside. If there had been a source of water nearby it would have been truly perfect, but even without that, it was exactly what they were looking for.

He parked his bike and trailer against the cleft of the hill and said, "This is good—let's camp here."

As he began to relax, his sweaty back immediately began to cool in the evening air. "Ripley, can you gather wood and kindling for a fire?"

She nodded blankly and moved off, ditching her own bike and then walking back down the creek bed about twenty yards or so until she found an easy path out of the ravine. "Watch out for snakes," Gabriel called to her as she clambered up the bank. Then he turned to Tam. "Time to teach you how to set up a tent?"

Tam grinned and said, "Sure, although I think I did it once

or twice when I was a kid." Gabriel pulled his tent out and had almost finished putting it up by the time Tam had located and produced his own from his bag.

When Ripley returned with a huge armload of branches and sticks, Gabriel was showing Tam how to secure his tent to the ground with the pegs. They all pitched in to help arrange the wood and kindling, then took turns using Tam's Swedish steel fire starter to try and kindle a fire. Gabriel offered a few pointers, culminating in the final words of wisdom, "You have to concentrate—and blow on it." At this point, Ripley looked at him quizzically and Tam laughed out loud, but the fire finally caught. It felt very good to Gabriel to hear Tam's laughter, but the feeling dried up when he saw that the flame was the wrong color again, the long blue tongues dancing too slowly for a normal fire.

Tam went to find some larger logs, and Gabriel showed Ripley how to pitch her tent. Soon they were all sprawled out on the ground around the fire, passing around bags and cans of their trail food. They had only eaten snacks during the day, so they set about their dinner with a quiet but ruthless enthusiasm.

As they slowly finished their meal, they sat in what seemed to Gabriel a companionable silence. He felt strangely removed from the horrors of the past two days. Just traveling and being on a mission to do *something* about all this was really helping to ease his worries. He was doing what he could. He glanced at Ripley's face—and its still-shell-shocked expression—and decided that not all of them were feeling as okay as he was.

"We should get some sleep. We've got another long day of pedaling tomorrow," he said. Ripley stood up and walked down the path, presumably to relieve herself.

Tam murmured, "Me too," and got up, moving off in the opposite direction. Gabriel dug around in his backpack for his toothbrush and toothpaste. He was just finishing up when Tam and then Ripley returned. He walked a few steps away from the camp to spit and then continued into the darkness to do his own business. Away from the fire, the night was cool and the insects seemed louder. At least they hadn't all died out. He gazed up at the stars, millions of hard points of light, almost painfully bright. There were so many more stars than you could normally see. *It is so peaceful out here*, he marveled.

Gabriel thought about what would happen if their mission failed—if the whole country was like this. If his family was beyond saving. What would they do then? Make a new life, camping out in the woods? Find a cabin somewhere and some land to farm? There were worse things, sure, but he was already feeling the painful loss of a thousand years of technological progress. Television, modern medicine, cell phones. He shook his head. Hopefully, if they went far enough, they could leave this field of the dead behind. He sighed and turned back to the campfire.

Ripley was scrubbing her face with a damp cloth when he got back. Tam was halfway inside his tent, arranging his sleeping bag, pack, and weapons to his satisfaction. When he was done, he backed stiffly out of the tent and stood, his hand moving absently to his lower back. "I'm going to be sore tomorrow," he remarked.

"Yeah, I think we all will," Gabriel replied, nodding slowly. After a moment he continued, "I suggest you keep your boots inside your tents and close the tent flap fully, otherwise you might find snakes and scorpions and whatnot in them," he said, suppressing a grin at the falling faces of his two travel companions. He turned to look at his tent—he had already put his gear inside except for his axe and the clothes he was wearing. He reached in and pulled out his jacket, hanging it over the front. "I'm going to stay up for a while and keep watch," he said.

Tam's and Ripley's expressions turned serious. Tam nodded slowly, then said, "Wake me when it's my turn."

Gabriel nodded. "Goodnight, guys."

"Goodnight, John-Boy!" Tam replied.

It sounded familiar, but he couldn't place it. "What's that even from?" he asked.

Tam was already zipping his tent closed behind him. "Now you're the uncultured one," Tam clucked. "*The Waltons!*" Gabriel shook his head, a bemused smile on his face.

"Goodnight," Ripley said quietly, then zipped up her own tent.

Gabriel stared at the fire. *Not a very good idea for a sentry, since it ruins your night vision*, he thought, but something about fire mesmerized him, now more than ever. The base of the blue flames sometimes shone a dull red. They still flickered and danced, but the beat was slower, the movements more sensual. He closed his eyes and listened instead. The fire dominated there too, with its crackling and snapping, but behind it he could hear crickets and other insects in the night, the slight breeze blowing through the trees and across the grass, and even the slowing breathing of Tam and Ripley. In less than twenty minutes, they both seemed to be sound asleep. Gabriel relished having this time to himself to think about everything that had happened— to the world and to him. He wanted to tell himself that none of it made sense, that it was all some kind of horrible dream, but the trouble was that it did make some kind of sense.

The experiment he had been brought here to keep in stasis at all costs had been even more dangerous than anyone had feared, even Tam. It had released a novel particle into this world that had caused some strange and terrible effects, including an EMP-like impact on electronics and changing the way fire burned. It had also killed or sickened thousands of people. Or more.

The creatures, however, were a different story. That was *definitely* not something they had foreseen as a possible result of their experiment. He had been puzzling over this question since before they had even seen their first... demon or alien or whatever. Even the wildest theory he could come up with that might explain the facts as he knew them—that the experiment had created a wormhole-like rift connecting this universe to a different one—fell short. How could living beings of that size pop through that hole and emerge here intact? He didn't have any clue about dimensional theory, especially now that it could be tested by observation, but he had to imagine that his universe was most likely completely inhospitable to these outsiders. And yet, murderous though they were, they seemed to feel quite at home.

And then there were the changes in himself and Tam. Also a function of the particles? Perhaps they had received a high dose, but there was no way to know how the new particle proliferated. Its effect on electronics was fast but not instantaneous, judging by the printouts they had seen back at the lab. The brief moments of data recorded after the stasis field had failed seemed to indicate that the particle was propagating at a tremendous speed and volume. It could be everywhere by now. Gabriel guessed it could have been worse—an Earth-sized hydrogen bomb, for instance. Or a new, universe-wide Big Bang.

The snap of a branch jarred him out of his reverie. He turned to where he thought the sound had come from and quietly put a hand on the handle of his axe. For a long moment, he didn't see or hear anything else, and he was almost ready to relax again when he heard a low noise, almost like a groan, along with another branch snapping. The sounds were coming from about forty yards away, uphill from their camp and through some trees—whatever was there could almost definitely see their campfire. Gabriel felt his heart thumping in his chest. He strained his eyes toward the source of the sounds and thought he could make out some movement in the dark—at least a couple of large shapes. He stood up and took a single step toward the intruders. Were they demons? Should he wake the others? He was still frozen, trying to figure out the best thing to do, when he saw a pair of reflective eyes in the dark—brown and large, blinking lazily. He heard the low moan again, but this time it was clearer.

Mooo.

Gabriel grinned broadly, relief flooding his limbs. He walked toward the cows, still carrying his axe.

Even though he was backlit by the fire, the cows sensed his approach and had turned and trundled thirty yards farther away by the time he crested the edge of the depression. He peered through the starlit night and saw the backs of four or five cows trotting off into the dark. They were surprisingly quiet for such large animals, though he heard another branch snap as they shambled off, clinging to the limited tree cover as they went. Gabriel stood in the dark looking after the departing animals with a smile on his face. He was glad that at least some cows had survived. He thought about what the world was going to be like with over ninety percent of its people missing. The fences were still up, but he imagined that cows might become a wild species nonetheless, filling the niche once occupied by the American bison. Deer, now—*they* would surely proliferate. Not enough hunters or traffic to thin them out. Feral dogs would probably hunt them. Maybe other predators as well. Wolves and mountain lions. Then he sobered, thinking that maybe the demons would take over as apex predators if there were enough of them. He hoped not, but it seemed possible, or even likely, given the ones he'd seen so far. His stomach knotted with the fear that his family back east might be in danger—might be prey. *Please let this whole thing be limited to this area*, he thought, but that felt like willful optimism. He wished there were something he could do about it right now—*tonight*.

Instead, he sat down with his back against a tree, zipped his jacket the rest of the way up and set out not to fall asleep. The night was quiet after that, and he nodded off a few times, scolding himself harshly each time. But at least he remained upright. After the last such lapse, he checked his watch in the starlight and decided that it was probably Tam's turn to replace him. He stood, joints creaking and muscles sore, and walked back to camp. He stopped at Tam's tent and slapped it with the flat of his hand near where he thought Tam's head might be. "Tam," he whispered hoarsely.

There was no response at first, but after he repeated his slap and whisper, Tam's voice floated out of the tent, "What?"

"It's your turn to keep watch," Gabriel said.

"Oh," Tam replied, sounding sad. "Okay, I'm up."

Gabriel turned and found his own tent, crawling inside and zipping up the flap behind himself. He took off his boots, climbed into his sleeping bag fully dressed, and was already more than half asleep by the time he heard Tam climb out into the night.

TWENTY—ONE

HAKK'RIX

Hakk'rix stepped cautiously out from between two tall trees and turned some of its eyes to scan the structures below. It didn't sense any rivals nearby, but it could make out several prey animals scurrying about in the area.

The structures ahead were similar to the hundreds or thousands Hakk'rix had already seen on this side of the rift. They were *constructed dwellings* for these strange, foolhardy prey. Out in the open! Most of them offered very little protection from anything other than this world's surprisingly pleasant version of emberfall. Rather, it was as if this whole world were a domesticated prey pen claimed by a most powerful Apex—a preserve where the prey fed only one rival and had lost the need or ability to hide. But no such Apex had yet claimed any territory here. Hakk'rix had sensed several on this side, including an immense and powerful airborne one that had swooped down on a formidable rival right in front of Hakk'rix shortly after they had all passed through. The rivals had scattered far and wide immediately after emerging from the strange metal burrow in the ground, fleeing from each other as much as feasting on the plentiful prey.

In reality, the terrain on this side of the hole resembled the southern lowlands back home in only one respect: it was dry and dusty. Everything else was new and incomprehensibly different. Even the rivals themselves were different—it was harder to think or change here, and many of them had become little more than hungry animals. There was not much need for logic in a place such as this.

Hakk'rix, however, had gradually gotten used to being in this place and had begun to reason more clearly again. Its frequent feeding had caused it to molt twice already, keeping the same shape but growing larger and more powerful. It was as if it had settled on its final form and was becoming an Apex, though Hakk'rix wasn't nearly large enough to make the leap yet. It also had none of the radiance aura or powers of control that had characterized all the Apex it had ever sensed. Hakk'rix rocked back and forth for a moment to clear its unruly mind. Its intelligence had reached the point where it was sometimes a distraction. It tested the air again for any sign of rivals. Finding none, it stepped down toward the most isolated of the inhabited dwellings, crossing a tiny, cultivated patch of organic life whose soulspark was almost too faint to sense even from this close, though there were animals in this world that consumed the stuff.

It crept silently toward the dwelling, questing out with its senses to find the best way to access the prey inside. It sensed at least two creatures inside, shuffling fitfully around, neither sleeping nor socializing. The easiest path was through one of the clear viewports—Hakk'rix could simply walk through those—but it had learned how noisy that was, alerting the prey within and in all the other dwellings nearby. It was better to go through the entrances the animals used, which depended entirely on a tiny piece of metal to bar access. It was easy enough to punch through the material and disable the latch, but that was also loud. Hakk'rix had come upon a solution to this particular problem early on, however. Its power could be concentrated against the material surrounding the metal latch, rotting it until it crumbled into dust. While a particularly observant nearby rival might sense the use of its power, these prey animals apparently couldn't.

Hakk'rix found the entrance on the closest side of the dwelling and then inspiration struck. Hakk'rix vibrated softly with excitement. Instead of charging in immediately, it raised a limb gently to the metal of the security latch and released its power in a tightly controlled burst to fuse the metal together. Then it quickly circled the building to find the entrance on the other side.

This time it broke in physically, not bothering to use its power. The sounds of the door slamming open and Hakk'rix squeezing forcefully inside alerted the prey, sending them scrambling to the first entrance, screaming and trying in vain to open it and escape. Hakk'rix met them there and subdued the three of them with a wide pulse of extreme disorientation. Two of them fell over immediately, as bipeds everywhere were wont to do, and Hakk'rix pounced on the biggest one, which resisted to some degree. The creature was terrified and... *angry*. That was probably why it hadn't fallen over like the others, and it delighted Hakk'rix immensely.

Hakk'rix lowered itself onto the irate animal, which was snarling and yelling ineffectually, and settled its maw onto one of the beast's shoulders. The small connecting bones snapped like twigs as it took its first bite, releasing overwhelming flavors, fear, and pain. The creature screamed loudly, and Hakk'rix bit down harder until it opened the creature's chest cavity and robbed it of its ability to make noise.

Hakk'rix fed until the organism died, then stepped over to

the smallest one and brought it to fuller, if temporary, consciousness by thrusting a sharpened appendage through its midsection. The animal screamed, but weakly, bereft and frightened—so different from the larger one. Hakk'rix took only small bites from this one, savoring its fear and confusion for as long as its life force endured.

Though it was already well sated, Hakk'rix moved on to the third, reviving it with an invigorating shock. As soon as it came to, the animal threw itself onto the remains of the smallest one. It didn't even scream as Hakk'rix began to eat from it. The emotional bouquet of this creature was intense—abject, feverish loss and then surrender. Its surprising lack of fear made the sensation different and vaguely unsettling for some reason.

Hakk'rix finished it off quickly and wondered if this experience was common for rivals that ate cultivated animals. Perhaps prey were too different here. Or maybe the problem was that Hakk'rix was changing—coming to understand the prey too well. Hakk'rix hoped this wasn't the start of a metamorphosis into a form or mentality more akin to these prey animals. Major form changes sometimes began this way, and it wasn't uncommon for rivals to start exhibiting similarities to the prey species they consumed frequently. It didn't mind the extra intelligence, but if it lost limbs, eyes, or its chitinous shell, that would be a distinct disadvantage when it came up against other rivals.

Hakk'rix squeezed through the short passage into another room of the dwelling and settled onto the floor to rest. Its last thought as it succumbed to torpor was that if it grew much more during its next molt, it would no longer be able to fit through the passages inside these narrow dwellings.

TWENTY—TWO

GABRIEL

The next morning, Gabriel awoke thinking he smelled bacon, and his mouth immediately began to water. He slowly climbed out into the morning light, dew thickly coating the outside of the tent. He slipped his feet back into his boots and walked over to the campfire that had either been kept alive through the night or rekindled this morning. Ripley was cooking over it. Not actual slabs of bacon, unfortunately, but apparently there were bits of pork in the cans of beans she was warming, hobo style, in the fire. The depths of Gabriel's disappointment at the lack of real bacon shocked him. *Would he ever have bacon again?*

The morning sun was peeking over the horizon, and the light streamed through their little canyon like a visual trumpet blast, making the dew sparkle brilliantly on their bikes and the tents, and causing Ripley's hair to shine as if on fire.

"Good morning, Ripley," Gabriel said, smiling at her.

"Good morning," she responded, her voice a quiet songbird compared to his frog croak. She smiled back at him—truly a staggering weapon—and then turned her attention back to her beans, stirring them gently.

Gabriel stood still for a moment, then shook his head briefly to clear his senses of the effects of Ripley's beauty and turned to walk up the hill into the trees to relieve himself. He wondered if her attractiveness was going to be a problem. Gabriel remembered that demons weren't the only monsters they might encounter.

He broke away from these dark thoughts and returned to camp. As he passed Tam's tent, he called the man's name loudly enough to wake him, which seemed to work, judging by Tam's bleary-eyed emergence shortly thereafter. Apparently he'd gone to bed as soon as Ripley had woken up, but if they were going to make any sort of decent time, they needed to take advantage of all the daylight available.

"Let's get a good meal into us—protein and carbs—we've a long ride ahead, though I believe it's mostly flat or downhill today," Gabriel said.

"Yes, it should be flat all the way to Mesa, which I hear is located on a large, flat-topped hill," Tam confirmed. Ripley wrinkled her nose at what passed for Tam's sense of humor and took her beans off the fire, stirring them vigorously.

Tam and Gabriel each dug through their own stores of food and the three of them shared their meals companionably around the fire. When they were done, Tam gathered up their trash—a couple of cans and a plastic bag—stuffing the bag into the smaller can and then the smaller can into the larger one, and put it in his pack. Gabriel shared a quizzical look with Ripley, which Tam noticed.

He responded somewhat defensively, "We can find a better place to dump this than here."

Gabriel nodded his head. "Certainly, eco-warrior Tam, friend of Gaia."

Tam turned to his tent, mumbling something about "doing our part" and began getting ready for the road. Within ten minutes, all three were taking down their tents, Tam whistling as he worked.

The next two days passed similarly, the party losing itself in the rhythms of travel. They spoke infrequently throughout the day—mostly during breaks. They passed more "carsoleums," as they had come to call them, dead bodies decomposing slowly even in the dry, desert-like air. They also saw a few more abandoned cars, the occupants apparently having fled on foot. None of the vehicles were old enough to have avoided the EMP effect, or to be suitable for attempting a rolling start. Nevertheless, they all hoped to find a candidate as soon as possible. Driving already seemed like a distant extravagance, and Gabriel hungered for it, spending long stretches of his day thinking about how great it would be to throw their bikes in the back of a pickup truck and cruise the rest of the way to their destination in comfort.

Tam, on the other hand, seemed oddly content with the current situation. He clearly liked traveling by bicycle, didn't mind not being connected to the outside world, and didn't seem troubled by the fact that humanity, as far as they knew, might no longer be mass producing food and goods.

During their only extended conversation in two days of traveling, as they sat in some brown grass beside the road, relaxing over a late afternoon lunch, Gabriel remarked on Tam's ready acceptance of the new way of things, to which Tam responded with a shrug, saying, "I don't know. The mass deaths and monsters are terrible, of course, but I don't think technology and interconnectivity are the things that make life worthwhile or interesting for humankind. It would be a harder life, and probably a shorter one, too, if it's like this everywhere, but no less important or even less fun."

"I didn't realize you were such a hippie!" exclaimed Gabriel, but Tam shook his head gravely.

"The hippie movement was a reactionary rejection of the buttoned-up, forcibly homogenized fifties and an open embracing of what its members thought of as the real human experiences of love, sex, civil rights, and individuality. I'm just saying that life and its achievements—and the enjoyment of them—are just as important, if not more so, now that we have lost access to all our previous technological advances and long life spans.

"Uh, longer lives would necessarily mean more life to enjoy," said Gabriel, "but in any case, if you had the power to wave your hand and make everything go back to the way it was, wouldn't you?"

Tam didn't answer right away. After some thought, he said, "To stop people from getting sick, maybe. To get the lights back on and the cars running, probably not. I don't know. It would depend on other factors."

"Such as?"

"Such as what else I could do with that magic power, or what it cost me or the world at large to use it in that way. How much I was disadvantaging people or animals who had already adapted to the new way of things."

Gabriel shook his head. There was no arguing with him when it came to his moral compass. He was a strange bird.

"Here's an example," Tam continued, seemingly oblivious to Gabriel's waning interest in the topic. "Back when I was a kid, I used to read comic books and think about superpowers and stuff like that, and I would try to decide what power I would most like to have—flying, telekinesis, teleportation, lasers, or whatever." Gabriel nodded—his favorite had been teleportation, which just seemed incredibly practical in so many circumstances.

"Then one day I saw a commercial trying to raise money to help feed starving children in Africa; I wondered if I should feel guilty for not even thinking about using my imaginary power to help fix real problems like hunger." He shook his head, half-amused. "But then I thought, if I picked some kind of power that allowed me to generate an infinite amount of food, the end result would be enormous population growth until some other limited resource was exhausted and even *more* people suffered and died. Is our goal to have as many people on the planet as possible? Is that what our morality would have us do? Choke this planet with so many people that the sole purpose of Earth is to birth humans? I don't think so. Life is precious—or interesting, at least—to those living it, but it's not inherently and objectively valuable—it doesn't justify anything that's otherwise immoral or reckless, and the purpose of the universe is not to make more people at the expense of other forms of life. That's just what we want to do as competitive animals. That's a base urge—hardly remarkable—and not a moral cause. People dying of starvation is the ugly face of natural population pressure, not a call to dedicate all our resources to solving world hunger. Or our make-believe superpowers."

Gabriel thought about that for a moment. The implications of Tam's argument were so typical of him—rejecting a common aspect of the human experience because it went against his logic and his own moral compass. But Gabriel knew him well enough to see that Tam was being genuine—he really didn't think of a starving child as a wrong to be righted. Faced with such a situation in real life, he would probably sacrifice his own food to give to the child, but only because he was capriciously generous, not because he saw a starving child as a *wrong* per se. Sometimes Tam seemed to be something other than human in the way he thought about humanity—apart from it somehow.

"I don't think we have any higher moral calling than to protect the weak and help those who can't help themselves," Ripley said, out of the blue. Gabriel couldn't have been any more stunned if she had sprouted wings. She had been sitting next to them, clearly following the conversation, but had never contributed anything other than a nod or shrugs to their talks before. This was the longest sentence she had ever uttered to either of them.

Tam bowed his head but was otherwise silent. Gabriel grinned at Ripley, wanting to encourage her, and he also liked that her statement seemed to point out a flaw in Tam's argument in a very earnest and simple way. He turned back to Tam, grinning.

"Yeah, Tam," he said. "Isn't that the case? Shouldn't we protect the weak and suffering when it is in our power to do so?"

Tam's brow furrowed further, and he glanced back and forth between them defensively, somehow managing to look even more stubborn than before. "As normal, individual members of society, yes, I'd agree that should be part of moral behavior, but as superpowered beings capable of shifting the natural balance of things, we would have additional responsibilities that might conflict with our urges on a small scale. Helping to ensure one child doesn't suffer is right, but helping a hundred children who couldn't survive on their own—who will go on to consume resources that would otherwise go to better adapted creatures—might be wrong. Maximizing the number of humans on this planet simply *can't* be the highest moral calling."

Gabriel didn't know what to say to that, but now Ripley's face was the one that looked stubborn. "Having a superpower doesn't change your moral responsibilities," she exclaimed. "You're not a god just because you can fly or generate infinite food or whatever." She looked from Tam to Gabriel and back, her eyes wide with indignation. "You're still part of society, still responsible for helping those who need it to the extent that you can."

"What about my responsibility to the Earth? To the rabbits and deer that would be just fine-or better off-without extra hamburgers or cell towers or Tupperware?" Tam asked. "What if I make it possible for a billion more people to live, and they go on to kill ten billion deer and rabbits a year until *they* go extinct? And then the two billion children of those humans all start to suffer and die of starvation?" They were both really into this argument, which was beginning to strike Gabriel as a ridiculously silly hypothetical debate, but Tam plowed on. "Have I served any moral purpose then, or have I just shifted resources around and increased the absolute amount of suffering in the world?"

Ripley was taken aback momentarily by his screed. After a second, she opened her mouth to respond, but Tam interrupted. "Just because I'm human doesn't mean that humans deserve to live more than rabbits and deer. We have no greater right to life than they do, or even than the bacteria that would feast on our corpses."

Gabriel expected her to fold in the face of Tam's bizarre polemic, or to ignore it, or maybe even to curse at him. God knew Gabriel had felt that way many times. But she didn't do any of those things.

"Even if we agree that your hierarchy of good is valid, which I don't *at all*," she said, "your argument suffers from the same fundamental flaw as all utilitarian beliefs, which is that you don't know the full consequences of your actions ahead of time. By choosing to let a child starve, you are already in the wrong, and you may end up creating more suffering anyway."

Gabriel, a broad grin of enjoyment lighting up his face, turned to Tam expectantly. The man was silent for a moment, then lowered his eyes. "I'll have to think about that," he said with more grace than Gabriel could usually muster when being schooled unexpectedly.

Gabriel looked back at Ripley, who, after a moment more of staring Tam down, smiled and gave Gabriel a sly wink. "I was in the middle of an online philosophy class," she admitted.

It was a terrific moment, and the best Gabriel had felt since this whole thing had started, but they had to get back on the road, so he sighed and stood up. The others joined him and they all picked up their packs and hauled them back to the two pull-behind carts.

The road was still brutally hot, even though it was late in the day. They had only been pedaling for about twenty minutes when they saw movement near some cars up ahead.

A pale, dark-haired woman in her thirties or forties was trying desperately to flag them down, waving her arms above her head, calling out for them to stop.

TWENTY—THREE

RIPLEY

As Ripley and the others came to a stop in front of the woman, she began murmuring "Oh, thank God" over and over, but her eyes darted back and forth almost frantically between Gabriel and Tam's weapons and Ripley. Finally seeming to come to a decision after examining Ripley's face, the woman collected herself and addressed them.

"Thank you. Thank you for stopping," she said, her words tumbling out on top of each other, as if she'd practiced them so many times that they'd lost their individual meanings. "My husband and I are stranded, and he's sick. We're out of water. We have children."

Tam responded, "Well, we'll try to help however we can, but I'm the wrong kind of doctor for medical work."

No one laughed. *For someone so smart, Tam sure is clueless sometimes,* Ripley thought. She swung her leg off the bike and laid it down, then faced the woman.

"What's your name?" she asked. Her voice wasn't used to talking anymore, but this was the first woman she had seen alive since her mom had died in the living room the night of the storm.

The woman looked back at Ripley and her shoulder pads, then seemed to make an effort to calm herself. "Marcia," she said. "I'm Marcia Feldman."

The men looked at Ripley, surprised that she had spoken, but apparently hoping that she would continue.

Before she could, Marcia blurted out, "Do you know what's going on? Why have all the cars and cell phones stopped working?"

Ripley turned to Gabriel, wordlessly nominating him to explain recent events. The woman's eyes followed hers. Gabriel took a moment to gather his thoughts. Then he said, "Um."

Very eloquent, that one, Ripley thought.

After a second, he started again. "Well, we've been traveling for a couple of days, and none of the electronic equipment we've come across seems to be working." He paused, deciding what to say next. "A lot of people have died—a majority, in fact." Marcia's eyes welled with tears, but she didn't interrupt, so Gabriel continued. "They get feverish, start looking infected, and then die in a couple of days, but I don't think it spreads the way disease usually does—it's like they all got it at once."

At that, Marcia choked back a half-sob and put a hand on the car beside her to steady herself. Gabriel said nothing more. He didn't mention the dangerous or desperate people out there, which Ripley assumed was obvious, but he also didn't say anything about the creatures—or demons, as he called them. Marcia probably wouldn't have believed that part anyway, and the farther away from Betelgeuse they got, the more fervently Ripley hoped they would never see another one. Everything else was bad enough—worse than bad. But to think about those creatures and those torn bodies, that was the stuff of madness, and this woman looked half mad already. Ripley could sympathize.

"Marcia, would you like us to take a look at your husband?" Ripley asked, prompting her as gently as she could.

"Yes, please," Marcia said automatically, her wild eyes darting again. "This way."

She led them away from the road into the brown, tall grass. Once they were far enough from the road, the three left their bikes in the grass and shouldered their packs. Marcia led them over an old wire fence, one section of which had been knocked loose. A few trees grew along the fence line, stunted and gnarled with small waxy leaves. On the other side, the taller grass gave way to an open field—more of a prairie, really. Ripley wiped the sweat from her brow with the back of her hand, then gently shooed a fly away from her hair, which was getting pretty rank.

"He's gotten a lot better," Marcia said to Ripley with a sniff. "But he's still weak, and we didn't know where to go." This admission seemed to upset her again, and tears spilled freely down her cheeks.

Ripley reached out, turned the woman toward her, and enfolded her in a tight embrace. "We'll take a look at him and figure it out together," Ripley said, hoping her voice sounded confident. She felt the woman finally relax a little before she released her.

Marcia nodded, wiping the tears from her cheeks.

"Thank you," the woman said, squaring her shoulders to continue their walk. They followed the fence line for a short distance further before Ripley saw the woman's camp under the scant shade of a largish tree. In addition to a man lying on a sweaty sleeping bag, there were two children—a boy and a girl. The boy was older, perhaps ten or eleven, and eyed the newcomers warily. He had unkempt brown hair and was holding a stout stick in his hand. The daughter, maybe seven or eight, had long blonde hair and stood on the opposite side of the camp, poised to run.

The moment hung nervously in the air; everyone seemed to

be trying to think of something safe to say. Ripley felt a surge of compassion and sadness for these people.

"Don't be afraid," she said. "We're here to see if we can help." She motioned Gabriel toward the father and strode the rest of the way into the camp, where she took off her backpack and sat down beside it, rummaging until she pulled out a bright red bag of Skittles. She smiled at the little girl and gestured with the bag in a general invitation. The little girl took a step toward Ripley before stopping and glancing to her mother for permission. The mother thought about it briefly, then nodded and walked over to Ripley herself. Both kids, relieved, came as well. Soon they were all sitting together, sharing Skittles and watching Gabriel and Tam, who had gone over to see to the father.

The man had eyed them warily as they approached, his eyes glassy. It was clear he had been unwell. He shifted slightly when they drew near but made no effort to rise. "Hello," he said, awkwardly, looking up. "Pardon me if I don't get up. I'm Sam."

"Hey, Sam," Gabriel said, smiling. "Your wife said you've been sick. We'll help you if we can. Can you tell us what happened?" As he said this, Tam took off his pack and pulled out a plastic water bottle opening it and offering it to the man.

Sam accepted it with a nod of thanks and took a long swig before gathering himself to speak. Ripley handed the bag of candy to Marcia, who seemed calmer now, and then stood up to walk over to the men.

"Thanks," the man said to Gabriel. He took another, smaller sip. Then he sighed. "I started feeling sick almost immediately after the car died. We were behind another car on the road when ours conked out, and I guess theirs died too." He shook his head.

"The old man and woman in it were already pretty sick, and they didn't want to leave their car—they said someone would come for them. We tried to at least get them out of the heat, but the old man cursed us out in front of the kids, and I was feeling worse and worse, so my wife and I took the kids a little ways away off the road. I had to lie down in the grass there, couldn't go any further, and my wife and kids were worried about me." He took another swig of water.

"Anyway, by nightfall the old couple were both dead, and we still hadn't seen anyone else come by. We all needed sleep, so my wife got our camping stuff out of the car and set up the tent here, away from the road. She got me up and we all stumbled over here and fell asleep. I slept for about twenty-four hours. Fever, chills, nausea, cramps. I've been in and out ever since. I'm not really sure how much time has passed, actually…" He trailed off here and looked at them.

"About four or five days," Ripley offered.

Sam sighed and nodded. "That seems about right, I guess." He paused. "Are all the cars and phones dead everywhere?"

Gabriel nodded. "We've been riding our bikes for a couple of days from over in New Mexico, and it's been like that between there and here, anyway."

Sam took another drink. "That's discouraging," he managed. "Anyway, we were just about at our wit's end. We haven't been as regular as we should have been in going to synagogue and all, but they all prayed over me yesterday, and I know how this sounds, but God answered their prayers and the fever broke." He watched their expressions. "Like, right away. Like a miracle," he said earnestly.

"Okaaay," Gabriel said, his voice carefully neutral. *Clearly not a believer*, Ripley thought. After all the crazy things they had seen over the past few days, she was not about to doubt anyone's claim that they had witnessed a miracle. *If there's one thing I've learned from this mess, it's that anything is possible*, she thought.

Sam seemed to accept their silence as an invitation to continue. "I'm feeling much better than I did, but I'm still a little weak, and we're out of water and food."

"You still look sick to me," Tam said bluntly, "but can you walk?" He started digging through his pack for something.

"I feel weak, and a little cold," Sam said. "But so much better than before. We wanted to leave once my fever broke, but we weren't sure where to go, and we kept hoping someone would come." He wiped his brow, still covered in sweat. "I think I'm dehydrated."

"When's the last time you took any medicine?" Ripley asked him.

"I took our last Tylenol yesterday, Marcia tells me."

Ripley produced a bottle of Tylenol, took out two pills, and handed them to the man. "We can spare some water, but is there a river nearby? Or a creek or something?"

Sam shook his head.

Gabriel watched Ripley give away the medicine with concern plainly written all over his face. In her mind, however, the guy clearly needed it more than they did, and they could get more in the next town.

Tam glanced at Gabriel, who held his gaze, as if they were mentally communicating about how much or how little they should help these people. The meaningful look they shared was not lost on Ripley. *I'm here too, guys*, she thought with a touch of annoyance as she watched them.

Gabriel's face was comically easy to read. He was trying to come up with an excuse not to help. So Ripley spoke again.

"We'll help you get somewhere safe," she said. "We have a little food and water that we can share with you until we get to a town or a store."

Gabriel glared at Ripley, his face still laden with obvious

meaning, but he didn't argue. Tam, however, standing just behind Gabriel, winked at her and smiled.

Sam sighed with relief. "Thank you," he said simply. "We appreciate that so much. I worry about keeping them safe with me in this state," he said.

"With a group this large, I think we should be okay even if we see someone else," Gabriel said. "Although we haven't seen anybody alive for a few days now."

"We're close to Safford," Tam said. "But towns don't seem to be any safer in our limited experience."

Gabriel eyed the man critically. "Do you feel up to traveling now? We really should get you guys moving and find a better place to camp and some water."

Ripley smiled. She had suspected that all Gabriel needed was a gentle nudge to get him to agree to help. He seemed like he could be a decent person, even if he was far too intense—so much so that she still felt wary around him.

Gabriel held out his hand to Sam, who gripped it and used it to haul himself upright. Once he was standing, he bent over and rested his hands on his knees for a moment but remained on his feet.

"Whoo," he said. "Head rush, but I'm okay." His wife and kids all watched him worriedly. He slowly straightened until he was standing fully upright, and his wife walked over to him as if to hold him up, but he waved her off with a rueful smile.

"I'm okay," he repeated. "Let's pack up and go for a walk."

As the family rolled up their sleeping bags, took down their tent, and packed their meager belongings, Gabriel took Tam aside, walking halfway back toward the road. He leaned in to speak quietly. Ripley followed and stood nearby, watching the family and the path to the road alternately.

"We should help them find some water and a place with some shelter," Gabriel began quietly, "but we can't stay with them. They'll add days to our journey and seriously reduce our chances of making it at all."

Tam frowned irritably. "That's bullshit. They can walk, unlike that officer back in Betelgeuse. We're not leaving a family with children alone and sick in the desert!" His voice was quiet but intense. His glare was hot, and he and Gabriel locked eyes for a strained moment. Then Gabriel glanced to the side and saw Ripley standing there, listening. She gazed into his flashing eyes in a way that she hoped conveyed how important this was to her.

Gabriel broke off his glare, nodded once, and sighed.

"Fine, we can help them find someplace safe, but Ripley, we are on a mission. We know some people who might be able to help with all of this," he said, gesturing around at the world. "We have critical information that we need to get to them." Then he turned back to help the Feldmans pack.

What are these two hiding? she wondered.

TWENTY-FOUR

GABRIEL

I t was much harder to walk their bikes with the carts attached than it was to ride, Gabriel complained inwardly, but the road here was flat and even slightly downhill in places, so it was manageable. Sam actually seemed to gain strength from walking, though he never exactly looked well. He didn't talk much at first, saving his strength for the physical effort of putting one foot in front of the other, but occasionally he would laugh at something the kids were doing. And whenever Marcia or Gabriel asked him how he was doing, he responded with a smile that was meant to be reassuring. His wife seemed pleased with his improvement—apparently he had been at death's door a couple of days back so it was a tremendous relief for the whole family to see him so well recovered.

Ripley, meanwhile, was simply transformed. Just watching her bounce around with the children and talk to Marcia warmed Gabriel's heart. She had obviously been through terrible things—she had never said who the man was in the school with her that the demon had killed, but Gabriel suspected that he might have been holding her against her will. And worse. She certainly hadn't mourned him at the time, nor had she mentioned him again. Thinking about it made Gabriel angry. So angry, in fact, that it was hard to think straight when he dwelt on it.

Generally, though, everyone's mood was good. The children, Travis and Miri, initially stayed close to their parents, but gradually became more comfortable with the new dynamic and were soon ranging ahead, looking into every car as they passed. Their mother had told them not to the first twenty times, but there was no avoiding the cars on the road, some empty, others with their dead occupants inside, and Marcia eventually got tired of trying to keep them from looking.

They continued like that for three sun-baked hours before they found a stash of water and snacks in one of the cars–four full water bottles, trail mix, pork rinds, assorted candy, and a zip-lock bag of saltines with peanut butter, all of which they allocated to the Feldmans.

After a short, sweaty lunch break, Gabriel got everyone back on their feet.

"Tam, could you scout ahead and keep a lookout for us in front?" he asked. "I'd like to know about any new potential developments before the kids walk into a problem."

"Sure, you got it," the man responded, throwing his leg awkwardly over his bike and lurching into motion.

"Don't get too close to anything—just report back if you see something," Gabriel said.

"Yes, Mom," Tam said over his shoulder as he pedaled off. The little girl, Miri, laughed out loud and Travis grinned. Gabriel smiled to himself. *It's nice to have an audience*, he thought. Ripley smiled too.

Sam Feldman quickened his pace to fall in beside Gabriel. *He seems so much better*, Gabriel thought.

"Hey Gabriel," Sam said conversationally. "Where did you guys start out? I take it you weren't all together before this happened."

Gabriel nodded, considering what he was going to say. There was no way anyone could know that Betelgeuse was ground zero, so he decided to stick as close to the truth as possible.

"We started out in Betelgeuse—a tiny town to the east, off Route 180 in New Mexico," he said.

"We must have driven right past there," Sam said. "We were on a little family road trip to Roswell, and I decided to take the back roads."

Gabriel glanced at him and Sam gave a tired grin in response. "I thought it would be fun for the kids, and I'd never been there," he said a little defensively.

They walked in silence for a moment before Gabriel spoke again.

"Was it? Fun, I mean?"

Sam laughed, quickly and easily. Feeling much better, then.

"It was okay—just as cheesy as you'd expect. It's a huge tourist trap, but the kids enjoyed it, so it was a good trip."

Gabriel smiled back, Sam's humor infecting him. "I've never been there—aliens aren't really my thing. I go camping in my free time. Or play video games at home."

Sam nodded sagely. "Spoken like a true bachelor."

Gabriel cocked an eyebrow, waiting for Sam to elaborate.

"It's not like the sitcoms make it out," Sam said, glancing over his shoulder at his wife and kids, who were far enough back not to overhear. "Wives aren't sadists who want you to stop having fun immediately after the wedding—it's more like once you're married and especially after you have kids, there just aren't enough hours in the day to do all the stuff you used to do." He sighed. "Too many new responsibilities." Then he smiled absently at his children, who were scampering toward the windows of another car.

"But I've never regretted it, not even for a single minute," Sam continued warmly. Gabriel believed him. He hoped he would be able to say the same thing someday, but he couldn't help but think that with the world the way it was now, he might never settle down like that—for all he knew, maybe settling down wouldn't be a thing the human race would do anymore. Maybe people would go extinct. On the other hand, biology wasn't going to go down without a fight. Humans had survived and multiplied when they were living in caves and hunting saber-toothed tigers, so they could probably survive this.

"So what about you?" Sam asked.

"What about me what?"

"Have you ever been married?"

Gabriel shook his head. "Between work and fun, I never felt like I had the time. I move around a lot for work; I'm generally assigned to a new location every few months or so."

"What do you do?" Sam asked.

"I'm a contractor for the federal government," Gabriel replied, trying not to sound evasive. "Basically a traveling risk assessor and problem solver." Strictly speaking, he wasn't even supposed to give that much detail about his role, but he didn't think it mattered much now. Besides, he hated telling people that he was an HR consultant, which was the official cover story assigned to him by Colonel Broadnax when he had first joined.

"That sounds awesome!" Sam said. "And you work with Tam, right?"

"Yeah," Gabriel said. "We've been working together for the past six months or so."

"And Ripley?" He glanced over his shoulder to where Ripley was walking with the kids, who were orbiting around her, seeking her ever-patient approval of and interest in everything they were doing. Gabriel had not seen Ripley looking this normal—happy, even—since they'd found her.

Gabriel lowered his voice a bit more. "We only met her a few days ago, after all this started. She's had a rough time—lost her family, I think, among other things. But it looks like she's enjoying herself now."

Sam looked back and saw his daughter bringing a flower she had picked from the side of the road to give to Ripley, who took it with an earnest-looking reverence.

"I wasn't sure if she was with one of you or what," Sam said with a grin.

Gabriel chuckled. "No, just traveling companions, or friends, I guess you could say. We couldn't leave her behind where we found her. We wanted to find a safer place to take her. Maybe she'll want to stay with you guys."

They passed the rest of the day like that, Gabriel and Sam walking and talking together, though occasionally Sam's wife or one of the kids would join them for a while. Gabriel thought that Sam would probably have become a good friend right away if they'd worked together before all this. They enjoyed one another's humor, and a mutual respect had rapidly developed between the pair.

But as the sun began to sink toward the horizon, Sam began to struggle to keep up and spent more and more time in silence, concentrating more on the act of keeping his feet moving.

Tam rode back toward the main group and reported that there were several cars ahead that had already been looted, but he hadn't seen the looters yet.

Gabriel led the group off the road, thinking they should camp far enough away to be out of sight. He considered saying something about not leaving footprints near the road that would indicate their presence, but it would be dark before long, so he let it go.

After they found a good campsite and all the tents had been set up near a group of stunted trees, Tam began to gather sticks to build a fire, but Gabriel held up his hand and said, "No fire."

Tam cocked his head to the side. "It's getting cool already," he said, his tone indicating that Gabriel was talking crazy.

Gabriel shook his head. "We just saw some cars that have obviously been looted—there may be strangers nearby, and we don't want to set up a beacon for them to come find us all unawares."

No one said anything to that, though Tam put down the twigs he had been gathering. Eventually, everyone settled in a circle around the spot where a fire would have been, and quiet conversation resumed over a cold meal of snacks and canned goods. The kids and Ripley sat on one side, while the other adults sat on the other, with Sam slumped between his wife and Gabriel.

After everyone had finished eating, Marcia set the kids to brushing their teeth and going to bed, then helped Sam stand up to do the same. He looked a little feverish again. Once upright, he staggered and almost fell to the ground before his wife rushed to his side and he threw an arm around her shoulders. She helped him back to their tent, fixing Gabriel with a pained and vaguely accusatory look as they started walking. Gabriel stared after them, worried. He hoped Sam was just tired.

Gabriel felt fine, though pushing the bike had been more taxing than riding it, so he took first watch. He walked to what passed for the highest ground near their camp, a small rise of weathered stone no taller than a low bench and sat down. He perched there in silence, listening to nature, mostly obscured by the sounds of his group settling in for the night. The plop of boots being taken off, whispered conversations, and tent zippers being drawn all quickly faded into silence.

Gabriel stared off into the softly lit landscape around them, seeing the desert in all its stark and mystical beauty. It was like an alien landscape, not truly flat or featureless, but filled with details that caught the eye: dry creek beds, small hills, stony outcroppings, and boulders. A number of short, hardy trees that stood silently around their camp along with patches of wildflowers and even grass. Gabriel found it beautiful. Intoxicating, even. He had always loved the desert, although they would need to find a water source tomorrow or they would all start going thirsty.

He glanced up at the moon but noticed that it wasn't there. Either it hadn't risen yet, or it was behind a thick blanket of flat, light-devouring clouds. In fact, there were no stars or light sources anywhere. Gabriel had been staring fondly out into the pitch black, seeing everything as if it were still twilight. *Huh*, he thought, shifting his weight uneasily. *That's... neat.*

Staring around, he tried to verify that he was actually seeing what he thought he was seeing. To him, the landscape was evenly visible, though certainly not bright. He saw details that he didn't think he was imagining. He tried to make an educated guess at the mechanism of his night vision. All he could come up with was that either the ground itself was emitting small amounts of visible light, or else he was perceiving some other wavelength that was passing through the clouds, bathing everything in some strange *unlight*. He didn't know which would be weirder. In any case, he couldn't decide between the two hypotheses. The only other thing that struck him was the fact that he couldn't see any shadows anywhere.

When Gabriel finally estimated that it had been four hours, he went to Tam's tent and tapped on the frame, repeating Tam's name in a low voice at regular intervals until he heard a groggy, faint "coming" in response. Gabriel retreated to his small vantage point. A few minutes later, Tam emerged from his tent, and from the direct, unhesitating path he took as he walked over to Gabriel, it was clear that he could also see quite well in the dark.

"Fancy meeting you here," Tam quipped, his voice low.

"Hola, amigo," Gabriel murmured back.

"What time is it?" Tam said, stretching his arms languorously above his head.

"Not exactly sure. Maybe two?"

"What's up?" Tam asked, realizing that Gabriel wanted to talk about something.

"Tam, you can see okay, right?"

Tam was quiet for a moment, looking out into the desert before turning back to Gabriel. "Yeah, it's dark, but I can see you, anyway. And the ground around us."

Gabriel could see more than that, but it was still the same phenomenon. "*How* are we seeing?" he asked.

Tam looked around again, then upward, pausing for a longer time now. Eventually, he turned back to Gabriel and spoke again, deadly serious. "Are my eyeballs glowing?"

Gabriel laughed softly. "Not particularly, although I can see them," he responded.

Tam thought some more, turning back to the desert around them. "That's a good question, then. Flashlights for eyeballs was my best guess. If not that, I'd say that we, along with the ground, are giving off a faintly visible quantity of radiation."

"Yeah, I couldn't think of anything better, either," Gabriel said. "Well, goodnight!" Just hearing that Tam was experiencing the same thing somehow made it less threatening. He wanted to discuss it and all the other weird things they had come across in more detail with the man, but his exhaustion was stronger than his desire to do so. *Maybe tomorrow*, he thought as he yawned.

But the next morning he woke up to the sound of Marcia Feldman yelling Sam's name over and over again, fear and worry thick in her voice, and all thoughts of magical night vision were forgotten. He dressed hurriedly and dashed out into the morning light, only to stop and stare at the Feldmans' tent flap in tense indecision. Ripley sat nearby, a half-eaten can of fruit forgotten in her hand.

A moment later, Marcia appeared, propping up Sam as he struggled out of the tent and gingerly stood upright. He looked like death warmed over, sweaty and pale, with dark circles under his eyes. He met Gabriel's eyes and gave what was probably meant to be a brave smile, or maybe some kind of apology. He was sick again. Silent tears were streaming down Marcia's face as she stood at her husband's side. Gabriel felt as though she were glaring at *him*. He felt defensive, but he didn't know what he had done—she was probably just upset and needed someone to blame.

Marcia helped her husband over to a rock where she eased him down. She returned to the tent, grabbed his boots, and returned with them before lifting up their bag of food. The kids came over as well, somber-faced and quiet. Marcia handed out some snacks to the children and then pushed bite after bite onto Sam, who seemed to rally a bit now that he was out in the morning sun. At least he was trying to.

"How's it going, Sam?" Gabriel said, immediately thinking what a lame question that was. Indeed, it seemed to elicit a renewed glare from Marcia, though she didn't answer for her husband.

"'Sokay," Sam responded. "I may have to slow down today… if we're heading out," he continued.

Gabriel nodded. "I think we'd better. There's no water here and we'll have to find some in the next day or two." He left out the *or else*. "But let's get you some ibuprofen and start a course of antibiotics before we head out."

"Hopefully, there'll be a store or something before we get to Safford," Tam chimed in.

"I would say that you could stay here while we go find some water," Gabriel went on, "but I don't want us to split up—I think we'll be safer in a larger group."

Sam nodded, and even Marcia's glare softened into concern.

"Let's pack up and we'll be ready to move whenever Sam can manage it," Gabriel said.

Within fifteen minutes, they had given Sam some of their precious supply of meds, and all their tents and other things were stowed away in their packs. Then, however, Marcia realized that Travis wasn't wearing socks, so she had to unpack his bag again to get a pair, delaying them by a further ten minutes. The whole time, Travis stared at the ground, or anywhere but at Ripley, terribly embarrassed. When he was finally squared away, Sam nodded and stood up, still with one arm over his wife's shoulders, and they started back toward the road.

Just as they reached the pavement, Gabriel held up a hand, his heart in his throat. There was another set of tracks beside the road, crossing their own footprints from the night before. It looked to Gabriel as if someone in large boots had left the road to examine their tracks, then returned to it, walking in the direction they were headed.

Gabriel made eye contact with Tam and then glanced back at the tracks, trying to silently alert him. He had to repeat the process twice more before Tam caught on, and by then Marcia had noticed as well, tightening her lips in additional worry.

Still, there was nothing they could do but press on—they had to find water soon.

"Let's all walk together today," Gabriel suggested neutrally, and they all traipsed onto the road. Gabriel surreptitiously checked to see if he could quickly free his axe from his belt, then pushed his bike onto the road, heading west.

The day got rapidly hotter once the full sun was beating down on them. The cloud cover from the night before had already burned off, and it would have been a stunning, perfect day if they hadn't been walking down the road with no shade in sight. Gabriel wished for a sun hat and worried about their remaining water. He noticed that Ripley was sweating profusely under her football pads.

They passed a number of other cars that had been broken into, windows smashed and doors left wide open, oftentimes with the bodies dragged out onto the road and left there. Several of these had been worried by coyotes or other scavengers, and the Feldmans tried to cover their children's eyes as they passed. Worry was on everyone's face, and even the kids' talk was muted, lapsing into silence as they struggled to keep walking. Sam, especially, looked rough.

Just before noon, a gas station and a few other buildings came into view at a lonely intersection. Gabriel glanced over at his friend, whose eyes said that he was worried. "I'm worried," Tam's mouth said as well. "I've got a bad feeling about this, but I'm out of water, and I think we have to go in."

Gabriel nodded. "The next store might be another day's walk away. We have to check it out."

Gabriel examined Sam, who was in really bad shape. He had been shambling along with them silently for the past two hours, mostly with his arm slung over his wife's shoulders.

"Maybe we can hole up there out of the sun for the rest of the day," Gabriel said.

Ripley walked her bike up next to the kids. "I hope the store still has some candy!" she said, smiling at the little girl, Miri. Miri smiled back and put her hand on Ripley's handlebars as they walked. After a minute, she said, "Do you think they have Peeps?"

"Or Pop Rocks?" Travis asked.

"What are Pop Rocks?" Tam asked.

Now Gabriel was smiling too. "We'll get you some, Tam—there's no way to describe them properly, and it would be better as a surprise."

"I call dibs on the Butterfingers," Sam said suddenly, shaking off his lassitude. The kids looked up at him and grinned.

"Butterfingers are gross, Dad," Travis said. "They stick to your braces."

"That's why I had my braces removed," his father replied matter-of-factly. "The Butterfinger company almost went out of business until I got my braces off." His sweaty, flushed face brightened as he smiled at his own joke, though he kept his voice serious.

"*Daa—aad*!" Miri said, stretching the word into two syllables.

Soon they were within sight of the shop, which was an old gas station with a large awning and a couple of folding chairs outside the glass doors. There were a few vehicles around, including a pickup truck parked in a dirt lot on their side of the road that would provide some cover.

Gabriel led them over to the pickup truck and left his bike there, out of sight of the store. He took his staff from where he had strapped it to the frame and waited for his companions. Taking his cue, Tam unholstered his machete and Ripley picked up her aluminum baseball bat. Gabriel removed his tomahawk from his belt and gave it to Marcia. Tam handed Sam his knife and Ripley passed one to Travis. She looked the boy in the eye and said, "Show this if anyone comes toward you, but don't try to use it. Get your sister and run away and hide instead, got it?" Travis nodded solemnly, his eyes as big as saucers.

"If there's trouble, and you see us go down, take our bikes and ride straight away without stopping. One of you will have to run behind, switching off when you get tired," Gabriel said to Sam and Marcia.

Ripley turned and walked back to her bike, where she took her football helmet out of its basket and pulled it down over her head. She looked at Gabriel and Tam and nodded. Tam nodded as well. Gabriel checked that he could get to his axe, then said, "Let's do this."

He started walking toward the store, holding his staff in front of him. Ripley and Tam followed a few steps behind on either side. Gabriel thought he could feel his skin tingling and his muscles bulging in anticipation of danger, but he didn't see any flames coming from his skin yet, which he was glad about; that would have been pretty difficult to explain to the Feldmans.

They got closer and were soon under the awning that covered the pumps. Still, there was no sound or sign of movement. The place looked deserted. An old metal chair and two canvas folding chairs stood by the door, facing the pumps. Several empty beer bottles sat on the pavement next to them. *Probably not deserted, then*, Gabriel thought.

They reached the door and peered inside—still no movement, although it was hard to see through the dirty glass into the darker interior. Gabriel tried the door, but it was locked.

"That's both good and bad," Tam remarked quietly.

Gabriel brought the head of the staff down to the lock, shielding it with his body so the Feldmans couldn't see. He envisioned the rune they now associated with opening things, and he felt energy course down his arm through the staff and into the lock, which promptly clicked. He smelled a faint scent of ozone. *Or maybe coppery blood*, he thought. Ripley watched him closely, a strange expression on her face, but Gabriel didn't stop to explain. He had no idea what he'd say, anyway.

He glanced at Tam, who was standing ready, and then jerked the door open and quickly stepped inside, his companions hard on his heels.

The interior seemed deserted, and though it was darker inside, several dirty windows let in enough light to see. The place had clearly been ransacked, and precious few items of food or drink remained. The few things that were left would not sustain them for long unless they took almost everything.

Gabriel guessed that it was or had been someone's cache and

base of operations, and that it might still be guarded even now. He motioned Tam and Ripley toward the far wall on the left while he went to the right, past the cash register. He looked behind the counter where he saw a few dollar bills and some candy wrappers. He reached the back wall at about the same time as Tam and Ripley. They approached the small hallway that housed the bathrooms and another door that could have been a cleaning closet or maybe an office. Gabriel held up his hand to stop for a moment, and they listened for any sound, but heard nothing. Gabriel pointed Tam and Ripley to the first door, the women's restroom, and he approached the men's room. He held up three fingers and silently counted, slowly bobbing his hand up and down like he was playing a solo game of rock, paper, scissors.

Three. Two. One. Go—and they pushed both doors open simultaneously, entering the bathrooms. Gabriel's was empty, and from the lack of yelling, he assumed Tam and Ripley's was as well. He ducked back out of the men's room, his eye on the last door. Tam and Ripley emerged from their restroom. Together they slowly approached the door. Gabriel tried the knob, but it was locked, so he once again used his staff to unlock it. There was a soft *click* and he swiftly turned the knob and threw open the door.

Inside was a fairly large office, empty of people, but piled high with sleeping bags, rifles, ammo, and the odd piece of survival gear. Gabriel stared, taking it all in. Out of the corner of his eye, he saw a tiny lick of flame escape his skin and flit up his arm over his shirt. No one mentioned it, though. They all stood for a moment and stared at the room.

"I think we should grab some food and water and get out of here," Tam said. "These people are planning on coming back." Gabriel nodded, and they all backed out of the room and headed back to the main part of the store.

Gabriel started giving orders. "Tam, you gather some food. Ripley…" He stopped as Ripley ducked back into the women's restroom without a word. Tam shrugged and moved off to look over the shelves. Gabriel went first to the counter, where he grabbed four bags, and then to where the water and other drinks were in the now-defunct coolers.

He began grabbing water bottles and a few sodas and tossing them into the bags. He was careful to leave a couple of bottles in each row to make their intrusion less obvious. Ripley joined him after a few minutes and picked up two of the full bags. By the time they were done, Tam was behind them with two small bags of his own, stuffed with beef jerky and mixed nuts from the looks of it. He nodded.

Gabriel slid his two bags onto his staff and put it on his shoulder. "Okay, let's get the hell out of here," he said, and they pushed open the door.

Together, they stepped out into the bright sunshine, squinting as their eyes adjusted to the glare. Gabriel looked back to where they had left the Feldmans and stopped dead in his tracks.

"Trouble," he said, dropping his staff and drawing his axe.

TWENTY—FIVE

Aman in camo pants and an oversized button-down shirt was standing close behind Marcia Feldman, holding her arm forcefully behind her back with one hand while restraining her in a loose chokehold with his other forearm. Marcia screamed and struggled but couldn't break free. Another man was gripping little Miri, who was crying and thrashing about, while a third, who wielded a wicked-looking survival knife longer than his hand, faced Travis. The boy gripped Ripley's knife in front of him as menacingly as he could manage. Sam sat on the ground, slumped against the wheel of the abandoned pickup truck, a red mark on the side of his face visible from forty yards away.

Before the scene had fully registered, Gabriel had dropped everything and begun running toward the little family, drawing out his axe. Tam and Ripley did the same and were only a short distance behind him. They ran quietly, hoping to catch the men by surprise. But before they had crossed even half of the distance, three more armed men came out onto the road behind Travis, who didn't seem to notice them. They spotted Gabriel, however, and began shouting and pointing.

Travis, startled, whipped around toward the new threat

behind him, leaving his back exposed to the man who had been facing him. The man did not hesitate. He took a quick, jerky step in Travis' direction, and before Gabriel could even scream, he plunged his knife into the boy's back. Travis immediately crumpled to the ground with a wet cry.

Gabriel's vision blurred and his mind emptied of thought, filling instead with pure, unreasoning rage that left no room for anything else. He could feel the stinging flames explode up his arms, back, and head. He heard a terrible sound, and as all the men turned to face him, he realized it was his own hoarse scream. Judging by the expressions on their faces, he made for a frightening sight. One of the three men who had just come over the rise turned immediately and ran. The men holding Marcia and Miri tightened their grips and shielded themselves with their hostages. The rest drew closer together almost unconsciously, brandishing their weapons as if to ward off evil.

Gabriel changed his trajectory at the last moment, veering suddenly into one of the men who had come up behind Travis like a derailed freight train. The man held a long machete, but Gabriel swatted it aside with ease and brought his flame-hardened forearm up into the man's face as he crashed into him. He knew from the sickening crunch that he had broken the man's nose and perhaps more, and his opponent barely managed to stay on his feet as he staggered backward. Before the man could even finish bringing his hands uselessly to his ruined face, Gabriel pivoted in front of him with a vicious swing of his axe, sinking it deep into his arm just below the shoulder. By the time Gabriel realized the axe had gone all the way into the man's rib cage, the arm had been sheared off completely and slid out of what was left of the man's shirt sleeve to fall on the ground. Gabriel jerked the axe free, turning back to the two men holding Marcia and Miri. He dully noted the man behind him slumping heavily to the ground, already unconscious or dead.

Now it was suddenly quiet as everyone's bulging eyes fixed on Gabriel. In his peripheral vision, he could see that blue flames were licking up from every part of his body that he could see; he could feel—and smell—them singeing his skin. Another of the bandits turned and fled, running past Tam, who let him go, concentrating instead on the hostage-takers. Gabriel bent down and put his fingers to Travis' neck to check for a pulse.

Nothing. He held his fingers there for a full minute as everyone stared at him. No one moved or made a sound until his rage got the better of him again and he screamed—a primal, anguished bellow.

He straightened up to the sound of Marcia's agonized wails. Gabriel pointed at the three remaining men, his voice hard and loud. "You two are free to go if you leave the women unharmed, but the one who killed the boy stays."

The man he pointed to took a step toward Miri and her captor, but Ripley stepped between them, her back dangerously exposed to the man holding Miri. Tam took two slow steps closer. The men holding the hostages exchanged panicked glances.

"Why would you let us go?" the man holding Marcia asked plaintively. Marcia's eyes stared blankly at her fallen son.

"Because we don't care about you," Tam responded, his voice low and reasonable. "We just want our friends here safe— we already let two of you go."

The man who had killed Travis spoke up. "More likely, you'll kill us all as soon as we let the women go," he said gruffly, desperate. His intentions were obvious, but his companions appeared to consider his words carefully. "How about you let us walk slowly over to our store, and you can follow, and once we're inside, we'll let the women go?"

"The one who killed the boy has to pay," Gabriel said, his voice detached from the rage roiling inside of him. "The other two can go back to the store, but you'll let our people go once you get within twenty feet of the door."

The bandits were silent for a moment, considering. The murderer in question seemed to sense things were going against him, because he stood still for about a second before sprinting back toward the dry, empty grassland.

Gabriel's flames flared up higher along his arms and hands. He could feel the heat billowing up around his head, crisping his hair and feeding his anger and frustration at seeing this killer trying to get away.

"Tam!" he shouted, "Get him!" Tam's weight shifted toward the man for half a second, but then he stopped, remaining focused on the man holding Miri. Gabriel tried willing Tam to chase the fleeing bandit, but to no avail. Frustrated, he thought about throwing his axe, but he didn't think he could hit anyone from more than about ten feet away, and even that might require them to promise to stand still. Instead, frustration and anger raged even higher within him. The bizarre blue flames jumped around on his skin and scorched his clothes, seemingly in response to his inner turmoil. He pointed uselessly at the man's receding back in impotent fury, wishing him dead. It was almost as if he could reach out and grab him, snuffing out his life from thirty yards away. Then, he felt something move in his mind and thought he saw a point of darkness form hazily in front of him, surrounded by its own flames. He suddenly felt dizzy, like he was about to pass out, and shook his head to clear it, taking a deep breath. He turned his attention back to the situation before him. They needed to get these predators away from Marcia and her daughter.

"You're running out of allies," he said through clenched teeth. "The only way you get out of this alive is to let these people go right now and leave. Back to the store or following your friends." He paused to let that sink in. "Every other choice ends with your guts spilling out on the sand right here in the next two minutes."

The words fell like a final pronouncement, and the men seemed to take it with all the gravity Gabriel intended. The man holding Marcia thought it over for about eight interminable seconds before letting her go and taking a step backward. Marcia immediately flew to her son, who lay in a pool of his own blood. When Gabriel didn't immediately attack, the man took another step back. Then another. Then he turned and ran off into the desert.

The man restraining little Miri tightened his grip on the girl. She was sobbing uncontrollably now, a high, loud sound that tore at Gabriel's heart and, along with Marcia's keening, made it hard to think.

The man held her close, knife at her throat. He was crying too, tears streaming freely down his face. His eyes darted from Tam and his wicked-looking machete back to Gabriel. He seemed to ignore Ripley, who stood between him and the store.

Hunched over as if trying to hide behind the little girl, he began walking toward the gas station, turning his body to keep Miri between him and the men. As he approached Ripley, instead of angling to keep all three companions on one side of him, he kept his direct path toward the store, turning his back to Ripley as he passed her.

"Think for a minute, man," Tam said. "You could walk away from this if you just let the girl go this second."

The man glared back, still dragging Miri toward the store.

"I'm not letting her go, and if you touch me, she dies," he hissed, spitting the words out like poison. But before he could take another shuffling step, Ripley's bat caved in the back of his skull, sending him stumbling forward, his dead weight falling over Miri's screaming form.

A second later, Ripley had dropped her bat and was

kneeling on the road, holding Miri and comforting her. Gabriel sighed, some of the tension leaving his body. He looked around for any of the bandits who had fled, but he didn't see any.

He walked over to the man Ripley had felled and knelt to check his pulse. Surprisingly, his heart was still beating fitfully, though Gabriel could see that the man's skull was severely fractured and sunken. His open eyes stared blankly into the dirt, shooting wildly from side to side as if in panic, but his face was now smooth and blank, his body stilling. Gabriel shuddered, revulsion turning his stomach. The man was almost certainly going to die, and the longer it took him, the worse it would be. Gabriel glanced up at Miri and then over to her mother and father. Ripley was only a couple of feet away, but her back was to him. Marcia was absorbed in grieving her son, and Sam seemed catatonic. No one was watching except for Tam.

Without allowing himself any time to think about it, he drew his belt knife and opened the man's jugular with a quick, short cut. Blood spurted out immediately and began to pool on the pavement beneath the man's neck. Gabriel glanced up at Tam, who stared for a moment, eyes wide and watery, before giving a sharp nod and turning away.

Gabriel wiped his knife and axe on the man's shirt and stowed them safely, then grabbed Ripley's bat and cleaned it off as well. His flames slowly began to gutter out, which somehow seemed to hurt worse than when he was burning. He got up and walked over to Tam, speaking quietly so the Feldmans wouldn't hear him. "We should get Sam into the shade and see what's wrong with him, and we need to bury Travis, but I don't want to spend the night in that store—I doubt the others will abandon it, and we might wake up with their knives at our throats."

Tam nodded. "Or to them burning it down around us."

"See if you can get Marcia to bring Miri into the shade and tell her that you and I are going to bury Travis," Gabriel said.

"I'll take Sam to the shade by the store." He touched his head absently, and was surprised to feel rough stubble, as if his hair had been burned off and was already growing back. *Because that's exactly what's happening*, he thought incredulously.

Tam turned to Marcia, who was holding her dead son against her breast and rocking back and forth, talking softly to herself or to him. Gabriel walked over to where Sam was sitting, still slumped against the wheel of the car. He was awake, but clearly dazed. He sat staring blankly at his wife and son.

"Sam," Gabriel said, reaching out to touch his shoulder. There was no reaction. The man's face was bruised and swollen, but Gabriel felt his illness was the main problem—that and the trauma of seeing his son killed.

"Sam," he said louder, giving his shoulder a shake. Sam's eyes snapped around and he looked scared. "Sam, we need to get you into the shade over there and get you some water, okay?"

Taking Sam's lack of objection as assent, Gabriel reached down, grabbed his shirt and hauled him upright. He slid in under Sam's left arm and grabbed Sam's wrist with his own left hand. From there, he half helped and half dragged Sam toward the store, stopping once they reached the shade of the awning and sitting him down in the chair by the door. He entered the store, grabbed a bottle of water from a shelf, and brought it back outside to Sam. Unscrewing the cap, he handed it to the man, who took it absently.

"Take this," Gabriel said succinctly, handing him another dose of antibiotics. He watched as Sam automatically put the pills in his mouth, then raised the bottle to his lips and took a sip. Gabriel saw that Sam was shivering despite the heat. That worried him, but he didn't know if it was a fever or shock.

He looked back at the others and saw that they had more or less gathered themselves and were walking toward him. Tam led the way, followed by Marcia, who was now carrying the sobbing Miri, while Ripley brought up the rear, Travis's lifeless body cradled tenderly in her arms.

Marcia walked all the way to Gabriel and stopped, looking at him with tortured eyes. "Can you help him?" she asked.

Gabriel shook his head slowly. "No, I'm sorry. No one can help him anymore." Marcia started tearing up again and just stood there. She seemed at a complete loss as to what to do next.

"Marcia, we need to bury Travis and leave this place."

No response.

"I'm afraid the men who got away will come back for us." At this, Marcia's eyes flicked briefly back to Gabriel's face. "They aren't going to abandon the store—their stuff is in there," he said, "so I think they'll try to come back tonight to finish us off."

She nodded absently, still in shock. "We should go," she mumbled.

"Marcia," Gabriel continued, "Tam and I are going to bury Travis right now, but you have to help get Sam to eat and drink and cool down. Can you do that?"

Slowly, finally, Marcia began to focus on his words. She nodded and looked down at Sam, whose eyes were closed, tears leaking from the corners. She went to him.

"Tam," Gabriel said, "can you get our camping shovels and check inside to see if they have anything better, please?"

Tam nodded silently and ducked into the store.

"Ripley," he said, "can you put him down and bring our bikes and gear over and keep an eye out for those guys sneaking up on us, please?"

Ripley didn't answer, but closed her eyes, tears trickling down her nose and cheeks and leaving tracks in the dust that covered her face. She hugged the boy's dead body to her even more tightly, her shoulders hunched and working as if she were about to scream. Now that they were in the shade, Gabriel thought that both Ripley's and Travis' bodies looked like they were… *sparkling*?

Gabriel was about to repeat his request when Travis' eyes opened over her shoulder and he drew a ragged breath. His panicked eyes searched frantically before landing on Marcia's shocked face.

"Mama? Am I alive?"

TWENTY–SIX

Marcia flew to Ripley and wrested Travis into her own arms, all the while howling the boy's name over and over, her voice breaking and tears streaming down her blotchy red cheeks.

Gabriel watched Ripley's face, though, because something seemed wrong with her. She suddenly looked terribly confused and sweaty, her eyes darting around without settling on anything.

"Ripley?" Gabriel asked. "Are you okay?"

She turned toward the sound of his voice and opened her mouth to say something, but then paused and instead craned her neck to try to look at her own back. She turned slightly as she did so, exposing her back to Gabriel. It was wet with blood, and as he watched, still more blood seeped through and pattered to the ground behind her. A *lot* of blood. He took a step toward her, but she collapsed forward onto the concrete before he could grab her.

Gabriel slid to his knees beside her and pulled up the back of her shirt, which clung wetly to her skin. There on her ribcage, in the same place that Travis had been stabbed, was a puckered, open gash—as if Ripley had been skewered just like the boy. Dark, thick blood oozed from the wound.

"Tam, get me a clean cloth!" yelled Gabriel, and Tam, who had returned from the store at some point, produced an oversized, fresh-looking handkerchief as if from thin air. Gabriel pressed it to Ripley's wound, willing it to close. The wound felt hot and immediately soaked the handkerchief with blood. *Hadn't she healed unnaturally fast when the demon had sliced her side at the school?*

"C'mon, Ripley," Gabriel urged. "Wake up and heal!"

But there was no reaction from the young woman—she lay senseless and bleeding on the filthy concrete.

The Feldmans had noticed what was happening, and Miri left her mother and brother to come over and crouch down next to Ripley. The little girl put her hand on Ripley's shoulder and shook her gently.

"Ripley, please wake up," the girl whispered, tears slipping down her cheeks.

Gabriel kept pressure on the wound, and though the cloth and his hands were soaked in blood, he thought maybe his efforts had helped to stem the flow to some extent—it was no longer spilling down Ripley's side to the ground, at least, but there was a pool of it under both of them now. He could feel her breathing shallowly, but her eyes were closed. She appeared to be sleeping there on the concrete.

After another agonizing minute or two of keeping the pressure on because he couldn't think of anything else to do, Gabriel risked looking at the wound again and saw that it had finally begun to close, pink and red edges drawing together slightly to form what looked like the beginnings of a terrible scar, even as Gabriel watched in fascination. The blood flow had slowed to a gruesome trickle. He tried to use the cloth to wipe the remaining blood from Ripley's skin, but quickly gave it up as futile as there was now more blood in the cloth than on her skin. Finally, he climbed unsteadily to his feet, feeling useless.

"Let's give her a little while to recover," he suggested lamely. His heart still thudded heavily in his chest, and he prayed silently to himself that he wasn't being naively optimistic. No one else volunteered a better plan.

The Feldmans, too, seemed to be slowly recovering. Even Sam looked marginally more alive, hugging his son so tightly that the boy was beginning to squirm.

Gabriel looked over at Tam, who stared back in mute amazement.

"I know he was dead," Gabriel insisted quietly, nodding toward Travis. "I know how to take a pulse. She brought him back—she must have."

Tam, his eyes still wide, just nodded.

Gabriel wanted to talk about it, wanted to pepper Ripley and even Travis with questions, but one was unconscious and the other was being fussed over by his extremely overwrought parents. Instead, he eyed Tam.

"I'm waiting for your comprehensive theory on how we can do these things," he said, only half joking, trying to distract himself from Ripley's state.

Tam collected himself and nodded. "We've always known that Ripley has at least one ability-an evocation—like you, allowing her to heal herself. Apparently she can also heal others," he managed weakly, his voice cracking. "Or at least absorb their injuries."

Gabriel stood and just marveled for a moment. Magic was real. What was more, he and Ripley could do magic. And Tam...

"You, too, I think," he said, meeting Tam's eyes.

His friend's face fell, his eyebrows furrowed stubbornly.

"I'm not sure," the man said, his eyes shifting to the side.

"The way you went *through* that demon at the school?" Gabriel pressed. "And you never told me how you got into your house without unlocking the door."

Tam shrugged. "If I have some sort of ability, I haven't figured it out yet," he mumbled at the ground.

Gabriel frowned. It was unlike Tam to bury his head in the sand. He needed to talk about it.

Tam looked up. "You, though," he said, clearly changing the subject from his own powers to Gabriel's—his voice now animated and enthusiastic. "You've got six evocations that I've observed so far."

"Six?"

"Depending on how you categorize things, yes. The flames on your body, your physical and performance enhancements when you light up, then quickly going back to normal when you calm down, unlocking doors, the creation of the rune on the staff that enables others, or at least me, to replicate that effect, and now the new one."

"What new one?"

Instead of answering, Tam walked over to the staff, picked it up and examined it.

"I was right!" he exclaimed. "There's a new mark."

"I assume you don't mean a scuff mark from where I dropped it," Gabriel said.

"No. Well, maybe, but there's also a new symbol near the unlocking one. What was that thing you did during the standoff where you pointed at the guy and made the air burn in front of you?"

Gabriel felt his stomach drop. "I actually thought I had imagined that."

"Well, that's the only *new* weird thing I've seen you do lately." Then he looked over at Ripley, who still hadn't stirred, though she looked a bit less pale and sweaty now.

Tam turned and walked just around the corner of the store, staff in hand, out of sight of the Feldmans, but still within view of Gabriel.

Tam held the staff up, pointing it into the distance, and touched the new symbol with his thumb, seeming to concentrate on it. Gabriel again felt a movement in his head, almost like something poking at his brain from inside his sinus cavity. A bright sphere formed in front of Tam, a thick corona of fire crackling around a strangely dark center. Tam's brows knitted with effort, and the sphere grew. Then his shoulder jerked forward as if to shove it away from him, and the ball shot off in the direction he was facing, crashing into a dirt hill some hundred feet away, where it exploded with a thunderous boom, tearing a great gouge out of the mound.

Tam turned around, with a grin as wide as his face. "That was cool!" he exclaimed with childlike glee. Gabriel's mouth hung open in stunned surprise.

Before he could say anything, however, he heard Ripley moaning raggedly and saw her start to stir, as if trying to roll over. He fell to his knees beside her and put his hand on her lower back.

"Try not to move," he murmured. "You need to let your wound heal."

She stopped moving, and her body seemed to relax. She opened one of her eyes a slit to look up at him blearily.

"How's Travis?" she croaked.

"He seems okay now, thanks to you," Gabriel replied. "And your own wound is healing. It looked as bad as Travis' at first, though, and didn't heal right away."

Ripley just sighed in response, her relief audible. Then she groaned again pitifully. "It hurts," she breathed.

Marcia shuffled over with Miri and Travis, who, other than looking ashen-faced, seemed fairly hale for someone who had recently been a corpse.

"What was that noise?" Marcia asked, her eyes wide with concern.

"That was just Tam messing around," Gabriel said. "But as

soon as we can get Sam and Ripley on their feet, we need to get out of here before the rest of those guys come back for their stuff and for revenge. You guys go in and get whatever water and snacks you can easily carry."

Marcia, clearly still overwhelmed, simply nodded her head and went into the store, leading her children.

"Keep resting and give yourself a chance to finish healing," Gabriel said to Ripley, then stood and walked over to Tam.

Keeping his back to the door and to Sam, he said, "Show me what you did."

Ripley propped herself up on her elbows very gingerly and watched them both.

Tam held the staff out between them and placed his thumb over the new rune burned into the wood below and to the right of the opening rune.

"I touched here with my thumb and imagined the ball you made... it seemed natural that I should be able to shoot it at a target, and when I thought about how to do that, it just kind of happened." He paused, still speaking quietly; Ripley could probably hear them, but Sam was farther away and staring blankly at the ground.

"There you go, jumping into another experiment," Gabriel remarked. "What if it had blown up in your hands?"

Tam shrugged. "Just trying something new. Caution hasn't worked out for me," he said blandly.

Gabriel snorted.

"Anyway," Tam continued, "I think you did it first, and the staff recorded it somehow." His tone got more animated. "And I felt cold—the air and the ground around me! Not as cold as it should have been to make that ball, but still, I am irrationally excited that at least one aspect of this almost makes sense!"

He handed the staff back to Gabriel, who held it warily in

front of him for a moment more, then gripped it with his hand covering the two runes. Nothing happened and he shrugged.

"I hope it only happens when I want it to," he whispered, half to himself, and then turned to walk back to his pack.

"We need to talk about all this and do more experiments so we can understand everything!" Tam exclaimed. His tone suggested that Gabriel was already arguing with him.

Gabriel nodded slowly. "You're right, of course, but we can't do that here or now. We need to go—those people will come back." He held Tam's eyes for a moment, and the scientist eventually nodded.

By the time the three of them got their new supplies squared away, Marcia and the kids came out of the store with their own bags. Marcia also had one of the bandits' backpacks, stuffed full of supplies. Gabriel nodded to her and said, "Ripley, Sam, Travis, can all of you walk? We really can't stay here."

He went over to Ripley to help her stand if she could, while Marcia went over to assist Sam. When Ripley gained her feet, she winced in pain and then held onto Gabriel's arm for a long moment as her head cleared, her body pressed against him and trembling. Gabriel was flooded with what he assumed were protective endorphins, and the effect on him was both tender and almost overwhelming.

Eventually she stood up straighter and nodded. She dropped her arm from his and said, "I'm ready." Tam brought her a warm energy drink, which she accepted with a quiet thanks.

Marcia got Sam and Travis up, and Tam handed them both energy drinks as well. At last everyone was shuffling off in the direction Gabriel indicated, Ripley holding on to the handlebars of her bike as much to steady herself as anything else. Gabriel brought up the rear, glancing frequently over his shoulder at the road and the horizon behind them.

Though he was worried about being followed and murdered, his head was abuzz with Tam's theory.

"Evocation," he mouthed to himself, trying out the word. *All three of us can do magic!*

TWENTY—SEVEN

RIPLEY

Ripley's back ached with every shuffling step. No, not just her back—the pain went all the way through to her front. She kept thinking it was getting better, but it still wasn't what she would consider *okay*. At least stabs of agony no longer shot up and down her spine with every beat of her heart.

When she'd first stood up, her entire torso had throbbed angrily—from neck to nethers, as her grandmother would say—and she'd been so light-headed that she'd almost fallen over. There was no doubt that it *was* getting better.

As the pain slowly subsided, she was able to think more clearly about what had happened—how it had felt to focus her will on bringing Travis back, on taking his wound into herself. *How did I do that,* she wondered. *How is it possible? And even given that it clearly* was *possible, how did I know how?*

She shook her head in renewed amazement and watched as Travis walked along beside his mother on his own two feet, apparently none the worse for his experience.

She felt… *powerful.* Exhilarated. *She* had saved this boy. Not Gabriel or Tam or his mother. She had. She welcomed the pain—relished it, even. It was evidence, if Travis himself wasn't evidence enough, of what she had done. It was *real*.

Tam had called what she had done an *evocation* and likened it to the things Gabriel had done. Maybe that was true, but it didn't seem to capture it completely. It wasn't just 'calling into being' or whatever evocation meant by definition. It had felt specifically like a natural progression of her own experiences. As if she somehow wouldn't have been able to do it without having so intimately and thoroughly experienced such incredible anguish, depression, and even terror. She had taken control of those emotions—harnessed them and used them for what she wanted instead of being their object or victim. It felt *good*. Unbelievably so. That she could turn her absolute worst experiences and feelings—her parents, her life, her rape and abduction—into something so positive made her want to share that feeling with everyone who was hurting. It was like the cutting she did, but it actually *helped* people. It made her want to bounce off the walls and hug everything.

She smiled softly to herself, bemused by the warm glow of her feelings and the joy of finally feeling in control of her life.

"How are you doing, Ripley?" asked Tam.

She nodded. "I'm okay."

Once they were on Route 191, they made poor time for the next two hours—herself, Sam, and Travis all shuffling along like zombies. The breeze had picked up and cooled things down a little, which helped. They were heading into country that looked more like true desert, though there was a lot of scrub around. Red rocks were everywhere, with small mesas and ridges visible—off in the distance at first, but before long, the road was running right through them.

Gabriel tried to talk to Sam once, but the poor man appeared almost oblivious to what was going on around him, barely looking up and only slowly seeming to recognize Gabriel before responding with a monosyllabic grunt. At least he was still walking, though. Marcia's glare returned and Gabriel quickly took the hint that she wanted him to leave Sam alone.

During their first break, Marcia approached to ask if there was anything she could do to help Sam.

Gabriel walked over toward Sam as well, but Marcia held up her hand to stop him in his tracks.

"Please don't," she said. "He was getting better before he started walking with you."

Gabriel halted, obviously stunned, unable to formulate a response.

"I don't think you're doing anything to him intentionally," Marcia, "but I saw how you caught on fire when those men had us, and that fireball you made." She paused for a moment before she found her next words, seeming to be experiencing some kind of internal struggle. "Are you…" she began before stopping again and shaking her head.

Finally, she seemed to settle on what she wanted to ask. "Have you been irradiated or something?"

Gabriel's shoulders slumped. "Possibly," he admitted. "Probably."

She nodded, strangely satisfied. Her voice was flat and hollow as she continued, "I don't mean any offense, and I really do appreciate all that you've done for us, but I would prefer that you stay at least ten feet away from my family."

Ripley's eyes went to Gabriel's face, and Tam looked on as well. Miri pretended not to hear and concentrated carefully on eating a packet of trail mix, but Travis was clearly disappointed.

Gabriel looked back at Marcia and nodded, numbly. He turned, stiffly, and walked up the road a bit to stare off in the direction they had been traveling.

I'll need to talk to him later, Ripley thought. But for now, she just knelt over Sam, who lay panting on the ground with his eyes closed. She placed her hand, still pale white even after all this time in the sun, delicately on his ribcage and closed her eyes in concentration.

She could feel... something. She found her powerful emotions easily enough—they still haunted the recesses of her soul—but when she called them forth to try to use them, to direct them to absorb Sam's physical and mental pain, it was like they were scrabbling at a wall. Or maybe like trying to grow flowers in a desert. She sat there trying for several minutes, her eyebrows knitted in concentration, but eventually she sighed and sat back. She looked up and shook her head at Marcia.

"I can kind of *feel* that he's sick, but we already knew that," she said, frustration cracking her voice. "It's like his body is fighting itself instead of working to heal, and I... I can't get it to listen to me."

A tear escaped Marcia's eye and rolled down her cheek, but she just nodded as if that was exactly what she had expected to hear.

"I think he needs to make his body listen to *him*," Ripley said quietly, a little embarrassed to say such a thing out loud. She hoped that a night's rest would be just what Sam needed, but in her heart she feared it wouldn't be enough.

TWENTY—EIGHT

GABRIEL

S am died that night.
 A ragged, guttural wail woke the group just as the sky began to lighten in the east. Though it came from Marcia, it sounded almost inhuman, as if her throat were ripping itself to shreds. Gabriel was on watch, ruminating sourly on the idea that he could be considered dangerous or contagious, but before he could think of what to do, Marcia staggered out of the tent, clutching her two children to her legs, almost dragging them outside with her. They all staggered a few feet from the tent flap before falling to the dusty ground in a heap, clutching each other and sobbing. Little Miri struggled to get up and go back into the tent, but Marcia held her tightly, one arm wrapped around the girl's chest.

"Ripleeee," Marcia wailed, and Ripley came at a run, slipping inside their tent flap.

Gabriel exhaled, a lifeless weight settling on his chest as he slowly approached. Tam ran up and wordlessly held back the tent flap so they could all see.

Sam lay atop his sleeping bag, his eyes staring blankly at the tent ceiling, mouth ajar and his body completely still. Ripley clung tightly to the man's chest, her face pressed into the hollow of his neck, her own eyes screwed shut in concentration. She was still as death herself, and Gabriel shivered with a sudden fear that Ripley might kill herself trying to bring Sam back to life. He started to tell her to stop, but then held his tongue, knowing she wouldn't listen.

A small sound escaped Ripley—a cross between a grunt and a whimper—and Gabriel saw tears begin to trickle from her still-closed eyes. She adjusted her grip on Sam and bore down again, as if trying to move a mountain through desire alone.

After another few minutes of intolerably helpless waiting, she finally relaxed her grip and raised her head from Sam's chest.

"I can't get him back," she said, her voice bereft. "It's not working, like he's just not *there* anymore." She had spoken softly, but Marcia must have heard her nevertheless, because the woman began to wail anew, her cries now joined by Miri's piercing voice as well.

Gabriel blinked back tears as Ripley closed Sam's eyes with her fingers. He felt a terrible need to do *something*.

"Ripley," he said, "could you go up the hill and keep watch for us while we take care of Sam, please?" She looked up uncertainly, then nodded miserably and backed out of the tent.

He walked over to his pack and retrieved his folding camping shovel. He looked around for the least rocky ground he could find and immediately set to digging, not even allowing himself to think. Instead, he focused all of his energies on the task at hand. After a moment, Tam joined him, bringing his own camping shovel.

They dug for over an hour, pausing only to lever large rocks out of the ground and take the occasional drink of water. When they were finished, Gabriel glanced over at Marcia and the children. Marcia hadn't moved much and now lay supine in the dust, her eyes closed tightly. Miri lay across her body, pleading with her mother to get up, while Travis sat next to them, his face pale and glassy-eyed.

Gabriel stretched his worn-out muscles and tight back, then he and Tam went to pick up Sam's body. They slid him out of the tent and then carried him carefully to the grave, lowering him in as gently as they could.

Tam broke the silence, saying "Marcia, Miri, Travis, can you come say goodbye? Help us bury him?" The kids looked at their mother, who still would not move. Miri was the first to stand, whimpering pitiably as she did so, and then Travis got up as well. They walked slowly and somberly over to stand beside the grave. Tam glanced meaningfully at Gabriel.

Gabriel nodded. *We need some words.* Suddenly this was all happening too fast. Gabriel had thought that having a burial plan would give them all direction and allow them time to process and grieve, but now that the time had come to say their final farewells to Sam and leave him behind—it all seemed woefully brief and inadequate. *But what else can we do?* He sighed, gathering his thoughts as best he could.

"I didn't know Sam very long, "Gabriel began. "But I know he was a good man and a good father. He was kind, smart, and funny, and he will be sorely missed." He paused, searching for more words. "In the short time I knew him, we became friends. I wish I could have saved him somehow." He glanced over his shoulder at Marcia, who was still lying on the ground, though she was no longer crying aloud.

"We will never forget Sam, and we will always carry his memory with us. We will all live in part for him, and he in turn will now live through us—especially through his family." He remained silent for a moment, hoping that what he had said had made sense.

Miri grabbed Tam's hand and began to cry again—long, wordless sobs. They stood like that for a few minutes while everyone's tears flowed, then subsided, and dried in the arid desert air.

Gabriel stood in silence, wanting to let the Feldmans grieve for as long as they wanted. Inside, however, he was fighting sadness, anger, and a desire to get moving—to get back to their mission—until he felt like he was going to explode. Finally, he could hold it in no longer.

He bent down to pick his shovel back up, and he and Tam began to cover Sam's body. The children, quiet now, each brought stones to add to the grave. They were done almost too quickly, and then there was nothing left to do but pack up their things and go—if they could get Marcia to leave at all.

Gabriel stood quietly, contemplating the grave. "Goodbye, my friend," he said.

"Goodbye, abba," Miri echoed. Tam said goodbye as well, and Ripley, who had come down the hill for the ceremony, hugged the children. Travis couldn't speak, but bent down and hugged the mound of rocks and dirt for a long, silent minute.

After that, they drifted back to their tents and began putting things away, finding purpose, if not comfort, in the routine. Soon they were all ready for the road except for Marcia, who still lay motionless on the ground with her eyes closed. Gabriel saw the tracks of tears from the corners of her eyes, streaking across her ears and into her hair. She looked pale and sickly, and it occurred to Gabriel that she might be suffering from more than just a broken heart. He was about to go over to check on her when Miri ran to her mother and grabbed the woman's hand.

"Mama, we have to go—please get up," she said, her voice cracked and hoarse from crying. "We can't stay here."

Marcia's eyes opened and finally focused on her daughter's face. She sat up suddenly and clutched her daughter to her tightly.

"I'm okay, baby, I'm okay," she murmured into the girl's

hair as they both rocked back and forth, crying. They stayed that way for several minutes until Marcia finally relaxed her grip on her daughter and climbed haltingly to her feet.

Ten short minutes later, they and Travis were packed up and staring at the pile of rocks that marked Sam's grave. After a while, Gabriel spoke. He felt terrible and guilty for even suggesting it, but they had to move on—and not just for the sake of completing their mission. Their water would run out soon, too.

"Let's go," he said quietly, and began walking down the hill toward the road. To his surprise, everyone eventually followed him, the Feldmans trailing well behind, but plodding resolutely onward, their eyes downcast.

TWENTY—NINE

The group continued on in tortuous silence for the next three days, trudging west through the desert along Route 191. Ripley and Travis quickly returned to full health, and Gabriel stayed far away from the Feldmans. Their pace gradually improved from pitiful to slow. Gabriel ranged out ahead to scout, but even when he was with the group for meals and camp, he kept his distance.

In general, no one spoke much at camp; everyone seemed to be lost in their own thoughts. Even Miri was mostly quiet, staying close to her mother, though she did occasionally smile at Ripley. Travis seemed quieter than before—somber—but no more than was to be expected. He appeared to have come back from the dead without suffering any lingering effects. It was Marcia who was in the worst shape of the group. She spoke to her children only in terse, barely audible commands and completely ignored the others and her surroundings.

Meanwhile, Gabriel couldn't stop wondering whether he had contributed to Sam's death. He didn't think it was very likely, but Marcia's feelings on the matter were insidious. She hadn't said anything else to him about it, but neither had she spoken to him or allowed him within ten feet of her children.

He mulled over the timeline and how Sam had looked when Gabriel had been near him. *Surely, it's a case of correlation, not causation*, he thought. But how could he prove it? He could not. It was a miserable, guilt-ridden line of thinking from which he could not break free.

The weather didn't help any, either—it was brutally hot and dry during the day and cold every night. They tried, some of them in vain, to avoid getting burned by the sun, as they had used up almost all of their sunblock and were saving the last bottle for the children. Tam, Gabriel, and Ripley wore long sleeves, which helped some, though Gabriel's skin was becoming as dark as that of his abuelo, who had worked as a gardener all his life.

One morning, Tam approached him before they set off. "Is your skin getting darker?" he asked, with a strange furtiveness.

"Yes," Gabriel answered, somewhat confused.

"Like," Tam murmured, "from the particles or the fire?"

Gabriel's expression betrayed his confusion as he tried to make sense of what Tam was saying. Tam tried again. "Are you... *changing*?" The last word was almost a whisper.

Finally understanding what Tam was asking, Gabriel laughed out loud. The noise drew everyone's attention, so unexpected and unusual had it become for any of their group to laugh since Sam had died.

Gabriel quickly regained control of himself. "Are you asking me if my skin has gotten so much darker because I've been cooking myself with blue fire?" he asked, his voice dripping with incredulity.

Tam shrugged uncomfortably, but still looked questioningly at Gabriel.

"No!" Gabriel finally exclaimed. "My skin gets darker the longer I'm in the sun because I'm human. I'm only darker than you because I'm Mexican."

"You're Mexican?" Tam asked. Now he was the incredulous one.

Gabriel searched Tam's face to see if the man was joking, but could not discern the slightest hint of humor.

Gabriel arched an eyebrow in irritation. "Yes, I am a Mexican-American," he said with a patience he didn't feel. "My name is Rodriguez, for Christ's sake."

"Names don't mean anything," Tam mumbled stubbornly, but let the matter drop and turned back toward his bike, still muttering. Gabriel heard him say "I'm not Scottish" over his shoulder as he walked away.

Gabriel shook his head in wonder. Had it been anyone else, he wouldn't have believed they could be so clueless. But Tam? Maybe. Gabriel wouldn't put it past Tam to have achieved true post-racial consciousness through some combination of force of will and inattentiveness to things that didn't fit his highly rational worldview. Gabriel blew out a breath and walked to his own bike.

He rode off, pulling far ahead of the others, looking for signs of life and danger. The routine they had fallen into was to keep going until just after noon, then take a long siesta during the hottest part of the day, and then ride as late as possible before setting up camp. Gabriel itched at the lack of pace, but this was the best way he could think of to cover ground with this group.

On the third night after the bandit attack, Gabriel finally decided they could risk a fire if they were careful. That night they walked a mile or more off the road and around a small rise to ensure they were out of sight and hopefully far enough away not to be heard by anyone passing by. The ground here was hard and dry, which at least made it easier to walk their bikes. He used a branch from a scrubby bush to sweep their footprints away from near the road.

Once they had set up camp, the small blaze seemed to lift

the group's spirits considerably, blue though the flames were, and Tam broke the oppressive silence that had settled in by starting to sing. He began quietly, blue light dancing in his eyes. Gabriel had never heard him sing before, and his voice wasn't half bad, though it wandered a bit on its way to the notes. He sang some song about putting a birdhouse in your soul that Gabriel had heard before but couldn't remember where or when. Young Miri stared at Tam with rapt attention from across the fire and even smiled a couple of times. Marcia, holding Travis tightly, watched her daughter enjoy herself for those fleeting moments with a look of such intense hope that it hurt Gabriel to observe it.

Gabriel quietly joined in the chorus after hearing it a few times, trying to harmonize, and Ripley, who was sitting next to him, smiled, leaned over, and gave him a spontaneous, one-armed hug. Gabriel stiffened for a moment in surprise, but then hugged her back chastely around the shoulders, although he couldn't help but be incredibly conscious of her left breast, which was pressing against his side. Gabriel felt himself blushing, which was very unusual for him, and he laughed, half in surprise. Ripley laughed too as they released each other and straightened. Her laugh, so seldom heard, seemed all the more magical for its rarity. Gabriel experienced a sudden and unexpected arousal, as if he had just brought a date to park on Lovers Lane for the first time. He surreptitiously adjusted his posture to hide his erection and continued singing.

That night, as everyone settled down to watch the bluish, slowly dancing campfire, Gabriel thought about how beautiful and distracting Ripley was, with her long, silky hair, her flawless skin and fine features, and her lithe, healthy body. Lately he had found himself watching her instead of looking out for danger, and more than once he had caught himself daydreaming about her rather than thinking about their route and their needs.

During their breaks from the road, he concentrated on attending her softly spoken words, which were rare treasures, rather than listening for the sound of approaching danger. *In short, I'm getting distracted, and that's a problem*, he thought. He shook his head, trying again to banish her from his thoughts. He wasn't some teenager with a ridiculous crush—he had a mission. Hopefully they would soon find a safe place for Ripley and the Feldmans to stay. *And anyway, it's not like she has shown any interest in me*, he thought.

He arose from his position near the fire and went over to his pack, where he dug around until he found his roll of twine. He went to the edge of the camp and tied one end around a larger rock a few inches off the ground, then unwound the length around the rest of the camp, looping the string around the necks of a few empty water bottles they had kept. He anchored the tripwire around a couple of scrubby trees and another larger rock until the line encircled the entire perimeter. Empty cans would have been better than the plastic bottles, but unfortunately, they hadn't thought to keep any of those.

Once he was done, he turned to the others. "Everyone should go to the bathroom before bed while we still have the firelight—if you go in the night, be sure to step over the wire," he said. "I'll keep first watch, but then I won't wake any of you— I think we should be all right here."

The others nodded and each began their evening rituals. Gabriel thought they were doing better. Coping. It was good.

He thought he caught Ripley looking at him more than usual and gave her a small smile, which she returned before spitting out her mouthful of toothpaste. Somehow she made even that seem cute.

THIRTY

HAKK'RIX

The rival in the distance paused, peering through the gloom at the large group of prey making loud socializing noises at the entrance to their den.

Hidden at the edge of the roof directly above the animals, Hakk'rix suppressed its aura even further, standing as still as the large gray boulder beside it, which it had dragged painstakingly up here over three cycles ago.

The strange rival crouched and slunk forward, stalking the prey below. It certainly wasn't an Apex, but it was powerful and large. It had five long, spindly legs that tapered at the ends into whip-like, prehensile tentacles, which constantly twitched and quested around it, scraping dryly across the smooth, hard ground and mindlessly touching every surface nearby. It would have reach on Hakk'rix and was probably both stronger and faster. The tentacles could wrap around Hakk'rix's legs, though the serrated edges on Hakk'rix's armored appendages would help prevent it holding on for long.

Although the creature's maw was on the smaller side, it

looked strong enough to crack Hakk'rix's chitin if given the opportunity, and its soulspark was strong and thoroughly unsubtle. It smacked of a single note—hunger. No curiosity or caution. Hakk'rix's own hunger rose in response, and it suppressed its soulspark so as to not give itself away. It would kill and eat this one if it could. It had been a very long time since it had consumed a rival, and this trap had been something Hakk'rix had wanted to try for several sun-cycles, ever since it had found the strange prey-made web.

Hakk'rix could sense no other rivals nearby, which was not unusual—there was plenty of territory to spread out in, and abundant prey everywhere. Hakk'rix had chosen this spot for its vantage point over the large group of prey below, which had made a permanent settlement at the front of this building. From their foolish trust in their numbers and their tiny weapons to keep them safe, it seemed obvious that they had not yet been attacked by any rivals, but Hakk'rix had known it couldn't be long—they were too loud and numerous to go unnoticed forever. It was the perfect opportunity to lure and trap a truly enriching meal.

And now it was coming to pass, just as Hakk'rix had planned. The strange rival approached rapidly, barely keeping out of sight of its targets. It rounded a corner and immediately sprang into the throng of prey with a loud, disorienting chirp that added to the effectiveness of its ambush. Hakk'rix was far enough away to avoid the effect, but still it waited. *-One more moment-*

The rival, now about six body lengths below Hakk'rix, grabbed three, then four of the animals with its tentacle-tipped legs. Still Hakk'rix waited. Another prey animal shook its head and stumbled away past the rival's last remaining free leg, and the predator, unable to help itself, snatched the animal by the neck and dragged it backward to its doom. *-Predictable-*, thought Hakk'rix. All the other animals shook off their mental fog and bolted, scurrying away as fast as they could.

-*Now*-. Hakk'rix used three of its legs to throw the web it had found on a floating vessel tethered to a platform at the edge of a seemingly endless body of deep water. The web seemed perfect for catching prey, and Hakk'rix had conceived of this trap as soon as it understood what it was looking at. It had once encountered a rival long ago that had made its own webs by producing and weaving the material from its abdomen, and it had seen a few similar creatures in this place, though on a miniature scale.

The web unfurled as it fell, landing heavily across the entire body of the feasting rival, which gave a pulse of surprise that quickly turned to angry dismay. Hakk'rix scurried behind the boulder and pushed it off the edge of the building as well. It plummeted toward the rival, gaining tremendous momentum and smashing into its carapace, breaking rigid internal structures and opening the leathery flesh before bouncing off onto the hard ground. Hakk'rix wasted no time, stepping off the roof itself to follow in the rock's wake.

It sailed downward through the air and crashed on top of the damaged, entrapped rival, inflicting more pain on the dazed creature. Hakk'rix unleashed a massive jolt of disorientation and electricity into the opponent, hoping to prevent it from using any of its own abilities and also to identify the location of its nerve center. The creature convulsed and mewled, thrashing in the web and trying to release the captured prey to free its appendages. But the electricity still coursing through its body prevented it from relaxing its tentacles, and it only succeeded in entangling itself further in the web.

Meanwhile, Hakk'rix sensed the rival's nerve center, rich with powerful animus and desire despite the creature's stupidity and lack of caution. Hakk'rix wasted no time, seizing a firmer perch and pressing his searching maw against the perfect spot on the rival's body. It bit down hard, opening the flesh, then again, deeper than before. Then a third time, this time closing on the brain. The creature wasn't as juicy as those prey animals, but its soulspark was marvelously vivid and palatable, and as the rival finally began to panic and fear, the flavor grew into an orgiastic crescendo of sensation that began to flow into Hakk'rix's own soulspark as a torrent of ecstasy.

Hakk'rix soaked up the power as it fed on the creature's soft matter, and the rival quickly began to flag. The creature tried one last time to shake Hakk'rix off, using its final reserves of power to try to form a protective shield around itself, but with Hakk'rix already draining it, the effort fizzled and was overcome by Hakk'rix's own desire to eat. Hakk'rix was surprised that this rival had any defensive powers at all, however ineffective and untrained they might be.

After draining the rival entirely of its soulspark, a power-drunk Hakk'rix staggered off, not even bothering to eat the two prey animals still held fast in the rival's clenched tentacles and the web. The others must have gotten away during the struggle. Hakk'rix made its way unsteadily to a building some two hundred spans away, out of sight of the rival's corpse. It smashed through a tinkling clear wall and burrowed into the back, bringing down enough material around it to partially cover it up. Then, damping down its aura again, it fell into an uneasy slumber, distracted by a slew of strange and unrelenting visions and impressions that had begun to swirl through its mind.

After almost a quarter cycle of disorientation, Hakk'rix realized that these impressions were coming directly from the minds of other creatures, mostly prey, but also a different rival. After another quarter cycle, Hakk'rix had integrated this new power and gained some measure of control, rifling through the nearby minds of these alien beings as its own body recuperated lethargically. *It could read the minds of creatures from afar!* This would change everything—both hunting and defense. As

Hakk'rix examined the minds it could sense more closely, it gradually grasped that the distant rival it had detected wasn't a rival at all, but a prey animal, or something in between, something *becoming*. A curiosity, then. Something truly new.

It already knew that it must investigate this creature—learn about it. *What would it taste like?*

THIRTY—ONE

GABRIEL

By the next afternoon, they had finally reached Safford, a remarkably flat and one-storied town. They stopped just short of the first buildings, looking out for any threats or movement. The town began suddenly, random brown business premises sprouting like dry mushrooms along the roadside—a shocking change after the days they had spent traversing empty, dry plains. After only three or four small blocks of dirty, seemingly deserted-looking houses and buildings, they spotted a huge parking lot in front of an enormous, beautiful Walmart.

The group evaluated the scene from behind a scattering of deserted vehicles for a few minutes but couldn't see anything moving. Gabriel got off his bike and told the rest of the group to wait and hide while he scouted. He left his staff behind, but made sure his axe was loose on his belt.

He walked slowly—alert but not stealthy. As he passed the first few buildings, he peered in the windows, many of which were broken—though why anyone would want to loot a travel agency, for example, was a mystery to him. The auto parts store next door made more sense as a target, and Gabriel briefly wondered if there was anything in the store that might help them get a car started. He doubted it, but reminded himself to discuss it with Tam.

He walked over the curb into the Walmart parking lot, which had maybe thirty vehicles in it. Every car was empty, and there were no bodies to be seen, though several windows had been smashed in. Gabriel continued to the main entrance, where the sliding glass doors had been forced open slightly and hung askew against the relative darkness inside. He paused at the door and stood there silently for one, then two long minutes, listening intently for movement, but hearing nothing. Just as he began to move again, turning back toward his companions, an opossum waddled out of the store and scurried past his feet, hissing as it went. Startled, he smiled fiercely as his heart galloped for a moment.

After taking another minute or so to calm down, he squeezed through the broken sliding door and into the entryway of the store, stopping to listen again and taking off his sunglasses. The inner doors were open, and after a moment he walked through them as well, all the way in, until he was just past the cash registers. There was no movement or other sign of life.

He walked quietly along the entire width of the eerie store, looking down each aisle. He passed racks of batteries, assorted snacks, camouflage tank tops, control top pantyhose, and hot pink shorts. A lot of things had clearly been taken, particularly food, and unfortunately all the water, but there were no people around.

Walking back outside, he slipped his sunglasses back down over his now squinting eyes. He looked around the parking lot and the surrounding area, and seeing nothing amiss, finally signaled for the others to approach. They started toward him immediately. Marcia was even pushing Gabriel's bike, which made him smile for some reason.

When the others made it to the entrance, they huddled in the area between the inner and outer doors, bringing the bicycles into the shopping cart vestibule after forcing the doors open a bit further. Tam handed over Gabriel's staff.

"It seems clear," Gabriel began, "but it doesn't feel right—this stuff is too valuable and this place too obvious a target to be empty." He regarded their worried expressions. "Let's reprovision and get out of here quickly. Go pick up anything you need or want to replace. Gear, sleeping bags, weapons, clothes, and shoes. Then grab as much nutritious food as you can and some drinks if you can find them—but I haven't seen any water around. Remember, you may have to run with your bag, so don't let it get too heavy."

He paused long enough to see most of them nod in understanding. Marcia, however, wouldn't meet his eyes or acknowledge his suggestion.

"I'll wait here and keep watch at this door," he added. "There are probably other entrances that are open, so stay together, or at least with a partner, and keep your eyes open. You've got twenty minutes."

And with that, they were off. Tam grabbed a shopping cart and Marcia did the same. As they headed down the aisles on their free shopping spree, Gabriel could hear giggling—Miri and, oddly enough, Tam. Gabriel shook his head and went back outside to look out over the parking lot.

Nothing was stirring as far as he could see. He considered that he would be less conspicuous if he stood inside the outer doors, but then he couldn't see the corners of this side of the building, and he was more afraid of someone coming around the corner and catching them off guard than he was of drawing attention by being seen.

Fifteen or twenty minutes passed, and finally Tam came back out, slicing the last moldy edges off a block of cheddar with a pocket knife to expose the unspoiled cheese inside before taking a bite. He chewed thoughtfully, then nodded and smiled as he swallowed. "I can take over as lookout now if you want to grab some things inside," he said, his mouth still full.

Gabriel nodded. "Thanks."

Inside, Gabriel saw that Tam's shopping cart still had several things in it that he must have grabbed before deciding they were too heavy—or maybe Tam had grabbed extras for him or the others. Gabriel went through the items in the cart, selecting a pocketknife that was a twin to the one Tam was using, two packs of athletic underwear and socks, and the real find—another plastic-wrapped block of cheese that was almost mold-free.

He put these items in his own cart, then wound his way through the checkout lanes. He saw the Feldmans making their way back to the front of the store with their cart packed with far too many items—hopefully Tam could help them whittle their haul down a bit.

Gabriel decided that he would throw away pretty much all his dirty clothes and replace them—including the ones he was wearing. He had noticed scorch marks on two of his shirts where the flames from his skin had browned the fabric, making it brittle and scratchy. He made his way to the men's clothing section, imagining a cloud of dust emanating from him as he moved, like the Peanuts character Pigpen. He worked his way through the racks of men's clothes until he was surrounded by a wall of socks and underwear on one side and plaid button-down shirts on the other. He looked back toward the cash registers where he could hear the others, but his line of sight was completely blocked. Then, setting down his axe, he removed his belt, tomahawk, and knife, followed by his shirt, which was just as burned and filthy as he had feared. His sweaty undershirt was even worse. He dropped them in a new pile, farther away. His boots went into the keep pile, and then he put his pants, socks, and underwear into the discard pile. The air, which had seemed stagnant and close when he had first come in, now felt cool and refreshing on his bare skin.

He stepped over to the shirt rack and picked out the ugliest one to use to wipe himself down—a huge brown T-shirt that said, "Real Men Smell Like BBQ" and seemed to come pre-stained.

Starting with his face and hair, he worked his way down to his shoulders and arms. He scrubbed the shirt vigorously over his sweat-dampened skin, trying to clean himself with physical force in the absence of soap and water. He figured it was better than nothing, and there was certainly no shortage of ugly shirts here. He had already gotten the first one pretty dirty, so he threw it down next to him and grabbed another, starting at the top again and working his way down to his torso, undercarriage, and legs before finally sitting down on the first shirt and tending to each foot with the makeshift towel. The thought occurred to him, belatedly, that an actual towel probably would have worked a little better, but he was done now and already in the right place to change into fresh clothes.

He stood back up and wiped his armpits one last time, his skin tingling all over from the rough scrubbing. He turned his head toward the back of the store, thinking he had heard a sound, and saw Ripley.

She stood in the next department over, clearly visible between two racks of colorful women's shirts despite the dimness. Like Gabriel, she was completely nude, and was scrubbing herself down distractedly with a wet towel. He knew he should turn away, but her beauty was mesmerizing as she stood there, unselfconscious and full of vitality. From her sun-darkened neck, to her pale and perfectly smooth breasts with their pink areolas and erect nipples, to her tautly-muscled stomach and hip bones, to the fine blonde hair on her sex, to her long, athletic legs… she was *glorious*. Gabriel had never seen anyone or anything so beautiful. He felt his own body respond, his breath quickening and his cock immediately hardening into an erection so powerful that it ached with a wicked urgency.

Summoning all his willpower, he reminded himself of Ripley's vulnerability, her recent horrific experiences, and his mission. He began to turn away, but elbowed into some clothes hangers in his distraction.

Ripley's head shot up and she looked right at Gabriel, an expression of shock on her face as she hugged the towel to herself. Gabriel became intensely aware of his own nakedness, but resisted the urge to scamper behind the rack of shirts. Instead, he simply stood a little straighter and returned Ripley's now-unreadable gaze, which seemed to travel over every muscle and sinew of his body and everything else as well. She didn't turn away, though. Gabriel thought the corners of her mouth might be turned up in the hint of a smile, but at this distance he had to admit that could be wishful thinking. He turned to pick up and open a package of underwear. He drew out a pair and stooped to put them on, stuffing his eager and conscienceless penis uncomfortably into them, pointing down against his leg. He glanced up at Ripley, who was still looking at him, now wrapped in her towel. She was definitely smiling as she waved lightly and darted back farther into the women's section, her thighs flashing as she went.

Gabriel shook his head, clearing it of what already seemed like some kind of dream. He sighed, wondering whether he should feel guilty, and what, if anything, she had meant by ogling him back like that, before giving himself over to the task of finding replacement clothes that wouldn't make him look too silly. His erection, however, was very slow to subside.

He finished outfitting himself with decent-enough clothes

and was making his way through the rest of the store looking for anything else that might be of use when he heard Tam's shout. Gabriel ran to the front of the store, axe in hand.

Tam motioned him toward the front door, and he went and stood just inside it. The women stood nearby, geared up and ready to go, including Ripley, who gave him a very subtle smile. Or so he thought.

"We've got company," Tam said, pointing out across the parking lot. Gabriel shielded his eyes before remembering his sunglasses and putting them on. He didn't see anyone at first, but then he spotted movement. A man stood behind a car in the street outside the parking lot, with a pair of binoculars trained on them. A woman was standing beside him, and two boys were running in the other direction, toward town. Gabriel guessed they were on their way to get reinforcements.

"We need to get out of here now," Gabriel said. "We should get bikes for the Feldmans and ride away before more of them come."

Tam motioned nonchalantly behind them, pointing to the three additional bicycles. Gabriel nodded in appreciation.

"Okay, good. Marcia, your job is keeping your family together and moving as fast as they can. Tam and Ripley will ride ahead and find a safe path—we want to head west eventually, but any place that looks safe will do for now. I'll ride at the back and deal with anyone who gets too close. No one stops for me—I'll catch up."

Everyone nodded and went to their bicycles. Once the Feldmans were ready, Tam and Ripley rode out through the doors. The Feldmans followed, and Gabriel went last. As he cleared the doors, he looked for the people watching them and saw that they had both walked forward. Each had weapons on their hips—machetes from the looks of them—but both had their hands free and seemed to mean no immediate harm. The man was shouting at Tam and Ripley, who, instead of riding away as Gabriel had instructed, were pulling up and stopping about twenty yards shy of the strangers. The Feldmans and Gabriel quickly caught up, Gabriel looking all around in case this was a trap. The man and woman both looked healthy and friendly, dressed less like road warriors and more like people about to do their Saturday chores, but you couldn't be too careful.

"Hulloooo!" the man yelled again. He looked fit and seemed to be in his fifties. He had an anchor tattoo, which was partially exposed under the short sleeve of his shirt. "Where y'all from?"

His accent was out of place here—he sounded like he was from the Southeast—maybe North Carolina.

Tam replied, "New Mexico! Up around Betelgeuse, about a week's ride northeast of here." Gabriel wasn't sure it was a good idea to tell everyone where they were from, but it was done now.

The man shrugged absently. "I don't know whereabouts that is, but that ain't saying much." He glanced at the woman, who nodded—apparently confirming the existence of such a place. Her eyes were on Marcia, the kids, and Ripley.

The man turned back to the group. "My name's Bill, and this here is Susan. I know trust is in short supply these days, but we've set up a little community where people who act like they're supposed to and try to avoid violence are welcome. We got hot meals, some real beds, and safety. Perimeter security. Plus, we've got intelligence about the surrounding roads and areas—which could be important, seein' as how there are gangs of folks who've done went crazy to the west of us, including downtown here—people indulging in whatever dark whim strikes 'em." He paused. "All we ask is that you behave like your parents taughtcha and supply any information you got—we haven't had many people come in from the east yet."

Marcia had her hand on Miri's shoulder, and Gabriel saw her take half a step toward the strangers before looking over her shoulder at Gabriel. It sounded like a risk worth taking—possibly the solution he had been hoping for, so he gave a slight nod. It didn't feel like a trap. At best, it would be a safe place to leave the Feldmans—and Ripley, though the idea of leaving her behind caused Gabriel a sudden and surprising pang of disappointment.

Tam turned back to the couple. "That sounds good to us. We prefer to avoid violence ourselves. But we want to hang on to our weapons, gear, and bicycles."

The man and woman smiled at each other. He nodded and said, "That sounds fine—pretty much everyone is armed these days, at least outside the camp, even some of the kids." Gabriel saw Miri shoot her mother a look of delight at the mention of other children, and Marcia nodded back.

Bill came forward and shook Tam's hand, then everyone else's. When he finally got to Gabriel, his smile faded just a little, and the handshake was very firm and a little longer than necessary. Gabriel assumed that he must look more like trouble than the others. He smiled, trying to look reassuring but not obsequious, which probably didn't work, because the man snorted softly before turning to address the group. "If y'all are ready, let's head back to the village—it'll be dark soon and we try not to be out and about too much at night. Things go bump in the night."

Gabriel found the comment odd and worrisome. He wondered if they had seen any of the creatures here. He assumed not—at least not up close, since the man and his community were still here, but he wanted to ask them about it.

As Bill led them south, just inside the edge of town, he told them that the downtown area was controlled by a gang and wasn't safe for anyone, even in numbers. He also explained that his community claimed this side of town and that they patrolled it during the day. There were more of them than of the bandits, and they'd even had some deserters from the bandits join them.

"Which is all well and good," Bill continued. "There's more than enough on this side of the town to support us for as long as it takes—or, frankly, forever if the lights never come back on. We've got the Walmart, another little grocery store, a seed store, and the biggest water tank in town other than the municipal one, both of which we're plannin' on hookin' up to if things don't get better soon."

"So nothing works here either?" Gabriel asked.

The man shot him an appraising look, then shook his head. "No, and it's the damnedest thing, begging your pardon, ladies. A few of us are purty good with cars, and we've tried to get a couple older vehicles going that don't rely on anything electric, and they still won't run. We can't figure any reason for them not to work." He paused and shook his head. "We've had a lot of talk over what caused all this, but no real answers."

Gabriel and Tam exchanged a quick glance while Bill looked out over the road ahead. "Anyway," he continued, "our little community would love to hear your stories and share what information we have." He pointed ahead and said, "Here we are."

Set in the center of the sparse, partially developed industrial park they had entered was a vast, fenced-in parking lot fronting a large, two-story office building and warehouse. Off to one side was a small surface water pond that probably used to have a fountain in the center. On top of the building was a huge water tank and what Gabriel assumed was a rainwater catcher. A row of porta-potties stood along the fence line on the opposite side of the pond.

Gabriel whistled. "That's a pretty great setup you got there, Bill," he said. "And you set it up fast."

Bill smiled. "Thankee kindly," he said. "When we were worried the power might not come back on, me and a couple of others figured this'd be a good place to wait it out for as long as it took. We came for the water and the porta-potties, but the fence has come in real handy. If we're stuck here for more than another couple of weeks, we'll come up with a way to build some partitions for individual apartments. People keep turning up." He glanced at Gabriel and his group. "We go out and look for folks and offer them a place to rest—there's safety in numbers these days."

As they approached the fence, which was topped with barbed wire in places, the gate rolled open with a screech. A few men with hatchets at their belts and hunting bows propped next to their lawn chairs stood by, ready to close it again. Gabriel paused at the gate and scanned the encampment for signs of anything sinister—he didn't want to be stuck inside if this was some kind of trap. There were people working on some hand pumps attached to hoses that ran down into the pond and a few others tending to a large roasting spit over a good-sized fire built in a makeshift fire pit right in the middle of the parking lot. A small group of children were playing nearby, running from one group of adults to the next in what looked like a modified game of tag. Gabriel heard their laughter and saw one of the men working the pumps smile paternally at the children.

"Good enough for me," he said, half to himself, and walked his bike and cart inside the gates, followed by the others.

"Philip, Jose, this is Gabriel, Tam, Marcia, Travis, Miri, and... I'm sorry, young lady, I didn't catch your name," Bill said, indicating them each in turn to the guards at the gate. Ripley looked up, hesitated, then said, "Ripley." She flashed a grin at Gabriel and Tam and they both smiled back at her.

Bill smiled too, not quite getting the joke, but said, "Ripley it is then. These two are Philip and Jose, on guard duty today— we try to keep two or three stalwarts patrollin' the fence at all times, though in truth the downtown folks have only been out here in force once and we chased them back out of this side of town.

"You're free to come and go just as you please durin' the day," he continued. "But the gate stays locked at night. Supper will probably be served soon, and you can see how many of us there are. Then we'll talk. For beddin' down, y'all can pitch your tents inside in the loading dock or in the parking lot—wherever you feel more comfortable. The ground is hard in either place, I'm afraid. If you stay a while, we might be able to scare up some mattresses and maybe squeeze you into an empty office inside," he said, gesturing toward the central edifice.

"Thank you," said Marcia, her voice choked. "Thank you so much." She gathered herself and fought back her tears as best she could.

Bill came over and put his hands on her shoulders. "You're all welcome here as long as you want, and you should be safer here than anywhere else I know of. Seems like a lot of folks went crazy when the lights went out, but we got a couple of cops here, a few who served this country in the military, and two or three fellers who always liked to be prepared for anything. Plus the families who survived the sickness and quite a few stragglers. There are already nearly fifty of us. We've all lost people here, but the Good Lord willin', the rest of us will survive."

With what looked like a tear in his own eye, Bill turned away and began walking toward the large cookfire. "Now, let's see about supper!"

THIRTY—TWO

That night they sat around one side of a crowded fire eating the most delicious food they had tasted in a long time—weeks, perhaps, though it was becoming difficult to remember the everyday life of before. Even the fire didn't seem quite as blue, though perhaps it was just all the happy faces around it that made it seem more normal. The remaining Feldmans still kept a distance between themselves and Gabriel, but their relief at finding apparent safety was obvious even from afar.

Dinner that night was a plate of some kind of juicy rotisserie-style meat and green beans. They even had salt, and Tam accepted an offer to use one man's bottle of A1 sauce, although the meat didn't really need it.

"It's the principle of the thing," declared Tam, sounding half-drunk on good food and safety. "I'm doing it because I *can*—I don't even like A1 sauce!" Gabriel heard a man laugh good-naturedly.

Once the food had been distributed, everyone was quiet for a while, even the kids. Then, as some folks finished eating, Bill or one of the others who seemed to have influence here would take turns talking about their plans—more mattresses, putting up structures in the parking lot, the food choices they had for tomorrow, and more. Susan, the woman they had first met with Bill, suggested that the community formalize some kind of temporary school program for the children. Apparently, most of the children were already grouped together during the day while the adults worked, although some of the older ones acted as gatherers and runners alongside their elders. Susan was a high school science teacher, and the others generally agreed that she should be the one to set something up. Some of the children complained about this plan, but they were quickly overruled. A sense of community and civic responsibility positively radiated from both Bill and Susan, and Gabriel decided that they were the reason this place was the way it was, while so many others he had encountered elsewhere had given in to their baser impulses. Bill and Susan were giving all these people a purpose and providing them with the framework they needed to create something decent. People stuck out there, alone, surrounded by death and predation, were reacting to that. This community was a quintessential light on the hill.

After the talk of day-to-day plans had died down, Bill turned to a couple of kids, both with the tanned skin and almost black hair that indicated a similar ancestry to Gabriel, and asked them to tell their story. They had been living in Pearce, due south of Safford, when the lights went out, and had only just arrived the day before.

"Almost everyone got sick real fast," said the more talkative one, whose name was Lucia. Gabriel guessed her age at thirteen. "By the third day, my family was all dead. Angel's, too," she added, nodding at her friend.

"We knowed each other since we were kids," Lucia said. "We spent the first few days hiding in my house, waiting for the power to come back on and the government to show up. We didn't know what to do." She swallowed, then continued more quietly. "Two days after my tío died, we ran out of food in the house, so we decided to sneak over to the grocery store. It was only three blocks away." She paused again, and Bill encouraged her to continue.

"Well, we seen five or six people from one of the gangs there. It figures that they would be the only other people left alive," she said with a cynicism that was beyond her years. "And they had crowbars and bats, so we hid behind some cars, hoping they would leave. But they didn't leave for a long time. Two of them were out in the parking lot, busting car windows just for fun. The others were in the store—maybe they were living there, I don't know." She was trembling now, and the whole community was focused intently on her story.

"We had been waiting maybe over an hour—it's hard to tell—watching from across the street, when we saw the *demonio*." She looked up and around at her audience. "I know it sounds crazy," she said. "But we both saw it. This monster, covered in blood. It run up to them faster than anyone, on all fours like a bull or something. It had huge horns, like one of those boy sheep. At first I thought maybe it was a chupacabra, but that's not real, right?" She looked around, as if hoping someone would agree, but no one said anything, and she continued reluctantly.

"When it got close to the cholos, it stood up like a man, and it was way tall. Like eight feet maybe. Maybe more." Her voice was breathy, almost panting. "When it stood up, it grabbed one of those dudes and ripped his throat out with its teeth! So fast. The other guy hit the thing with his bat, but it turned and killed him, too. It was over so quick, you know? The thing just started eating them, then rolled over on top of them, there was blood and stuff all over..." She stopped short, looking at some of the younger children who were listening in stunned horror, then continued.

"Then the others in the store must have saw it and made

some noise, because the thing took off toward the doors and went inside. It had to crouch down to fit inside the door." She paused again. "Angel hit me in the shoulder—I was so scared I didn't hear him shouting—and we took off running. We ran all the way home, packed a bag, then we ran some more—away from that thing. We spent that night in a van, and the next day we kept going as fast as we could. We got here yesterday. It seems like a dream now, but it happened just like I said." She swallowed hard, looking defensive, as if she expected not to be believed. "We in the end times, man!"

She stopped and looked around, meeting looks of horror from some and incredulity from others. Bill gathered his thoughts for a second, his bushy eyebrows knitted over his dark eyes.

"Thank you for your story, Lucia. It's quite a tale—I haven't known you very long, but I don't think you're the type to make up stories," he said.

"I told you!" someone behind Bill said in a stage whisper, but whoever it was fell silent when Bill glanced backward. A few in the group looked around worriedly, but many others shook their heads in disbelief or began to smile indulgently.

Gabriel decided to speak up even though he hadn't planned to. "We saw something similar," he said, almost grudgingly, into the silence before anyone else spoke. It was hard to talk about these crazy things, but now that he had the chance, he realized that he really, really wanted to. "A couple of them. And I heard from a police officer that she had seen another one, different from the ones Tam and I saw."

All eyes turned to him, waiting. So, he launched into an abbreviated version of their journey, skipping the lab and their role in the event that had kicked all of this off and ending with the demon in the school. That he described in all its unnatural detail, but he left out the fact that they had killed it, instead implying that they had seen it from farther off and then slunk away. He wasn't quite sure why he left that information out. It might give some of these people heart to know the creatures could be killed, but he wasn't even sure how he had managed it and he thought that hiding and running was the tactic of choice against these things. Tam took his cue and described a few things about the creature that Gabriel had left out, but didn't correct the story. They both left out the fact that Ripley had been there at all.

When they were done with their abridged tale, there was a moment of silence. No one was shaking their head now, at least, although Gabriel doubted that everyone believed them. Bill eventually spoke up, saying, "Thanks Gabriel, Tam, and thanks again Lucia. Very disturbing indeed." He paused again, clearing his throat, and looking out over all the frightened, expectant faces.

"I have never seen one of those things, but I believe you. We've heard tell of such creatures from a couple of others, too. There's even a rumor that the group downtown captured one. All I can say is that we're making this place as safe as we can. The fence goes all the way around, and we patrol it day and night. We've got fifty-odd people armed to the teeth and willing to fight for our little patch of land and the people on it. Lord only knows if it will be enough, but we're gathering more all the time, and we're doing everything we can think of."

He looked around at the group and nodded to himself. Gabriel thought the speech had done the trick, reassuring most of the worried faces.

Bill turned to Gabriel's group and spoke again. "I promised information about the roads out of here in exchange for your stories. I assume you all were headed west." Gabriel nodded and Bill continued. "If you mean to continue that way, we've had a few people come here all the way from Phoenix and I'd advise you to avoid it. Too many people and not enough water, plus they said the entire downtown area was on fire." He glanced at two or three members of the circle, who each nodded glumly.

"So many desperate people means danger—some people will take what others have by brute force," Bill continued grimly. "If'n you do go west regardless, we recommend you head north through the desert from here and then cut west after a day or so. The ground is rough in places, and you probably won't be able to ride over some of it, but at least you'll avoid the roads through town here. We think the gang in town probably has about thirty people, most of them desperate or depraved, and they are not shy about taking whatever they want at the point of a knife. They've looted every sharp item in town that we didn't already have, and they pretty much own all of downtown and the roads out to the west." He looked at Marcia and Miri and added, seemingly reluctantly, "We hear they take women and girls captive when they can. Not fellers you want to have any truck with, I reckon. A few folks have made it through to our side of town without running into them, but I wouldn't risk it if I were you."

He looked at each of them in turn, then spoke again. "I'd propose that you all stay with us. We'll put you to work, true, but we'll feed you and shelter you, and you'll be safer here than in any other place I know of."

Marcia spoke up, her eyes fixed on Bill. "My children and I would like to stay." Gabriel was relieved to hear that. He couldn't think of a better place to end up right now.

"You and yours are welcome here," Bill said simply.

Miri made a noise and ran to Ripley, threw her arms around Ripley's neck and said, "Can you stay with us, too? *Please*?" Ripley didn't say anything, but seemed to give in to the child's enthusiastic hug-tackle, smiling and hugging her back. Gabriel was glad, but also undeniably disappointed. He had been hoping... but that was ridiculous.

"Well, that's settled then," Bill said, smiling at the girls. Then he turned expectantly to Gabriel and Tam.

Gabriel shifted uncomfortably. "Tam and I need to head on tomorrow," he said.

Bill looked them both over, then nodded somberly. "Well, if that's how it is, that's how it is, but I'll ask you again tomorrow and hope you've changed your minds," he said with a wink before turning back to the group.

"Okay, enough glum talk for one night—let's relax and enjoy being alive and together." Bill stood slowly, his knees popping loudly enough for Gabriel to hear over the sound of the fire. "I, however, am old and going to bed. Goodnight, all!"

He retreated to the sound of a few dozen "goodnights." Gabriel wanted to stay up and enjoy the company, but he was exhausted. He supposed that was a rational response to the relative safety they found themselves in after spending so long constantly looking over one shoulder, and certainly to eating real food for the first time in what felt like an eternity. He got up and waved to Tam and Ripley. Tam waved back but seemed content to sit by the fire. Ripley was listening raptly to Miri, who was talking to some older children. Gabriel couldn't help but notice two or three young men nearby who seemed to be lurking around trying to find a casual way to approach Ripley.

With that deeply uncomfortable thought, he walked back to his tent on the other side of the parking lot. He unzipped it and backed in, taking off his boots and putting them in the corner before zipping the tent shut behind him. He was relieved that Ripley and the Feldmans were finally safe, but the thought of leaving Ripley behind brought a twinge of anticipatory longing.

THIRTY—THREE

TAM

When Tam awoke, his sleep-addled mind struggled momentarily with the sounds he was hearing. It dawned on him like a revelation that it was *people*—a community—waking up and beginning their daily interactions. He grinned drinking in the muffled but glorious sounds of morning greetings and breakfast conversations as he crawled out of his sleeping bag and pulled on his hiking boots. The smell of food made his stomach rumble so loudly and sharply that he laughed softly to himself. He scooted out of his tent and stood up, looking around to soak it all in. The same cookfire from the night before was still burning, now with a pot hanging over it and a man stirring it and adding something from a bag. He stirred again and tasted it, then dished out a bowl to a teenager standing nearby. *Could it be grits?*

As he crossed the parking lot to investigate, he heard a voice call out from behind him. "Tam!"

He turned and smiled at Bill. "Good morning," he greeted the older man.

"Mornin'!" Bill replied enthusiastically. "Are you and

Gabriel going to stay with us for a while? We'll feed you and put you to work, but nothing too difficult, don't worry." He said the last with a wink. Tam liked the man—he seemed to radiate positivity and organization. More importantly, it wasn't right to accept someone's hospitality and not pitch in to help. It was *impolite*, and in his mind, there was no greater transgression.

"I'll talk to Gabriel about it—I guess we could stick around for a day and help out," he responded, hoping Gabriel would be of the same opinion—but surely Gabriel would agree that they couldn't just take and not give back.

"Great! Go grab some food. Once you and Gabriel have eaten, you can join Jose and those others over there," he pointed vaguely toward the fence to the left of the gate they had come in the night before. "They're reinforcing the rest of our fence with some barbed wire—they've got some extra work gloves and cutters and everything you'll need."

Tam smiled and nodded distractedly, eying the breakfast table again. Bill clapped him on the back before moving off to a group of three women and a teenage boy standing in a circle discussing one project or another. Tam could see how this group of people had accomplished so much so quickly. Bill was a natural leader. He shook his head to clear his mind and walked over to the man stirring the pot of what most certainly smelled like grits, although it might have been oatmeal. The man handed Tam a bowl, responding with a gruff "Yer welcome" when Tam offered his thanks.

It was a little gelatinous, and Tam still couldn't tell exactly what it was, but it was hot, filling, and delicious. After a while, he found himself wondering if it could do with a little salt, but then realized that he was already almost done.

Just then he saw Gabriel, who was himself approaching the breakfast table, and Tam walked over to stand in line beside him.

"Good morning!" he exclaimed, and Gabriel nodded in

response, his intense gaze sweeping over the place and taking in everything in turn. *Probably looking for threats,* Tam thought.

"Bill asked us to stick around for a day and do some work here," he said.

Gabriel gave him a sideways glance. "Is that right?"

Tam grinned. "We're on fence reinforcement duty after breakfast," he announced, unable to keep the excitement out of his voice. He'd never worked with barbed wire before and was looking forward to the experience.

Gabriel frowned but didn't immediately object. "I don't like waiting another day, but it would be good to check the fence and get the lay of the land. I'd like to know a bit more about how safe and stable things really are before we leave Ripley here... and the Feldmans," he added belatedly.

They each stepped forward in turn and received a bowl of the morning's concoction along with a small bottle of orange juice, which Tam hadn't seen his first time through.

Tam walked over to a bare patch of pavement and sat down cross-legged. Gabriel followed, sitting down smoothly beside him.

"This is good," Gabriel said, savoring a bite of what Tam had decided was actually porridge.

"Yeah, I thought so," Tam said. "This is my second helping."

"I figured," Gabriel offered. "My keen powers of observation noticed that you were holding a dirty bowl when you joined me in line," he added dryly.

"That *is* unusually observant of you," Tam said absently as he looked around the camp, taking in the sights and sounds of the little society. Pretty much everyone seemed to be up and about now. The line for food was already longer than it had been. He saw Marcia and the kids emerge from their tent. They had set up quite a ways away from Gabriel and Tam last night, but still within sight.

Marcia looked much better than she had in days. Her eyes searched the camp until she saw Gabriel and Tam, then she gave a small wave but didn't smile.

"She's a tough woman," Gabriel said, and Tam nodded.

"That she is," Tam said. "Not the friendliest, but I do like her."

"Do you think being around me, or us, could have made Sam sicker?" he asked.

Tam chewed a bite and squinted at Marcia, thinking. "It's hard to say for certain," he began. "There's not nearly enough data—he could have gotten sicker for any number of reasons."

Gabriel was about to respond in agreement, but Tam continued.

"That being said, it stands to reason that we may have received a larger dose of those particles than anyone else, and we don't know if they were dispersed uniformly or concentrated in pockets or if it was lumpy and localized. It also seems possible, if not likely, that exposure to the new particles may have caused the sickness we've seen—directly or not." He paused to think. "And the degree and localization of your… *unusual* effects suggest that you may be a greater locus for them." He paused. "So, I'd say it's a decent working theory, but with a very low degree of certainty."

Gabriel's face turned sour. "So, your decent working theory is that being around the two of us might cause people to become sick, or sicker?" He said this as something between a question and a restatement, failing to keep the flatness and dismay out of his voice.

Tam shrugged. "Like I said, it could be anything—it's far from certain that we're still saturated and radiating, or even that the particles we've detected are actually responsible for any of this rather than being a symptom of something else. If there's a physics model that adequately explains the effects we've observed, I can't imagine it yet. We need more data."

Gabriel nodded glumly. He lowered his voice. "Someone in our organization had a model that predicted and enabled mass pairing of particles at a distance, though—there may be more to that work."

Tam had considered that, of course. "Ainsley could have a theory that envisions some of this," he admitted.

"Maybe she or her team could help us figure out how to fix it," Gabriel murmured, his voice so full of naive hope that it was almost a whine.

"I doubt we can put the toothpaste back in the tube," Tam began, but Gabriel cut him off, low and insistent.

"But it might be possible, and anyway, we have to try. We need to get our data to her, if she's still alive, even if we have to ride our bikes all the way to LA." His voice wavered, as if pleading for some modicum of support or agreement.

Tam just nodded. His willingness to go was not an issue—he would ride a bike to LA for no other reason than because it would have been so completely unimaginable a few weeks ago. It was a real adventure. But there was no fixing this, he felt sure, and his role in this suffering and death was a sour and painful cancer that he was always aware of, lurking just beneath the surface. Another reason he had to go to LA was that his parents and brother all lived near there, if they still lived at all. He would need to visit them and be there to help his mom with his brother, who was... difficult even at the best of times. *There's no way Ryan is gone—he's far too stubborn to die.* The thought might have been wishful thinking, but it also just seemed *right*.

They sat in uneasy silence for a moment, finishing their orange juice and watching the rest of the community go about their business.

"Did I mention that I volunteered us for manual labor?" Tam asked.

Gabriel made a face, but seemed happy enough with the

change of topic. "Well, I was planning on ordering Indian food and watching TV all day, but I guess I can squeeze some manual labor into my schedule."

"That's good," Tam said. "Manual labor builds character."

"That must be why all our most respected public figures are ditch diggers," Gabriel responded dryly.

"There's no accounting for public taste," Tam rejoined, "but I once met a ditch digger whom I respect more than anyone else I've ever known."

Gabriel turned to face Tam, disbelief plastered across his face. "Bullshit."

"It's true," Tam said. "His name was Bud, and he worked for Santa Clara County doing road construction. He had dual degrees in economics and philosophy from Stanford and had worked for a consulting firm before making a conscious decision to leave that life and work for the public—improving roads, controlling erosion, and maintaining public land. He had achieved true happiness, lived free of self-doubt, and his labor definitively added value to the world. He-"

"He burned out and dropped out of a high-pressure career to do mindless, low-value manual labor," Gabriel finished. "As anyone could do. Like the main character in the movie Office Space."

Tam's brow wrinkled. "I'm not familiar with that movie, but I don't think you're fully grasping the intentionality of his choice, or the beauty of truly pursuing the impossible dream of a perfectly lived life."

"I apologize for casting aspersions on Saint Bud," Gabriel replied, the corners of his mouth turning up involuntarily. "I'm sure he was an interesting guy."

Tam opened his mouth to agree, but Gabriel cut him off by pointing to a group of people gathered around a large pile of barbed wire rolls.

"Is that where we're supposed to report to?" It was a blatant attempt to distract Tam from explaining why he respected Bud, but Tam allowed it. You couldn't *force* people to learn things that didn't fit their world view.

"Yes, I imagine so."

"Well, let's get on with it," Gabriel said, apparently warming to the idea now that he'd had some breakfast.

They took their dishes to the washing station and then strode over to the fence repair crew.

A man looked over at them—Tam thought it might be Jose, whom they had met yesterday, but he wasn't sure enough to use the man's name. The fellow was tall and thin, and his skin was slathered with white, greasy streaks of sunscreen.

"Good morning," he said cheerily. "Here to help with the fence?"

Gabriel nodded. "Good morning, and yes, we are," he said.

The man smiled. "Great!" He pointed to a small pile of gloves, some of them thick and elbow-length, which lay next to several huge bundles of barbed wire.

"You guys are going to string this through the top of the fence all the way around the compound to discourage climbing."

Gabriel sighed loudly, which Tam found a little embarrassing. It *was* a big compound, but that was a fair price for a good breakfast, he reasoned.

But then Gabriel looked the man in the eyes and nodded. "We'll get to it."

"Good man!" Jose said with a grin.

THIRTY—FOUR

GABRIEL

When Gabriel woke up the following day, their second morning in camp, he lay there for a while listening to the now surreal sounds of humanity stirring. The noises already seemed so strange to him after their time on the road, and he worried that he would never hear them again when he and Tam got back on their way.

He crawled out of his tent and looked around. A man and a woman toiled over the cooking fire, which the community kept going even through the night. They had hung the huge pot over the fire again and were taking turns stirring something in it with the biggest wooden spoon Gabriel had ever seen. Periodically, one or the other would dish out a bowl of what looked like cheesy macaroni. Gabriel watched one young man take a bowl and then squirt a generous quantity of spray cheese onto it. Gabriel wasn't normally a fan of canned dairy products, but his stomach seemed to have other ideas.

He made his way over to the food and was greeted with smiles and a warm bowl of noodles, along with a lukewarm mini-bottle of V-8 juice. He even added a little spray cheese himself. *When in Rome*, he thought.

He picked up a plastic spoon and walked over to a curb to sit in the sun, which was already warming the air nicely after a chilly night. He took his time eating, enjoying the still novel feeling of relaxing in relative safety. He hadn't quite finished his breakfast when Tam joined him. They sat in companionable silence while Tam worked on his meal. After a few minutes, Gabriel looked sideways at his companion. "Did you make the acquaintance of any nice local ladies last night?"

Tam shrugged. "It wouldn't be hard," he said. "It's like math camp out here, and we're the new kids. If we stayed, I think we would do pretty well in the acquaintance department." He paused, reflecting. "Though, from a sentimental perspective, I think all the single people here are only recently single, if you know what I mean. Right now, most of them seem to want to talk about their dearly departed ex-lovers. I'm not sure they're even aware of the evolutionary biology that inspires their social cues— reaching out eagerly for new connections. But sexual urges are part of our animal brains; I prefer to operate from my rational mind."

Gabriel shook his head quietly to himself. Tam certainly was… unique. He let the matter drop, not wanting to defend the rationality and appropriateness of physical attraction. Instead, he said, "Unless this breakfast obligates us to do more work, I think we should get back on the road. We've got to get this data to Ainsley."

"Aye aye, Cap'n," Tam said gravely.

Gabriel paused and Tam looked at him, aware that Gabriel wanted to say something more. Finally, Gabriel spoke.

"I'd like to tell Ripley about our mission and why we have to leave."

He wasn't sure if he expected Tam to argue or shrug, but the man surprised him by smiling broadly instead.

"It's about time!"

Gabriel hesitated, then said, "Okay, I'll go do that now."

"Okay then," Tam said, still grinning.

He found Ripley easily enough, as she was already making her way to the breakfast line after checking on Marcia and the kids.

He led her toward the side fence, away from the others and into what passed for privacy here. Then he turned to her, searching for the words to explain it all properly. Nothing immediately came to mind—he really should have thought about this ahead of time—but he started talking anyway.

"Ripley, Tam and I have to leave."

She nodded gravely and continued to look at him, her big, beautiful eyes blinking once as she waited for him to continue.

"Um," he said. "We have to go because we have a mission."

Still she said nothing, and Gabriel couldn't blame her, as he hadn't yet told her anything she didn't already know. *Why is this so hard?*

"Tam and I, no, I mean me specifically, I feel responsible for all of this. Everything that's happened."

And once he'd said that—admitted it aloud—everything else came pouring out. He told her about the experiment and the zero field, how he had been called in, what he and Tam had tried to do, and how they had failed. How they had ushered in the end of the world.

Her face grew pale and her body language stilled as he went on. She seemed to appreciate the gravity of what he was saying, seemed to accept that he was ultimately responsible for what had happened.

"We're hoping that the people who designed the experiment and understand the physics of what was happening in the beginning can look at our data and figure out exactly what went wrong and how we might be able to fix it."

It sounded pathetically naïve to him when he said it out loud like that, but it was all he had now.

"Even if they can't make things go back to the way they were before," he said, trying to be realistic, "they might be able to figure out how we can get technology to work again, or work in a different way, maybe."

He trailed off into silence, waiting for her to explode, to rain condemnation and curses down on him.

Her face and posture were stiff, and twin tears trickled unevenly down her cheeks.

"Thank you for telling me," she said. "Good luck."

With that, she turned and took a wooden step away from him, then another, slightly smoother one before falling into a more natural gait as she strode away, back in the direction of her tent instead of toward the breakfast line.

Gabriel wanted to go after her, to say he was just kidding, or that it wasn't his fault, but there was nothing else to say. He had given her the truth, and it felt a little like parachuting— three parts plummeting to your death and one part freedom.

By the time he found Tam again, he was resolute and calm—eager to get back to their mission and make better time on the road.

They gathered and packed their things and went to find Bill. Gabriel told him that they were heading out, and rather than argue, Bill shook both their hands and wished them well, thanking them for their help with the fence. He seemed completely sincere in his invitation for them to stay, but didn't try to change their minds once they said they were sure.

Then they sought out Ripley, Marcia, and the kids to say goodbye. Ripley remained stiff and wouldn't look Gabriel in the eye, but she gave each of them a brief hug and seemed sad or torn. Gabriel waved to little Miri and Travis and nodded his head to Marcia. Miri cried, and Marcia looked relieved, which was to be expected at this point. Gabriel had deeply mixed feelings about saying goodbye to Ripley, but he knew it was the right thing to do. She probably hated him now—he couldn't blame her. *Anyway, it's easier and better this way*, he told himself. He hoped she would be alright here. Hearing that there had been one of those creatures within walking distance a week or so ago worried him, but on the other hand, this place was certainly safer than traveling with them. And other than that one baffling and beautiful instance of flirtation in Walmart, he had no indication that she had any romantic interest in him. She didn't want—*shouldn't* want—to leave this haven to accompany Gabriel on his mission.

"Take care of yourself, Ripley," said Gabriel, turning away quickly and walking back to his tent before he could make more of a fool of himself by saying anything else.

He and Tam packed up their bike trailers, grabbed all their weapons and headed for the main gate. Several groups of people stopped what they were doing and watched them leave. Some had faces of concern or even sadness, but the younger children were excited about the event. Even that felt good to Gabriel—just being noticed as they left reinforced the feeling that they could belong to this community if they wanted to.

Mounting their bikes once again, they rode north. Gabriel had been inclined to take Bill's advice and avoid downtown, but now that he was riding again, he really didn't want to go off-road and have to walk their bikes. After their conversation about getting to Ainsley and the facility in Long Beach, he felt the need to make better time. And the wind in his hair felt nice. So he had suggested, and Tam had agreed, that they head north first, but then take the last road they saw going west, skirting the northern edge of town.

They rode cautiously, stopping at crossroads to look and listen for any sign of hostiles. Once Gabriel thought he heard something and held up his hand for a longer pause, but whatever the sound had been, it didn't repeat, so they continued on.

Eventually they came to the northern edge of town—only open desert, boulders, and gullies lay ahead to the north. They had just passed a likely looking road to the west a couple of minutes earlier, so they backtracked to take it, turning smoothly onto it and riding slowly past small white houses and bare dirt yards, alert for any potential danger.

After only ten minutes or so of slow riding west, they came to a stop. Ahead, the houses gave way to a small collection of low, single-story, metal-walled storage units and warehouses that crowded the road on both sides. Their only alternative to riding through this restrictive route was to turn south, back toward downtown. They had seen another road that seemed to lead west a couple of blocks farther down that way.

"Well, what do you..." Tam began to say, but Gabriel held up his hand, cutting him off. There was a sound behind them and it was getting closer. Someone or some*thing* was definitely coming for them.

THIRTY—FIVE

T am pulled out his machete and Gabriel drew his axe, though he thought about the practicality of trying the fireball thing. He was still leaning toward not using any of his... *unusual* powers where people could see them, but wondered if he would regret not using all the tools available to him in times of need.

Before he could make up his mind, the sound grew louder and a figure in a football helmet and shoulder pads rode out of a side street behind them on a pink bicycle.

"Ripley?" Tam said loudly.

She sped up to them and slammed on her brakes, coming to an abrupt halt. Gabriel had already begun warning her, "Ripley, you can't come with us," before she had even stopped fully, and he intended to continue in that vein, but Ripley uncharacteristically interrupted him.

"Some people are chasing me," she said. Indeed, Gabriel could now hear something else. He looked in the direction she had come from and saw a group of six people on foot armed with crowbars and baseball bats coming around a corner and loping toward them.

"Let's ride!" Gabriel said, jumping on his bike and setting

off as quickly as possible. He chose the path in front of them, accelerating through the warehouses with Tam and Ripley following closely behind. Glancing over his shoulder at their pursuers, Gabriel was encouraged to see that rather than sprinting after them, they seemed—whether from exhaustion or lack of desire—to be trotting slowly and would soon be left far behind.

He turned his attention back to the path ahead. The road was clear and smooth and should allow them to outrun their pursuers easily. He wondered how far they would have to ride before it would be safe to camp.

But just as he was beginning to relax, his eyes fell on a construction site at the end of the buildings, where an out-of-commission excavator perched at the side of a large pit that spanned almost the entire roadway.

A figure stepped out into the road in front of the pit, followed by a second, a third, and then four more. They carried chains, machetes, clubs, and two of them wielded homemade spears, maybe fifteen feet in length. Two others had hunting bows.

Gabriel slammed on his brakes and turned to look over his shoulder at their pursuers, who had already made it as far as the first warehouse.

"An effective trap," Tam remarked detachedly, taking the words right out of Gabriel's mouth, though he said them aloud and with less cursing. Gabriel silently berated himself for leading them straight into it.

A voice called from the group ahead. "Welcome to our territory," one of the men shouted. "Give up your bikes, weapons, and food and you can go free and unharmed. All of you."

Gabriel could *hear* the lie in the man's voice. It sounded strangely modulated, as if someone had recorded the "go free and unharmed" part and played it at almost exactly the same time, so that the minute differences interfered with each other, creating an audible beading. Gabriel could hear the malice in it. The man had no intention of keeping his word—Gabriel would have bet anything in the world on that. He didn't know how, but he was certain he was right. He glanced back at the faces of his companions to see if they had heard the same thing, but they hadn't reacted any more unusually than one would expect after being trapped in an alley by an entire evil football team.

"He's lying," he said to his companions. "We're going to have to fight our way out of this—I don't think we can ride past them."

He caught sight of Tam nodding his head subtly out of the corner of his eye. "Follow my lead and when I yell, attack hard and fast. Show no mercy—I can tell they won't show us any."

With that, he slowly got off his bike. He faced the men in front of them and raised his hands in the air. He shouted, "We surrender!" and began walking toward them, hands still in the air.

As they approached, the speaker's contemptuous smile grew wider. He was dressed in dirty tan canvas work pants with lots of pockets, like a carpenter or plumber might wear, and a loose, light tan button-down shirt that was mostly open in the front, exposing a muscled, hairless chest covered in tattoos. His head was shaved and darkly tanned. He carried a machete and, Gabriel noted to his bemusement, had an Indiana Jones-style bullwhip tied to his belt. His companions seemed an incongruous mix of redneck farmers, bearded bikers, and Michoacán drug cartel enforcers.

Gabriel saw movement at the lip of the pit behind the men and stopped short. A metal pole as thick as Gabriel's arm had been driven into the rock in the center of the surprisingly deep excavation. Attached to the pole was a thick metal chain, and as Gabriel's blood drained from his head in shock and horror, he saw that the other end of the chain was connected to a thick band straining around the neck of a skittering, brown, insect-like demon. Its body looked like a cross between a fifteen-foot centipede and a shark, but with extra pincer arms protruding haphazardly from its back. Its head was bulbous and bi-directional, like a hammerhead, but with a much larger, tusked jaw and several emotionless, shark-black eyes of varying sizes at the top and bottom of its head. Its spiky carapace was sticky with blood, dirt, and viscera. The creature darted up and fell back down the wall of the pit, moving counterclockwise in frenzied fits and starts, dragging the clanking chain behind it.

"You like our pet?" the leader said, grinning madly. "It killed five of us when we caught it, and that was after it had picked off four others in our camp." He held his chin high and his shoulders back—his pride practically rolled off him. Even as he spoke, the creature behind him began scrambling up the side of the pit to the rim. The two men with the long spears jabbed at it until it dropped back to the ground, where it resumed its erratic progress along the bottom.

"But we caught that fucker!" he yelled down at the demon, a fleck of spit flying from his upper lip. "We're the bosses now—of this monster and of this whole fucking town!" He looked back at Gabriel, seemingly surprised and disappointed that Gabriel wasn't cheering or smiling.

"We've fed it a few times since then," he said, conspiratorially, as if letting Gabriel in on a secret family recipe. "Chaining it here like this keeps the others away—maybe 'cause they don't want to fight this one, or maybe they're scared of getting caught, too." He watched Gabriel's face closely for a reaction, and Gabriel was suddenly and jarringly reminded of Colonel Broadnax back in DC. He hoped the woman was alive—surely nothing could kill her. *And my family*, he thought. *Que Dios les salve a mi familia.*

"It grew bigger with each one we fed it," the man continued.

"Smarter, too." His gaze turned briefly to Tam before settling uncomfortably on Ripley.

"We got a tiger by the tail, boys. I don't really want to feed you to it," he said. "It's hard enough to control at this size." He paused.

"But I will if you don't do exactly what I say."

Gabriel stood there, shocked and angry at himself for not seeing this coming as soon as he had seen the demon chained up. *How could anyone even threaten to feed a human being to one of those things?*

"You send your football player lady friend over here with us, and if she minds her manners, she can stay," the gang leader continued. His expression was somber, but not overtly menacing, which somehow made it worse.

"God, you talk a lot," Ripley said. The man ignored her comment, although Gabriel thought he saw his eyes flash.

"Then you two put down your weapons and walk away. Leave your stuff. You can go back to the old man's camp." Gabriel heard the lie again. The man had no intention of letting him and Tam live.

Gabriel ground his teeth and felt heat begin to suffuse his body. He thought he sensed something similar from the demon in the pit—an echo of the manic, driven fury that blazed in his own gut, igniting his ever-combustible rage into an internal fireball. *They think they can control me with* FEAR? *They think they can take Ripley hostage with* WORDS?

He began to grin as the overwhelming feeling of righteous anger flooded his bones. It was a blinding, comforting, mind-blanking rage. He took a shaky step forward, still holding his axe in front of him.

"Hold it right there, homes," the leader said, raising his machete slightly. Some of the others took more aggressive stances as well, and the two with the bows kept their arrows trained on Gabriel. *I need to deal with them first*, he thought, sobering slightly. Tam came up to stand beside him, and Ripley followed close behind, wearing her helmet and carrying her baseball bat. He glanced farther back and was surprised to see that the group who had chased Ripley hadn't come much closer. They were still pretty much at the entrance of the trap, and advancing very slowly. A small positive, then.

"Don't make me say it again, vato," the leader said. "We got no problem feeding you to it, or just killing you."

Gabriel put his hand behind his back and summoned his will to try to create a fireball.

"So we can go if we give you our weapons, just like that?"

"Yeah, just like that," the man responded. Another lie.

Gabriel thought the fireball had begun. He started to feel cold and then heard some confused and distant shouts from the men behind them, which probably confirmed it.

"What you got behind your back, man?" the leader said angrily, taking a step toward them.

"Nothing. See?" Gabriel slowly brought his hand around from behind his back. Exhilaratingly, an ugly blue and black ball of fire, flickering with uncanny life, hovered a couple of inches above his palm.

"What the *fuck*..." the man began, and Gabriel willed the fireball toward the man as hard as he could. It shot out of his hand and straight into the man's chest, just below his sternum, where it punched a hole in his exposed flesh and detonated inside his body. Gabriel thought he could see the flame of the explosion through both the man's mouth and the hole in his chest. It made a sick, wet popping sound as it exploded, and the man went rigid for a moment, then slumped all the way to the ground, eyes open.

There was a split second of stunned, frozen silence, then just about everyone present started screaming and the scene exploded into motion. Gabriel looked at the men with the bows just in time to see them release their arrows. At a distance of fifteen feet, they were unlikely to miss, but at that moment he didn't care—he knew he was going to kill them anyway.

He felt Tam's hand on his shoulder, and the world immediately turned gray and misty. His stomach lurched as if he were floating and he wondered if he had been hit. The thought flittered through his mind that perhaps he had died.

Then, as quickly as the strange sensation had started, it was over, and there was no time to think. Tam charged at the bowmen, and someone swung a ridged cudgel at Gabriel's head.

THIRTY—SIX

TAM

As soon as Gabriel started summoning the otherworldly sphere of fire behind his back, Tam had known that the very next thing to happen after Gabriel threw it was that the archers would unleash their arrows. So when Gabriel launched the thing at the gang leader, Tam acted on instinct, putting his hand on his friend's shoulder. He didn't have a conscious plan, except that they had to somehow avoid being hit by said arrows. A strange feeling came over him, a lightheadedness, and he lost his balance a little. The arrows that streaked at them from barely a dozen feet away somehow missed, however, and Tam felt a fleeting moment of pleased surprise. He knew he had caused them to miss, but wasn't exactly clear on how.

He shook his head, trying to clear the fuzzy, disconnected feeling from his brain, and then Gabriel, already engulfed in the eerie hellfire, was moving, and so was everyone else. Tam shifted his machete back to his right hand and thought, *I've got to focus!* Then, because it seemed necessary, he charged at the bowmen. One was already nocking another arrow, and the other, still standing and staring at them with his mouth agape, would surely remember to do so soon.

Before Tam could reach them, however, another man, who had dropped the long spear he'd been using on the demon, came roaring at him with a wicked-looking spiked baseball bat raised in the air and a manic grin on his face. Tam's momentum carried him right toward the man, and without thinking, he ducked and rolled, hoping to maybe knock him off his feet, or at least make himself a smaller target and avoid being brained by the man's weapon.

He didn't feel the impact of the man's legs, which was very disorienting. As he righted himself and regained his footing, he realized that he must have wildly overestimated the speed and angle of his roll, as he had somehow shot well past the man and was now crouching beside the archers, who whirled to face him. He felt drunk and somehow disassociated from the world, as if he were watching someone else's life.

His physical body didn't waste the opportunity, though, and without a thought beyond "*bows bad*," he slashed at the drawn bow of the one on the right. The tip of his machete made contact with the taut bowstring, which snapped immediately, sending the bow bucking and flopping out of the man's hand before it clattered to the dusty pavement. Wide-eyed, the man took an involuntary step backward and promptly fell into the pit behind him, arms pinwheeling ineffectually as he disappeared from view. He must have barely hit the bottom before the demon had him, and the man began to scream in earnest. The other spearman ran over and stabbed frantically at the creature, but he was too late.

Tam didn't waste his moment and promptly swung at the other bowman, who was now trying to draw a new arrow from his quiver, his wide, petrified eyes darting between Tam and the pit.

The first swing missed the man and his bow completely, but Tam quickly followed up with another, connecting solidly with the man's forearm as he tried to ward off the blow. The serrated machete bit deep into the flesh, causing the man to drop his bow and clutch his arm to his chest. His blood splattered onto the pavement at his feet, and the man crouched down, glaring at Tam but making no move to lift another weapon, so Tam held off.

Another second or two passed, then the man turned and sprinted away from Tam and the pit, back toward the people standing at the entrance to the trap. After three steps he fell, feet still scrambling, and rose again.

Tam could spare him no more thought because the spearman, having given up on saving his friend, nearly caught him by surprise in the back. He saw the spear tip out of his peripheral vision at the last second and danced sideways, somehow knocking the spear aside with an instinctive swing of his machete. He spun around to face its wielder, whose face was a mask of grief and anger, tears visibly streaming down his cheeks.

"I'll kill you for that," the man rasped. The man jabbed at him again, but Tam scrambled back and to the side, realizing almost too late that he himself had come dangerously close to the edge of the pit.

His attacker kept coming forward, and Tam saw that, strategically speaking, he should have charged the man to get inside the effective range of the spear tip. Right now, he was at a complete disadvantage, since his machete wasn't nearly long enough to do anything. He tried to think of a better way to tackle his opponent, but nothing immediately came to mind.

Their brief detente ended abruptly when Gabriel crashed into the side of the spearman, large blue flames flickering hungrily over his legs, arms, shoulders, and now almost his entire head. The flames extended up into the air, forming an uncanny, angry blue halo. *How does that not hurt? I bet it hurts.*

Gabriel twisted and slammed the axe savagely into the spearman's side, hewing him to the pavement like a dropped sack of groceries.

Tam stood up straighter and stared at Gabriel, who was a frighteningly inhuman sight. *Like a demon himself*, Tam had to admit, but there was no time to dwell on that—he and Gabriel heard another man scream, and they both looked over to see the demon snap its chain as it crested the lip of the pit, a shrieking man dangling from the thing's bony jaws.

Gabriel was the first to move, of course, launching himself at the monster, which was a quarter of the way around the pit.

Tam sighed, then followed. He wasn't sure what he was supposed to do exactly, but he theorized that he would probably need to be close to Gabriel and the demon if he was going to be of any help at all.

The demon dropped its latest victim, who had been the last of the attackers on this end of the trap, and reared up, its wide head swaying in the air as it assessed Gabriel's approach. It was huge—considerably taller than Gabriel—and it began to make a loud hissing noise that jarred Tam's ears and brain so badly that he stumbled and fell painfully to one knee. He saw Gabriel fall sideways onto the road in front of him, but couldn't think beyond the excruciating noise in his head.

The creature lowered its head back to the ground and skittered over toward Gabriel. The sound it was making abated somewhat, and Tam was able to struggle back to his feet. He looked up in time to see the demon pounce on his friend, latching on with its jaws and rolling him over, coiling its body around him like a boa constrictor.

Tam had taken three anguished steps toward the demon, trying to figure out where best to slash with his machete, when both Gabriel and the demon went up in a hungry blue blaze of Gabriel's skin fire.

The demon squealed angrily, trying at first to hold onto Gabriel's body despite the fire, but then quickly letting go to get away. Tam saw that the eyes on the underside of its broad head were now completely white, as if cooked like hard-boiled eggs.

Gabriel stood up. The flames burned so brightly it was hard to look at him for long. They dripped with burning blood from a wound in his arm and fell like puffs of volcanic ash onto the roadway. He was a terrible sight to behold. He coiled up to swing his axe, stepped forward to close with the demon, and caught the creature just below its head. Ichor spurted out and the beast hissed in rage.

It gathered itself for another lunge, but Gabriel was ready, catching it squarely as it launched itself, hitting it with an axe blow that split its head open from top to bottom.

Even that didn't kill it, but the thing went wild, apparently unable to sense where Gabriel was. After a few near misses from the creature's thrashing limbs, Gabriel finished it off by hewing its body into three segments, which finally and mercifully fell still before catching on fire. Orange-red and beautiful.

Tam and Gabriel watched it dazedly for a moment, then both recalled Ripley at the same time and turned as one to see if she was okay.

At first she appeared fine and stood looking at them with a calm but deeply troubled expression. Tam wondered if she was as scared of Gabriel as he was right now. Then they noticed the arrow sticking out of her stomach.

THIRTY—SEVEN

RIPLEY

When Gabriel killed the leader with his fireball, Sarah's mouth went dry with fear. *No, my name is Ripley now*, she admonished herself, and there was no room for fear in her anymore. These men trying to trap them reminded her gratingly of the man who had abducted her, and she knew that she had to defend herself and her companions, but seeing the bald man explode from the inside was a sickening jolt to her system. There wasn't time to think about that or anything else, though, because then the fighting began.

Standing behind Gabriel and Tam, she couldn't see exactly what was happening directly ahead, but she saw Tam put his hand on Gabriel's shoulder, and then they just... *turned into mist*. And then, all at once, a freaking arrow slammed into her stomach, punching into her belly like a fist, just above and to the right of her belly button. She wondered for a second how badly it was going to hurt, but then Gabriel became solid again and stepped out to the right, and Tam launched himself at and somehow through the feet of a towering monster of a man, and suddenly she was face to face, or football helmet to midsection anyway, with a huge man holding a spiked baseball bat. The man turned to look at Tam and raised his bat to go after him, but before he could take a step, Ripley slammed her own bat into the side of his leg as hard as she could. It worked—the man crumpled to his knees mid stride. She was surprised by her own strength.

She stepped around in front of him and hit him again, this time in the side of the head, and he fell heavily the rest of the way. It seemed to take forever for him to finish falling. She hoped he wouldn't die like the other man she'd hit like this.

Ripley looked up, somewhat dazed, to see a man running right past her as he fled the fight. He tripped and spilled to the ground a few feet away, but then scrambled back to his feet and continued his flight. Tam was squared off with the last spearman, leaving the demon unguarded, and Gabriel, now wickedly aflame, had already dispatched two—no, three—of the men and was leaping toward the one Tam was fighting. Gabriel was a truly terrifying, fiery spectacle. It looked like his entire head and back were burning bright blue. She felt the urge to find a blanket to smother the fire, but it didn't seem to be harming him. As if he was somehow a part of the fire, not its victim. She wondered what that meant—if his responsibility for all of this was somehow causing this change in him, or if maybe it was just that he and Tam had been so close to the origin—but in any case, it was deeply unsettling. It was as if he weren't of this world.

She turned to look back at the men behind them, but three of them had already turned to run, several disappearing around the corner of the first warehouse as she watched. She nodded to herself—she would have run, too. She looked back at Gabriel, wondering idly whether he was even aware that he was on fire, like pretty much fully on fire, and had been since the beginning of the fight. He was also bigger than usual—he had grown half a foot taller or more. She thought she was probably in shock because none of this felt as strange and awful as it undoubtedly was—instead, she just felt numb. Her rescuer was a fiery, murderous, magical monster and had been involved in the destruction of what she was increasingly sure was the whole world. And she herself had probably just killed a man. Again. Her stomach turned in disgust.

She was about to walk over and stand next to Tam when the demon lunged up over the far side of the pit to attack the last remaining gang member.

Gabriel took off toward it like a shot and she moved to follow, but the monster stood up tall and began making a deafening noise that caused the world to come crashing in on her head and lungs, and she slumped backward onto the ground.

She lay there for a few moments, fighting for consciousness and trying not to throw up before the sensation finally subsided and she was able to think and breathe again. She gathered her wits and eventually clambered clumsily back to her feet.

Gabriel was finishing off the demon, fire and blood everywhere. Tam seemed to be more or less okay, though he was staring vacantly at Gabriel and the monster. Everyone else lay murdered on the ground. Her head began to spin again.

Gabriel and Tam both turned to look at her, as if sensing her distress. She remembered the arrow in her belly, which started hurting on cue. It was a deep ache and uncomfortable. She knew she should wait until someone could cut it out—if there was a barb on the arrow, it would do more damage coming out than going in, but she couldn't stand the thought of it inside her body a minute longer, so she grasped the shaft firmly and jerked it out in one motion. She was not going to worry about something as trivial as this. Not after what she'd been through. She was a survivor. A small spurt of blood followed the arrow as it came out, and her head swam a little more. She took a slow, deep breath and tossed the arrow—thankfully not barbed—

aside. As it clattered to the ground, Gabriel and Tam sprinted to her aid. She stayed upright, though it felt like a near thing.

Gabriel, no longer angry or on fire, looked panicked instead. He ran to the man she had taken down and used a belt knife to cut off a strip of the man's shirt. Then he ran back to his pack and dug around it until he found a bottle of hydrogen peroxide. His rushing around, overreacting to her wound, would have been cute if she hadn't just watched him burn and kill like a grim reaper of souls straight from hell. Now it was just jarring. She knew she should speak up and stop him, but she felt trapped in her own thoughts. *Who is this man? And am I really any better?* She'd just killed, too. She glanced over at Tam, but the man just stood there, lost in thought and staring at the ground.

"This might hurt a bit if your wound is still open," Gabriel said, his voice tender and concerned. He gently helped her lie down on her back. Sometimes Ripley thought she might have a crush on Gabriel, but other times she couldn't even imagine it. Like now. He was covered in burnt blood and… other stuff that had been someone's insides moments before. He was breathing hard, at least, and he looked worried about her, but his face betrayed no remorse for hacking *several* people to death with an *axe* in a handful of seconds. Nor did he seem to feel any kind of regret for all the thousands of other people who had suffered and died like her parents.

He pushed up her shirt to expose the blood around her wound and then poured some hydrogen peroxide onto the area. It helped wash away some of the blood, showing that there wasn't even a scratch underneath. The liquid tickled as it dribbled down onto her stomach and around to her back. Ripley found the whole scene ridiculous, and a wild, strange laugh escaped her throat, shocking everyone, including herself.

At this, Gabriel seemed to come to himself and calm down. She was feeling better herself, too, she decided. She prodded around the area where the wound had been—it was tender, but seemed sound enough. The skin of her stomach was smooth, with only a pale white star of scar tissue to show where the arrow had gone in. She had always healed very quickly, but her healing was obviously much more extreme now—she knew she would bounce back easily from such a minor thing. Nothing like when she had healed Travis—she had genuinely thought she had been dying then. But no stupid arrow was going to cause her any lasting problems. She mourned the hole in her shirt, though. It wasn't like she just could order another one online, and she had liked this one.

Gabriel looked at her and shrugged sheepishly. He stood and held out his hand to help her up. She accepted it graciously.

"Are you okay? Can you ride?" he asked. *Very direct, this one.* The fight in which he had slaughtered several people hadn't ended more than two minutes ago, and he was now acting as if it were of no concern. She knew that those bandits or whatever they were would have done the same and maybe worse to all of them, and Gabriel had protected them once again, but still. Maybe they should take a moment.

Instead of saying anything, however, she simply replied, "Yes." She was exhausted and wrung out, but she would manage.

She turned back to the man she had killed and whispered to him that she was sorry and that she forgave him. Then she wiped her bat off on what was left of his shirt. Gabriel did the same with his gruesome axe. It was a hateful-looking thing, all wicked, sharp edges, and so black that it somehow stood out from everything around it.

At some point, Tam was able to focus long enough to pick up the undamaged bow, a quiver, and all the arrows he could find. He stowed it all beside his bag in the wagon he was pulling.

And then they rode off again—simple as that. They kept a careful eye out for any more trouble, both ahead and behind, but they didn't see another soul. After barely thirty minutes of riding, they were leaving the town behind them and heading west into the desert again. Of course, it was already brutally hot and sweat was dripping uncomfortably from just about every one of her pores.

Ripley figured they were far enough out now that there was no chance they would try to make her go back to the encampment. She was going to help them, whether they liked it or not, and do something important with her life. She raised her voice to call for a halt. Gabriel and Tam both came over, eyeing her stomach with a concern that was entirely unwarranted.

"That's not why I stopped," she said, cutting them off, even though she felt exhausted. She walked over to her pack, which was now safely back in Gabriel's pull-behind. She opened the largest outside pocket and exclaimed, "I have presents!"

She pulled out three brand new, floppy, wide-brimmed hats in desert camouflage. She put hers on—it was much less sweltering, albeit less safe, than her stupid-looking football helmet—and handed the other two to Gabriel and Tam, who were rendered momentarily speechless.

After accepting the hats with appropriate reverence, they both thanked her profusely. She had gone out the day before and looted them from a forgotten bin at the back of a thrift store, but explaining all that would have spoiled the magic of her gift, so instead she just smiled at them.

Both men seemed overwhelmed, and she felt a warmth that she hadn't felt in ages. Gabriel practically had a tear in his eye! Tam even hugged her, kind of sideways, around her shoulders. She used to hate it when people hugged like that, or the way some girls hugged that somehow kept their boobs from touching the other person—pretty amazing when you thought about the mechanics—but now she was glad for the less intimate contact. Maybe she did have intimacy issues after her terrible experience, but there was also the fact that everyone was sweaty and smelly these days, especially right now. As the men put on their hats, she sighed contentedly and waited for the signal to move on.

The two men thanked her again, for the third time, and then they all mounted back up and rode off into the desert, wearing some new, very fine hats.

THIRTY—EIGHT

HAKK'RIX

The immense, glaring star hung directly overhead, bathing everything in its unrelenting light and shrouding the terrain in a pregnant silence. Even the tiny, barely-souled flying creatures that usually filled the air with their raucous calls anytime the fiery orb was in the sky had fallen silent.

Hakk'rix had found a semi-sheltered hiding place in a pile of boulders, from which it observed the strange prey animals it had tracked here.

In the distance, the trio moved smoothly across the ground on their wheeled conveyances. Their small, bipedal appendages pumped up and down, somehow propelling forward the metal devices on which they traveled. They weren't moving very fast, but it looked like they could keep it up for a long time.

Hakk'rix shifted uneasily, marveling at the cleverness of this species of prey.

But that was the fascinating oddity. These *were* prey animals. Like other prey it had hunted, they were delicate, unarmored bipeds. They socialized in small groups. Two of them had radiated fear before and during the clash that Hakk'rix had just witnessed.

But Hakk'rix had followed them here because it had sensed the mind of the other one from afar, and it was... familiar. At first, Hakk'rix had thought it must be a rival—one that was new, or sickly, or hiding its presence for some reason by disguising itself as prey. Or perhaps Hakk'rix was confusing it for the young rival that the other group of prey had captured and imprisoned here.

But when it had finally found these animals and watched them fight the other group and kill the young rival, Hakk'rix was certain. They had used their surprisingly vibrant soulsparks just like rivals would, though unconsciously, it seemed, to help them in their battle. And the one—it *felt* like a rival. Or maybe like it was becoming one.

Hakk'rix did not fear it—in fact, its body thrummed with a deep urge to consume the creature. Would it be as nourishing as devouring a true rival? Hakk'rix suspected it would. It could easily destroy all three at once, but Hakk'rix had not lived this long by taking unnecessary risks. The strange rival-like feel of this prey animal was something completely new, and its soulspark was already sharp and deep.

Hakk'rix clicked softly to itself, imagining what it might become once it consumed these unique beings.

There was no risk of losing the animals anymore—it could easily find the mind of the one. It could trail them for as long as it wanted, learning what it could, living undetected in the creature's mind.

And then, in the darkness, it would come for them while they slept.

HERE ENDS THE INFERNAL AGE – DEMON GATE

A NOTE TO MY READERS

First of all, *Thank you!* Writing these books and putting them out there always seemed like a foregone requirement inherent in my soul, but that next step of having someone want to read them was (and remains) unknowable, scary, and exciting. I recently read that there are over two million books published PER YEAR now, so you picking this one to read is an honor, and it's appreciated.

Please please please rate and review this book where you bought it, so that others can find it (or avoid it, if you didn't care for it) and look for book two coming soon! I read all my reviews. Also check out my website at www.ansonjoaquin.com and reach out to me there to let me know what you thought.